Australian author **Ally Blake** loves reading and strong coffee, porch swings and dappled sunshine, beautiful notebooks and soft, dark pencils. Her inquisitive, rum- ' un:ctious, spectacular children are her exquisite delight. And she adores writing love stories so much she'd write them even if nobody read them. No wonder, then, having sold over four million copies of her romance novels worldwide, Ally is living her bliss. Find out more about Ally's books at allyblake.com.

**Helen Lacey** grew up reading *Black Beauty* and *Little House on the Prairie*. These childhood classics inspired her to write her first book when she was seven, a story about a girl and her horse. She loves writing for Mills & Boon, where she can create strong heroes with soft hearts and heroines with gumption who get their happily-ever-afters. For more about Helen, visit her website, helenlacey.com.

D1627769

Discover more at millsandboon.co.uk

# HIRED BY THE MYSTERIOUS MILLIONAIRE

## ALLY BLAKE

# HER SECRET TEXAS VALENTINE

## HELEN LACEY

## MILLS & BOON

First Published in Great Britain 2019
by Mills & Boon, an imprint of HarperCollinsPublishers,
1 London Bridge Street, London, SE1 9GF

*Hired by the Mysterious Millionaire* © 2019 Ally Blake
*Her Secret Texas Valentine* © 2019 Harlequin Books S.A.

Special thanks and acknowledgement are given to Helen Lacey for her contribution to the Fortunes of Texas: The Lost Fortunes series.

ISBN: 978-0-263-27212-3

0219

MIX
Paper from
responsible sources
FSC™ C007454

This book is produced from independently certified FSC™ paper to ensure responsible forest management.

For more information visit: www.harpercollins.co.uk/green

Printed and bound in Spain
by CPI, Barcelona

# HIRED BY THE MYSTERIOUS MILLIONAIRE

**ALLY BLAKE**

The seed of this story came to me fifteen years ago
and would not have survived had I not written it down.
Therefore I dedicate this book to the scraps of paper,
backs of receipts and many beautiful notebooks
that have given themselves over to my career.

# CHAPTER ONE

"IT'S HIM. It has to be."

Ignoring her friend's imploring voice, Evie Croft let her body rock with the soothing motion of the morning train as it rumbled along the Frankston Line. Swiping through the ads in the Room Rent app, she tried really hard to feel enthused about exorbitant rent, alarming-sounding housemates, or both.

"Evie!" Zoe whispered, loudly enough that the schools boys sitting across from them actually looked up from their phones. "You know who I mean. He's nose-deep in a book the size of a house brick, so you can look. *Look*. Look *now*."

Evie knew Zoe was talking about her "train boyfriend" and she had no intention of looking. She'd already accidentally made eye contact with Hot Stuff in the Swanky Suit today, and many more times since he'd started taking her train.

It was hard not to. With his overlong hair and rugged stubble, the man was a study in the kind of dark, broody countenance you just couldn't fake.

"Stop looking at that stupid app," said Zoe. "You are not moving out of my apartment just because Lance is moving in and that's final."

Evie gave her oldest friend a squeezy one-armed hug. "I love you because you truly believe it. You and Lance have been waiting for this moment since you were sixteen years old. He's home from deployment next week and it's finally happening."

Zoe sat back, closed her eyes and sighed. "It really is, isn't it?"

Either way, Evie gave up on looking for a new place to stay. Only half an hour out from the biggest job interview of her life—with Game Plan, no less, a coder's Holy Grail—she instead practised answering interview questions in her head.

At least, she tried. Until Zoe leaned over, reaching for her phone. "Click back to that other app. No, the other one. Go back."

"Gah!" Evie held her phone up high, out in front, then opened the neck of her top and slipped her phone between sternum and bra.

Zoe cocked an eyebrow. "You really think that's going to stop me?"

Evie did not. With only a super-quick glance in the direction of Hot Stuff in the Swanky Suit to make sure he wasn't watching, she dug beneath her vintage pea coat and warm winter top to fish out her phone, shivering as her chilly fingers grazed her skin. And rocking into the older man sardined in beside her. She sent him an apologetic smile. The barest flicker of his cheek was a tale of eternal sufferance.

The train commute took all sorts. The bored schoolkids, the frazzled mums with toddlers and prams in tow, women in piercings leaning on men with tattoos, creative office types with their smooth hair and manicured nails. It was a delicious microcosm of the city at large.

Evie had grown up in a small dairy community, just north of Echuca, and her favourite memory of her mother was listening to her wax lyrical about the short time she'd lived in Melbourne—the electric hum of creativity, the eclectic fashion, the epicurean delights. She remembered tracing the delicate "Adventure" tattoo etched into her mother's fine wrist.

After her mum died Evie had promised herself she'd end up there one day too and have the life her mother had never had.

Though the past couple of weeks the city had been making her work for it.

"Seriously?" Evie cried when Zoe whipped her phone away with a delighted, "Aha! Now, let's see what Hot Stuff in the Swanky Suit has to say."

Zoe didn't mean "in person". For she and Hot Stuff had never had an actual conversation.

Well, unless you counted that first day. She'd made it to the train doors right as they'd pulled up to their city stop when the train had lurched to a halt. Shoved from behind, Evie had tripped and elbowed Hot Stuff in the gut.

Mortified, she'd crouched to pick up the book he'd dropped. The autobiography of Jonathon Montrose, the man behind Game Plan, no less. Cowboy tech investor, IT savant, Evie's actual hero.

Funny. She'd forgotten that detail. Had that given her the seed of the idea to dare apply for a job with the great man himself? Huh.

Anyway, handing over the book to Hot Stuff, she'd apologised like crazy, while trying not to swoon in his glorious presence, until he'd taken her by both shoulders, strong hands holding her still. He was even bigger up close. And he'd smelled *so* good. When he'd looked down into her eyes, the stormy blue depths of his own holding her in their thrall, she'd forgotten how to breathe until he'd let her go and disappeared into the station with the bustling morning crowd.

Evie let out a soft sigh and glanced his way just as he ran a hand through his overlong dark hair, leaving finger tracks in its wake. All that indolent grace, the sexy stubble and those deeply intelligent-looking eyes—he really added an extra something to the daily commute.

Other commuters came and went, took different trains, adopted random seats, but Hot Stuff always chose the same spot: across the aisle and down three rows from hers. Evie had always been a fan of patterns. It was comforting to know she wasn't the only creature of habit in their little train universe.

"How many apps do you have open at one time?" Zoe

fussed, and she swiped them into oblivion. "How does your brain not scramble?"

"It's called multitasking."

Zoe snorted. Then found the Urban Rambler app. Developed by Game Plan, of course. His apps were seriously the best. Evie would be first in line to sign up to Game On—the revolutionary new mobile communication app everyone in the biz was excited about.

Zoe clicked on the *Let's Get Personal* column, flipped the phone so the words were nice and readable and read out loud.

"'*Frankston Line.*' That's us. '*Carriage Three.*' Ditto us. '*To the Bewitching Brunette in the Beauteous Beanies.*'"

Zoe paused a moment for drama before lifting her gaze to Evie's knitted beanie. One of the billion she'd knitted herself. For she really was a fan of patterns.

Today's was silver, with a rainbow pom-pom on top. It didn't *exactly* go with her interview outfit—pea coat over black top and slouchy black pants with fake zips and pockets—all belonging to fashion-plate Zoe, as even computer-nerd Evie wasn't about to turn up to an interview in a Han Solo "I Know" T-shirt, boyfriend jeans and Converse boots—but it did the job.

Zoe said, "Now, hold on to your hat, my friend, because this is going to blow your mind. It says:

*New to your orbit, I find myself struck*
*By your raven locks, your starlit eyes. What luck*
*That I find myself able to see you twice a day.*
*A beacon in a sea of strangers. I must say*
*Your sunshine smiles are my good morning.*
*Your evening sighs my goodnight.*
*If I had the courage I'd say hello.*
*Till then I remain alone in my delight.*
*From Your Appreciative Admirer.*

"Wow," Evie mouthed.

"It's *you*!" Zoe cried. "You are the Bewitching Brunette!"

The schoolboys looked up again, their eyes unglazing this time, enough to give Evie a second glance.

"Well, isn't she?" Zoe asked the boys, waving her hands up and down as if Evie were the prize in a game show. "If this poem wasn't written for you I'll eat your beanie."

Evie tugged off her beanie and shoved it under her butt cheek. Only to have to deal with long strands of dark hair now crackling with static as they stuck to her face.

So, she did have a thing for beanies. She ran naturally cold. Her mum had been the same, needing blankets all through summer. Calling Evie Froglet because of her constantly chilly feet. But it was her granddad who'd taught her how to knit. He'd also taught her how to tie her laces, fix a tractor, cook a perfect steak. To follow her curiosity wherever it might lead her.

Zoe went on. "Lance, for all his good points, is not a romantic man. Telling me my backside looks hot in certain dresses is about as schmaltzy as he gets, bless him. Keeping in mind Lance is a pretty good marker for the average guy, can you see any man on this train who *does* look capable of writing poetry?"

Together they looked. At the scruffy schoolboys now poking wet fingers into one another's ears. The dour gang of goths hanging morosely near the door. The harried working dads with their crooked ties and tired eyes.

As one they turned to the dashing, Byronesque gentleman in the impeccable suit lounging in his seat, reading a book.

Evie swept a hand self-consciously over her hair. It crackled so loudly she quickly put her beanie back on. "Poetry or not, it doesn't matter."

"Why on earth not?"

Evie took her wallet out of her backpack, found a small, crinkled bit of paper and handed it over to Zoe.

"A fortune cookie fortune?" Zoe deadpanned. "From your birthday dinner last week?"

Evie nodded.

"And what does this have to do with Hot Stuff and his undying love for you?"

"Read it."

Zoe did. "'*Bad luck comes in threes. Monkeys, though, they come in trees.*'" After which she burst out laughing. "I…can't…even…"

Evie plucked the piece of paper out of Zoe's shaking fingers and shoved it into the coin compartment of her wallet. "Ever since I read that stupid fortune things have been weird."

"Weird how?" Zoe asked, wiping her eyes.

"Think."

"Your job!"

"And the sudden losing thereof. The very next day."

"The day after your birthday? You didn't tell me for a week!"

"Because as I stood in the office watching the police take away the computers, you rang to tell me Lance was coming home. You were happy. And rightly so."

Evie knew it was nonsensical, but it felt good to finally be talking about it. Hopefully it would relieve the persistent pressure that had been sitting on her chest since the night of her birthday.

"'*Bad luck comes in threes*,'" Zoe said, scratching her chin. "Losing your job was number one."

"Having to move out is number two."

"I told you, you don't have to—"

Evie flapped a *shut up* hand at her friend.

Zoe buttoned her lips. Then promptly unbuttoned them. "There are rules to fortunes, you know. You have to have eaten the entire cookie, I think. You can't tear the paper. And once you tell someone it no longer comes true!"

"Zoe, it can't 'come true' because it's a computer-generated missive stuck in a random dry cookie." Evie slowly shook her head. "And yet, I feel like it would be remiss of me not to keep an eye out for falling pianos."

Zoe nodded sagely.

Not that Evie was taking it lying down. No, sir. There was the Game Plan interview. One she would never have had the nerve to go for if she hadn't been desperate for work. She was too young, too inexperienced, her only long-term tech job having been for a company who were under investigation for embezzlement and fraud.

Or more specifically Eric—the son of the managing director and her ex-boyfriend—who had pilfered her every last dollar before attempting to flee the country.

Zoe coughed. Then burst into laughter again.

The schoolboys squirmed and sank deeper into their seats, no doubt embarrassed by the loud twenty-somethings in their midst. One perked up enough to realise they were at their stop, and in a rush and flurry they gathered their huge, dirty, dishevelled bags and snaked their way to the doors right as the train lumbered to a halt.

While the carriage emptied and filled, the crowd a seething mass of elbows and wet shoes, of jostling and repositioning, a microcosm of Darwin's survival of the fittest, Evie snuck a glance at Hot Stuff.

He'd glanced up, not at her but at the crowd. He did this every time there was a big shift in people, offering up his seat if he had the chance. Because he was beautiful, well-read *and* a gentleman.

Was it possible—even remotely—*he* had written her a lonely-hearts poem on an app?

The timing fit—morning and evening. The train line too. And there were other hints, clues she couldn't ignore.

"*New to your orbit.*" They'd been catching the same train a couple of weeks at most.

"*I find myself struck.*" Was that a nod towards the time she'd winded him?

"*Starlit eyes.*" She did have an impressive collection of *Star Wars*, *Star Trek*, even *Starman* T-shirts.

She usually went for nice-looking men, with easy smiles and busy mid-level jobs. Men who had no hope of spinning her off course as her mother had been spun. She was only just finding her feet in this town after all. Quietly following her curiosity as her granddad had encouraged her to do.

Hot Stuff was fun to moon over *because* he was out of her league. The thought of him reciprocating—heck, the thought of him even knowing who she was—made her belly turn warm and wobbly.

"Now, hang on a second," said Zoe. "What does this have to do with Hot Stuff and the poem? Ah, I get it. After home and work going up the spout, you don't really think a falling piano is in your future. You believe the logical third spate of bad luck involves your love life. But that's a good thing!"

"In what universe?"

"You can cross messed-up love life off the list. You've already had the *worst* luck there. Eric was a douche. Dumping you. Using you. Framing you—"

"Yep, okay. I hereby concede that point to the prosecution." Evie shook her head. "It doesn't count. He doesn't count. We've been kaput for months. '*Bad luck comes in threes*' means it has to happen after I opened the cookie."

"You've arbitrarily decided a man who looks like Byron's hotter descendant is off-limits because a fortune cookie says it will turn to crap."

Evie looked over at Bryon's hotter descendant. She couldn't help it. Heck, at that very moment the train rounded a bend and a slash of sunlight lit him up like something out of an old film.

"He's dreamy, Evie," said Zoe, though Evie hadn't said a word. "And he wrote you a lonely heart."

Evie blinked, only to find she'd been staring too long as a pair of stormy blue eyes caught on hers. Her breath lodged in her throat. Her cheeks burned as her very blood went haywire.

*Look away,* her subconscious begged. *Look. Away. Now!*

Instead habit overcame instinct, and she smiled.

Growing up in a country town, she'd been smiling at strangers since she'd learned how. Saying hello to anyone who made eye contact. Waving in thanks to cars that stopped to let her cross the street. It was simple good manners.

Now, on a packed train hurtling towards the big city, she felt like an utter fool, her smile frozen into place as those fiercely blue eyes stuck on hers and didn't let up.

Then a small miracle happened. The man blinked, as if coming to from a faraway place. The corner of his mouth kicking north into what could only be a return smile. And then he nodded. Nodded! Sending her a private hello from across the way.

She felt the train concertina as everything beyond the tunnel between their gazes turned fuzzy and out of focus. And then those eyes slid north, pausing at the top of her head. Catching on her beanie, the wool suddenly itching like crazy against her scalp, the bob of the pom-pom like a pulse at the top of her head.

He blinked again, then those stormy eyes slid away.

"Oh, my ever-loving gods," Zoe said. "Did you see that?"

Hell, yeah, she had.

"He couldn't take his eyes off you. Proof he's your Appreciative Admirer!"

Heart kicking against her ribs, Evie let herself follow the possibility of Hot Stuff in the Swanky Suit having a secret crush on *her* to its logical conclusion.

By the look of him he'd eat in fine restaurants, read and

understand prize-winning literature, know the actual difference between bottles of wine. From the feel of him when she'd elbowed him then checked him for injury he also wrestled crocodiles, chopped wood for fun and rescued newborn puppies from warehouse fires.

While she lived on cheap cold pizza, spending all weekend in the same holey PJs obliterating strangers gaming online, and she currently slept on an ancient lumpy futon in her best friend's lounge room.

She didn't need a fortune cookie to tell her it would all end in tears.

She looked down at the phone she was spinning over and over in her cold hands.

Her granddad had always insisted her flair for coding was a result of her mum's creative mind. But she'd inherited his practicality too.

Working for Game Plan would be a dream job. Even getting an interview was akin to finding a unicorn in your cornflakes. Especially when no one else would even take her call. She might have been cleared by the feds, but her connection to the embarrassment at her last job made her untouchable.

She couldn't go into that room with thoughts of Hot Stuff filling her head with cotton wool.

Evie glanced up at the electronic readout denoting which stop was next. Real or imagined, the fortune was messing with her head and she had two more stops to put an end to it once and for all.

"You know what I think?" said Evie.

"Rarely."

"If there is even the slightest chance the fortune is real, and I am to be hit with a third blast of bad luck, and it *is* linked to my love life, wouldn't the smart thing be to get it over and done with?"

Zoe grinned. "Only one way to find out."

Which was why, before she had even hatched any kind

of plan, Evie pressed herself to her feet and excused herself as she squeezed past the others in her row. Buoyed by Zoe's, "Atta girl!" as she made her way down the carriage.

Armand breathed in deep.

He'd been trying to read a tome on Australian patent law all morning, knowing there was something—some key, some clue—that would unlock the problem he'd been hired to unearth, but the tattooed youth to his left bumped him yet again. He couldn't care less about the piercings and symbols carved into the kid's hair, if only he'd damn well sit still.

Armand willed himself to focus. It was why he'd agreed to uproot himself after all. A challenge, a mystery to sink his teeth into, to deflect his thoughts from hurtling down darker, more twisty paths until it became harder and harder to find his way back.

When the words on the page blurred back at him he gave up. Rubbed his eyes. Looked up.

*People watching,* he had told Jonathon when his oldest friend had asked, expression pained, why he insisted on taking public transport instead of the car and driver he could well afford. A childhood hobby, it had been a useful survival skill once he was an adult.

Armand glanced around the cabin as it rocked gently along the tracks.

There was the Schoolgirl Who Sniffs. Behind her the Man Who Has Not Heard of Deodorant. The Women Who Talked About Everyone They'd Ever Met. The Man Who Carried an Umbrella Even When It Had Not Been Raining.

Now he could add the Boy Who Could Not Sit Still.

A glance out the window showed Armand he was nearing town. Frustrated with his lack of progress, he picked up the book again, opening it just as a shadow poured over the pages.

Armand glanced up, past black jeans tucked into knee-high black boots. Black-painted fingernails on a hand grip-ping the handle of the backpack slung over a shoulder. Long dark hair pouring over the shoulders of a jacket. Wind-pinked cheeks. And a heavy silver knitted cap with a huge rainbow pom-pom atop, bobbing in time with the swaying of the train.

Fingers lifted off the strap of the bag in a quick wave as the owner of the hat said, "Hi."

"*Bonjour.*"

"You're French?" She glanced sideways, and out of the side of her mouth said, "*Of course he's French.*"

Armand looked past her, but no. She was talking to her-self.

When he looked back, she tugged the knitted hat further back on her head and he recognised her as the Girl Who Sang to Herself.

A regular, she often sat deeper back in the carriage with her loud, fair-haired friend. On the days she rode alone she wore big white headphones, mouth moving as she hummed, even giving in to the occasional shoulder wiggle or hand movement.

With her wide, dark eyes and uptilted mouth, she had one of those faces that always smiled, even in repose. Add the headphones and she was practically asking to have her bag stolen. No wonder he'd felt the need to keep an eye on her. He'd seen all too often misfortune descending on those who deserved it least.

When his gaze once more connected with hers it was to find she was watching him still.

"You like to read?" she asked.

Armand blinked. He'd been riding the train for a little over two weeks and it was the first time anyone had tried to strike up a conversation with him. Another reason he'd enjoyed the ride.

"I do."

Her dark gaze slid over his hair, down the arm of his

jacket, towards the cover of his book. He turned it over and covered the spine. One didn't become head of an international security firm for nothing.

Armand checked the sign above. With relief he saw his stop was next. She followed his gaze, her mouth twitching before her eyes darted back to his. "How about writing?" she asked, the pace of her words speeding up. "Do you like to write?"

When he didn't leap in with an instant answer, she nibbled on her lip a moment before saying, "I guess there is writing and then there is writing. Texting is wildly different from a thousand-page novel. Or to-do lists compared with…"

As she continued to list the multiple kinds of writing the train slowed and the screech of metal on metal filled his ears, cutting out every other word. The sound dissipating into a hiss as she said, "Or, of course, poetry."

"Poetry?"

She swallowed. Nodded. Her eyes wide. Expectant.

Was he meant to respond in some way? It hadn't felt like a question. In fact, it felt as if he'd stumbled into the middle of someone else's conversation.

And suddenly the singing, the constant smile, the talking to herself, the novelty backpack, his persistent urge to keep an eye on her—it all made sense.

She was a Van Gogh short of a gallery.

He felt his shoulders relax just a little.

"Are you asking if I like poetry?"

She nodded.

"The greats can make you laugh, cry, think, ache, but it depends on the poet. You?"

"I've never really thought about it. I appreciate the skill it must take. Finding words that rhyme. Creating patterns in sound and cadence."

"Look closer. You'll find it's never about a cat who sat on a mat," he said as he pulled himself to his feet.

The woman gripped harder to her backpack strap as she looked up, up, up into his eyes. Her pupils all but disappearing into the edges of her dark irises.

"What is it about?" she asked.

He leaned in a fraction and said, "Wooing."

"Wooing?" she said, her voice a little rough. Her fingers gripping the strap of her bag. "Right. But the thing is, I'm in a transitional period. My life is kind of in upheaval right now. No room for wooing."

"Then my advice would be to stay away from poetry."

The train bumped to a halt, putting an end to the exchange either way. He slid his book into his briefcase.

But she didn't budge an inch.

He angled his chin towards the door. "This is my stop."

"I know." *Blink.* "I mean, right, okay."

She looked as if she had more to say, but the words were locked behind whatever traps and mazes had befallen her afflicted mind.

*"Excusez-moi."*

A frown flickered over her forehead as the occupants of the carriage swarmed towards the door. Gripping tightly onto the loop hanging from the bar above kept her from smacking bodily against him, but not from stamping down on his foot with the heel of her boot.

He winced, sucking in a sharp breath as pain lanced his toes.

She spun, grabbed him by the arm and said, "Oh, no! Oh, sorry! Sorry, sorry, sorry!"

Then he remembered.

They had spoken once before. His first day on the train she'd elbowed him right in the solar plexus.

If he'd been a man who looked for signs he'd have taken it to mean he'd made a grave error in travelling halfway across the earth in the hopes of being led out of his fugue.

"The Girl with the Perfect Aim," Armand muttered.

"I'm sorry?"

The doors opened, bringing with them a burst of light and chill, rain-scented air. Armand put a hand on the girl's elbow as he squeezed around her, joining the river of people heading out the train doors.

*Strange young woman*, he thought. Yet, he conceded, compelling enough to distract him with alacrity no book or challenge or mystery had yet managed.

He felt those burnished eyes on him long after he'd left the darkness of the station and headed into the grey light of the chilly Melbourne winter's day.

## CHAPTER TWO

EVIE GOT LOST—twice—while trying to find the front door to the Game Plan offices.

For starters, she'd stayed on the train till the next station. No way was she about to follow Hot Stuff in the Swanky Suit. If he'd seen her and was smart—and he certainly appeared to be—he'd have called the police. For oh, how she'd bungled that conversation royally.

Once she'd found the funky, arty little alleyway listed on the Game Plan website, she walked to the end and back without finding the door.

Not her fault. She blamed those stormy blue eyes. That accent. The scent—mysterious, masculine, drinkable. The serious don't-poke-the-bear vibes rippling off the man like a mirage. Wondered if the ten-day stubble sweeping over his hard jaw was rough or soft. How could she make thoughts when he'd held her by the elbow and her nerves had been replaced by fireworks?

Every second of the encounter had been cringeworthy and it had all been for naught.

Born with a talent for seeing patterns in numbers, in lines of text, in architecture and nature, Evie did not have the same gift for reading people—a theory backed up by her choice of boyfriends in the past. But she had no doubt Hot Stuff believed her a chip short of a motherboard.

As to whether—or not—he'd written the poem... Who knew?

Stupid fortune cookie. Whether its powers were mystical or merely persuasive, she hadn't been the same since she'd set eyes on it. The sooner she put the whole thing behind her and got on with her life the better.

She stopped in the middle of the alley, looked up into the overcast sky and breathed. "Get it together, kid. And fast."

When she looked back down she found herself in front of a white door tucked into the white brick wall. It had to be the place.

"Okay. You can do this. You want this. You need this."

She'd only just started making a name for herself, working on government contracts, really intricate work. She was most proud of finding and fixing a fissure in the Federal Reserve's security system. One they hadn't even known was there.

But after the way things went downhill in her last job she was tainted by association. Most of her contacts wouldn't take her calls. Those who did wished her luck and got off the phone. Fast.

She had to convince Game Plan to give her a chance by sheer force of personality alone.

Taking a deep breath, she lifted a finger to press the buzzer when the door opened. Of course, they had video surveillance. This was Game Plan. Meaning somewhere some security dude had seen her talking to herself.

Super.

Her heart played a staccato against her ribs as she stepped into a waiting area with white walls, bright fluorescent lighting, potted plants. Needless to say, her jaw dropped an inch when instead of an HR clone an invisible door finally opened to reveal Jonathon Montrose, Mr Game Plan himself.

He looked exactly like he did on the jacket of his autobiography. Rugged. Imposing. Tall. Not as tall as Hot Stuff in the Swanky Suit, mind you.

*Really? You want to go there now?*

*No, I don't!*

*Then focus.*

Evie whipped her beanie off her head, and once more felt the static turn her into a human generator. Madly patting her hair back down, she walked to the man and held out a hand.

"Mr Montrose, I'm Evie Croft. It's an honour. Your *Code of Ethics* textbook is my bible." Evie imagined Zoe holding out both hands, urging her to pace herself.

"From what I hear you can also tear apart code like a demon."

Evie's heart whumped, wondering who he'd heard it from. Her ex-boss? Her ex? The federal police? No way was she getting the job. Nevertheless, she said, "You hear right."

"Shall we?" Montrose held out a hand, ushering her through another door. "Welcome to the Bullpen."

And, while she would have liked to appear even slightly cool, her feet ground to a halt a metre inside the room and she gawped at the sight before her.

Despite the modest entry, the place was gargantuan. Two storeys of glass-walled offices circled the outer rim of the floors above, while the ground floor looked as if it had been hit with a paintball explosion. White walls and floors were splattered with brightly coloured beanbags, cubicles, desks, couches, exercise balls, computers, TVs and in between slouched dozens of guys in jeans, T-shirts and baseball caps, laughing, arguing, creating.

When she found her feet again, Evie followed Montrose along a wall of nooks filled with gaming rooms, VR rigs, darts, pinball machines. One room had rows of bunk beds like a camp dorm.

"When can I move in?"

Montrose laughed. While Evie took it all in—every rivet, every light fitting, every gumball machine, in case she never saw its like again.

Right when Evie felt as if she'd hit sensory overload, Montrose led her up a set of stairs to a huge but relatively subdued office on the second floor, tinted windows looking over the Bullpen below. When he shut the door, everything went quiet.

Evie breathed out in relief when the first woman she'd seen in the place popped her head into Montrose's office and said, "I'm grabbing a coffee. Can I get you guys anything?"

Evie shook her head, frantically gentling her mind. "No, thanks, I'm fine."

"Nothing for me. Thanks, Imogen," said Montrose, and the woman walked back out the door, leaving them alone.

Montrose motioned to a leather tub chair. Evie slid her backpack to the floor and sat.

Montrose sat on the edge of his desk—very much in the power position—crossed his feet at the ankles and began. "Tell me, Evie, why did you leave your last job?"

Evie opened her mouth to give the sensible answer Zoe had forced her to rehearse. Something along the lines of, *After several years of loyal service, I felt I'd achieved all I could and needed a new challenge.*

But she'd always been sensible. Taken small, considered steps. Choosing work she could do with her eyes closed, saving her pennies by sleeping on Zoe's futon. And it had all come crashing down around her ears anyway.

Because luck was out of her hands. Just ask the fortune cookie.

Hang on a second. If losing her last job ticked off the career part of her fortune's portent of "bad luck", this opportunity was uncontaminated. Clean. A fresh start.

And if she truly wanted to make an impression on the likes of Jonathon Montrose, playing it safe wasn't going to work this time.

Forgoing baby steps for a blind leap off a tall cliff, she looked her idol in the eye and jumped.

"You already know why I left, Mr Montrose."

The edge of his mouth twerked. She hoped it was a good sign.

He said, "Indulge me."

Okay then. "I worked for Binary Logistics until my ex-boss's son, Eric—who also happens to be my ex-boyfriend—embezzled from the company. That company is now under investigation by every federal agency there is and, considering my position, my access level, my connection to the guilty party, I was a suspect for co-conspiracy. Thankfully they caught Eric at the airport and he confessed to everything, their forensic decoders followed his trail with ease and I was cleared. But mud like that sticks. Which means you are the only person who has taken my call, much less asked me in for an interview."

She would love to have made it to the end without swallowing but if she didn't wet her dry throat she'd probably pass out.

"And why do you think I would do that?" he asked.

"You're a risk-taker, Mr Montrose. You actually like that I am marginalised. Perhaps I wouldn't have piqued your interest otherwise. You like that it has made me hungry and desperate, because I'll push to prove myself. Qualities you value within yourself."

A muscle flickered at the corner of his mouth. "Maybe. Or maybe I appreciated the gumption it took to even try to get an interview with me, knowing what I know."

Evie's laugh was a little shaky. "Every bit of gumption I have."

From there the interview took a turn into the normal, with Montrose asking about her family—her beloved granddad who'd moved into a retirement village, leaving his farming days behind him—and hobbies—gaming, knitting, hanging with Zoe.

And suddenly it was all over.

Montrose stood and so did she. Grabbing her backpack. And popping her beanie back on her head.

He blinked at the rainbow pom-pom but to his credit said nothing about it. Though he did say, "You are clearly a very bright young woman, Evie. Someone whose name has appeared on my radar more than once. I've heard men with far greater experience gasp over the work you've done, without knowing whose it was."

Evie held her breath.

"Unfortunately, though, I don't have anything for you at this time. I'd suggest you see this career break as an opportunity to look up and out. Read a book, travel, get your hands dirty. In the meantime, we will certainly keep you in mind for future work."

*What? Wait. No. No!*

Evie opened her mouth to state her case. To ask to be given a chance. To drop to her knees and beg if that was what it took. Because, having taken the leap, she could feel the wind in her hair and she wanted more.

But Jonathon was already distracted, and old habits were hard to break. Evie stood, put her beanie back on, grabbed her backpack and—

White noise from downstairs burst into the room as the office door was opened and a voice said, "Do you have a second? I need you to look at…"

The voice came to an abrupt halt.

But it was too late. The accent, the gravel in the tone, the huge amount of air that had been displaced—Evie knew who she'd find when she spun on her heel.

A small noise left her throat as she found herself staring down Hot Stuff in the Swanky Suit. He filled the doorway, the light from below tracing his broad shoulders, his wide stance, his mussed hair.

But gone was the bare hint of that smile he'd given as she'd babbled on about poetry and wooing. The one that had scrambled her brain, making it impossible for her to work out what was real and what wasn't.

Instead his entire body was taut as he glared as if he'd found her in his kitchen boiling his bunny.

"You," Hot Stuff accused, his voice deep and rumbling. Feeling like a squished bug under the microscope of a stranger's unflattering glare, Evie was finally overcome by the dire reality of her situation and something snapped. "Oh, my God, did you *follow* me here?"

"I believe that is a question I should be asking."

"*Pfft*. Why would I follow *you*?"

The self-assurance in his gaze made her knees go a little weak. And fine, he had a point. But still!

"Excuse me," said Evie. "I made it perfectly clear I'm not interested in your…" She flapped a hand at him, taking in his tousled hair, his arresting face, his slick suit, before blurting, "Your poetry."

Perhaps "perfectly clear" was pushing it, but it had been her intention, which had to count for something.

Yet the man glowered at her, *Why me?* written all over his face.

Seeing him with Montrose's book might have given her the idea to apply for a job with Game Plan. And, come to think of it, had she seen him reading a file with the Game Plan logo on the front? Either way, it didn't seem like admitting it would help her cause in that moment, so she kept her mouth shut.

She saw something move out of the corner of her eye, and was reminded that they weren't alone. She slowly turned to find Jonathon leaning against his desk, looking as if he was enjoying himself immensely.

"I take it you two know one another?" Montrose asked.

Hot Stuff had gone all silent and broody once more, forcing Evie to answer. "We don't know each other, exactly. We catch the same train. Every day. Morning and night. Across the aisle and three rows down."

She took a deep breath in though her nose and caught a scent. Like sailing. And sunshine. Serious masculine heat. Evie knew Hot Stuff had moved to stand next to her. Trying to intimidate her with his presence, no doubt. Arrogant so-and-so.

She half-closed her right eye to block him out as she said,

"Though I did elbow him in the gut once. Stood on his foot as well. And that about covers it."

"Is that right?" Jonathon asked, eyes bright.

When Hot Stuff cleared his throat, Evie leapt into the silence with, "Maybe you could do me one favour, Mr Montrose, and say the bit again about how bright you think I am. For I believe your friend has other ideas."

Montrose turned to the man at her side. "Do you?" he asked, laughter lighting his voice. "Do you have other ideas about Evie?"

She glanced sideways to find Hot Stuff gritting his teeth so hard he could pull a muscle.

Deciding to give the guy a tiny break—he had to be as much in shock as she was, after all—she cleared her throat and held out a hand. "I'm Evie, by the way. Evie Croft."

Hot Stuff blinked at her hand, then his gaze lifted to tangle with hers. For a beat. Another. Something dark swirled behind those stormy eyes before he took her hand in his. Of course, it was warm and smooth. The moment they touched a little shock ran up her arm and landed with a sizzle in her chest.

"Armand Debussey," he said in his deep French drawl. Then he took his hand back and looked, deliberately, at Montrose. "What's she doing here?"

Evie scoffed. So much for letting bygones be bygones. "*She* is in the middle of an interview for a coder's dream job," Evie said. Well, it had officially been the end of the interview. Semantics.

"What job might that be?" Hot Stuff asked.

Evie opened her mouth, only to discover she had no idea. She looked at Montrose. And smiled. *Like me! Want me! In a purely professional sense. Okay, stop thinking before you accidentally say any of this out loud.*

Montrose pushed away from his desk and ambled around the edge until he was behind it. Showing who was boss.

Then he looked to Armand and said, "She's a forensic code investigator."

Evie bit her bottom lip so hard it hurt. For something in the way he said it made her wonder, made her hope—

"You cannot be serious," said Armand, his voice taut. "She cannot do it. She can't. She's too..." Armand looked at her then, the fire in his eyes filled with danger. And warning.

Evie was a good girl, a smart girl. She kept her goals manageable and took her wins where she could. For her mother had been the exact opposite and it hadn't worked out well for her at all.

But here, now, instead of taking a rational step back, she felt herself sway towards Armand. Her hands went to her hips, she looked him dead in the eye, and said, "I'm too what?"

The man didn't flinch. If not for his radiating warmth he could have been a statue. The statue said, "You're a dewy-eyed *naïf*, Ms Croft. This place will eat you alive."

As she gawped at him his eyes went to her head. Or, more precisely, her beanie. Then, as if she were three years old, he reached out and tugged on the rainbow pom-pom, no doubt sending it wobbling like crazy.

She smacked his hand away but it was already gone. The man had lightning reflexes. "Well, you, Mr Debussey, are seriously hostile. And what do dewy eyes have to do with my ability to ferret out secret passages, hidden codes, keystones, Easter eggs, back doors in code? With cutting viruses from the flesh of a program without spilling a single drop of blood?"

Armand looked at her as if she was the one talking a foreign language.

"Just because I don't wear fancy suits, or come from a big city, or get my hair to look all perfectly wind-mussed, and finger-fussed, at Ooh-La-La Salon, doesn't mean I'm not killer at what I do. I am the best forensic code investigator you will ever meet, my friend. Put that in your pipe and smoke it."

*Put that in your pipe and smoke it?* Who said that? *Dewy-eyed naïfs, that's who.* As Evie's words swirled around the room like crazy little whirlwinds, she stopped to catch her breath. And wished with all her might she'd never leapt in in the first place. For ever since she'd struggled to regain solid ground.

Biting both lips together now, Evie slowly turned back to Montrose with the full intention of apologising. Only to find something had lit up behind Montrose's eyes. Even with her poor ability to decipher such subtleties, deep inside her instincts shook.

"Right," said Montrose. "Now you've both cleared the air of whatever that was, I'm sure it will make working together all the easier."

"I'm sorry?" said Armand, his voice rich with warning.

"Working together?" Evie asked, her voice sounding as though she were on helium.

"I'm putting you on contract. One project. A trial run, if you will. Congratulations, Evie, the job is yours."

Evie rushed over to the desk and shook Montrose's hand. "Thank you. I won't let you down."

Montrose nodded. "I know you won't. Take a right outside my door and you'll find Imogen's office. She'll get you set up with employee paperwork, security card, pay details etc. Be back here at eight tomorrow."

"Yes, sir. Thank you, sir." Evie spun in a circle—beanie, check, backpack, check—before darting out the door and shutting it behind her. The murmur of rising male voices faded as she hotfooted it to the office next door.

So what if she'd be working in the same building as Armand Debussey? And hadn't asked about pay, benefits, hours? She had a job! And not just any job! Forensic code investigation for Game Plan!

Her luck had surely turned.

She'd just have to steer clear of Armand Debussey as much as humanly possible, which shouldn't be hard in a company this size. And over time, her discomfort around him would fade.

And she'd remember this day not as one of her most bumbling but as one of her best.

Frustration riding every inch of him, Armand stalked behind Jonathon's desk, opened the mini-bar and pulled out a bottle of Scotch. He didn't bother asking Jonathon if he wanted one. He could get his own damn drink.

Armand poured himself just enough to cover the bottom of the glass, needing the burn in his throat to take the edge off whatever had just yanked him so vehemently from the mouth of *ennui*. Had made him burn.

He glanced at the screen embedded in Jonathon's desk to see the note Jonathon sent to Imogen about Evie Croft. A contract, as promised. One project. Armand translated Australian dollars to Euros and scowled at the pay offer. Why anyone chose to work for the man he had no idea.

"It's not even ten in the morning," Jonathon noted.

Armand tossed back the drink, wincing at the heat. "It's midnight in Paris."

"Then go for your life. And to answer your burning question," said Jonathon, "she did not follow you here, she applied for the job a few days ago. Nice girl. Next-level intelligence. Yet I had decided not to hire her when you came storming in."

"What the hell changed?"

"You tell me."

Armand knew Jonathon was baiting him. And why. Armand took a long, deep breath and waited. He could wait for ever, if that was what it took. One good thing about not giving a damn—his indifference knew no bounds.

Jonathon squinted his way. "Is it hard for you to believe I hired her on her merits? Is it because she's a woman?"

"*Non*," Armand scoffed, wounded by the accusation. "*Mon Dieu*—"

"English, please."

"No."

"Is it because she's young?" Jonathon asked.

"How old is she?"

"I didn't ask. We're not allowed to these days."

Armand looked to the ceiling and muttered.

"*En Anglais, s'il vous plaît*," said Jonathon.

"You understood every word."

Jonathon grinned. "Mid-twenties, I'd say. The age of blissful ignorance and creative hubris. An advantage in her line of work. While you, five years older at most, bear the weight of the entire world on your well-bred shoulders."

Not any more, Armand thought, tipping the last drop of Scotch onto his tongue before putting the glass on the desk.

"How did it come about on your daily train trips, morning and night, across the aisle and three rows down, you came to think her not clever?"

Armand merely slanted him a look.

"Save it for another time, then. Until then I assure you— Evie Croft is special."

Armand railed against the thought as the embers inside him flared. But he listened, as the mountain of paperwork— legal documents, in-house communications, news articles, company reports—Jonathon had foisted on him had not yet yielded results.

Jonathon went on. "One of my guys picked up on her chatter online a couple of years back. Tough talk about cracking one of our most complicated games. Turned out it wasn't just talk. The last company she worked for was a lumbering dinosaur, a house of cards waiting to tumble, but her work therein was inspired. I'd go so far as saying she's a prodigy."

Armand ran a hand down his face. He knew that look

in Jonathon's eye. The gleam. For Jonathon was no longer pulling his leg.

"If it's not because she's a woman," said Jonathon, "and it's not because she's young, and now you know she can do the work, do we still have a problem here?"

Armand wanted to say *no problem*. To accept the inevitable. For all he wanted was to fix Jonathon's problem and go home. Back to the familiar, the safe. But for some reason he couldn't say the words.

"It's the dewy-eyed *naïf* thing, isn't it?"

Armand dropped his face into his palm and laughed, the sound hollow, humourless. "I knew that would come back to haunt me."

"I'd go as far as to say that's exactly why Ms Croft got under your skin just now. You are worried when you bump into her in the hall she might spark some proof of life within you. You didn't die that day, my friend, no matter how it might sometimes feel you did..."

Armand shook his head. Just once. But it was enough. Enough for his old friend to know he'd hit the edge of that which Armand would accept.

"What are we to do?" Jonathon asked. "I will not launch my very expensive, very important program until you assure me it is safe. If you believe you don't need Ms Croft and her special skills in order to make that happen then I'll tell Imogen to send her home right now. It's completely up to you."

With his high-level contacts, hands-on experience tracking the worst kinds of men, even his very name, Armand could chase down public information and private conversations, money and mayhem, promises made in huts and boardrooms. He had blown open drug deals, illegal gun sales, fraud rings and worse. He could speak five languages and understand many more.

But when it came to the inner workings of computer code, he was at a loss.

And yet Armand's nostrils flared as he fought against

the overwhelming need to make the call that meant not having to deal with the likes of Evie Croft. Those big dark eyes that hid nothing of what she felt. The tip-tilted mouth with the full bottom lip she nibbled on more than could possibly be necessary. That constant frisson of energy that crackled around her. Those odd knitted hats. The woman was a magnet for trouble.

Armand breathed deep, only to find himself enveloped in a lingering cloud of feminine perfume. Or perhaps it was shampoo. It smelled like cherries, of all things.

The women of his experience wore designer scents. They did not smell like *fruit*. Or wear pom-poms on their headwear. Or have cartoon characters printed on their backpacks. They did not have backpacks at all.

He pictured Evie Croft leaning towards him, hands on hips, lips pressed together, dark eyes flashing, making fun of his suits, his haircut. All while in the midst of a job interview.

She might be dangerously naïve, she might even be a bit of a head case, but she had fortitude. He had to give her that.

Then, before he saw it coming, her image was replaced with another—little black dresses, diamonds and pearls, pale blue eyes filled with judgement, the swing of a neat blonde ponytail heading out the door.

Armand wiped a hand down his face.

At least he could be sure Jonathon had it wrong on one score—Evie Croft was as far from his type as it was possible to be.

"Give her a shot," Armand said. Hearing the rawness of his voice, he took a moment to swallow. "But she is on trial."

"Why do you think I put her on contract? Now go forth. Find out why my perfect program is glitching so that I can launch the damn thing. Knowing nothing that happens between you and Ms Croft will concern HR."

Armand opened his mouth to vehemently deny the accusation.

"Read my lips," said Jonathon. "I Do Not Care. Now that's settled, why did you come storming in? You wanted me to look at something."

Armand searched back through the quagmire of the past ten minutes for the answer then remembered the piece of paper. He found it scrunched up on the floor near his feet. He pressed it open, saw the lines of code he'd hoped Jonathon could explain to him, before folding it neatly and putting it back in his pocket.

Jonathon laughed. "Something for your new workmate to sort out tomorrow, then?"

"So it would seem." Armand pulled himself out of the chair and ambled to the door, pausing with his hand on the frame. "You know what made that whole debacle worth it?"

"I can't wait to hear."

"*Yes, sir. Thank you, sir.*"

Jonathon's face fell to his desk, landing with a thud. "I felt like a dinosaur."

"Serves you right. Sir."

Armand shut the door behind him with a soft click and moved to the railing to look out over that which the staff called the Bullpen.

He took a step back when he saw a rainbow-coloured pom-pom bobbing through the space.

Used as he was to working with serious men—men who in another era would be warriors and guerrillas and pirates and Vikings, men with scars covering every inch of their bodies, inside and out—working around the kids down below in their running shoes and cheap deodorant had been a stretch.

And now he'd been lumbered with the Girl Who Sang to Herself.

He told himself he did not find her whimsy charming. That it was to her detriment. But the truth was he hadn't only kept an eye on her to make sure no one robbed her blind while she listened to music with her eyes closed.

The moment he first set eyes on her he'd not been able to look away. The way she smiled, the way she laughed— she had surely been lit from within. Making the train trips home in the chill Melbourne evenings feel not so dark at a time when he'd thought he'd never feel warm again.

When a man had lived with ice in his veins as long as Armand had, warmth was not a relief. As his sluggish blood heated, straining to pulse faster through his stiff, cold arteries, every part of him ached.

Now she'd be here, every day, till he got the job done.

He wasn't sure how to bear it.

Worse, he wasn't sure he had it in him any more to try.

# CHAPTER THREE

EVIE USUALLY LOVED the train ride into the city.

The rocking of the carriage, the soft *chooga-chooga* of the train rumbling over the tracks, the pockets of suburbia swishing by.

Unable to bring such sensitive work home, she'd had no choice but to chat, listen to music and let her mind wander, riding those blissful streams of creative consciousness that only come with doing nothing. To daydream.

On her own today—as Zoe had been picked up early to take a plane to Sydney for a meeting with the head designers at her work—Evie was a bundle of nerves, counting the stops till one Armand Debussey was due to hop on.

Instead of staring at the train doors all the way into town she worked on her latest beanie.

Her mother had died when she was six, so Evie's granddad had raised her. An old-school gent with a quick mind and flashes of accidental feminism, he'd taught her how to tie her shoelaces, how to fix a tractor, and how to knit.

Right now all she had was a square of yellow, but in the end it would have ear flaps with plaits on the end that could be tied under the chin. Granddad's request for a woman named Corinne who'd just moved into his retirement village on the outskirts of her home town.

But her mind was so scattered, she had to unravel a row and start over three times.

Giving up, she took out her phone and scrolled despondently through the real-estate app until she found three share houses that didn't seem too awful to contemplate.

She called the first to find it already taken.

She called the second. The phone rang out.

She called the third. The ring tone buzzed in her ear as the train doors opened. It was Armand's stop.

For a moment Evie thought he might not appear. He could have taken a different train. Hopped on a different carriage—

"Hello? Hello?" a chipper female voice called in her ear.

"Oh, hello," Evie said into her phone. "Hi. My name's Evie and I'm calling about the share room."

"Super. Well, the fee listed is weekly. The place is freshly painted. Bed supplied, but BYO linen. The room is a double. Has a view of the park."

Evie sat taller as the voice continued extolling the virtues of what sounded like the perfect set-up.

But then her brain hit *pause* as a familiar dark form punched a hole in the sunny doorway. All sexy mussed hair and beastly countenance, the form lingered a beat before moving into the carriage, the fluorescent lights playing over the hard angles of his unfairly beautiful face.

In the back of her mind Evie heard, "Halves-ies on Wi-Fi, electrics and water. Walk to train, shops and bars."

Armand's unerring gaze had found hers, with that potent mix of stormy blue and a French sense of not giving a hoot. And the voice faded to a distant whir.

Evie braced herself for a nod hello before he would no doubt take his usual seat. She could then spend the next ten minutes ignoring him before they got off at the same stop. Then she'd pause to tie her non-existent laces before walking in the same direction but not with him—

Wait. Oh, no. He was coming her way.

Evie's knitting slipped on her lap and the last three casts slid from the needle. Muttering under her breath, she quickly swaddled the mass of yellow wool, one-handed, and shoved it into her backpack.

"Is your friend not here?"

*Good morning to you too*, Evie thought as she looked up.

Only when her eyes met his—to find him staring blankly at the greenery on top of her pumpkin-shaped beanie—did it hit her that he knew she usually sat with a friend.

Meaning he *had* noticed her too. And paid attention.

*"New to your orbit, I find myself struck/By your raven locks, your starlit eyes. What luck..."* The accent reciting the poem in her head was very definitely French and she shook her head hard to make it go away.

Armand took it as an answer. Pointing at the spare seat across from her, he asked, "May I?"

Evie swallowed. "All yours."

"Sorry?" said the voice in her ear.

"Sorry," Evie parroted back. "Sorry, you dropped out for a second. I'm on the train."

Evie crossed her legs as Armand took a seat, tugging on her ruffled skirt, which hadn't seemed short when she'd put it on that morning. Her high brown boots with the even longer socks were no protection, as his legs were so long her bare knees rested in between his.

Not that he seemed to notice. As usual he had a book in his hand and simply got on with reading. Beauty and brains. It was seriously hard not to sigh.

And then the train took off, rocking Evie's legs into Armand's, the shift of his suit pants rubbing roughly against the bare skin of her knees. This was going to be the longest ride of her life.

"Though the rats are gluten-free," said the chipper voice in her ear. "Dairy intolerant and the smell of fruit makes them gag. Any housemate must respect that."

"I'm sorry, did you say rats?"

Armand looked up, frowning. It was his default face. Evie pointed at her phone. He nodded and went back to his book.

After a pause, the voice in her ear said, "Yes."

"You have pet rats?"

The voice scoffed. "I am no more their master than they are mine."

Evie bit her lip and thought about the supplied bed, the walk to the train, the view of a park. "How many rats?"

"I couldn't say. Their numbers ebb and flow. Though Rowena is pregnant right now so a swell is imminent."

Scrunching her eyes tight, Evie said, "Okay, well, thanks. I'll get back to you." And then she hung up.

When she opened her eyes it was to find Armand watching her. The frown was still in place, but it seemed to have softened. Just a little.

Evie waved her phone at him. "Looking for a new place to live."

"With rats?"

"I'm hoping they'll be optional."

"A new job and a new home," he noted.

"You could say I'm in a transitional period."

"Yes, you mentioned that. Yesterday on the train."

"Did I? Well. Any chance we could forget that entire conversation?"

"Already done."

"Super." She smiled, then bit down on her lip.

His gaze dropped to her mouth and a crease formed above his nose. His eyes darkened, as if a cloud had passed over the sun, then he looked away and out the window. Conversation over.

Evie rolled her eyes at herself. Get a grip! Then the train tilted as it rocketed around a corner and Evie's knee slammed into Armand's, before sliding a good inch or two up his leg.

Evie grabbed her seat and shuffled back as deep as she could. While Armand's only reaction was the slide of his gaze to the point of impact.

Did it not bother him the way it bothered her? Or did he not move because he liked it? Could it be, despite evidence to the contrary, he had a little crush on her too? Had he in fact written a poem about her? To her? For her?

There was one way to find out—she could just ask. *Hey, Armand, did you write me a love poem and publish it on Urban Rambler's lonely-hearts page?*

But if it was a no she'd not only have to see him on the train, but at work as well. And mixing personal life and work life was a recipe for disaster. She'd learned that lesson the hard way.

And what about the slim chance he'd say *yes*?

She came over a little wobbly in the belly, tingly behind the knees. Which was more than enough of a reason for a case of don't ask, don't tell.

Needing to say something lest she say the one thing she could not, she said, "No Australian patent-law book today?"

A few moments went by before Armand looked up. He lifted the cover of his book—this one by a certain Nathaniel Hawthorne.

"Any good?"

Armand surprised her by asking, "You haven't read it?"

"Might have seen the movie."

Armand's sigh was long-suffering.

"Don't panic. I do read. I'm in my granddad's retirement-village book club. This month we're reading a JD Robb. Futuristic cop romance. They're awesome."

Armand's face remained impassive. But Evie swore she saw a flash of sufferance behind his eyes. The guy had no idea what he was missing. "And when you're not reading?"

"I game."

Armand winced. This time it was obvious even to her, the queen of misreading people.

"Don't knock it till you try it. The good games, the really great ones—it's not about the effects, or the amazing CGI, it's about the story. Those ones get under your skin, make you think. Make you laugh, cry, even sigh."

She realised all too late she'd mirrored his words from the day before when he'd spoken of great poetry.

Maybe it was best to get it out there, to be sure. Otherwise the energy used to keep a lid on it might cause her to implode.

She sat forward, her hands draping over her knees. "Armand. Can I call you Armand? Of course I can; it's your name."

His gaze remained on hers, his eyes so dark she could not make out the colour at all.

"About yesterday, on the train, when I asked if you like poetry…"

He sat forward too. He smelled amazing. Clean, laundered. Edible. "Didn't we already agree it was forgotten?"

"Mmm-hmm."

A sunbeam chose that moment to hit the window of the train, sending shards of diffused light over his face. The man looked like a prince. One who had left the palace long ago, heading off on a thankless crusade to slay a dragon or rescue a princess or free a kingdom. Only he'd got lost along the way—head injury? Magic spell?—and couldn't reconcile how he found himself on a train heading towards inner-city Melbourne.

"Ms Croft," he said, "Jonathon does not hire lightly. He does so with recklessness, at times, but always in the hope of creating magic. You have been given a chance to be a part of something important. Make it count."

The train lurched and her fingers grazed his knee. She jerked them back.

Then he was standing, moving through the crowd, and she realised the train had reached their stop.

Evie grabbed her bag, apologised as she squeezed past legs, stepped over bags. Once outside the train she caught up to Armand.

He turned quickly, and she nearly banged into him.

"I have a stop to make first," he said.

She took another step back. "Right. Okay. Well, I might see you around work."

He looked at her in that long, slow, considering way he had, then with a nod he slipped through the crowd and was gone.

Reading normal people was hard enough. Reading a man who acted like Yoda had had a makeover and ended up on the cover of *GQ* was impossible.

Leaving Evie to lift her arms in a shrug of utter confusion.

But nobody paid her any heed.

She shifted her backpack into a more comfortable position and headed off to the first day of the rest of her life.

Having used her shiny new security key to enter the Game Plan building, Evie walked into the Bullpen. The colour, the noise, the light like an elixir to her soul.

Armand had hit on something. She'd been given a second chance here. A chance to do things differently this time. It might even be time to forgo the baby steps for bigger strides. For third chances were rare.

So, rather than hiding herself away, she introduced herself to anyone who looked up from their work, determined not to take cover from office politics. Anything to make sure she wasn't blindsided like last time.

"You're Evie Croft, right?" asked a guy about her age.

"Um, yes."

"Your arrival was pinged in the daily company email alongside a Roger and a Phil. Pretty easy guess. You might not have noticed but this place is testosterone-heavy."

By the looks of the room, the testosterone levels were pretty mild, but she just smiled and shrugged. "Used to it."

"I'm Jamie."

Evie shook his hand. Felt the familiar rough thumb pads of a guy who gamed. Caught the gleam of interest in his eyes and let go.

Fortune cookie or no fortune cookie, she was going to make good decisions, the first of which was to keep work and monkey business a million miles apart.

"I'd better get started," she said, backing away. "Nice to meet you."

"See you around, Evie."

Evie followed the instructions Imogen had given her the day before, heading back up the stairs that led to Jonathon's office, before heading down a dark hall with a single door at the very end. No glass here. Very mysterious.

She went to open the door to find it locked. Now what?

Then she noticed a small discreet pad lodged into the wall, with buttons the same colour as the paint. A keycode? Fingerprint? She tried hers but nothing happened.

She turned, thinking to head…somewhere, when the door opened inward with a flourish.

Evie jumped back as a dark figure appeared in the doorway, backlit by a dim glow. "Jeez, you scared me!"

"Apologies."

That voice… "Armand?"

Without another word, he pressed the door open wider and motioned for her to come inside. A golden glow created a halo around his profile—strong nose, sombre forehead, unkempt hair shading his stormy blue eyes.

"I'm really not following you, I promise."

He opened the door a fraction wider, giving her a glimpse of dark wood and low lamplight, a pair of small lounge chairs—elegant dark brown to match the rest of the room. Coffee table, ditto. Bookshelves. It was like something out of a gothic novel. It suited him to a T.

She kept her feet firmly planted in the hall.

"Are you waiting for a formal invitation, Ms Croft?"

"To what? Here?" She poked her head inside, and counted the desks—one, two. "With you? I'm to be working in here with you?"

"For me," he qualified.

Well, that was way better.

"Of course, if you are second-guessing your decision to take on the role, I can let Jonathon know—"

"Are you kidding? I'm delighted. Thrilled! Look at me." She stretched a huge smile across her face to prove it. Then, hitching her backpack higher onto her shoulder, she nudged past, catching a waft of lemongrass, of cedar, of clean, groomed man.

Evie took off her beanie and blew out a breath, a wave of hair sweeping away from her face. "Any chance you might have told me this morning?"

The edge of Armand's mouth flickered, before his face settled into its usual blank cool. One hand slid into the pocket of his suit pants, his scruffy hair slipping over one eye. "The work is sensitive. We will not be discussing such things in public venues."

She opened her mouth to say *Won't we, now?* but, considering the kind of work she was used to doing, she believed him.

When Evie turned Armand had moved deeper into the room. She tipped back so fast she had to take a step away. "Look, you were right. This morning in the train. Today is a new beginning for me. As such I'd like for us to start again too." She held out a hand. "Hi, I'm Evie Croft. Nice to meet you."

The pools of golden light created shadows upon shadows over his dark form, so she nearly missed the spark that flickered to life in his eyes before he reached out and took her hand in his.

Once again, a zap of electricity shot from his hand through hers like a delicious little shock.

"Armand Debussey," he drawled. "*Enchanté.*"

She offered a most professional nod, then quickly pulled her hand away. "So, what now?"

Armand glanced at her a beat longer before his dark

gaze swept past her and he motioned with a tilt of his chin. "Now we get to work."

She moved to follow the direction of his gaze, but at the last moment saw him surreptitiously rub his thumb into the palm, as if trying to rid himself of pins and needles.

Had he felt it too? The zap? No. Surely not. It was probably just nerves. Or static electricity from the commercial carpet.

A small voice in the back of her head said, *Work, monkey business, a million miles apart*. Her train crush and his poem—or not—could not matter from this moment on. They were colleagues, nothing more. Zip. The end.

One of the desks had a single yellow banker's lamp, paper calendar, a pristine notebook, pencils lined up just so. Definitely his.

In the other corner, the second desk was big, shiny and black. Hinged for sitting or standing. Ergonomic chair. Linked to three huge monitors. And was that…? It was! An encrypted solid-state hard drive, the likes of which she'd only heard rumoured.

"Please tell me that's mine."

"It's certainly not mine."

That was all she needed to hear.

She all but ran across the room, dumping her backpack, gaze dancing from one glorious technological wonder to the next. Whatever she had been hired to do, she'd been given state-of-the-art hardware with which to do it.

She'd set up employee name, password, fingerprint and retinal ID with Imogen the day before. With a single swipe of her finger, the system turned on.

"Pinch me," she muttered.

"*Pardon?*" Armand said, now leaning back against the edge of his desk, hands gripped lightly around the wood, watching her settle in.

Her heart fluttered like a butterfly at the sight. But she pushed the feeling back down.

"Okay, then, boss. Where do I begin?"

Armand did the chin-tilt thing, motioning to a note on her desk. Apparently, she was to click on the only icon on the screen and follow the prompts.

She'd been so untethered by the events of her past week she couldn't wait to get her teeth stuck into something solid.

As for Hot Stuff in the Swanky Suit? She'd find a way to work with him without swooning, or snapping, or she'd die trying.

Armand, who wished to get back to the slew of work he had to get through, instead watched as Evie brought a flexible plastic rectangle out of her backpack, uncurled a thin cord from one corner and plugged it into the hard drive of the main computer.

He might not know much about software, but he had a handle on mechanics. And this was not regulation. "May I ask what it is you think you are doing?"

"Hmm?"

He pointed to the foreign object on her desk.

"Cool, right? Not a Qwerty keyboard. Programmed so that only I know the order of the keys."

Armand, who typed with two fingers and only when forced, asked, "Why?"

"Security."

"I'm not sure Jonathon would concur—"

"He knows. I emailed him the specs last night."

"Again, why?"

Evie's fingers stretched as they hovered over the shiny black contraption. "Fair question, since I'll be working with…sorry, *for* you. In my last job, someone used my access code to embezzle from the company."

The hairs rose on the back of Armand's neck and his fingers curled in on themselves as he glanced in the direction of his friend's office.

"It's okay," Evie said. "Jonathon knows."

Armand glanced back at her and stretched out his hands. It wasn't okay. It wasn't even close to being okay.

"How did it happen?"

"The person, the embezzler, was the boss's son. And my ex-boyfriend. Turned out he'd hidden cameras in my office so he could copy my key strokes."

She rested her hands gently over her blank keyboard then blinked at him, her eyes big, shining, sombre. "I was a total dewy-eyed *naïf*. The only reason I don't still lie awake at night berating myself is that the authorities are confident the money will all be recovered."

She'd been worse than naïve. As Armand saw it, she'd been grossly negligent. But he also knew about lying awake at night, riddled with regret.

"If he'd been smart enough to code, if he'd even touched my computer I'd have known it. I could have stopped him. Ironically it was the fact he was clueless that gave him the advantage over me."

Armand bristled. He had degrees in law, economics and art history. He owned an internationally renowned private-security company. He could defuse a bomb with his bare hands. But if a computer locked up he'd have to call Tech Support.

Not that he'd been near a bomb in some time. Now he spent his days sorting fake Picassos from real for his family's art collections, his mother claiming the genteel world of art was where someone with his intellect ought to be. Not out "playing the hero", nearly killing them all with worry.

"Anyway," Evie went on, "it taught me to be extra-vigilant. No one's ever going to pull the wool over my eyes again. If you'd like I can show you how this thing works…"

Armand held up both hands. But it was shiny and space-age and he was a man. Curious despite himself, he asked, "Where did you find such a thing?"

"It's a prototype. I invented it."

"You?"

She nodded slowly. "Yeah, me. Ironically if I'd not worked all those extra hours at my last job, I'd have had more spare time to finish this baby and Eric would never have had the chance to do what he did. Anyway, while I can only hope you don't plan to frame me for embezzlement, I'm using the keyboard and that's that."

Armand waved a hand in acquiescence. "Have it."

Which she did.

Leaving Armand to wonder what the hell Jonathon was thinking.

Perhaps she was innocent, but she'd been duped. Her instincts were less than exemplary. Her relative youth might be an asset when it came to the job at hand, but her naivety was a proven liability. She jeopardised the entire team.

Armand sat behind his desk, running a hand over the bristles on his chin. He knew exactly what Jonathon was thinking. The hero complex that terrified his parents would have him fall head over heels for one ingenuous brunette.

Jonathon had been a player his whole life. Gambling with ideas, with investment and invention. Only this time he was playing with people.

One who wanted this job with her whole heart.

One who had no heart left.

Meaning the sooner the job was done, the sooner he could leave the game. Go back to Paris. And sink back into a life of ease and comfort where he'd never put a loved one in the path of danger again.

Two hours later Evie's leg ached from jiggling.

The icon on the smaller screen had led to a slew of training videos covering everything from how to turn on a computer to proper workplace language, each finishing with twenty-five inane multiple questions to answer at the end. It was mind-numbing. Life-sapping.

She glanced up to find Armand still poring over the papers on his desk. The man's focus was impressive. Figuring he could keep it up for hours, she wriggled on her seat, and with a few relatively easy clicks found her way into the back end of the program she'd been forced to undergo. Another half an hour and she was done. Each program now registered as complete.

"Done!" she called out.

Armand took a moment to glance up at the analogue clock on the wall beside his desk. "You're finished?"

"Yep. What's next? Unless I've been put in this room with you as some kind of scientific experiment. See how long it takes me to crack. Or you!"

Armand slowly leant back in his chair. "Am I to expect this level of chatter to continue?"

"Oh, yeah. My granddad was a big one for curiosity. Whether I was keen to know about tractor engines, or constellations, or ant hills, or bones in the wrist, he'd take time to answer any questions I posed. I posed a lot."

Ah, Granddad. Evie wondered what he was doing in that moment. He seemed to truly be enjoying life in the lovely local retirement village, which was so wonderful. Costing her every spare penny to cover the rental, but better that than sell the farm—his lifeblood, her home.

She blinked back to the present to find Armand sitting still, breathing slowly, exuding such an air of rakish sophistication he could well have been part-vampire. She'd always had a thing for vampires.

"My turn," Evie trilled. "If I'm Chatty Cathy, why are you taciturn?"

He blinked. For him that was as telling as a flinch. "I don't see the point in speaking unless one has something of worth to say."

"Ouch. That was a dig at me, right?"

The edge of his mouth flickered and Evie held her breath. A smile? Was it coming? But no, his face eased back into its usual watchful repose.

"Here's something worth discussing," said Evie. "Tell me about the project I'll be working on."

Armand blanked, and sat up tall. "We'll get to that. Why don't you take a break?"

Evie rolled her eyes and stood, grabbing her backpack and heading for the door. But she stopped before she made it past his desk. "You will have to tell me eventually, you know. Give me full and proper access to all the boxes with the wires and engines and microchips."

She paused, deciding how best to put a dent in her co-hort's perfect façade. "It's not a big leap to figure out what I'll be doing. I'm a hacker. Jonathon needs me to hack. Find errors and to clean up the mess. Right?"

Anything? A glimmer of surprise? Of admiration at her powers of deduction? Nope. *Nada.*

"Here's something to mull over—while I have yet to find a system, a program, a game, a brand of software that I cannot infiltrate, I can't analyse that code unless I actually see the code."

Armand rose, forcing Evie's chin to tilt as she looked up into his shadowed face. Only he moved to the shelves, where he picked out a heavy-looking text and brought it back to his desk, where once again he sat.

Evie felt totally flustered. Not that there was anything rushed about him—more an overwhelming sense of power well-leashed.

He picked up a pencil, perfectly sharpened, and gripped it between his teeth as he sat back in his chair and began to read.

Which was when it hit her. "Where's your computer, Armand? Your cell phone? I see pencils, I see notebooks, I see a lot of paper. You're a technophobe!"

She clapped her hands together before jumping out into a star. *Ta-da!* Only her audience wasn't clapping. She shuffled her feet back together. "I'm going on a break now. Want anything? Coffee? Tea?"

She—very smartly—stopped herself from saying *Me?* Even in jest. She hadn't needed to take a quiz on Appropriate Interpersonal Office Relations to know it was best to steer clear of those kinds of conversations with Armand from now on.

"No? Then I'll see you in half an hour."

Evie headed down the stairs, grabbed an apple from her bag and made her way towards the exit in search of fresh air. Though she soon found herself waylaid by the noise and bling of the Bullpen.

She slowed, dawdling past the little alcoves to find a couple of guys duelling on pinball machines, a couple talking string theory while playing vintage Ataris, and—

"Evie."

Evie spun on her heel. "Jamie. Hi."

"Looking for someone?"

"Break time," she said, holding up her apple.

He blinked as if he'd never seen such a strange food. "I'm thinking you've not yet found the Yum Lounge."

"I have not."

Jamie cocked his head, motioning for her to follow. Follow she did, but not before glancing up the stairs as if expecting to see Armand hiding in the shadows, watching over her like her own personal avenging angel.

The "Yum Lounge" turned out to be Game Plan's private restaurant. Jamie pointed the way to a two-seater table together in the corner of the room. When their meals came out they looked and tasted like something out of *Masterchef.*

Evie sat back, holding a hand over her belly. "Amazing. But I do not want to ask what that just cost me."

"Not a cent," said Jamie with a grin.

She sat up straight. *Oh, no. No, no, no.* "No, Jamie, you can't… This wasn't…"

He grinned. "Relax. I didn't. It's all part of the package."

"Seriously? Pinch me." Evie held out her arm.

Jamie grinned at her. Then reached out and gave her arm a pinch. Right as a shadow fell over the table.

As one they looked up to find Armand looming over them. Hands in his pockets, face dark and stormy.

Cheeks heating like crazy, Evie tugged her arm back to check her watch. She'd been gone for thirty-five minutes. Dammit.

"Back to the grindstone," she said, quickly wiping her mouth with a napkin and pushing back her chair.

"Stay," Armand commanded.

Evie made a point of sitting upright like a good girl.

Something flickered behind Armand's dark eyes before he added, "I am not your keeper, Ms Croft. You were not answering your phone, therefore I sought you out to let you know I will not be in the office when you return."

"Oh. Okay." Glancing at Jamie, who was watching them carefully, she was judicious in her choice of words. "This morning, the keypad…"

"Programmed."

"And what should I work on while you're gone?"

"I've left a note."

"Cool. Great!" she effused, his soberness somehow making her want to double up on the sunshine factor. "I'll get on it right away."

As if he knew exactly what she was doing, Armand drawled, "Enjoy your lunch, Ms Croft," before walking away.

"I did thanks," she called. Then after a pause added, "Mr Debussey."

His next step may have faltered slightly. He was too far away to truly tell.

"Wow," said Jamie, drawing out the word. "Wait a minute—you're working with *him*?"

"I am."

"Huh. He's been lurking around here for a few weeks, holed up in Jonathon's office. Very cloak and dagger. In fact, there's a pool going. Is he an auditor? A psychic? Private eye? I have fifty bucks on bodyguard."

Despite not enjoying Armand's clear hesitation in giving up the details to her, she had to figure he had good reason. With a friendly shrug she went with, "First day—still not quite sure."

Jamie squinted, but took her word for it. "Is he as big a stiff as he seems?"

Evie opened her mouth before snapping it shut as a strange kind of protectionist sensibility washed over her.

Armand might be difficult, but she had to trust that Jonathon Montrose had put them together for a reason. And, well, something about him made her feel as though he was used to looking out for other people rather than the other way around.

"First day, remember," she said.

"Right."

Evie glanced through the restaurant in the direction Armand had gone. She could practically see the trail of his mysterious aura. Wondered what stories, what secrets lurked beneath the elegant façade. Such as…had he ever written a lonely heart?

"Jamie?"

"Yes, Evie?"

"Have you ever written poetry?"

"Poetry? Good God, no. Unless…would you like me to?"

Her gaze slammed back to his. "What? No! I didn't mean it that way. It was just a random query…" She shook her head and pressed herself to standing. "Anyway, I'd better get back to work. I'll see you round."

Jamie opened his mouth as if he had more to add, but she spun on her heel and bolted.

# CHAPTER FOUR

ARMAND KNOCKED ONCE before striding into Jonathon's office.

Imogen looked up from where she was taking notes. Without a word she unfolded herself from the chair and melted from the room. Why couldn't Evie be more like her? Dignified, mindful, not disturbing in any way?

Jonathon checked the contraption on his wrist where a watch ought to be. "A little over three hours till you stormed into my office. My money was on one. How goes it?"

"Interminably."

"You don't say."

"She can't sit still. She's always shifting position. Twirling, stretching, rocking back and forth."

Armand had had a kid in his first platoon with an attention-deficit condition. A good kid—super-fit, keen, but a total daydreamer. Armand was sure he'd lost years off his life trying to keep the kid alive. Until the day the kid's number was up.

He ran a hand down his face. Not going there. Not any more.

"Are you punishing me for something? Did I bruise your delicate feelings in some way?"

"When will you realise Evie Croft is not penance, she's a gift. Learn from her. Guide her. Find common ground. Find a way to work together. You'll thank me."

Armand slouched into the chair across from Jonathon's desk. "She's on to me."

"She's into you?"

"*On to*," Armand enunciated, certain Jonathon had heard him just fine. "She called me out for not having a computer."

"Armand, old friend, anyone with eyes could tell you're a Luddite. Your watch is ancient."

"It's vintage."

"Your phone is arcane."

"It makes and receives phone calls. Anything else is superfluous to requirements. The moment I feel myself pining for a selfie stick I'll upgrade. She also did something to your computer."

Jonathon's face lit up. "As in…?"

"After rolling her eyes at the screen so often I thought she'd burst a blood vessel suddenly she was done. Twenty-four hours of videos finished in a morning."

Jonathon barked with laughter. "Told you I can pick them."

"Why are you smiling? She cheated."

"She's industrious."

"You act as if this is a trifling consideration. She is the kind of character I would usually be hired to uncover, not someone I would ever choose to work alongside."

Jonathon waited for Armand to finish his denouncement. "You done?"

"Quite."

"Did she sit back and stare at the ceiling once she was done…?" Jonathon waved a hand.

"Being industrious?" Armand helped. "She did not."

"Did she pretend to work while surreptitiously checking her phone?"

No, and neither did she appear furtive or nervous. Check over her shoulder or blink excessively. All signs of guilt. "She appeared utterly delighted with herself. Then asked to be put to work."

Jonathon held out his hands in supplication before his phone rang.

"A moment," said Jonathan, holding up a finger. He pressed a button and took a call, leaving Armand with his thoughts.

Armand brought out his phone. He did indeed have one. Though he mainly used it to ignore concerned messages from his family back in Paris who were terrified he was working on something dangerous.

He wasn't a technophobe, as Evie had declared. He'd built a ham radio while at uni. Fixed a walkie-talkie once in the middle of a mortar attack.

His brain worked better with the tactile feel of paper and pencil in hand. No doubt an echo of growing up in a family of art lovers, gallery owners, generations of Debussey auctioneers, where the senses were meant for the appreciation of beauty, form, history, not for looking into a person's eyes, peeling back layers of their soul and seeing to their darkest heart.

"Everything okay?" Jonathon asked.

Tired of having to assure people he was "fine", Armand didn't deign to answer. He stood. Said, "What now?"

"Regarding…?"

"Ms Croft."

"I meant it when I said that is entirely up to you. Whatever it takes for you to get to the bottom of whatever the hell is wrong with my shiny new app. It's the only reason I brought you here after all."

"Really? From memory you brought me here because… Let me try to bring up the exact words. I was 'wasting away in my big, ivy-covered chateau like some tragic hero in a gothic novel'."

"Heroine. I believe I used the word heroine."

Armand moved to the door.

"Evie can help you, Armand. If you don't believe me, kick her to the kerb."

With that Jonathon pressed another button on his desk and took another call, and this time Armand walked away and kept going, all the way to his room at the end of the hall.

The door was shut, but he could hear noise from within.

A throb, like a heartbeat. He pressed his thumb onto the discreet pad and the lock clicked open.

In the short time she'd been back from her break, Evie had made herself at home. She'd figured out the lamps had dimmers and had switched them all to bright. She'd plugged her phone into a tiny speaker in the shape of a pineapple, and it was pumping out music.

She'd pulled her hair into a messy knot on top of her head and it bounced from side to side as she swayed on her feet, fingers tapping over her keyboard. The light from the monitors shining on her contented face.

And the whole room smelled like cherries.

"Ms Croft. Evie."

Clearly not having heard him enter, she nearly jumped out of her boots, her short skirt flapping and swishing around the tops of her long legs. In the brighter light the instant rush of pink to her cheeks was clear.

She pressed something on her phone and the music went dead. "I saw you in Jonathon's office. Am I fired?"

"Did you do something that would make that a concern?"

She held up the Post-it note. In his handwriting it read, "Finish the training videos."

"I believe Jonathon would have been disappointed if you hadn't found a way around them."

She held a hand to her chest as she laughed, clearly relieved. "I get why HR would insist—it's the age of the lawsuit after all. But he needs to invest in better videos."

"Feel free to tell him."

"Did you have to watch them?"

Armand breathed out before saying, "Of course."

She pointed a finger his way and laughed. "Liar!"

He'd held eye contact. He'd not shifted his feet. His nostrils had not flared. Every sign of lying subjugated by years of specialised training in the Legion. And yet she'd seen through him.

He could tell himself his heart had not speeded up, his

hands did not sweat. Those feelings, that level of care, had been worn down to the nub.

Which had nothing at all to do with his change of subject. "Your lunch companion seemed fond of you."

"Jamie? No. Do you think?"

"There was no need to think. He made it perfectly clear."

"How? No. Don't tell me. It wouldn't matter if he was… fond."

"And why not?"

"Work and play don't mix. Lines become blurred. Trust misconstrued. Boundaries breeched. And when things fall apart…" Evie turned her fist into a bomb which exploded with accompanying sound effects.

Her mouth quirked. Such a pretty mouth. Light, soft, prone to laughter.

"You Australians are too uptight," Armand chided. "In France such things are not a concern. Lovers are found where they are found. In a bar, at a party, at work. The location is merely scenery."

"Right," she said, her huge brown eyes no longer blinking. Instead they held on to his in such a way he found it hard to disengage. "I'll make sure to remember that."

Growling, mostly beneath his breath, he said, "Would you like to know what you are going to do with all that stuff or not?"

Instantly deflected, she placed her hands on either side of a screen as if covering a pair of sensitive ears. "This stuff, I'll have you know, is beyond your wildest imaginings. Yes, I would like to know what I am going to be doing with all this stuff!"

"You signed the confidentiality agreement?"

Her eyes narrowed, temper crackling. "Of course I did."

All that energy, Armand thought. Was there ever a time when he'd burned with such passion? About anything good?

He held out a hand, motioning to the lounge. She took one end, he took the other. A face-off.

"Jonathon has recently purchased a start-up app and wishes for us to give it a once-over before it launches."

Evie was up, moving back to the middle of the room, where she stretched her arms over her head, did a small pirouette before stopping and pinning him with those dark eyes of hers. "He's already bought it?"

Armand nodded.

"And now he wants me to have a look?"

"Yes."

"That's like buying a house and then checking for termites."

"I believe I have mentioned Jonathon can be reckless when over excited."

"Any one of the guys downstairs could check the code, could Beta-test. Why would he need me? Armand?"

"Yes, Evie."

"Does Montrose's shiny new app have termites?"

"We believe so."

Evie slapped her hands together, then had the good grace to look chagrined. "It's not uncommon. No program is perfect. Unless… Unless he's concerned that the problem is systemic. Or deliberate. Is that why he has us holed up here? He believes his app was sabotaged?"

Armand ran a hand over the bristle on his chin, chiding himself on how staunchly he'd resisted. It was time to stop thinking of her in terms of her relative youth. Her innocence. Just because he'd lived a dozen more lifetimes than she had, it did not diminish her resourcefulness, her value.

"Jeez," she said, pacing now. "Who would do such a thing?"

"People whose proposals he has rejected. People whose companies he has bought and dismantled. Competitors. Anonymous…"

"Okay. I get it. You've had to cast the net wide."

"You have no idea."

"If I'm finding termites, what's your part in all this?"

"I figure out who put them there and why."

"How?"

"My background is in history. Finance. Law. I talk to people. Comb through online chatter, phone records, bank statements." Mostly above board. A man with his responsibilities had to do what he had to do. "They'll have given themselves away at some point. Via a pay-out, a boast in a pub, a line in a contract. Everyone does."

She glanced over his shoulder to the pile of folders on his desk, the legal books on the shelves behind. "Clever. A little scary, but impressive. And you've been doing all this on your own?"

He nodded.

She twisted her fingers together. Cracked a few knuckles. "Well, you're not alone anymore. Point the way, partner."

Armand felt a skitter of something flicker to life behind his ribs. He wouldn't go so far as calling it zeal, or gusto, but it was something. An echo. A memory. The thrill of the hunt. "What do you need?"

Her mouth curved into a Cheshire cat grin. "Nothing that's not already there. Programmers always leave breadcrumbs. Snail trails. Their personal signature. If they've left tracks I'll find them. Wow, I sounded pretty fierce just now. I bet you're not used to that kind of talk in your field."

Before he even felt the words coming they came. "Ah, but I wasn't always the dashing paper pusher you see before you. Not all that long ago I worked in search and rescue."

Evie stopped her pacing and slowly sat on the armrest, drinking him in like a sponge. "You? How?"

"A family friend's little girl had gone missing."

"Come on, you can't leave me hanging. What happened? How on earth did you get involved?"

Realising he'd put himself in it, Armand saw only one way out: the truth.

"I'd had…experience tracking bad people down. My father's friends begged my family to ask me to help. I put together a team of colleagues from my previous employ whom I believed would have the requisite skills, the emotional stamina, the trustworthiness. For her father was prominent. French government. A good man, with divisive left-wing views. The chances of recovery, even if we tracked her, were slim."

"Then what?" Evie asked, her face grim, her voice a mite breathless. "Please tell me there's a happy ending coming."

"We—as you said—followed the breadcrumbs and recovered the little girl in less than twenty-four hours. Alive. Unhurt. Happy ending."

For all his covertness word had spread through the highest echelons of power. Problem on the down-low? He was the man to fix it. Without even meaning to, Armand had built himself a posse of men like him: skilled but untethered, having witnessed a lot of bad and now looking to do some good.

And it had been good. The perfect blend of his experience and education.

No matter how hard he tried to cap the recollection there, to the good times, his mind flowed to its logical conclusion. To Lucia. The little girl's aunt. They'd met the day he'd brought her niece home. Coolly beautiful, polished, and from a family as venerated as his own, she would, he'd believed, be his way back to the real world. He'd been wrong.

"Wow, Armand," said Evie on an outward breath, her husky voice tugging him gently back to the present. "You're a real-life hero. You and your Action Adventure All-Stars."

Armand shook his head. "No more than anyone with skills who knows how to use them."

"Come on. You're allowed to feel a little smug. You did that! You saved a girl."

She was so chuffed at the thought, Armand felt a smile tug at the edges of his eyes. It caught, ached, as if those muscles had not been used in a very long time. He didn't realise he was sitting forward, leaning in, until he breathed in and caught the scent of cherry.

He rubbed both hands over his face before pulling his heavy body to standing then walked purposefully back to his desk and sat.

All the while thinking, *Breadcrumbs. Snail trails.*

Every life followed a path. Straight, meandering, going around in circles. Paths that were broad and gentle or treacherous and overstretched. Paths that were halted by sudden mountains, the traveller stopped, stymied, stuck before finding a way over, or around. Or not.

It made sense that computer programs—programmed by humans—would be the same. It made sense that Evie, knowing the terrain, would be able to follow the map and find Jonathon's mountain. Leaving Armand to find out who'd put it there.

He'd planned to give Evie only pieces of the puzzle, to ensure the security of the project. Now he found himself saying, "Blue icon."

Like a team member he'd worked with a hundred times, she had his shorthand down. She bounded back to her desk and beamed at the screen. "Got it."

He gave her the password. She typed it in and waggled her fingers as she waited for it to load.

He saw the moment she noted the name of the program. Not so much a new start-up app as Game On—Jonathon's new flagship telecommunications software. The one the entire country was waiting for.

Evie turned to him with comically wide eyes. "Are you kidding me?"

Armand shook his head.

Then watched as a calm came over Evie. As she breathed in and out. As she pressed her feet into the ground and shook the jitters from her hands. He'd seen those moves more times than he could count. She was preparing herself for battle.

"I can do this, Armand."

"I don't doubt it," he said, and meant it.

For the next several minutes they worked in silence—Evie tapping away, fingers flying over her customised keyboard, the mouse. Face a study in concentration.

Armand tried to find his rhythm. Marking up red flags in correspondence between Jonathon's lawyers and the company from whom he'd bought the base software. But he couldn't settle. "How's it going?"

Glints of gold snapped in her big brown eyes as she turned them on him. "No termites as yet, if that's what you wanted to hear."

Armand wasn't exactly sure what he wanted, so he let it go.

But after a few seconds, Evie asked, "If I'm the Exterminator, then what do we call you?"

"Armand will do just fine."

"Come on," she said, half closing one eye. "A title gives you focus. Even Napoleon wanted to be Emperor. So who are you?"

Evie couldn't possibly know how much that question had weighed on him his whole life. Who was he? A Debussey. A scholar. An art historian. Yes, but also a foot soldier. An enforcer. A leader. A helper. A shadow. A blade. Until the day he'd realised that even the most determined, most skilled, most focussed fighter for good could be brought to their knees by bad luck.

Right now he was a friend doing a friend a favour.

And to do that well he needed a partner on the mission. For that was what she was. Her knowledge of the playing field was stronger than his.

He'd believed Jonathon had given him this young woman as a move in one of his games. But there was far more to her than exuberance and a knack for being underestimated. Armand felt a flicker of self-reproach, when he'd thought he was done with feeling much at all.

He cleared his throat. "You can call me the Undertaker."

Evie laughed, the sound husky and sure. Then she shot him a sideways glance.

Another very different sliver of sensation shimmered to life in parts of him he'd thought were nothing but dust motes, pain and remorse.

She said, "I'll kill the problem and you'll bury it?"

"Something like that."

"Okay, then." She cocked her head and got back to work.

Her quiet focus became magnetic, as if she'd drawn all that cracking energy back inside of her. Headphones back on her head, she rocked from side to side.

Armand craned his head to listen. But it was a song he didn't know. A song young people liked. Young Australian people with no cares in the world.

When Armand realised he was staring he took his subconscious by the throat and gave it a good shake. Now was not the time for distraction. He'd been skirting around the edges of the playing field until today. Now it was game on.

He grabbed his paperwork and began to read.

Evie jiggled her key in the door of Zoe's apartment, bumped the door open with her shoulder and threw her backpack, beanie and scarf onto the futon before collapsing into a heap with a sigh.

"Work was that good, huh?" asked Zoe.

Evie lifted her eyes to find her flatmate standing in the door of her bedroom, one leg hooked up on the other knee, eating tuna from the tin.

Voice muffled by a cushion, Evie said, "It was amazing."

The code she'd been hired to investigate was brilliant. Elegant and clean. So neat it shone. Meaning any kind of error ought to stand out like a lump of coal. But the best part of her day? When she'd been gifted a glimpse behind Armand's hard outer shell to the private man beneath.

Zoe said, "Tell me all about it."

"The job itself… I can't talk about."

Zoe rolled her eyes. "Used to that."

"For all the laid-back, geek-boy first impression, the infrastructure is slick. Sharp. Fast. And the technology we are working with... I think I'm in love. No, I'm definitely in love."

"And the people?"

With the word *love* ringing in her ears, and Armand's deep voice rumbling in his ear as he told her about the time he'd saved that little girl... She cleared her throat. "Men. Pretty much all men."

"Lucky you."

"You think?"

Zoe loped back into the kitchenette. "Yeah, I get it. For me, in fashion, it's pretty much the opposite. Anytime we get a man at work, gay or straight, the poor guy's mobbed. Any particular men we need to talk about?"

Evie tried to pull up Jamie's face, but all she got was light hair, teeth, a general air of flirtation. Then the vague image instantly morphed into dark angles and stormy blue eyes. Elegant slouch and constant scowl. A ridiculously sexy accent saying, *"Lovers are found where they are found..."*

"Nope," Evie said. "Not a one."

Zoe slapped herself on the head. "I'd nearly forgotten. What about Mr Lonely Heart?"

Which was when Evie realised she'd forgotten to tell Zoe that whole tale. And there was no way she could see around it. Squeezing one eye shut, she said, "Turns out he works for Game Plan too."

Zoe's eyes near popped out of her head. "Noooo. Wow. That's...fate."

"Yes... No." She told Zoe about the book, the folders. "A simple case of subliminal messaging."

"But what about the lonely heart...?"

"Not him." She was almost one hundred percent sure.

"Bummer."

"It's a good thing. Means we can have a normal working

relationship—cool, distant, professional." Evie rolled off the futon and landed on her hands and knees before crawling into the bathroom, where she started up a hot bath.

Then, a moment later, Zoe's voice came through the keyhole. "If it wasn't him, then who? Any man who writes poetry should be given a chance."

Evie reached into the bath and turned the taps to full blast, the noise of the spray giving her the excuse not to answer.

# CHAPTER FIVE

THE NEXT MORNING Zoe and Evie sat in their usual seats on the train.

It was a gorgeous Melbourne winter's day—crisp blue skies and a brisk chill in the air. Yet Evie felt warm. Scratchy. She took off her bright red bomber jacket, then put it back on again. She fiddled with her beanie—black today, with double pom-poms that looked like teddy-bear ears. And she tried to stop staring at the electronic sign telling them how many stops to Armand's South Yarra stop.

Thankfully, Zoe was too busy sexting Lance, who'd landed back in Australia after his final overseas army posting. A few days, then, till Evie had to find somewhere else to live.

She rocked forward as the train came to a halt. Her eyes zoomed to the doors. And a familiar form filled the space like liquid darkness.

Cool, distant, professional, she told herself. But, as Armand's eyes swept over the carriage before landing on hers, her nerves zapped and zinged, the hairs on her arms standing on end.

Zoe's hand flapped in the corner of Evie's vision as she waved for Armand to join them.

"Zoe," Evie hissed. "Leave him be."

"You're kidding, right?"

Eyes still locked onto Armand, Evie saw the squaring of his shoulders before he excused himself as he made his way up the busy aisle.

"Good morning, Evie."

"Hey, Armand. Um, this is my friend Zoe. Zoe, Armand."

Zoe held out a hand and shook Armand's with relish. "Sit."

The schoolboys must have had a day off, as there was a spare seat across from them. While Armand settled in Evie rearranged herself so as not to spend the trip playing footsie with the guy.

Zoe said, "I hear you two are working together."

Evie caught Armand's gaze, inscrutable as ever. "I only mentioned we were working together, not what we're working on."

Zoe scoffed. "I wouldn't understand it anyway."

"She really wouldn't. Then again, neither would Armand."

Armand's intense gaze darkened, just a fraction. It was quite the thing.

After three solid seconds of eye contact, his gaze swept to Zoe. "She thinks I'm a Luddite."

"I thought you were French. Didn't you say he's French?"

"I did. He is." Evie's mouth kicked into a grin and Armand's eyes seemed to spark in shared amusement. A secret shared. Evie's heart took a little tumble.

She swallowed quickly and turned to Zoe—much safer—to explain the history of the Luddites and their aversion to new technology.

The conversation then moved on to the design program Zoe was being forced to learn for work, to when it might be cold enough for proper coats, to the underfloor heating in Armand's penthouse apartment in South Yarra.

"Posh," Zoe said. "Does it have an extra bedroom?"

It took Evie a moment to break free from the Zen of listening to Armand talk and realise where Zoe was going. She gave her friend an elbow in the ribs.

"Ouch. It's a perfectly reasonable question." Zoe sat forward. "Beneath the cool exterior, our girl here is brimming with panic as she is under the mistaken impression she has to move out of my place this week."

"She mentioned she was moving," Armand said.

"My boyfriend is moving in, so she thinks she has to leave."

"It's a one-bedroom place. I sleep on a futon in the lounge. When Lance moves in it will be a little…"

"Cramped," Evie said right as Armand joined in with, "Intimate."

"That too," Evie said, her voice a little rough. Their eyes locked. Evie swallowed. So much for "cool, distant, professional".

Taking Armand's loaded silence for disapproval, Zoe added, "Don't worry. It won't distract her from work."

He shook his head, his mussed hair unsettling and re-settling in an even more appealing alignment. "I've seen her work. It would take an air-strike siren to distract her."

Zoe laughed. "And you've only known her a day. I wish my boss saw me like that. I've been working there a year and a half and she still thinks my name is Zelda." Zoe nodded towards the door. "Your stop, guys."

Armand stood.

This time Evie knew better than to try to keep up, so she made a play out of slowly collecting her things.

"Don't be late," he instructed. Then with a nod he was gone.

Evie saluted his back, then scrambled to get her back-pack from under the seat.

"I like him," said Zoe as Evie stepped over her legs.

"Then you can have him."

Not wanting to look as if she was following Armand, Evie had dawdled to work. In the end she ran late, puffing by the time she reached the Bullpen.

Naturally the first person she banged into was her boss.

"Mr Montrose!"

"Evie. How goes it? Settling in all right? Making friends? Getting the lie of the land?"

"Great!" she enthused. "All is great!"

"I see. Armand has scared you witless, has he?"

Evie laughed. "He's rather intense." *Arrogant, short-tempered, closed-off. Mysterious, hunky, fascinating.*

"Can be. Comes from being a genius among mere mortals."

"Then how come you're so nice?"

Jonathon blinked, then looked at her. Really looked at her for the first time since they had met. *Notice me. See me. And please don't fire me.*

Thankfully he laughed. "You'll keep."

He looked ready to move on when he turned back to her. "Keep me in the loop, Evie."

"Of course."

"Not merely apropos the investigation. With regards to Armand."

Evie swallowed, not quite sure how to answer. "I'm not sure I understand."

"The usual. If he's playing nice, if he's giving you enough space to do your job, how goes his state of mind."

"State of mind?"

Jonathon glanced over her shoulder, the very image of nonchalant. "Has he spoken much about his life before he came here?"

Apart from the story about the little girl, he'd barely spoken at all. "We've mostly talked about the work."

"Is he settling in? Making friends?"

*Help.*

The only time she'd seen him interact with anyone was when he'd glared down at Jamie at lunch. "I can't really say."

A flash of a smile. "You're loyal to him already. Good to see."

Was it loyalty? Or the fact she didn't know him at all?

Suddenly Evie's stomach tightened and her ears began

to burn as she remembered a similar conversation with her last boss, asking her how things were going with Eric. On that occasion she'd completely misunderstood—blustering over the fact that they'd broken up, kind of, that they were in the process of moving on, not realising her boss was asking if she'd noticed anything untoward.

Not that Armand seemed *anything* like Eric. Polar opposite, in fact.

Eric had been affable, like a St Bernard puppy. He'd appeared harmless and wasn't.

While Armand… He was far more at the Doberman pinscher end of the scale. A stunning specimen, but instinct said it was best not to stray too close. And yet he read actual books. Stood on the train so old ladies could sit. Had seemed genuinely concerned—in his own intangible way—that she might soon be out on her ear.

Before she could come to any logical conclusions, Jonathon gave her a nod and left her to hurry to her office.

She went to press her thumbprint against the security pad, only to find it was missing, the door unlocked and Armand working on the security pad, coloured cords poking out every which way.

She edged in behind him, intrigued. Electrical circuits were one of the first things her granddad had taught her about when he'd realised it was easier to answer her zillion questions than hope they'd go away on their own.

Making to "play nice", she went to point out he had the wrong micro-screwdriver, when he reached into a small toolbox and pulled out the right one.

The man might not know a gigabyte from a bug bite, but he clearly was capable in countless other ways. Of course, it only served to make him even more intriguing when she really needed him to become less.

He grunted. Then said something in… Swedish? She realised he was also on the phone. A regular old landline tucked between ear and shoulder.

But it was the tone of his voice that was the biggest surprise. It could almost be mistaken for chipper.

She glanced towards Jonathon's office, wondering if she ought to tell him. But it didn't feel right. If Jonathon wanted them to get along, then she'd make it her focus to get along.

She caught Armand's eye as she moved to her desk to let him know she'd arrived. He gave her a small nod as she passed—practically a hug in Armand world.

Then stopped when she found a new addition to her little corner—a small cabinet, elegant, wooden, most likely antique, with enough room for her backpack and a shelf for personal touches she'd brought from home. And, above, a pair of fat knobs nailed to the wall, the perfect size for her scarf. And her beanie.

She turned to ask Armand if he knew who to thank but stopped short when she saw him leaning back in his chair, ankle hooked over the opposite knee, a hand waving through the air as he illustrated some point the person on the other end of the line could not see.

It was the smile that got her. Wide, crooked, creasing the edges of his eyes until they were no longer stormy. Her blood rushed so hard and fast she could hear it in her ears.

Gaze sweeping unseeingly over the room, those eyes caught on hers. A mercurial, sparkling blue-grey, like sunlight on water.

The swinging stopped. His hand dropped. The smile slowly melted away.

But the light in his eyes remained. Just for a moment. A breath really. But enough for something to rage to life deep in Evie's belly.

Then he blinked, his gaze sliding away from her as if it had never caught, his chair turned to face the other wall as he continued his discourse, the foreign words quieting, easing down the phone lines.

Evie sat. Switched on her computer. Got to work. But it was a while before her heart slowed. Before she could even see the screen.

A half-hour later she jumped when Armand said, in English this time, "Team meeting."

She turned to find him at the lounge. The halfway mark of the office. No-man's-land.

Evie played with the zip on her bomber jacket as she moved out to join him. Then sat primly on the edge of the couch. Her hands clasped together.

Armand said, "You go first."

"Who was on the phone?"

He baulked. "A colleague."

"A colleague…?"

"Performing background checks."

She waited for more, to get some insight into who in his life could make him smile that way. But nope. She got nothing. "Have they found anything to report?"

His eyebrow jumped.

Evie brought her hand to her chest. "Or am I not allowed to ask?"

Armand's inscrutable gaze flickered and she half expected him to say, no, she was not allowed to ask.

In the end he waved a conciliatory hand and went on to outline the work he'd done so far. The accounting errors that seemed just that. The dead ends he'd reached. The players he was targeting as suspicious. It was an impressive amount of work. She wondered that he'd had time to sleep, much less settle in, make friends.

"I bumped into Jonathon this morning," she said when he was done.

"And?"

"He asked me to keep him in the loop."

Armand stilled. No, he stiffened, his entire body going

rigid. But his voice was smooth, giving nothing away as he said, "It is his business."

"It wasn't about the *business*. He asked me to keep an eye on you."

Armand shot to his feet, pacing back and forth over the same small patch of floor, muttering in French and a little English about "trust" and "allegiance", with a few choice swear words thrown in for flavour. It was more emotion than she had ever seen him display—anger, disappointment, regret. The mix volatile, unexpected; she couldn't hope to pin each down.

Evie stood, running suddenly sweating palms down the front of her jacket. "Armand, I told you because I have no intention of following through."

Armand stopped mid-stride. "What do you mean?"

"The way I see it, we are a team. If one of us is playing the other it won't work. Been there, done that, don't ever want to go through it again. But if I'm wrong, if this is more than Jonathon stirring, if there's something about you I should know..."

Armand pinned her with a dark glare. "You said it yourself—we are a team. We are not friends. There is nothing you need to know bar the report I just gave."

The burn travelled fast, singeing her cheeks till they flared. She held up both hands in surrender. "Forget I said anything."

He gave her one last, long look before he walked slowly to his chair, where he sat and watched her from his place in the semi-darkness.

Evie crossed her arms. "I take it the team meeting is over?"

Armand waved a hand in agreement before he scraped his fingernails through his stubble.

Evie scooted back to her own desk, where she sat, stiff-backed, staring unseeingly at her monitors.

A few moments later, Armand's voice came to her.

"If this job is so important to you, why not do as Jonathon asked? Why tell me at all?"

She turned, keeping her fingers poised on the keyboard. "I didn't think it was fair." One thing she had taken out of the implosion of her last job and her part in it was that whatever happened she had to be able to live with herself.

Armand sank his face into his hands a moment before giving it a good scrub and looking at her with haunted eyes. "Bad things happen to good people in this world. I've seen it time and time again. If you don't toughen up, grow a thicker skin, I fear for you, Evie. I really do."

"If you'd prefer to sit over there in the darkness, glowering at nothing, keeping whatever has Jonathon so concerned all bottled up inside, you're going to have a stroke. I fear for you, Armand. I really do."

She glared at him and he glared back. When her eyes began to water at the stalemate she blinked, rolled her eyes and got back to work.

Her fingers slammed down on the keyboard, till she remembered it was her beloved prototype and took more care. Mind spinning in a dozen different directions, she forced herself to concentrate. To curb her anger. To do her job.

But, as the code finally drew her in, one niggling little thought kept flashing at the corner of her mind.

Evie might not know much about why people acted the way they did, but she did know family. She knew community. She knew fellowship.

She hadn't felt much of that in her last job. They had valued her but only for the skills she offered. They'd rated her so highly they'd stuck her in a secure office where no one bar top management—and Eric—could visit. Rather than feel appreciated, she'd felt isolated. Like a tool rather than a human being.

Armand said he feared for her, which meant she wasn't merely a cog in the corporate machine to him. To him, at least, she mattered.

She settled in with a small smile on her face, feeling as if they might not turn out to be the worst partnership ever assembled after all.

Evie's stomach rumbled.

After their earlier standoff, the office was deathly quiet. Armand must have heard. But when she looked up it was to find him in his regularly programmed position—frowning over his reports, the pool of golden light cast by the banker's lamp throwing craggy shadows over his deep, soulful eyes.

*This man worries about me. He'd care if something terrible happened to me.*

Armand looked up and Evie started at having been caught staring.

"Did you bring lunch?" she blurted.

"Lunch?" he asked, as if he'd never heard of such a concept that might take time away from glaring at paperwork. "*Non.*"

Even while she wasn't playing his game, Jonathon had hit on something when asking if Armand had made friends. She knew how it felt being the odd one out at work. Just because she'd decided not to report back, it didn't mean she couldn't help.

"I'm heading down to the Yum Lounge to find something decadent and delicious to eat." A pause, a deep breath, then, "Care to join me?"

Armand looked up, those dark eyes bringing on tingles and skitters and rising heat. Then he surprised the heck out of her by shutting his notebook and saying, "*Oui,* I will. *Merci.*"

"Really? Great. Okay. Let's go."

Evie held out a hand, motioning to the door. But Armand refused to go before her, waiting with barely reined patience for her to trot through.

Once out of the office, Armand locked the door, even though the security key pad meant that only select people had access anyway. No trust, that man. Since reading people wasn't her forte, she gave everyone the benefit of the doubt. Probably best he was in charge.

As they reached the Bullpen the energy, the laughter, the sense of chaos couldn't have been more different from the intense quiet of upstairs. She glanced towards Armand to find him tense, bristling, on high alert. For a moment it was easy to picture him as he might have once been, not hunting a problem, but the kind of man who'd take care of a scared little girl.

She shot him a smile. Turned it into a grin. Gave him a nudge with her elbow.

While his face said he was still considering her sanity, his shoulders relaxed and the tendons in his neck no longer looked like they might burst from his skin.

When he took a turn towards the Yum Lounge, Evie grabbed his wrist. He froze, as if shocked by human touch. Making a split-second decision, she slid her fingers into his and dragged him towards the Game Rooms, stopping when she found Jamie and a couple of colleagues battling it out to get past what looked like the penultimate level of *Insurgent: Jungle Fever III*

She called out, "Hey, guys."

Several heads turned. Some waved, others raised cans of energy drink. When some looked warily over her shoulder she glanced back at Armand, realising she was still holding his hand.

She let go. His hand immediately sank into the pocket of his suit pants. Then she tipped her head in the direction of the room, prompting him to acknowledge the crowd.

"These guys are on our team too," she murmured.

He muttered something in French. She did not believe it was complimentary.

"You guys game?" someone called.

"Totally," Armand responded.

Laughter bursting from her mouth, she turned to find

Armand had moved in closer. She rolled her shoulders, subtly, in an attempt to stave off the warmth washing over her at his nearness.

Jamie, who was sitting in a straight-backed chair, fingers flying over a controller, sweat beading on his forehead, didn't move as he said, "Miss Evie, nice to see you down here." Then, "Armand. Welcome to hell."

"Looks fairly close," Armand said, his hard gaze now locked on the huge screen where soldiers in camouflage gear, loaded up to the eyeballs in weapons, tried to shoot their way out of an ambush.

"How long have you been stuck there?" Evie asked.

"This session? Two hours and sixteen minutes."

Another guy added, "That's not including the several days before that."

"Jonathon pays you to do this?" Armand asked.

"We're about to launch *Jungle Fever IV* and need to make sure we haven't doubled up on any scenes."

"Do you use military consultants?"

One guy looked up. "My uncle was a lieutenant in Vietnam. We brought in a few of his mates to fill in the blanks."

Armand shot him a look. Gave him a single nod, appeased, before standing up straight.

Evie took a couple of steps into the room. Eyeballed the screen, catalogued the tools lists of each player. "You want help?"

Yet another guy hunched over a controller muttered, "We are beyond help. And I'm out."

He put down the controller and slumped over in the chair.

Evie held out a hand and someone passed the controller to her.

After a beat she offered it to Armand. "Care to show them how it's done?"

A flash passed over his eyes, a moment of connection, like lightning within a storm. A thrill shot down her spine, making her toes curl.

Then he slowly shook his head. "All yours."

"All righty, then," she said, taking a moment to shake off the pins and needles. She ran her fingers over the buttons, familiarising herself with the remote. Cricked her neck one way, then the other.

"Follow me," she commanded Jamie, then set to unlocking the level in a minute and a half.

The room erupted in a cheer befitting a gold medal performance.

Grinning, Evie bowed to the room, bowed to Jamie, then turned to bow to Armand. He leaned in the doorway, arms crossed, ankles too. Cool as you please.

He shook his head once, his eyes glinting. And then his face lit up with a smile. Teeth and all. A zing shot through her, head to toe, as if she'd been struck by lightning.

Good Lord, he was magnetic.

Smiling, the man was devastating.

Out of the corner of her eye she saw Jamie throw down his controller and pull off his baseball cap to run a hand over his damp hair. "How?" he asked.

Evie broke eye contact to give Jamie a shrug. "I'm just that good."

"Everyone," Jamie said as he pulled himself to standing, "this is Evie Croft. And she is just that good."

Each of the guys stood to introduce themselves, a flurry of names she'd struggle to remember. Evie laughed, feeling light, happy. Included. It was the best she'd felt since the Day of the Fortune Cookie.

Then her gaze slid back to the doorway to find Armand's smile now gone. He glanced behind him, as if looking for a way to escape.

With an, "Excuse me," Evie ducked through the crowd. She muttered, "Uh-uh, don't even think about it." Then, tucking her hand into his elbow, she dragged Armand bodily into the room.

Evie shook any hand that came her way and said, "And this is Armand Debussey."

Armand did surprisingly well in the end—he smiled politely, was charming despite his best efforts and was an adept conversationalist. After a few minutes, it felt as if they were all firm friends.

Fun now over, the crowd dissipated, small groups heading off in different directions, already talking about optic cables and firewalls.

"Well, that wasn't so hard, now, was it?" Evie asked, turning to Armand. "Even I started to believe you were an actual human person."

Armand smiled, just a little, and Evie found herself lost in a whirl of stormy blue. She'd never stood so close to him before, apart from elbowing him on the train. Toe to toe. Close enough to count his tangled lashes. The lines on his face that spoke of hardship, worry. Of care.

Her next breath in felt sharp and keen and far too shallow.

Her tongue slipped over her dry bottom lip and Armand's gaze dropped to her mouth. And stayed. The banked heat in his eyes had her knees giving way.

Then from one moment to the next the shutters closed over his eyes with a snap and he took an instant step back.

"Lunch?" she said, glad to remember what it was called.

He looked at her for a beat. Inscrutable once more. "No lunch. I have something urgent that needs attending to."

"Oh," she said, hearing the tinge of disappointment clear as day. "Okay. See you in the office afterwards, then."

With a nod, and a slight bow, he left the room.

Jamie sidled up to her to give her a bump with his shoulder. "Seems you're after a lunch companion."

She had to drag her eyes away from the doorway to give Jamie a chummy smile. The smile she got back was more than chummy.

While Armand was a study in elusiveness and restraint,

Jamie was not. There was a strong chance she was reading the signs wrong, but she didn't think so. The smoulder he was sending her was as subtle as a billboard.

She was hit with a revelation.

What if *Jamie* was the fortune cookie mistake? Was he the romantic entanglement she had to nip in the bud?

She felt a sudden lightness come over her. If it was true, it would be the easiest fix in the world!

He was nice-looking, smart and clearly keen, but she felt nothing for him beyond friendship. Nothing close to the way she felt when Armand even looked her way.

Suddenly her revelation didn't feel helpful after all.

"Thanks," she said to Jamie. "But I don't think that's a good idea."

His face dropped till he looked like a sad little boy and she knew she'd made the right decision.

"Look, I know I'm a novelty around here but, like you, I'm here to do my job. Just think of me as one of the guys."

Jamie perked up. "You sure played like one."

Evie bit the inside of her lip to stop herself from calling him out as a sexist pig. Hopefully she'd have the chance to show them all how wrong they were.

Jamie ran a hand up the back of his neck. "You and Mr Mysterious—you're not…?"

"God, no! No way! Nuh-uh." *Stop protesting. One "no" is plenty. Okay, one more for good measure.* "Nope. We are a project team. And that is all."

Jamie watched her a moment, then nodded. Backing away, he said, "Rematch?"

"Deal."

He shot her a salute and headed off.

Left alone in the Bullpen, Evie lifted her gaze up the stairs.

That was what she wanted, right? To quietly go about her job without making waves? Making a splash had been her mum's deal. Being lauded, applauded, recognised for her artistic talents. Her dreams had been so big that when she'd crashed she'd crashed hard.

Evie had never wanted standing ovations, she just wanted a seat at the table. And now she finally had one.

But, while half an hour before she'd been starving hungry, right then she felt strangely hollow.

# CHAPTER SIX

ARMAND SAT AT his desk, the lamp light as low as it would go.

Discomfort sat on his shoulder like a cloak—his nerves twitching with over-stimulation, making him realise how long he'd cut himself off, kept himself numb by thinking over his past, his choices, to remind himself why apathy was imperative.

Life had started well for Armand—a golden childhood spent in Saint-Germain-des-Prés, summering on the waters of the Côte d'Azur. He'd been an active child—rugby at school, excelling in track and field at university. Backpacking through Turkey with friends—including a young Jonathon Montrose—after graduation had been an easy choice. And one that had changed the course of his life.

He still remembered that day his life had flipped on a hinge with wretched clarity: late spring, bright, sunny sky. A bunch of rich kids hopping loudly off the dilapidated bus, dragging their matching luggage. To the band of rebels waiting in the rocky outcrops—their clothes tattered, their bellies empty—Armand and his friends must have looked ripe for the picking.

Armand remembered sitting on a bag, watching Jonathon chat with the bus driver, when Katrina, an American girl in their group, was suddenly grabbed from behind. Basking in the sunshine, in his lazy contentment, he'd only noted she was missing when he heard her scream.

By the time he turned, she had blood running down her face from where she'd been hit with the butt of a gun. Her eyes were rolling back in her head, her legs limp as she was dragged away.

Arms raised in the international sign of surrender, Armand went after them, shouting, begging them to let her go. He threw down his wallet, his passport, a pack of gum from his pocket.

As they yelled back in a language he did not then understand, waving their guns at him, sweat prickled on his back, his neck, his scalp. He remembered the hollow feeling in his stomach. The fact he could no longer feel his feet.

But mostly he remembered the sense of utter helplessness. He'd have followed her to the ends of the earth, offered himself in her place if it had helped. But he'd had no clue if that was the right thing to do. If it would ensure her safety or get his friend killed.

Heir to the Debussey gallery and auction-house fortune, he'd known a life of obscene wealth. He knew nothing of hardship and starvation, of soul-deep pain and fear. How dared he think he could negotiate with these people? He didn't even have the wherewithal to protect what was his.

Then Katrina was gone—tossed into the back of a truck, the vehicle bouncing over the dirt hills, heading who knew where, and Armand was left with his expensive luggage and no clue as to how to get her back.

Three days later—after a police hunt, intervention by the American Embassy and what he inferred was a monetary payment by her family—Katrina was returned; beaten, bruised, with several ribs broken and permanent hearing loss in her left ear.

She was an immigration lawyer now, in Washington. Fighting to provide food, shelter and hope to those who needed it most.

Jonathon had left Europe soon after, heading off into the wild blue yonder for a number of years, before coming home to Australia with a pile of money he'd earned doing goodness knew what, invested in start-ups and made a name for himself as a leading tech entrepreneur.

Armand had gone another way.

His family had not understood his decision to join the French Foreign Legion. They'd railed against it with all that they had. Threatening legal action, disinheritance, calling on every favour they had to bring him home.

But the Legion did not bend.

He'd joined up looking for answers. And absolution. To have the wild fury that had sent him there honed by pushing his body, his mind, to their absolute limits and beyond. Stripped bare, right down to his skin, to his basic humanity, he'd rebuilt himself. It was the only way he could have overcome the events in Turkey. What he'd faced in his own mind. He might even have stayed beyond the requisite five-year term if not for the timing of the kidnapping of a little girl.

That had been years ago now. So much had happened since.

Armand tried to remember how that felt. To be so sure about his sense of duty to his friends, his corps, his family. To be so certain that he could put measures in place to make sure those he cared for could never be hurt again.

As the swamp of memory and regret threatened to suffocate, Armand dragged himself back to the here and now.

He picked up a random piece of paper from his desk, only to find the letters swimming before his eyes. He looked up at the shelves with the bobble-headed figurines lined up below the knitted hat hanging from a hook on the wall.

Evie's trinkets. Evie's hat.

After all he'd seen and done in his life, he found the woman's lack of self-awareness exasperating. Her complete ingenuousness, her need to introduce herself to everyone she met, even the way she moved—floating across the floor as if in a permanent daydream…she may as well be walking through life with a target on her back.

Why it bothered him so much, he could not explain. For she was not his cross to bear. He barely knew her.

She was simply too young, too green, too obstreperous.

She didn't listen when she ought; her opinions were far too decided. How she'd managed to come out clean from under the rubble of her previous employment he had no idea.

The woman needed a full-time minder. Not him, though. Not his speciality.

He was a finder, not a keeper.

She required a bodyguard. Or a babysitter. Even a boyfriend would do. Again, not him. Though the thought of her with one of those fledglings downstairs made his kidneys ache.

No, a man who'd seen what he'd seen and done what he'd done was not for the likes of light, bright Evie Croft.

As if he'd conjured her out of thin air, Evie hustled through the door in a whirlwind of noise and light and energy.

"Oh, hi," she said, her wide, dark eyes taking him in.

Her legs were long in tight, torn denim and studded black boots. Dark hair streamed over the shoulders of her shiny red jacket and she looked luscious and warm, loose-limbed and effortlessly sexy.

Then she took another step and tripped over nothing. Like a fawn bumbling through a forest, snapping twigs and alerting every hunter within hearing distance she was coming their way.

Armand clenched his jaw so tight he swore he heard a tooth crack. "You all right?"

"Super," she said, fixing her hair. "Nice trip? Sure was. I'm here all week. Try the veal."

Despite himself, his mouth twitched. He wiped the evidence away with a hard swipe of his hand.

Before he'd even met her he'd believed her a sitting duck. He still did.

What he hadn't known about then was her knack for self-deprecation. The serious gumption ticking away behind her ribs. The startling scope of that brain behind those big

Bambi eyes. Or how fast that particular collection of attributes would reel him in.

"Did you take care of that urgent thing you suddenly remembered you had to do?" she asked.

"Not quite." *Not even close.* "What about you? Thought you'd be at the restaurant with your friends."

"The Yum Lounge, you mean?"

"I refuse to say those words in that order."

"Spoilsport." Her eyes narrowed. "They could be your friends too if you put in the tiniest effort. But alas, you are who you are."

The fact she realised it, and accepted it, when those who were meant to be his biggest supports had struggled to do the same, only made her more damn endearing.

"Anyway, I know you haven't eaten all day, so I brought the feast to you."

And now she'd brought him food.

Evie filled the silence. "No need to thank me. It was completely self-serving. The longer you go without eating, the grumpier you get, and this is a really small room. Sit. Eat. You can go back to brooding afterwards."

Without further ado, she placed a couple of linen napkins she'd clearly stolen from the dining room and laid them out as a tablecloth, then tipped a bunch of pastries—sweet and savoury—and whole fruits into the middle.

She then nabbed a couple of cushions from the couch and tossed them on the floor. She kneeled down on one, the low lamp light catching the side of her face. Those deep, dark eyes. Full lips gently pursed as she hummed under her breath. Not a single worry line marring her pale skin.

Like a moth to a flame he pressed away from the desk, pulled up a cushion and sat. Cross-legged. As if he was in preschool. Before he could demur, the scents curled beneath his nose and his hunger got the better of him.

He picked up a mini-quiche, paused with it near his mouth as he said, "Thank you."

She passed him a serviette then smiled at him with her eyes, her mouth full of chocolate croissant.

"I don't brood. Just by the by."

She chewed. Swallowed. "You're kidding, right?"

He waited.

"You sit at your desk and frown at those papers all day long. I bet the farm you were doing exactly the same for the few weeks before I got here."

She lifted onto her knees and bent over the table to get another chocolate croissant the same time as he reached for one. When he pulled his hand away she grabbed it, turned it over, plonked the croissant within it. Then went back to grab another for herself.

The feel of her hand wrapped around his, even for the briefest moment in time, burned like a brand.

Armand had been brought up in a family who showed affection through patent family pride. They were not huggers. His work in the military and later private security had hardly changed that.

But Evie was a hugger. A toucher. And it wasn't flirtatious. Not always. Not with everyone. Though, despite knowing how very different they were, there was something there—interest, intrigue, whatever one might call that glowing filament of fascination that burned between them.

He acknowledged it, but he would not act on it. Too many people he'd let past the outer shell had paid the price.

"Eat," Evie insisted. "Before I start turning into one of my granddad's lady friends, clucking about him not looking after himself."

"I'm eating," Armand growled.

"Good. Because whatever you were thinking about just now, you've unlocked another level of brooding," she said around a mouth full of pastry.

Armand leaned over the table to get a mini-pie. And looked up to find Evie's face close to his. Closer than it had ever been.

He'd never before noticed the spot of pure gold in her left eye. Or the freckle beneath her right. He was close enough to spot the pastry crumb stuck to her bottom lip. Before he even felt himself move Armand reached out, held her chin in his hand and used the edge of his thumb to wipe it away.

The flake fluttered to the table but his hand remained, cupping her chin.

Her skin was velvet-soft, and so very warm. Exactly as he'd imagined it would be.

Because, dammit, he had imagined. The feel of her, the taste of those sweet lips. How it might feel to wake up to that smile.

Her top teeth bit down on the spot where the crumb had been, looking for more crumbs. Or to ease the sensation where contact had been made. Either way she left a liquid sheen in its wake.

Eyes glued to her mouth, Armand once more grazed his thumb over the spot. Her smooth lip tugged against his calloused thumb. Heat swarmed through him in a sudden rush.

His eyes lifted to hers to find them huge and gleaming. A pulse beat by her temple.

This was no filament of attraction; it was a wildfire.

Armand dropped his hand away.

Evie's instant intake of breath was loud in the loaded silence. She opened her mouth to say something, but Armand held up a hand.

"Eat," he said.

She frowned. Paused. Then nodded.

And so they ate.

When she went for a third chocolate croissant Armand shoved a bowl of strawberries her way.

She shot him a look. A smile. A glimmer of challenge. Before she chose a strawberry and ate it whole. He'd never seen a person smile so widely with a mouthful of food.

Looking at her, you'd never know she'd lost her job and been under investigation for embezzlement a week earlier.

She'd have no place to live a week from now. Her problems, as he knew them, weren't small. And yet it didn't show.

She left them outside the office door and got on with getting on.

While he—older, wiser, having been through so much and come out the other side relatively intact—brooded. Not unlike an infamous French beast, best known for shutting himself away in his impenetrable castle, believing himself cursed.

Enough was enough. He could do better. Be better.

Armand stood, brushed himself off.

"So soon?" she asked.

"We are no closer to an answer now than I was the day I arrived. So we work."

"Armand," Evie said, from her spot on the floor. "Despite the occasional sidestep into whimsy, I am serious about this job. Whatever problem there is, I will find it. You will believe in me enough to recommend to Jonathon that I stay on."

She looked pure in the half-light, innocent and unspoilt, but the things she was saying between the lines were not. She was setting boundaries. Telling him she felt it too—this gravity drawing them together. But her job was her number-one focus.

It should have been a relief.

When Evie slowly reached out and grabbed another croissant, Armand unexpectedly felt laughter bubble into his throat. "How can you fit any more in?"

"It's sustenance," she said. "Now, stop watching me eat and go put your brooding to good use. We have work to do."

Armand nodded once more and went back to his desk.

And even while his awareness of the woman on the other side of the small room had deepened into a constant warm glow, the letters on the pages, the numbers in the columns, the tangled concepts were suddenly sharper, clearer.

Whatever was wrong with Jonathon's deal, Armand

would unearth it. For that was what he did. That was who he was.

Whether on a battlefield or in a boardroom, Armand was a man who protected his own.

Several hours later Armand sat forward, fisting his knuckles into his eye sockets.

Even with the new clarity of purpose, he felt no closer to finding the reason for Jonathon's concern bar a few items the tax office might wish to look at, but he wasn't working for them.

He looked up to find Evie pacing along the back wall, stretching out her shoulders and bouncing on the balls of her feet like a prize fighter warming up. Her hair had been piled up into a messy bun, her huge headphones were tucked over her ears and she mouthed the words to whatever song was playing.

As if she felt him watching her, she glanced over.

She stopped, hunched as she tipped the headphones backwards till they hung around her neck. And even in the semi-darkness of their cave he knew her cheeks had pinked.

"Sorry, did you say something?"

Armand shook his head.

"Anything I can do?"

"How much do you know about finance law?"

"Not a lot. But I'm a quick learner. How much do you know? Between rescuing little girls, brooding and learning multiple languages, I can't see how you manage to do anything else."

"I managed. Law and Economics at university with a side-note in Art History."

"Well, that's kind of random."

"Not when your family run a series of art auction houses."

"You're one of *those* Debusseys? I know as much about

fine art as you know about debugging, but even I've heard of them. Of you."

Armand bowed with a flourish.

"Why aren't you over in Paris doing this kind of thing for them?"

He'd spent the past year doing just that and it had sucked the life out of him. Or so he'd thought.

"Long story."

"I'll bet." With a smile she grabbed her laptop and sat cross-legged on the couch.

Armand stood; the crick in his shoulder and the ache in his legs felt good. Great even. As if his whole body was grateful for the chance to be of use.

He gave his desk a quick tidy and picked up his briefcase. "Evie."

"Hmm?" Evie balanced the laptop on her knees, finger scrolling quickly over her mouse, gaze like a laser on the screen.

"It's well after six. Time to go home."

"Can't."

Something in her voice flipped a switch in Armand's gut. "What have you found?"

She shrugged one shoulder. "Nothing. Maybe something. I didn't want to say until I was sure. A thorn. Or a knot. I can't tell which. Either way I'm snagged, and I'd like to keep going while I'm on a roll. Is that allowed?"

"It's encouraged. But you haven't had a break in hours."

"I'm all good." She shot him a quick glance before looking back at her work. "You don't have to stay. If you have somewhere to be."

"I have nowhere to be."

"You sure? No TV show you're desperate to binge-watch? No woman—or man—waiting for you back home?" She said it like a throwaway line but he could tell her gaze was no longer focused on the screen.

"No woman—or man—awaiting my return." He couldn't

believe he was about to ask this. "Do you need to call any-one?"

"Me? No! *No*."

"Will Zoe worry?"

"Zoe will not." She shot him a glance. "She'll be on the phone to Lance—the army boyfriend who is moving in any day now. Her place has very thin walls."

"Is your desire to stay here due to a desire to keep work-ing or to give them space?"

"Both."

He had nothing to say to that. His entire reason for being in the country was a severe case of avoidance.

He picked up the phone, called down to the restaurant and discovered the chef was French. It was a few moments before he realised Evie was watching him, her fingers now still, her gaze on his mouth.

"*Oui*," he drawled, agreeing to the chef's suggestion. "*Et le poivron rouge, champignons, olives. D'accord.*"

When he rang off, he cleared his throat. "Dinner will be here in fifteen minutes. I should have asked if you have al-lergies."

She put the laptop onto the coffee table and stretched her arms and legs out in front of her. "I can eat anything. Ex-cept mushrooms and olives and red something. Peppers?"

Armand baulked. Until he saw the smile at the edge of her mouth. The muscles around his eyes tugged, creaking from under-use. "You speak French?"

"Not a jot. I'm just good at seeing patterns."

"Patterns?"

"Patterns—patterns everywhere. In sounds, in texture, in numbers, in code. I'm not sure why. Or how. My grand-father says I always lined up my jelly beans in coloured rows as a kid. And I took to knitting like a duck to water." She motioned to the knitted hat hanging on the hook on the wall by her desk. "My brain is simply wired that way. You?"

"Are you asking if I see patterns? Or how my brain is wired?"

"Whatever you'd like to share. We have fifteen minutes to fill, after all."

Armand moved deeper into the room. "What would you like to know?"

Evie's eyes never left his. "I'd built you up in my head as this strong, silent type. I had no idea it would be that easy!"

Armand stopped, crossed his arms.

"Fine. Okay. Here's a question: I get that your skills and knowledge are wide and varied, but what makes you the one Jonathon called in to do this job when you clearly know nothing about the kinds of technology that are his bread and butter?"

Trust her to cut straight to the quick. For the answer was complicated. A mass of thorny tangles and dark alleys and the kind of moments in a man's life only the very oldest of friends could understand. And forgive.

"We've known one another for a long time."

"Since university."

"How did you—?"

"His autobiography. I was rereading it last night and saw he studied Economics in France. I'm clever that way."

Armand scoffed. "You've read that schlock? More than once?"

Evie blinked. "As have you."

When he didn't respond she turned towards him, tucking one leg beneath her, leaning her elbow on the back of the couch, her head dipping into her palm. "On the train. A couple of weeks back. I think it's what gave me the impetus to look into career opportunities here when my last job went belly-up."

She'd watched him on the train. Just as he'd noticed her. Days ago. The knowledge settled, sliding into the dry cracks inside him like the first raindrops after a drought.

"Then you are my fault," he said.

"Completely." A grin spread slowly across her lovely face, like a sunrise in fast-forward. "Which explains how you know him but not why he came to you. Why he trusted you."

"Are you always this impertinent?"

"Are you always this obstructive?"

Armand breathed in. Breathed out. This woman.

He sank down onto the armrest of the couch. "My family—"

"The Debusseys of Paris," she said swishing a hand across the sky. His mother would like that. Would like her.

He tucked that thought away, nice and deep. "The very same. Despite the fact we have been in the business of art for generations—curation, auctioneering, patronising and owning—I did not go into the family business, instead joining the Légion Étrangère."

"The strange legion... You were in the *French Foreign Legion*? Still waters, indeed." Her eyes ran over his suit, all the way down to his handmade loafers and back up again. Then, "On *purpose*?"

This time as he smiled the muscles around his eyes tugged not quite so hard. As if they were warming up. "That's how it works."

A beat, then, "I might be mistaken, but I always had the sense it was a bit of a renegade unit, filled with murderers and thieves, men running from the law. Called on to intervene in the world's most dangerous hot spots at a moment's notice. While wearing berets."

"You are not far off. Any man may enlist, running from the law or otherwise. Bar those who've committed blood crimes and drug crimes."

She held up both hands, palms out. "I stand mistaken. Sounds like a lovely bunch of guys. You said any *man*..."

"No women."

She rolled her eyes. "Why am I not surprised?"

Armand went on to explain why. "The factors as to why

are multiple: history; biological stamina. The men need to concentrate on the mission at hand, not concerning themselves with the safety of the women—"

But Evie held up a hand to stop him. "Spare me. And look around this place when you next get a chance. Tell me how many of the people working here are female and then explain to me what that has to do with biological stamina or the Safety of The Women."

*Touché.*

"So Armand Debussey of the art-loving Debusseys of Paris, how is it that you came to join this band of ne'er-do-wells?"

Till that moment the conversation had been light. Easy. For it was that time of night when the sky turned soft and voices gentled. Where words spilled readily as the last vestiges of daylight faded away. It was the time of night when soldiers had to be at their most diligent. When shadows could be men and men shadows.

"It's truly not that interesting."

She shifted, her hair spilling through her fingers, the light catching her cheekbones, her jaw, the curve of her lashes just so, her tone hushed as she said, "It is to me."

Armand felt the past creeping cold and slow up the back of his neck. For Lucia—his ex-wife—had felt the same. She'd fallen for the hero. Had never understood that at the end of a mission he didn't want to come home to a rent-a-crowd, to rehash the gritty details. Home for him was a place of quiet comfort, of warmth, clean sheets and locked doors.

When reality finally hit, she'd felt tricked. Perhaps even justifiably so. For he was very good at his job, his company growing exponentially in those early years, becoming the name in European private security and exposition of corporate espionage. But all the success in the world did not make up for the way dealing with the lowest of the low chipped away at a man's soul.

"If 'not interesting' means you don't want to talk about

it, that's okay. Granddad fought in the Korean War and he needed to be in the right place, right moment, for the stories to come out." Evie shifted so he saw her in a new light—those rich brown eyes, the sweet curve of her smile, the insouciance of torn jeans, messy hair and slightly chipped black fingernails.

She was no Lucia. She was wholly herself. Kind, hard-working, curious and genuine. No ulterior motives. No judgement.

Armand found himself saying, "Men come to the Legion for any number of reasons: travel, bloodlust, the desire to do good in the world, a second chance. There are seekers, there are hiders and there are the romantics. Only one in four makes it through the sit-down exam, medical, fitness, interview, psych test. Those who do are required to give up their nationality, and their name."

She sat forward, eyes wide, taking it all in.

"Training occurs for many months—in weapons, team-work, standing still, marching through snow, following orders. Deserters are not uncommon. Those who make it emerge clear-eyed and well-shaven. Reborn. One."

"Mmm…" she said, her mouth twisting. "I can proba-bly find everything you've just given me on their website. Tell me they didn't take one look at you and know they had something special."

"Turned out my family name was irrelevant."

"I wasn't talking about your name."

Armand's chest tightened. He breathed through it. Tried at least. It was becoming harder to steel himself against the onslaught that was Evie.

"Who I was didn't matter," he said, his voice coarse. "Only what I did from that moment on."

And within the ranks Armand found true *esprit de corps*—not based on where a person was from, who they knew, but how they conducted themselves.

He had learned faster, worked harder than anyone else

and soon, despite the levelling nature of the corps, he had risen fast, his affinity with languages, with anthropological nuances, seeing him promoted swiftly, until he was put at the helm of a sharply honed team. A dagger hidden within the end of a blunt tool.

"Those men," she said, "the ones you brought in to help you find that little girl. Your Action Adventure All-Stars. That's how you knew them, isn't it? No better way to learn who you can trust than living in the trenches together."

"As much as it's possible to trust a bunch of ne'er-do-wells."

Evie shifted again, this time unhooking the band from her hair till it spilled into her hands. She gave her scalp a scratch and hummed with pleasure.

With no window to show if it was night or day—a trick used in department stores and torture chambers—Armand felt the quiet settling, the sense of possibility, of intimacy hovering on the air.

"Did you ever consider becoming a ne'er-do-well yourself?" Armand asked. "With your skill it would be a lucrative choice."

"Nah. I've always been a good girl." She batted her lashes, as if butter wouldn't melt in her mouth. "Preferring to build rather than tear down."

"An idealist. Like Jonathon. No wonder this is your dream job."

Her mouth twisted, her brow furrowing as she glanced towards the door. "Well, not exactly."

Armand stilled. "You told Jonathon otherwise."

She held up a finger. "I said this was *a* dream job, not my dream job."

"There's a difference?"

"When I was little, like four or five, my dream was to become a dairy farmer. My mum and I both grew up on my granddad's dairy farm, so it wasn't a huge leap. Then I turned eight, started taking the bus to school, and realised there were other jobs in the world. Bus driver! Teacher! When Granddad had heart problems I was determined to become a cardiologist."

When Armand frowned, she said, "He's good. Doing great. Clucked over like a prime rooster by a plethora of single septuagenarians in a very posh retirement village."

"And your mother?"

A shadow fell over her eyes, and she slouched a little in her seat. Always sunny—or bolshie, or impertinent, or frustrated—she was vibrant in every guise. Only now she seemed leeched of colour.

She said, "Not everyone *has* an all-consuming dream that sticks with them their entire life. My mother did."

The greyness swept over her, all the way to her fingertips as they began fidgeting with the ends of her short nails.

"What was it? Her dream?"

Her eyes lifted to his and he caught a flash, the glow inside her pulsing back to life. He felt the same pulse in himself, a beat of heat and light. His hand moved to his belly. To put a stop to it, or to hold it close. He couldn't be entirely sure.

"My mother was one of a kind. A true free spirit. She wanted to be an artist from the moment she held a crayon. She moved to Melbourne to follow her dream, only she never quite got a foothold. Then I came along and she went back to the farm. She died when I was six. Suddenly. Ruptured cerebral aneurysm."

She shot him a smile to say it was okay, it was a long time ago, but it was short. Flat. "My granddad did become a dairy farmer but it wasn't his big dream either. But he found immense pleasure in following his curiosity—getting his pilot's licence, inventing a board game, writing a book about colonial Australia. When I was born in the dead of winter he asked the Country Women's Association to teach him how to knit. In every baby photo I'm wearing a different beanie."

She breathed deep, sat taller.

"Where I'm from most local girls marry the local boys and keep local house while raising local babies. The only thing I liked about the local boys was how easily I could whip them gaming. With one hand tied behind my back. Literally. One day Granddad read that programming was the way of the future and cleared out a corner of the attic for a desk and a computer; he signed us up for Wi-Fi, signed me up for an online course in programming games and I was hooked."

"Follow your curiosity," Armand repeated, the feel of the words on his tongue new and fresh. For it was a concept he had never considered before. Raised to strive, to succeed, he had done just that, equating failure in any of his endeavours as failure in himself.

But to step back, to look inward, to know oneself enough to be comfortable with change—change of circumstance, change of heart, change of mind—with simply following one's curiosity; what a powerful, yet devastatingly simple, view.

"And now?" he asked. "If you were given the chance to follow your curiosity right now, what would you do?"

Something capricious flashed over her eyes; hints of humour, intrigue, and heat. A feeling he understood too well. For he had been wrestling with the same curiosity about her too. Fighting to keep it contained, hidden, lest it create discord, drama, dissension.

In that moment he paused, breathed, and simply let it be.

"You mean work-wise, right?" she asked.

A smile slid onto his face. "Of course."

"Other than ballerina princess firefighter astronaut?"

"You tell me."

Her mouth twisted as she tried to decipher if he really wanted to know, then eventually said, "I'd love to have a team of my own. Hand-picked. Enthusiastic. Creative. Nice. To develop the million game and app ideas I have mapped out in my "One Day" file. Game apps. Health apps. Learning apps. Much like our esteemed employer, actually. Have you ever had a job like that? That made you feel like you were contributing in a real, honest way?"

As she asked it Armand realised that, at one time, he had.

"Those first months after the foiled kidnap, when we started getting work without even looking for it, I had no choice but to organise, to create a framework, a business model. To hire in. It was wild. Crazy busy. But fulfilling. Yes."

Not just the work but also the knowledge he was giving good men secure futures went soul-deep. Allowing him to fall into bed at night with a sense of exhausted contentment for the first time in his life.

And yet his sense of duty had meant he'd allowed himself to be pulled away. Driven by the deep-seated need to do the right thing by all those he cared for. Not just his men. To keep his family safe and happy. Lucia safe and happy. Putting himself and his own needs last, as he'd always known deep down he was the strongest of them all.

No wonder the cracks had set in. No wonder he'd begun to feel lost in the fog. He'd buried his idiosyncratic spark, his *curiosity*, so deep below the layers of duty he'd forgotten how to recognise it at all.

"Were none of your Action Adventure All-Stars available to help you on this job?"

Armand's brow twitched. The thought of any of the brutes who worked for him knowing how to turn on a computer, much less understand how one worked, was laughable. Besides, it had been many months since he'd handed over the day-to-day running of his company to his second in command, knowing the man would not bother him unless civilisation was on the brink of collapse.

"It's a one-man job."

Evie's eyebrow crept higher and higher.

"Apologies; one man and one woman."

A knock came at the door.

Evie and Armand's gazes caught. Evie bit back a smile and Armand laughed, his voice raw, as he ran a hand up the back of his neck. "More shadows than you'd bargained for going down that path?"

She shook her head. "I've never been afraid of the dark."

"Well, you should be."

All he got for his efforts was a hint of a smile, glinting dark eyes and a sense of unfurling heat deep within. Volcanic. Untapped. Vast.

He drew himself off the armrest and moved to the door. He gathered the pizzas and wine and put them on the coffee table, watching as Evie slowly lowered herself to her knees, then onto her backside on the floor. Her long legs tucked under her.

"Pizza and *wine*?" she asked.

Armand smiled. "Of course wine—I am French."

She held out a glass. "*Vive la France*."

They ate and drank in companionable silence. The room warm, the light golden. The curl of interest and attraction simmering between them.

When Armand offered Evie the last piece she didn't argue, taking it with a happy sigh.

After which they cleaned up and went back to their respective corners, Evie with her profile lit blue by the computer screen, Armand taking a break from the real world within the pages of a novel. Or pretending at the very least.

"Armand," said Evie a little while later.

"Yes, Evie."

"When you ran to the Legion, what kind of recruit were you? The seeker? The hider? Or the romantic?" The pause between her second guess and her third was infinitesimal. And thoroughly telling.

"Wasn't there something about a thorn, or a knot, that required your attention?"

She looked over at him. "There was. And you really don't have to stay. I'm a big girl. Tough as nails. No dew in these eyes."

"I'll stay till you're ready to leave."

"Because we've not been in the trenches long enough for you to trust me not to make off with all this fancy equipment?"

"Because we are in this together. A team. No man—or woman—left behind."

Her gaze widened a fraction—dewy as all get-out.

Her voice was a little rough as she said, "Okay, then."

Watching her settle into her chair, hooking a foot up onto the seat and resting her chin on her knee, all coltish and clever and keen, he no longer even trusted himself.

# CHAPTER SEVEN

EVIE FOUND AN error in the code. Not a virus, or a time bomb—and no evidence of sabotage—just a thread that could have been better written.

She was disappointed that it hadn't been incendiary. But also pretty impressed with the fact it was the first error she'd found. Seriously sophisticated coding. Which made sense, as Jonathon was far too savvy to put his name on anything less.

She fixed the problem, then left her own trail back in case she needed to show it to Jonathon later on.

She stretched her arms over her head and rocked her neck from side to side. Her brain thus no longer locked onto her work, Armand's last words found a nick and slid back into her mind.

*Because we are in this together. A team. No man—or woman—left behind.*

The fact she'd been able to concentrate at all after that little bombshell had been a small miracle. Her mother had passed away when she was six. She'd never met her father. Her granddad had practically kicked her out of home—after the local doctor had convinced him it was far better for him to be in a residential village, surrounded by his peers and medical help, than stuck on the farm with a bad heart. And now Zoe was moving into the next phase of her life.

She knew her granddad was in good hands where he was, which was why she was happy to pay extra for the rent. And she was delighted for Zoe and Lance. Didn't mean she didn't ache for the fact that everything was changing.

No, Evie was not new to the concept of being left behind.

And yet Armand had stayed. It was a little thing in comparison. Keeping her company for no other reason than he believed it was the right thing to do. She understood that when the job was done he'd go back to the far more exciting life he'd led before. Yet the man was making it terribly difficult to remember why she shouldn't be falling for him in a big way.

Once the first yawn hit, Evie knew she was done. She glanced at her phone to find it was nearing midnight. The witching hour. When shadows and noises and illicit thoughts sprang up where in daylight they would not. She found herself actually looking forward to falling into her futon, lumpy and less than private though it was.

She saved her work and set her own secret encryption protocols in place. Better safe than sorry.

Evie clumped heavily over to Armand's desk.

"Done?" he asked, looking up from his book.

"For now," she said, her voice husky from under-use. "My eyes are crossing and my fingers feel twice their normal size. Skiving off?"

"Skiving?"

"Playing truant. Cutting class. Instead of working, you're reading..."

She leaned further over his desk, tipped the cover towards her. And nearly fell over when she saw the title.

Armand noticed. He noticed everything. Now she knew he'd been in the French Foreign Legion of all things she had an inkling as to why.

If she wasn't great at reading people, she got her heart stomped on. If he wasn't great at reading people, people died.

He turned the book over to glance at the cover. Hardback, ivy scrolled over the borders. The title: *The Poetry of Elizabeth Browning*.

"Not a fan of Browning?" he asked.

"Hmm?" Evie squeaked, thinking, *Poetry, poetry, poetry…*

"Elizabeth Barrett Browning."

"Um… I'm not sure I know anything she wrote." *Think, Evie, think. Change the subject.*

*How 'bout them Cubs?* usually worked. But what did they even play? Baseball? Football? Lacrosse?

"I doubt that," he said.

She watched in growing horror as Armand flicked a few pages, pressed the open book to the table. In his deep, rough, lilting voice he read:

*How do I love thee? Let me count the ways.*
*I love thee to the depth and breadth and height*
*My soul can reach, when feeling out of sight*
*For the ends of being and ideal grace.*
*I love thee to the level of every day's*
*Most quiet need, by sun and candle-light.*
*I love thee freely, as men strive for right.*

"Oh," Evie managed through the pulse beating hard and fast in her throat. "*That* Elizabeth Barrett Browning. Sure, she's great."

*It's just a book*, her subconscious said. *The fact he's reading poetry doesn't mean anything. Heaps of guys read poetry. Educated French guys from pre-eminent artistic families, anyway. Now, say goodnight and go home.*

"Then you do like poetry," she said.

*Really? Are you trying to humiliate yourself?*

"Some. I speak several languages but I read them far less. While here I thought it best to brush up on my English vocabulary. Poetry, newspapers, literature, websites. It all helps."

"Cool."

*The man's reading Browning in a language that is not his own and all you can come up with is "Cool"?*

"Have you ever written poetry?" she asked. And her subconscious threw up its hands and left.

"Why do I feel as if we've covered this already?"

"We haven't," she insisted. "Not really. Have you ever written poetry?"

He pushed back his chair and collected his things. "Of course."

*Of course!* French, gorgeous, grouchy and an avid reader. How silly of her to even question him!

"Are you ready to go?" he asked.

And it took Evie a moment to realise he'd let her off the hook on which she'd been floundering. "Hmm? Yes. *Yes*. I'm done. All done."

Armand held out a hand towards the door, and Evie scooted by, holding her breath so as not to catch the scent of him—warm, elegant, inviting.

Downstairs, the Bullpen was like a sleeping giant: the hum of machines, the low lights, as if a good kick and it would rear back to comic-bright life in a second.

They hit the alley and walked side by side through the near-darkness, moonlight slanting over the artwork decorating the brickwork and over the angles of Armand's face. Their shoes making music against the cobblestones beneath their feet.

If they hurried they'd still make the last train. If they didn't hurry she could still call a cab and she'd get to enjoy the strange magic of walking with this man in the moonlight. Tuck it away like a little gift to bring out and admire as she lay on her lonely futon wherever she ended up.

"I have organised a car," said Armand.

And Evie realised they'd hit the street. A sleek black car with tinted windows rumbled to life against the kerb. She could just make out the outline of a driver in a peaked hat. "You take it. I live an easy walk from the station."

"Nevertheless." Armand opened the rear door for her.

The street lamps dropped perfect circles of golden light

on the footpath, a light breeze rustled the branches of a sapling planted in a hole in the concrete. And Evie found she couldn't move.

She felt as if she had to say something—more than a simple thank-you for the car. They'd made a kind of breakthrough tonight. She wouldn't say they were friends. More like interested observers. Visitors at the zoo, only neither could be sure which of them was the exhibit.

He watched her watching him—quietly, patiently. As if he too knew what it meant to require time to figure things out.

What if he had written her the poem? What if he'd been waiting for her to figure it out all along? But she couldn't ask. It would have been embarrassing a few days ago, but now—yes or no—it would change everything.

And yet the possibility snagged at something inside her. Some place warm and soft and fragile. For the crush she'd hoped would dissolve away the more she got to know him had instead evolved as she'd come to regard him with respect, with intrigue, with a yearning that never quite went away.

If it was him she *had* to let him down. To break the fortune cookie's curse.

He was tougher than he seemed. Seriously tough, she'd come to realise. Warrior-, hero-, soldier-level tough. He'd get over it.

The real question was: would she?

The breeze kicked up, lifting the hair not tucked into her beanie. She pushed it behind her ear.

Somewhere a clock struck, the chimes counting down to midnight.

As if a finger had been hooked into her shirt she felt herself sway away from the car. Towards Armand.

He noticed. He always noticed. Meaning he probably knew all about the crush. The intrigue. The respect. The yearning.

His hand tightened on the top of the door. Yeah, he knew.

His feet stayed where they were, moonlight shining off his nut-brown dress shoes. "Get in the car, Evie."

"In a minute."

When she took another step closer his nostrils flared but he still didn't move. The man was a rock.

And the way her life was floundering, maybe a rock was exactly what she needed. In the interim. Until she was back on solid ground.

Armand looked off to the side, his eyes full of shadows, the breeze sending waves through his hair. After a long, slow out-breath his gaze came back to hers.

The figurative finger hooked into her shirt gave another little yank and she stumbled forward one more step. "I wanted to thank you. For tonight. For sticking around and letting me do what I needed to do. For making me feel like part of a team."

A muscle twitched in his jaw.

The wind caught her hair again, catching in her eyelashes, on her lip. When she tugged it free, Armand's gaze dropped to her mouth. And stayed there.

"Whatever it takes to get the job done." His voice was deep, a rumble that shot through her body before zapping into the earth beneath her feet.

"See, that's exactly how I feel."

Yet her heart slammed against her ribs as if it was trying to break free. How could it not when he gazed at her lips as if haunted by the space between them? When he looked at her as if she was not only a curiosity, but also a disruption? As if he was confounded by the very fact of her?

The fortune cookie bobbed up in the corner of her mind like a final-warning sign. Danger Ahead! Though it was a bogus excuse. Or a case of apophenia. Sufferers looked for patterns in random data to make sense of the world. She'd looked it up. It had first been discovered during schizophrenia research. Good to know.

As she stood there in the moonlight, the breeze tugging at her hair, her clothes, with Armand clearly holding on so tight, she knew—if she believed in patterns as much as she claimed to, then ignoring them when it came to Armand was hypocritical.

She wasn't alone in this. She wasn't alone.

Before she could stop herself, Evie took a single step forward and pressed her lips against Armand's.

No other part of them touched. He still held on to the car door, her back foot resting toe down on the ground.

It was delicate, daring, and it took less than a second to know she'd stepped over a line.

But she didn't move. Couldn't. Her mouth remained gentle against his. Cool to warm. Dewy to dry. Her entire body alight with the most exquisite sensation she'd ever known.

*Kiss me back,* she thought. *Or push me away. Stop time. Rewind.* Anything but the beautiful agony of the in-between.

Then, just as the backs of Evie's eyes began to burn, Armand's slowly closed. His hand slid around her back. He pulled her into the hard length of his body and a fist of tightly held desire unfurled inside her.

Weighted, heavy, her eyelids lowered and she grabbed a hunk of his shirt as she tilted and pressed her lips more fully to his. Testing, tasting, drowning in release. The warmth of his mouth, his body, a stark contrast to the wintry breeze at her back.

His other hand sank into her hair, his thumb brushing her cheek, her ear, dislodging her beanie, before he nudged her lips apart and set her world on fire.

Her hands were running up his back, sliding through his hair, over his spectacular backside, her knee nudging between his until every part of her that could lean into every part of him did.

Minutes, hours, aeons—probably seconds—later Armand pulled back, tipping his forehead to hers. Bodies heaving, they found their breath.

Evie felt less as though she'd been kissed than as if she'd been hit by a train. She couldn't feel her feet and her vision spun with stars. She still gripped a fistful of his shirt but no way was she ready to let go. It was the only thing keeping her from sinking into a puddle at his feet.

A car horn beeped long and hard, young male voices whooping and laughing as their car cruised by.

Evie came back into her own body enough to press back and look into Armand's eyes.

After one more deep breath Armand looked up, his stormy gaze tangling with hers.

What she saw there brought her back to earth with a thud.

For the man was in pain. She could see it in the curve of his shoulders. In the furrow of his brow. In the tempest of emotion in his eyes.

While she felt wracked with lust, Armand looked as though someone had just discovered the bruise in the centre of his soul and jabbed it with a sharp stick.

It was too much.

He was too much.

What had she done?

Before he could say a word she yanked open the car door, leapt inside and gave the driver Zoe's address.

As the car eased smoothly out into the street Evie sank her face into her hands and screamed. Silently.

She'd *kissed* him. And he'd clearly wished she hadn't.

How the hell was she meant to face him again? At work? On the train? Every day? How was she meant to face herself? When acting contrary to her own interests over a man was the one thing she'd been determined she'd never do?

As the train neared Armand's usual pick-up spot the next morning Evie's leg jiggled so hard it was making her travel-sick.

"How much coffee did you drink this morning?" Zoe asked.

"One, two cups." Evie literally couldn't remember. "I didn't sleep well."

"Bad dreams?"

"Not exactly."

"Ah, I see." Zoe nudged her in the shoulder. "*Bad* dreams. I bet I know who's the leading man. And speaking of dreamy, look who it is."

Evie knew exactly who Zoe was talking about and kept her gaze trained determinedly on the window. If she didn't make eye contact perhaps he'd head to his old seat. And they could pretend the night before had never happened.

When she heard the pop of Zoe's phone taking a photo, her head snapped around. "What are you doing?"

Zoe showed her the picture and, yep, it was Armand. "Seriously. That man is the very definition of a long, cool drink of water."

Knowing it was a losing battle, Evie glanced up from the phone to find Armand making his way through the carriage towards her. Her insides came over all gooey at the sight of him. He looked so French in his dark suit, dark shirt, dark tie, stubble now hitting sexy-beard length.

When she remembered how it felt to kiss him—the soft scrape of his stubble, the heat of his lips, Evie struggled to remember how to breathe.

Zoe said, "Lucky he's not completely to my taste, or I'd be in big trouble. I like rogues. Bad boys. And my daring Lance is the baddest of them all."

Evie thought back to Armand's revelations of his past adventures and decided not to tell Zoe lest she implode on the spot.

"Love poem or not, you are a fool if you don't at least put your hat in the ring there. Let me be your go-between. A fairy godmother if you will."

"Not necessary."

By the time Armand made it to their seat, Evie's leg was cramping from shaking so much.

This was for the best. Get the mortification over and done with. When his gaze connected with hers she braced herself... Only to melt from the head down.

"Good morning," he said in that voice of his, his gaze locked on to hers.

"Good morning!" Zoe sing-songed before Evie was able to find her voice.

"Sleep well?" he asked.

"Our Evie had bad dreams," Zoe said, helpfully. "Or were they good?"

"Not important," Evie said, her voice raw.

She could have sworn she saw a flicker of light behind the clouds in Armand's eyes. But the vision of him looking so pained the night before wiped it out.

Then Armand said, "I believe this is yours." He held out her beanie. The one that had fallen off her head when he'd kissed her.

Strike that. She'd kissed him. With the excuse she was trying to discover if he was the poet or the one the fortune cookie had told of. The truth was, she'd wanted to kiss him. So badly. Consequences be damned.

"Thanks." Evie leaned past Zoe and took the beanie, shoving it into her backpack.

She caught Zoe's eye when she sat up, to find her oldest friend watching her with far too much understanding on her face.

"So tell me about yourself, Armand. Married? Single? Got your eye on someone?"

Evie shot Zoe a death stare but her friend refused to engage, too busy was she keeping an eye on Armand to test his reaction. Little did Zoe know that the man was a Zen master.

Glancing at Armand as briefly as humanly possible, Evie said, "Ignore her. She's of the mistaken impression that anyone but her would care about such things."

When Zoe went to say something else, Evie leapt in.

"Please leave him out of this. He already thinks Australians are too uptight about romance."

"Does he, now?"

"He's French. It came up."

"Hmm, he could be right," Zoe said. "Evie is being very circumspect about the prospects at work. Perhaps you can illuminate me."

"Zoe!" Evie wished she could climb under the train seats, despite whatever disgusting things lurked down there.

Then Armand said, "What about your young friend in the Bullpen? The one who always wears a cap."

Evie's jiggling leg came to a grinding halt. Was he seriously suggesting what she thought he was suggesting? And after he'd held her to him the way he had the night before, kissing her until her knees no longer worked?

"You mean Jamie?" Evie offered helpfully. "I do not want Jamie." Then something made her add, "But even if I did *want him*, I still have no intention of mixing work and play."

"Ah, you're still stuck on that, then."

Evie's leg started up again, now at double speed. "Not *stuck*. That makes it sound as if it's not my decision. I am completely determined."

"If you say so."

The train began to slow, the metal beneath the belly of the beast screeching as they came to a halt. Evie ducked under the strap of her cross-body bag and stood, stepping over the school bags at her feet, and over Zoe's knees.

Till she found herself behind Armand. She could smell his aftershave. Or maybe it was just him. She closed her eyes and breathed. Earthy, clean and delicious.

When she opened her eyes he'd moved away, heading towards the doors.

"Off you go, then," Zoe said. "Can't wait to hear what 'comes up' today."

Once she could no longer see him, Evie made a dash for the door, catching it just in time. Her beanie slipped sideways, one of the puppy-dog ears dipping into her eye. She fixed it then took off at lightning speed towards the office so as not to be late.

"Evie!" It was Armand.

Of course, he wanted to walk with her today. Right when she felt all strange and discombobulated, confused and raw.

"Evie, please wait."

Evie stopped and spun, only Armand hadn't seen it coming and barrelled into her.

He grabbed her by the upper arms, turning her, their legs entwining, the world going topsy-turvy until he found balance enough for the both of them. There they stood, breath intermingling, bodies slammed against one another as gravity and momentum settled back to a normal ratio.

"Look at me," he insisted.

"I'd rather not."

"Why? Are you afraid you'll kiss me again?"

Evie laughed, the sound only slightly hysterical. "Don't panic. I got your message. I won't be doing that again."

"Evie."

She flinched at the intensity in his voice, the way it rolled over her skin like a caress. And she couldn't help it. Her eyes found his.

"I'm sorry," she said.

"You have nothing to apologise for."

Evie rolled her eyes. Or at least she tried to. With Armand so close—close enough she could see the flecks of navy in his irises, could trace the shape of his jaw beneath his stubble—she was struggling to maintain control of herself.

Her voice was raw as she said, "I saw the look on your face last night, Armand. You don't need to throw Jamie in my face as a way to try to deal with me."

A muscle beneath his eye twitched. "He seems like a nice young man."

Evie laughed again. "You've barely said two words to the guy, so how would you know if he's a nice young man?"

Armand breathed out long and slow. "You're right. Most

people blur into one another in the end. A rare few have surprised me. Of which you are most definitely one."

Evie felt herself flush all over at the look in Armand's eyes, the rough note in his voice.

Then he let go of her with one hand to tug her beanie into place. "Jamie is off the table. You would never find contentment with a man of his ilk. You need someone who knows your worth."

Now what was he saying? That *he* was that man? No, there was still that sense of a bruise about him. As though if she looked beneath the sharp suit she'd find he'd been beaten black and blue.

She glanced between his eyes but found him as barricaded as ever. The colour in his eyes so dark she could no longer differentiate the blues from the greys.

And yet he still held her. Close. So close she couldn't stop trembling.

That line she'd stepped over the night before? In that moment she knew—there was no going back. Not for her.

"What if I'm not looking for contentment?" she asked.

Her conscience perked up. *That's* exactly *what you're looking for, kiddo. Keeping your dreams manageable, your expectations reasonable. No running back to the farm for you!*

"Evie…"

"You kissed me too, you know. Sure, I kissed you first, but you kissed me back. And it was a good kiss."

His eyebrow lifted in the international sign of, *Come on. It was better than good.*

"Fine. It was a great kiss." She'd still been floating three inches off the ground when she'd slunk into Zoe's apartment forty minutes later. "And yet it can't happen again."

*Why not?* she asked herself. But then he got that look in his eye again. As if kissing him was a death sentence.

"What do we do about it?" she asked.

"Why can't we do nothing?"

"Nothing." *Huh.*

"The moon was high," he said. "The hour was late. The wine was good. The work intense. And we kissed. Not everything in life has a deeper meaning."

Evie reared back. "When you were in the jungle with your men, and it was late, and you hadn't seen another soul in hours, and things were about as intense as things can ever get, did that kind of thing happen to you a lot?"

Evie stilled, imagining his next step would be to throw his hands up and pace away from her, railing at the gods in French.

Instead he threw back his head and laughed.

It was a hell of a thing. Rich, rough and sexy as hell. It was also more unexpected than the flinch. Because he'd let himself go. The containment field that protected him gone, leaving her feeling heady, weak, as if the bottom had dropped out of her life.

"Maybe this is a huge joke to you," Evie said, "but it wasn't to me. I don't just go around kissing random people."

*Random. Good one. Make it sound as if you haven't been crushing on him for weeks.*

"And," she continued, "while I'd put money on the fact that you are perfectly happy to slink back into your metaphorical cave, I'm not. I don't run from my mistakes—I face up to them."

The laughter slowly fled from his eyes as a new kind of darkness followed in its wake. Not a scary darkness, oh, no. The kind of darkness that sucked you in and tumbled you about and you didn't mind a single bit.

"You believe it was a mistake?" Armand asked, his voice deep and rough and devastating.

"Isn't that what *you* just said?"

Armand watched her with that darkly quiet way he had about him. She felt giddy, as if the spinning hadn't quite come to a stop. And the look in his eyes, those dark, stormy, intense, beautiful, warm, engaging eyes—

Then someone bumped them. And another person.

Another train had pulled in, the early-morning commuters swarming over the platform like water bursting from a dam. Jostling them apart.

His fingers curled away from her arms, the skin left behind turning cold, the nerves sharp.

And, seeing daylight, she turned and hustled towards work. And this time he didn't try to stop her.

# CHAPTER EIGHT

EVIE KEPT HER head down as she barrelled through the Bullpen so as not to get stuck chatting games or algorithms with any of the boys.

And they were boys. Boys who lived on pizza and hamburgers, who she knew would live in places any rightminded landlord would condemn.

Growing up with her granddad and his friends, she'd known men who could roof a house, cook a decent meal and talk about everything from historical Russian literature to modern-day Russian politics.

She hadn't realised how much she'd missed being around actual grown-ups until she'd met Armand. For he was serious. Experienced. Despite his stubborn determination not to enter the electronic age he was the most intelligent man she had ever met.

And there was no running away from the fact her feelings for Armand had well and truly tipped from playful crush to "it's complicated".

So much for not dating fellow employees. Not that they were dating. Ha! They could barely hold a civil conversation without disagreement or culture clash or retreating to their own corners to lick their wounds. Or holding one another. Looking deep into each other's eyes. Kissing.

Evie was up the stairs and halfway down the hall when she pulled up to a dead stop.

There was only one thing for it. She *had* to ask to be put onto another project. For she couldn't lose this job. Working for Jonathon Montrose was the pinnacle—being fired by Jonathon Montrose a career death knell. If it ever came to that she may as well hang up her shingle and go home.

She'd kept the farm after all—renting it out to cover rates repairs and not much more—in case her granddad ever wanted to return.

In that moment she realised how desperately she wanted to stay. This city had got under her skin. She wanted this. Melbourne was her dream. She was not a farm girl any more; she was already *home*.

She paced back to Jonathon's door, raised her hand to knock. Stopped herself just in time.

He'd ask why. What could she possibly say? The truth? Her eyes slammed shut and she let out a sob.

"Evie?"

Evie flinched and opened her eyes to find Jonathon standing beside her, coffee mug in hand, Imogen peeling off to her office.

"Hi, Mr Montrose. Good morning."

"Did you want to see me? Everything okay?"

*No. Everything's not okay. The man you've lumped me with is like a dormant volcano and I can't be sure if I'm in lust with him or so burnt by my last twisted working relationship I'm building castles in the sky.*

"Everything's great!"

"Glad to hear it. How's the project coming along? Any chance it'll be wrapped up soon?"

Evie thought of the knot she'd tripped over in the programming the night before. The one that had had her staying late in the first place. Until the little carpet picnic with Armand had scrambled her brain.

"I'm getting close. I can smell it."

"Just you?"

"I mean we. We're getting close."

*Real close. His lips touched mine and I saw stars.*

"Close to finding the problem, I mean."

Her boss's eyes narrowed, though she could have sworn

his mouth twitched with a smile. "Excellent. And the other things we spoke about?"

Despite the fact she wasn't feeling all that delighted with the man right now, she still wasn't about to turn on him with Jonathon.

"I can handle him." Evie backed away, then turned on her heel and fled.

Thankful her thumbprint now opened the lock on the first try, she ducked inside and shut the door.

After inhaling a few deep breaths she darted over to her desk, dumped her backpack, hung up her beanie and opened up the program, determined to have good news for Jonathon soon. For the sooner this project was over and done with, the sooner she and Armand would no longer be stuck in a tiny room together. She'd have hopefully impressed Jonathon enough to keep her on. And Armand could get on with his life of international intrigue.

Armand arrived on cue. He lurked darkly in the doorway. All scruffy hair and intense energy.

Evie turned up the music in her headphones and got scrolling, still hyperaware of the man as he dropped his briefcase to the floor with a thud, picked up the phone and proceeded to bark down the line in French.

She didn't bother trying to translate. Instead she did what she should have been doing the whole time and got to work.

She managed another minute and a half before Jonathon's voice suddenly filled the room. "Evie. Armand."

"Jeez!" Evie cried, tearing off her headphones, gaze darting about the room. "What the heck was that?"

Armand glanced at his phone, pressed a button that had lit up red and said, "Is this the great and powerful Oz?"

A beat went by before the disembodied voice once more boomed into the room. "You know damn well who this is, funny guy. You both need to clear your schedules tomorrow evening. Cancel plans. Postpone any dates."

Evie couldn't help herself. She glanced towards Armand, only to find him determinedly not looking her way.

"Anyone with eyes can see that the two of you are still butting heads."

*Well, that was one way to put it.*

"You two need to find a way to be in the same room together without it ending in tears."

Oh, God, was that what he thought? "Jonathon, we're getting along just great. At the very least, Armand has never made me cry."

Then she looked to Armand, who was staring at his desk as if trying to burn a hole in the top. She whispered, "Have I made *you* cry?"

Armand finally lifted his gaze to collide with hers. His eyes filled with humour and regret. Heat and sorrow. She wasn't sure what she wanted to do first—hug him or kiss him. Probably easiest to simply do both.

Jonathon went on. "I've organised a team-building exercise."

Evie's gaze shot to the phone as her entire body clenched in response. Not the horror of a grown-up "truth or dare" session. Or "two true things, one false thing". And the trust fall? The thought of having to fall into Armand's waiting arms in front of people was too disturbing for words.

"You can both wipe the grimaces from your faces," said the voice.

Evie looked frantically around her, searching for hidden cameras. She'd been there, after all.

"Jonathon—" Armand began.

But Jonathon had the luxury of not being in the room and cut him off. "Imogen has sent you both the details. I look forward to hearing your effusive thanks next week."

Armand's finger slowly lifted from the phone. It was moments before his gaze finally lifted to connect with hers.

"We don't really have to do this, do we?" Evie asked.

"I have found in life that we don't *have* to do anything.

Only that which we feel we should. Or that which we truly want."

Evie swallowed, heat curling in her belly like a creeping vine in fast motion. No two guesses as to why she'd kissed Armand. Though she couldn't be certain as to why he'd kissed her back.

Either way, now that she'd promised Jonathon they were close—close to finding the answer, that was—her position at Game Plan felt more precarious than ever.

"Maybe he has a point," said Evie. "Maybe if we got to know each other more we could make more efficient use of our time."

Even in the low light she could see Armand's eyes narrow. Was he agreeing? Or was he imagining the same ways of "using their time" she was?

Evie broke eye contact by grabbing her phone. She scrolled through her mail till she found the team-building details. "There's just an address. A time. And a dress code: comfortable for freedom of movement."

No matter what Armand said, it was hardly as if she had a choice.

"I'm in if you are," she said, wondering if everything she said from now on would feel like a double entendre.

Armand said, "So be it."

At six o'clock the next evening, Armand found himself standing outside a corrugated iron door covered in graffiti reading "Escape Room Challenge".

"Is this what I think it is?" he asked, not bothering to disguise the lack of enthusiasm towards the endeavour.

Evie's big, dark eyes roved frenetically over the list of rules posted beside the door: "*No one with heart conditions... No pregnant women... No children under sixteen years...*"

This vision of energy and light had kissed him.

And he'd kissed her. He could still taste her on his lips,

feel the way she had sunk into his body. Her body soft and pliable. Completely trusting.

He should have put a stop to it then. Knowing that their attraction couldn't go anywhere. He'd seen too much darkness. Was bitter. Brittle. While Evie was endearing, charming, lovely from the inside out.

His time in Melbourne had been restorative. As if the smaller cracks were beginning to smooth over. Much of that was thanks to her. But some scars went so deep they leeched colour from a man's soul.

He'd meant it when he'd told her to find someone who knew her worth. But that person was not him. Could not be him. He struggled to reconcile with the regrets of his past. He'd never forgive himself if anything happened to her.

"What the heck was Jonathon thinking?" she asked.

"I often wonder the same thing."

"You do realise he's merely moved us about to go from one small room to another." Her hands moved to her hips, stretching the words "All My Friends Are Dead" over the dinosaur on her T-shirt tight across her curves. "Only this time we'll be locked in."

Evie looked up at him and he wondered if he looked as deeply put out as she did. But then she blinked, twice, and burst out laughing. The sound like birdsong. Like spring time.

He felt a kick at the corner of his mouth. Then another behind his ribs. Within a heartbeat he found himself back there again, deep in the memory of her kiss.

The surprise as her lips pressed against his—cool and soft. Then realisation that it was no surprise at all. Inevitable as the sunrise. Inescapable as breath.

Then her hand curling into his shirt, her knuckles sliding down his chest. Until he'd felt like bottled lightning.

After spending the past year of his life doing everything in his power not to feel anything at all he'd been unprepared, his neglected instincts reacting incongruously to his wishes, giving in wholly to sensation instead of dashing for cover.

A green light lit up over a door a couple of metres down the hall. It opened with a click and out sauntered Jamie, followed by three of his ilk.

Before he even knew he'd moved, Armand's fingers curled into his palms, his feet shifting into position as if he had an enemy in his sights.

As the kid squinted despondently into the brightness, wiping sweat from his brow, Armand told himself to stand the hell down.

"Jamie?" Evie called.

When Jamie saw that they had an audience, he rallied admirably. Squaring himself, finding a grin. "Why, hello, old man. Evie, love."

He sauntered up and slapped Armand on the back, hard enough to rock another man off his heels. But Armand was not any other man. He dropped a shoulder at the last second, leaving Jamie wincing and rubbing at his hand. It felt rather good.

Then the guy leaned over to kiss Evie on the cheek.

And Armand could have taken him down. A single jab to the throat with a sharp hand ought to do it. A crack to the jaw with a closed fist if he felt like going old-school. Of course, a knee to the balls was foolproof.

"How was it?" Evie asked.

"Brilliant," Jamie said, as his cohorts muttered things along the lines of "impossible".

"First time?" Evie asked.

Jamie answered, "I've done VR versions, of course. But in the flesh? Never."

Armand scoffed.

"Problem?" Jamie asked.

"VR," he muttered. "What a cop-out."

There were gasps all around. Evie moved in closer, as if about to dive in front of him if the others attacked. Him.

A man who could have the lot of them unconscious in seconds if he saw fit.

A strange sensation came over him. Warmth sliding through his insides as if he'd eaten hot soup too fast. He protected his own. It wasn't often anyone thought to stand up for him. Or feed him. Or make sure he was okay.

Jamie said, "Wait till you get in there. You know it is not real, but it feels real. Gives you a great glimpse into how you react in a crisis."

The kid poked a finger towards Armand's chest and it took everything he had not to grab the kid's fingers and twist.

"Jamie," Evie said, sliding a hand into Armand's elbow, "Armand has a better handle on that kind of thing than you realise."

She glanced at Armand, looking for permission. His shrug was as good as.

"He was in the French Foreign Legion."

"Whoa," said a cohort. "You for real?"

"For real," Armand deadpanned.

"Actual on-the-ground stuff?"

Armand nodded.

The cohorts oohed and ahhed. Said, "Man, that's cool."

While Jamie crossed his arms. "Sitting behind a desk pushing papers all day must feel like quite the departure."

"A combatant is a combatant," said Armand, eyes on Jamie.

Evie squeezed his arm. He looked down to find her face impassive. Then the edge of her mouth curved. Heat slid through him, only this time, like after jumping into a hot shower on a cold winter's day, it ached.

Before he had the chance to unpack all that that might mean, the light above their door began to flash yellow, which—according to the rules—meant they had a minute to enter before the game began.

Evie gave him a tug. "Come on, then, partner. I'm a genius. You're…you. Let's show these monkeys how this is really done."

For reasons he could feel guilty about later, Armand tucked a hand over hers and pulled her closer, smiling down at her and shooting Jamie and his friends an even bigger smile before opening the door to the Escape Room and closing it behind them.

It was dark, the lack of eyesight heightening his other senses. A sensation not new for him after his military training and years of organised insurrection.

Evie's skills were to be found in other areas, so she turned and walked right into him.

He grabbed her by the shoulders. Steadied her. Breathed in the cherry scent of her hair. Sweet and ingenuous. Like her.

So much for "getting to know one another". Their awareness had ratcheted up to eleven, making the air crackle and the walls close in.

"Sorry," Evie breathed, her voice giving away the fact she was in the same state as he was. "I didn't expect it to be this dark."

"I believe that's the point."

Static crackled though a speaker and a TV flickered to life. Armand let Evie go and they both turned to watch a "news report" that set up the puzzle they had to work out. The name of their room was "Corporate Chaos" in which a thief embezzled from the International Monetary Fund, leaving the world broke and leading to World War III.

Images of the Wall Street stock market cut to shots of shredders and people crying and finally to men and women in combat gear climbing over the smoking rubble of a fallen city.

He was going to kill Jonathon. Using his bare hands. Nice and slow.

"You don't have PTSD, do you?" Evie asked.

His experiences in the Legion had never been an issue. The parameters were clear—make a plan, follow the plan, stay alive. It was the civilised world he'd struggled with. The tug of duty, the lure of freedom, the ache of disappointment. And the mind-bending pain of loss.

"No," Armand assured her. "Do you?"

"You're hilarious," she deadpanned.

And Armand felt himself smile.

Even in the deep darkness, the room lit only by the static now playing on the screen and a small green exit sign over the door, he saw Evie's gaze drop to his mouth and stay.

The room suddenly felt smaller. Warmer. Little shocks tingled across his skin. He felt like a teen, stuck in a closet playing Five Minutes in Heaven.

Only they were grown-ups. In a locked room. On their own. And they had half an hour.

"What do you reckon, soldier boy? Shall we do this?"

For a second, he imagined she'd read his mind.

Then she turned about, looking up and down and all around. "What do we need first? A key? A clue? A code?"

"Light," said Armand, watching the very same play over Evie's hair, the curve of her shoulders, the sweet planes of her lovely face. "What we need is light."

"That was amazing!"

Evie spun around, arms out to the side, revelling in the feel of the air-conditioning on her hot skin as they burst from the Escape Room twelve minutes and eighteen seconds after they'd entered.

For it had been ridiculously fun. Intense—for sure. Especially considering the size of the room—they couldn't move without brushing up against one another. Leaving Evie hot and flushed and wired. But the thrill of the game had taken them over, and once they'd found their beat it had been like a dance.

Armand had a labyrinthine mind, clever and flexible,

twisting and turning and unravelling the trickiest clues with frightening speed. Leaving Evie to do her thing, to follow the breadcrumbs which stood out to her like fireflies in the dark.

She stopped spinning, wiped her damp hair off her face and faced Armand.

While she felt as if her T-shirt was sticking to her back, he looked as if he'd stepped out of the pages of a catalogue; his idea of "comfortable" a red-checked button-down shirt, chinos and elegant chestnut-brown dress shoes.

Adrenaline still coursing through her veins, she took a big, bold step his way. He didn't budge, though his chin lifted, and he slid his hands into the pockets of his chinos.

"Come on, Armand. Admit it. That was fun. You, Mr Grouchy Pants, had fun. With me. Because we make a great team."

Nothing. Not a high five. Not even a nod.

"I think it has a lot to do with our motto," she said.

A single eyebrow kicked north. "We have a motto?"

"Yes, we do." She took another big step his way until she was close enough to nudge the toes of her polka-dot lace-ups against the toes of his fancy shoes. Then made a banner in the sky with her hand. "No man—or woman—left behind."

"I think you'll find that motto belongs to another. The American Army Rangers, I do believe."

"*Pfft.* Sharers are carers."

"You be sure and let them know that's how you feel."

Evie tipped a few millimetres closer. "For the last few years I've pretty much worked in a room all by myself. This kind of 'squad goal' moment is a rarity. And I plan to revel in it."

Armand looked down into her eyes. All dark and French and achingly gorgeous. Then his toe nudged against hers. Deliberately. And it was one of the sexiest moments of her life.

"Hey."

Evie glanced sideways to find Jamie and his cohorts rocking up to them, with a kid wearing an Escape Room Challenge T-shirt in tow. She leapt back a step. But it was too late. The look on Jamie's face said it all.

She held her breath as she awaited his reaction. When he gave her a smile and a wink the relief was palpable.

"You guys rocked," said the Escape Room kid, his voice breaking only a little. "That was totally a record, you know."

"A record, you say?" Evie bumped Armand with an elbow. "Doesn't that make us the best team that ever was?"

The kid said, "Um, yeah. I guess. Anyway, you win a certificate. A team laser-tag session."

"Seriously? That's awesome. Thanks!" She glanced up at Armand to find he was watching her, a small smile playing about his mouth. Not quite as big as the smile he'd smiled in the darkness of the Escape Room, but it made the butterflies kick up a notch all the same. "Hey, any chance we could use this now?"

The kid shrugged. "I guess. Next session starts in half an hour."

"Armand, Jamie, guys, what do you say?" Evie tugged her hair back into a ponytail. "We eat. We hydrate. And then we shoot at one another with lasers."

"We're in," said Jamie, bouncing about like a puppy. His crew concurred.

"Armand? Remember our motto."

She knew there was a chance he'd make an excuse. That his instinct was to edge away from the group. Then she saw the way the others looked up to him. Realised it would have been that way his whole life. The burden of leadership. She wondered then if he'd lost men during his Foreign Legion years. The chances were high. It would make making friends harder. Make letting people close harder still.

Before she could stop herself she reached out and took

his hand, curling her fingers into his and drawing him back into the group. Showing him he wasn't alone in this.

He looked down at her, the bruise in his eyes gentling.

After a few long beats, he cricked his neck. "Let's do this."

"Woohoo!"

# CHAPTER NINE

By THE TIME they left the arcade a light drizzle had begun to fall.

Once again Armand called a car and insisted Evie take it home. In the spirit of their motto, she insisted he do the same.

The ride was electric, buzzing with leftover adrenaline from their Escape Room win, their laser-tag demolition and whatever additives were in the chicken wings. Add the hum of tension that had been building between them all night—starting with small "accidental" touches and furtive glances and ending with their hands sitting millimetres from one another on the car seat—Evie felt as if her blood were filled with soda bubbles.

When the car pulled up outside Zoe's apartment, she turned to Armand. "Thanks for the ride. And for staying. It was a good night."

"Thanks for making me stay. And goodnight it is."

Evie shot him a look. He gave her one back.

"Fine. Goodnight. See you tomorrow."

He made the car wait until she'd run to the front of the building and opened the door.

Laughing, giddy, she waved him off, watching the car head around the corner to take him to wherever it was he spent his nights. She knew it was in South Yarra somewhere, as that was his train stop. But knowing some of his background now—from an idyllic childhood to growing up surrounded by priceless works of art, to his years living in the most basic, uncomfortable, dangerous places in the world—she had no clue as to the kind of place Armand would choose to call home.

She brushed raindrops off her puffer jacket and beanie and took the stairs two at a time to Zoe's third-floor apartment, unlocked the door and walked in on Zoe and Lance getting it on.

"Oh, no. Oh, jeez. Sorry, sorry, sorry!"

Eyes burning with the image of a naked backside and so many limbs writhing on the futon—*her* futon!—Evie somehow made it back out of the door and into the hall. She slammed the door shut and leant against it as if it might hold back the horror.

"Evie!" Zoe called, her voice muffled through the closed door. "I didn't know he was coming back. It was a surprise visit. I should have messaged you, or put a note on the door, but things kind of got out of hand fast."

"It's fine," said Evie flapping a hand in the direction of her friend's voice. "Look, I'll get out of your hair for the rest of the night."

"No! Don't be silly. Come back in."

"Not happening."

"Where will you stay?"

She hadn't made all that many friends since moving to Melbourne. Working on her own at her last job, she'd done little more than wave on her way in and out. After the Eric fallout, even those she'd been friends with on social media had slunk away.

But she'd never needed much. Been happy with little.

It hit her then how much things were about to change.

Keeping her voice as calm as humanly possible, Evie said, "I'll get a hotel room in the city for the night. Easy-peasy! Maybe something a little flash. A little gift to myself for getting the new job."

"Are you sure?" said Zoe, cricking open the door.

Evie looked over her shoulder to find Zoe wrapped in a blanket from the back of the futon. One she'd knitted. One she would never again pull over herself while watching TV. "Positive. It was always a matter of time."

Zoe sniffed. Her big blue eyes welling up. "I kind of imagined you living here for ever. Like a maiden aunt. Or a favourite pet."

Evie laughed, even as it turned into a sob. "I've loved every second of it."

"Me too."

"Lance better treat you like a princess."

"And I'll treat him like a prince."

Evie gave Zoe a quick kiss and hug before stepping back. "I'll talk to you tomorrow, okay? Bye, Lance!" she called through the door.

"Bye, Evie," he called back.

Hooking her backpack over her shoulder, Evie headed off back down the stairs, heart thundering in her chest, thoughts fluttering uselessly inside her skull. She checked her watch to find it close to ten.

With no car she did all she could do and walked to the train station.

The air was still filled with drizzle—the kind that seeped slowly into one's clothes until your entire body felt soggy. By the time she got to the station, rivulets of water dribbled down her back and her shoes were soaked through.

The platform was empty. Eerie. All concrete greys, mossy greens and sharp, gleaming blacks, as if the warmth function in a photo app had been turned right down.

Pulling her icy hands deeper into the sleeves of her jacket, Evie nudged her toes against the yellow safety line and sniffed. But it wasn't the cold. A tear leaked from the corner of her eye and she dashed it away.

What the heck was she doing? Where did she think she was going?

She might have convinced Zoe, but the truth was she didn't have money to burn on a last-minute hotel. Not with the fact she was only on a contract and the price of her granddad's accommodation. And now Lance was back, what about tomorrow night and the next and the next?

She'd have to dip into her Just in Case account. Just in Case everything went wrong. She was her mother's daughter after all.

Which was why the fortune cookie had hit her hard.

From the moment she'd arrived in Melbourne, Evie had been waiting for the other shoe to drop.

She'd done her best to mitigate any possible disasters.

Working at a job she could have done in her sleep.

Staying on Zoe's futon.

Dating men she had no hope of losing her head over.

Her mother had been the opposite, leaving home at seventeen. Refusing to "get a real job" as she held tight to her dream of being an artist, sketching portraits at markets, busking with chalk art on the streets, sleeping wherever she landed each night.

Till she'd fallen in love, fallen pregnant and fallen on hard times. All that potential was for naught because she'd been in such a rush to live she'd tripped over her own feet.

Evie stared down the train tracks towards the city.

Choosing the comfort of familiarity over the risk of adventure hadn't made a lick of difference to Evie's story. Life had risen up and smacked her on the head anyway.

And yet… Maybe that was exactly what she'd needed.

She'd never have presumed to try for a job at Game Plan if she hadn't lost her last job so spectacularly. She'd probably have lived on Zoe's awfully uncomfortable futon for ever if circumstance wasn't forcing her to get off her butt.

The fortune cookie hadn't been a curse. It had been a revelation.

What it came down to now was whether or not she could follow that through. Continue taking safe, small steps through life, or surrender to adventure? Leap and discover how high she could go?

The lights at the end of the track began to flash. The

screech of metal on metal cut through the chill night air and
the train rumbled up to the platform. When the train doors
opened she leapt inside. Found a random seat, tossed her
backpack next to her and pulled out her phone.

She rolled it around in her hand once, twice, then with
a hard, sharp out-breath pulled up the number she needed.

Three rings later, a delicious French voice answered.
"Evie? What's wrong? I saw you go inside—"

"I did. I'm fine. I'm sorry to call so late but—"

"What is it?"

"Lance is back. I walked in on him and Zoe…together."
She shut her eyes, but the image was indelible. "Anyway,
I've let them be for the night. I'm on the train heading back
into the city. And…"

And what, exactly? Her gut had told her to call Armand,
but to what end?

*Adventure!* her heart cried.

But she hadn't stopped to consider that there was a really
good chance he wasn't riding the same wave of revelation
she was. He was still Armand. A lone wolf, brooding over
internal bruises earned miles outside the boundaries of her
own realm of experience.

Seeing a sliver of time in which to still save face, she
opened her mouth to ask him to forget she had ever called
when his voice rumbled over the phone.

"Stay there," he said, 'I'll turn the car around."

"I'm already on the train."

"You walked there? It's raining."

"And I wondered why I was wet."

He mumbled something under his breath in French.

"Are you sure about this?" Evie asked.

"I have a spare room. You will stay with me."

He hadn't answered her question, but she let it be. "Thank
you. It'll be one night, I promise."

"Get off at South Yarra Station."

"Yes, sir."

"Evie," he chided.

"Fine. Yes. I'll do that. And I know which is your stop, Armand." And maybe it was the snug cocoon of the train with the rain drizzling down the windows, or the soothing rocking of the carriage, but Evie found herself adding, "I've been well aware since the day you started taking my train."

"Is that so?"

"I even remember what you were wearing."

His quiet was loaded. Electric. She half thought he'd change the subject and yet found herself unsurprised when he said, "I'm assuming it was a suit of some description."

"It was."

"Of course, I have no idea which, so I'd have no hope of confirming or denying."

"Grey," she said, remembering the way the sunlight dappled the thread. "Subtle checked shirt. Green tie with white polka dots and matching—"

"Pocket square," Armand cut in.

The train slowed. Evie pressed her feet into the floor to counter the rocking. "I'd never seen a real live contemporary human person with a pocket square before. I thought you so dashing."

"Dashing?" he growled.

"With a healthy dose of mad, bad and dangerous to know."

Soft, rough laughter eased through the phone, sending waves of warmth through her all the way to her numbed toes.

Then Armand's voice sounded far away as he said something to the driver, no doubt asking him to take a different turn.

Evie sat up as a handful of people hopped onto the train. She shot them a polite smile as they passed, settling into the seat a few up from hers.

"Armand?"

"Hmmm."

"Thanks for this. I really appreciate it. You won't even know I'm there."

Again with the pause. As if he very much believed otherwise.

"I'll see you soon," he said, the phone clicking as he rang off.

Evie breathed out hard.

It had been a conversation. About getting a lift. From a workmate. Then begging a room for the night. But in that moment she understood how Zoe's phone had kept her and Lance happily together for years.

Evie slowly dropped her phone into her lap, turning it over and over between her hands, before looking out of the window. With the night having well and truly closed in, all she saw was her reflection looking back at her. Dark eyes, dark hair, nuclear-green beanie with a radiation patch sewn into the front.

For a moment she caught a rare glimpse of her mother in her own face.

She remembered her more from photographs nowadays. But she knew she had her mother's jaw, the splotch of gold in one iris, the shape of her smile.

The night she'd opened the fortune cookie she was at a dinner celebrating her twenty-sixth birthday. The same age her mother had been when she'd died.

The burden of which was not lost on her. Quite the contrary.

Maybe that was the message the universe had been trying to send her. It was time to go hard or go home.

Armand stood in the entrance to his apartment, tossing his keys from one hand to the other as he watched Evie take a turn about the room.

Not one to stand back, she ran fingers over the back of the soft leather couch, opened cupboards as she meandered through the warm, modern kitchen, took a spin beneath the repurposed chandelier. Her big, blue, puffy jacket squeaked as the cheap fabric swished together, the pom-pom on top of her beanie bobbing soggily.

"Jonathon put you up here?" she asked.

"Not exactly."

He'd refused payment from Jonathon, even in the form of rent, choosing instead to invest in a property in his company's name. First thing he'd done in that capacity in over a year, and it had felt good.

Working as a favour was not something he made a habit of, knowing what his skills were worth. But he'd needed the sense of autonomy. The surety he could walk away at any time. In case it turned out he was more broken than he'd realised. In case he was beyond repair.

"It's lovely, Armand," she said. "Not what I expected at all."

"And what was that?"

"Either four bare walls, an army cot, a box full of rations. Or a mini-Versailles." She shot him a smile, the kind that always left him feeling winded.

Which was when he noticed how much she was shivering.

He swore beneath his breath then strode over to where she was. Without thinking he ran his hands down her arms, friction creating warmth.

"You're wet through."

"Rain will do that to a girl."

"How far did you walk?"

"A kilometre or so."

He looked around. "Where is your luggage? Did you leave it in the car?"

"I left in a bit of a hurry," she said, teeth chattering. "No clothes. Just my backpack and me."

He turned her around and moved her towards the spare room which came with its own *en suite* bathroom.

"Your bed," he said, facing her that way as they passed it, then he quickly turned her and walked her into the bathroom.

"Whoa. That's bigger than Zoe's whole apartment."

He peeled the backpack strap from her shoulder, dumped the bag on the stool at the end of the bed and then pressed her into the bathroom. When he realised the next step was stripping her down he let go. Took a step back.

She turned to face him, all damp lashes and hair dripping in straggled ribbons down the front of her jacket. Her make-up had smudged, making her big brown eyes look huge. Her lips were swollen, tipped slightly open as her teeth clattered together.

She took a deep breath in, the breath out rough and jagged. And there was a new light in her eyes—a mania, a hunger. As if a switch had been tripped.

Which was when Armand realised that while he had been blithely convinced he had a handle on his affections towards her, it had been she who'd been in charge of the pace. Giving him the room to want, to imagine, to lean in. To be less mindful of his own boundaries.

And now she'd taken her foot off the brake.

He could have put her up in a hotel. Or she could have slept at the office. Jonathon clearly did not have a problem with the practice, as Armand had walked into Montrose to find IT guys sleeping on beanbags, on couches, at their desks nearly every morning he'd been there.

Knowing she was in trouble, he'd wanted her safe. Needed her close. Because he'd doltishly let himself care.

Nonplussed, he dug deep, regathered his self-control and took another step back. Mumbled, "I'll put some clothes on the bed," and walked away, shutting the *en suite* bathroom door decisively behind him.

Evie stared at the space where Armand had been before he'd scampered away.

Did he think she was going to jump him? He'd been in

the French Foreign Legion, for Pete's sake. He could probably take her down with one finger.

She shivered at the thought, and not out of fear.

A quick reconnaissance uncovered a heat lamp in the bathroom. The difference was immediate, and welcome. She stripped off her jacket, her damp T-shirt. Nudged off her filthy, wet shoes and socks and climbed into the huge shower.

A long, hot shower brought her back to life, after which she wrapped herself in a fluffy bathrobe and tucked a towel around her damp hair.

She opened the bathroom door slowly, found herself alone.

Biting back a grin, she jumped into the bed—was there a size bigger than king? All those pillows! Oh, the sheets. The softest blanket she'd ever felt. After years spent sleeping on a futon, she nearly wept.

When she was done luxuriating she grabbed her backpack, fished out her phone and sent Zoe a quick message to let her know she had a roof over her head. After checking the time she made a quick call.

Her granddad—always an early bird on the farm, now very much a night owl at the retirement village—answered the phone with, "Well, if it isn't my little Evie Marie Saint. Christmas Evie. Happy Evie After."

"Hey, Granddady-O. I can hear noise. Where are you?"

"Playing Mah-Jong. Evie says hello!"

A chorus of voices met her. Mostly female.

"All right with you, love?"

"Sorry I didn't call this week. It's been a bit busier than usual here."

"Busy is good. Means you're settling in. Making a real life for yourself. That's all I need to know."

Evie rested her palm over her eyes, closing them against the knowledge she hadn't been doing that at all.

She asked after his friends in the village. Took the usual beanie requests. And finished off by saying, "If you need me, call my mobile."

"Problems with the landline?"

"Something like that."

She could have just told him she was staying with a friend, but the word felt all wrong. Though what else could you call someone who let you stay in their spare room without pause or hesitation? Maybe there was no word. Maybe it was bigger than words.

The conversation hit a pause. After which her granddad's voice softened. "Was there something else, love?"

"Um… I was thinking about Mum tonight. More than usual, I mean."

"Were you, love?"

Evie realised the background noise was quieting, meaning he'd found a private place to sit.

"I miss her," Evie said.

"As do I. There is no shame in that. Or in not thinking about her every day. Or in feeling like you've forgotten more than you can remember. It's normal. It's how it's meant to be."

"What about spending an inordinate amount of time making sure I don't make the same mistakes she made? Is that normal too?"

"And what mistakes would those be?"

"Falling for the wrong guy. Falling pregnant. Slinking home."

"Oh, love. She'd never have called any of those things mistakes. Your mother never did anything she didn't want to do. Including being with your father. Including having you. And yes, even including slinking back to the drudgery of the farm."

"I didn't mean—"

"I know, love. I was joshing with you. The years I had the both of you home with me were some of the best of my life. And hers. If you'd had the chance to ask her yourself she'd tell you the same."

Evie wiped a finger under her eye.

"Why do you think I keep telling you to sell the farm?" Granddad added. "I knew how much you wanted to go, while fretting I'd feel like you'd left me behind. Know that I'm happy here. Happier still knowing you're happy there."

Evie squeezed her eyes shut tight. He'd known, clever man. She hadn't been making a life for herself. She'd been preparing to flee at a moment's notice.

Well, no more.

"Thanks, Granddaddy-O."

"Anytime, All About Evie."

"Go back to your game. Show those ladies what it's all about."

"Will do."

Evie said her goodbyes and rang off. Feeling light and heavy. Young and old. As if she was at a tipping point in her life. Maybe it was the amazing bedding playing tricks with her mind.

A soft knock came at the door.

She wriggled off the end of the bed, fixed her gown, took the towel from her hair and ran quick fingers through the damp mess. Then said, "Come in."

Armand pressed the door open but did not enter—keeping himself very much on the right side of the threshold. He had a neat pile of what looked like flannel pyjamas in his arms.

"No suit?"

The corner of his mouth kicked up. And every part of her that hadn't yet defrosted did as a wave of heat rolled down her body.

"Heard you talking. Zoe?"

"My granddad. I make sure to call him a few times a week. Not that he needs me to. The man's more social than a teenager."

"I'm sure he needs you plenty," said Armand in that deep, delicious voice of his.

"Yeah. That's what I've always told myself. But he's the strongest man in the world."

"Did you tell him you are here?" Armand asked as he stepped into the room.

Evie's heart stuttered. "Ah, no. I haven't even told him I've changed jobs, either. He's strong but he's not young. If he knew I was in flux, he'd worry."

"You don't think he believes in you enough to know you would work it out?"

Evie's mouth twisted. "I'm just beginning to see that. Turns out I'm the one who didn't believe in myself."

His frown was so very French. "And what is there not to believe? You are resilient, no? Determined. When Jonathon hesitated, you did not take no for an answer. And you are stubborn, oh, yes. Sure of your talents. Loyal too. Look how much you care for Zoe and her man, walking through driving rain to give them space. You are inclusive and tolerant, lovely and kind."

Evie wondered if Armand realised his words had trailed off course there at the end. She had to swallow, her throat was so tight with emotion.

She walked over to him and slid the neat pile of pyjamas from his hands. Then she tossed them onto the bench at the end of the bed before turning back to him. "You think I'm lovely?"

Armand's eyes darkened and he breathed out hard through his nose. Evie's pulse responded with a scattered whumpety-whump.

"That's what you chose to take from all I said?"

She lifted one shoulder in a shrug. "Maybe a little more. And maybe it's not actually that I don't believe in myself. I do. But I've come to realise I've been *acting* as if I don't. I've been careful—with work, places, people. I've not backed myself and taken any risks."

Armand watched her closely. Close enough now she

could separate the shards of blue from grey in his volatile eyes. She could tell he was mulling over her words but she wasn't a mind-reader. She was rather glad of it as she said, "Except, that is, when I'm with you."

Armand's throat worked.

"I'm pushier, sharper, more bolshie. I don't know why."

She thought he might just stand there, all gorgeous and dark and impenetrable.

Then his voice came to her, soft and rough, as he said, "Don't you?"

"Because you push my buttons?"

"Because you sense that you can push mine as hard as you like and I won't break."

She breathed out hard. "Anyone can break."

His nostrils flared. His voice was barely a rumble as he said, "I've been close, so many times. Becoming so brittle I believed one more hit and I might shatter. Knowing too many people needed me to allow that to happen, I hid myself away, went deep into self-protect mode. Until I stepped onto a train one morning, heading him a foreign city, and saw a girl who looked as though she was made of light."

Evie's breaths were hard to come by. "Please don't say something like that just to make me feel better—"

"Your beanie was pink," he said, stepping forward to run a finger under a swathe of damp hair. His dark gaze followed the movement as he tucked her hair behind her ear. "The kind of pink that only exists in candyfloss."

Evie stopped breathing as her lungs shut down. She had a beanie in that colour. And had worn it a few weeks ago.

"There was something on top," said Armand, plucking at an imaginary tuft above Evie's head.

"A ball of feathers," Evie finished, her entire body pulsing with every heartbeat.

"You laughed as the train turned a corner, and the shaft of sunlight that washed over you seemed to bask in your warmth. Your laughter echoed inside me that entire first day at work. I hung on to it, like a vine at the edge of quicksand. You were a signpost showing me the way out. I could either continue to exist in a world of grey or decide to see the world through a new lens."

"Armand…" Evie began, but she had no idea what to say. Except the truth. "I've never met anyone like you before. You are far more than I'm used to."

"As are you to me," he said. "And yet here we are."

Then slowly, achingly slowly, he dropped his lips to hers. Pausing a millimetre from the promised land. His dark gaze capturing hers. "Is this what you want, *ma chérie*?"

She knew what he was asking. She'd made it clear how determined she was not to start anything with someone from work. But that train had left the station.

*Yes, yes, yes*, a voice whispered in the back of her mind, and this time it was her own.

She tipped up onto her toes and closed the gap, her mouth brushing against his. Once, twice. Tentative as a butterfly unfurling its wings for the first time.

And then Armand took over. Tilting her face to better fit his mouth to hers. Sipping on her, gently, slowly, tenderly—until her whole body whimpered with a need for more.

The hand on her cheek slid down her neck, over her collarbone, tracing the edge of the bulky gown.

Evie's head tipped back as Armand's mouth followed, so gentle, so thorough, she could barely keep her head. Air hard to come by, senses reeling, all she could do was feel. To risk. To live.

Shifting closer, his knee nudged hers and she stepped back, the backs of her knees knocking into the edge of her bed.

Without overthinking, following all possible paths in her mind in order to find the safest route, she let herself fall. And fall. And fall.

# CHAPTER TEN

EVIE WOKE THE next morning with an all-body stretch. When her hands and feet kept going without meeting lumps or edges of a futon her eyes snapped open.

Sunlight streamed through plantation shutters onto a moulded ceiling a mile above the bed. She looked over to find a second pillow with the indentation of a head. But no head. No Armand. The scent of freshly brewed coffee told her he was around somewhere.

She grabbed the pillow and hugged it to her chest, squeezing her eyes shut tight as memories of the night before bombarded her like a movie-highlights reel: the feel of his hot skin under her hands. The warmth of his mouth on her. The way he'd curled himself around her, protecting her as she slept.

Feeling herself dropping off in drowsy bliss, Evie forced herself to roll out of bed and turned on the shower. Only once she went to get dressed did she realise the only clothes she had were the ones she'd worn the night before. If she wasn't careful it was going to be a serious walk of shame.

She grabbed her phone to text Zoe, in the hopes they'd make the same train, but Zoe had already messaged:

Sorry about last night. But thank you. Taking a sickie today. Can't get out of bed.

So much for that idea. In the end she turned her dinosaur shirt inside out and back to front and hoped for the best.

Downstairs, Armand was already dressed—in the bottom half of a suit and a white T-shirt, his shirt, tie and jacket hanging over the back of a kitchen stool. He leant against the kitchen bench, eating a croissant and reading an actual old-fashioned newspaper.

Her heart clutched, sputtered and flipped over on itself. She tried to swallow but her throat was too tight.

What had she done to deserve such a man?

Not that he was *hers*. *Pfft*. Not at all! They'd spent a night together. The most wonderful, tender, amazing night of her life.

But no matter what happened from here, it paid to remind herself he'd be heading back to France when the job was done. Meaning this…whatever it was, had a ticking clock.

It would end—just as her last job had ended, her last apartment had ended. Being strong enough to be with Armand and then to watch him walk away—that was the last step in her transformation. Into knowing she was living her own life, for real.

She must have made a sound—probably something between a sigh and a sob—as Armand looked up. His eyes gleamed before his mouth curved into a smile. "Good morning, Evie."

She couldn't help herself; she grinned like an idiot. "Hi. Any more where that came from?"

He reached over and grabbed a plate piled high with croissants. And carried them over to her. She plucked one off the top—no, two—and took a bite. He put the plate back down, then leaned over and kissed the top of her head.

"Coffee?" Armand asked as he pushed away from the bench.

Evie pressed his back, her fingers lingering a moment as she remembered the glory of all that warm skin and hard, curving muscles beneath the shirt. "Let me."

She saw the fight in him, the difficulty he had letting someone else be in charge. Before something relaxed in him and he said, "*D'accord*."

She worked out how to use the espresso machine quick

smart, grabbed cream over milk and proceeded to make two coffees.

"*Merci*," he said when she handed his over, offering up the most glorious smile. Private, intense, scorching.

"Any time," she said.

Then Armand looked over her shoulder and swore, in French, and motioned to the clock.

She took a few quick gulps of yoghurt, downed her espresso in one steaming, bitter shot. Then ran around like a lunatic, tracking down her jacket, her beanie, her shoes. "Armand, have you seen my…? Oh." There they were, resting by the fireplace, all dry and toasty warm. She sank down onto the floor to pull her shoes over her chilly feet and she sighed in bliss. "Oh, I love you for this!"

The silence that met her was palpable. She slowly glanced over to find Armand watching her as he buttoned his shirt.

"I didn't mean—"

"I know."

"It just came out." She pulled herself to her feet. "I barely know you. You could have a wife and kids back in Paris for all I know." *Please don't let there be a wife and kids.* "These are things a person really should find out before falling into bed with some random guy."

Armand simply waited for her to finish, his gaze forbearing.

"Well, not *random*," she ameliorated. Not even close. If she could have picked any man in all the world to have spent the night before with she'd have picked him. Not that she was about to tell him. She might have been in the habit of making mediocre choices but she wasn't completely self-destructive.

"I'm single," he said. "Divorced, to be precise. No children."

"Really?" she said, one eyebrow raised. Maybe they should have labelled him Mr Mysterious. "Divorced, huh? What happened?"

He looked at her as if he had no intention of going there, before, for some reason, he relented. "I disappointed her. It's one of my more consistent skills. Disappointing those who do love me."

Evie swallowed. "Not possible."

"Believe it. Lucia was the aunt of the little girl on that first kidnapping rescue. She imagined my life was drama and heroism and fell for the romance of her vision. After five years of soldiering, I fell for the mirage of having someone to come home to. She never forgave me for refusing to play the hero. Just as my family never forgave me for refusing to play the good son in the first place and take over the Debussey auction houses."

Evie got one arm through her jacket before stopping. "That makes no sense to me. How could they all get you so wrong? You're not a player—in any sense of the word. *Hero* is an overused word, so I won't go there. But anyone who knew you and found themselves disappointed…? I'd like to meet them so they can tell me so to my face."

He watched her eyes as she spoke, his gaze hot and pointed, as if he was trying to see into her very soul. And something in his eyes made the next question one of the hardest she'd ever had to ask. "Where is she, Armand? Where's Lucia?"

"She was killed a little over a year ago."

Evie's hand swept up to her mouth but not in time to cover the groan. "Oh, jeez. Armand, I'm so sorry."

Armand fixed the face of his watch until it sat just so. "We'd parted years before. One day she packed her bags and left and it didn't even occur to me to stop her. Last year we reconnected at one of my family's charity events, both apologising for having not put an end to things far sooner. A week later she was mugged. Stabbed while trying to wrest back her handbag. She bled to death before the ambulance arrived."

Oh, Armand. No wonder he brooded. No wonder he'd

looked so bruised when she'd kissed him. He would have taken it all on himself.

Evie took a step his way. "She sounds like a very strong woman. To have fought back. Quite the hero herself."

He ran both hands down his face and looked her way again. "She'd have liked that."

"Do you think you might have become more to one another again, if…if it hadn't happened?"

Armand shook his head. "We were the result of a rare weak moment."

Evie felt as if a fist squeezed around her heart. Was that what was happening here? Would he look back and think the same of her one day?

Needing to lighten the room, to let him off the hook, she said, "Is that how Jonathon got you over here? Another moment of weakness?"

His mouth twitched. "Something like that."

"Well, I'm glad. About Jonathon. Bringing you here. Not the rest. Though without the rest you wouldn't be here. A butterfly flaps its wings…and I'm going to stop talking now." A beat then, "Except to say that I'm truly sorry. For all that happened. And that your family doesn't see you for all that you are. And I'm single too, in case you wondered."

She pulled a face and told herself to *please* stop talking. And she would, after she said one more thing. "Look, I want you to know that I didn't come here for…last night."

"And I didn't offer my room for…last night."

Her pause had been a case of sudden-onset modesty. His pause made her think of tangled sheets and slippery limbs and gasps of air as time held its breath.

"If you like we can shake hands and part ways, go back to annoying one another in our tiny office and pretend nothing happened."

"But something did happen," said Armand.

"Yes, it did."

"You were the one who said I'm not a player. It means I'm no good at pretending. Let's not attempt it."

Evie couldn't stop her grin. "Okay, then."

He tilted his chin. "Grab your things, *ma chérie*, it's time to go."

Evie quickly made sure she had everything she'd come with, looking around in case it was the last time she saw the place. Her heart squeezed at the thought. But she knew it wasn't the lovely apartment she would miss.

Armand pulled on his jacket with an elegant swish, then met her at the door. Where he took her by the hand and pulled her into his arms.

Her eyes opened in surprise in time to see his close as he kissed her, hard and strong, his tongue sliding over the seam of her mouth until she opened to him and allowed him to sweep her away.

No sign of the tender touch and slow burn of the night before. He had her so hot she didn't even realise she was trying to climb him like a tree until he loosened his grip.

When he pulled back her legs had gone limp and she grabbed him by the lapels of his jacket, giving her time to find her feet.

"Stay here tonight."

It was not a question.

"No. It'll be fine. I'll check in with Zoe to see if we can make it work for a bit, till I find a new place."

Armand just looked at her.

"What?" she said.

"Lance has been on tour for how long?"

"I'll find a cheap hotel on a train line in the suburbs."

"Not necessary."

"I can't stay here, Armand. The noticeboard at work has a couple of rooms-to-let notices. I think one might be Jamie's—"

Evie squealed as Armand wrapped an arm around her

waist and hauled her in close, his nose pressed up against hers. Forehead too.

"You are not staying with that *goujat*."

"*Goujat?* What's that?"

"Bounder. Hound. Woof-woof."

"Ah. I thought you two had made friends."

"My friend is a hound. It's decided; you stay here. *Oui*?"

"*Oui*," she said, and he grinned, his eyes squinting a little, giving him smile lines. And just like that she fell a little more. A lot more. So hard and fast her head swam.

She'd only just started this adventure kick and already felt as if she had to hang on for dear life.

"No fancy car and driver today?" she asked when Armand strode towards the station.

"I like the train."

"Honestly? It's not some form of penance? Or undercover research?"

"Honestly."

Just when she thought she had a handle on him. She liked the train, but if she had the choice she'd totally take the luxury of a driver.

After another minute he said, "The train makes the travel time feel faster. The quiet in the car can be too much."

"Don't like to be left alone with your own thoughts?"

He glanced at her, that now familiar expression of surprise. Then, "Yes. White noise is better."

Before she could stop herself, Evie slid a hand into the crook of Armand's elbow. He put a hand over the top and tucked her in tight. It had to be a French thing—this absolute self-confidence. No game-playing, no post-sex masculine posturing. It was a little overwhelming. And a whole lot lovely.

"I like seeing the same people each day," said Evie. "It's like following a soap opera."

"Soap opera?"

"A daytime drama. Where you become invested in their lives."

Armand smiled at her again and ushered her through the turnstile right as their train came along. By the time they got on, Armand's usual seat was free. Coincidentally so was hers. By unspoken agreement they remained standing somewhere in the middle.

"Careworn Mum," said Armand.

Evie glanced at the woman across the aisle with triplets climbing over her. "You name them? *I* name them!"

Though "careworn" was a far nicer way of labelling the other woman's predicament than "frazzled".

"I wonder how she attempts this run every week," said Armand.

"The neighbours who rent my granddad's farm have young boys. Wildlings. Always better in open spaces than confined. What about those guys?" she asked, motioning to her usual pack of schoolboys on their phones.

Armand said, "I call them Fear for Our Future."

Evie laughed. "Even you were like that when you were fifteen."

"I was never like that."

She laughed, believing him.

But then she wondered—*had* he always been so self-contained? Or had the big, dark moments of his life shaped him so drastically they had hacked at his compassion, rubbed away any softness, leaving him unrelentingly un-moved?

Was that why she had ultimately been so drawn to him? Because it was clear any "moments of weakness" would be rare. A man like that could never break your heart, as a man like that would never hold it in the first place.

Armand caught her eye, his eyebrow rising in question. He saw right through her and always had. Meaning he probably knew exactly how she felt. Even before she did.

She cleared her throat before saying, "Do you think that means that they all name us too?"

"It's possible."

"What might we be? I'm probably Knitting Woman. Or Beanie Girl. Or... Hang on a second. You've called me something a couple of times now. What was it?"

"The Girl with the Perfect Aim."

Evie grimaced then laughed. "Right. Your foot."

"And my solar plexus."

"I was hoping you'd forgotten that."

"Never."

Another gap of quiet, though this one felt less empty. There was a strange kind of hum there now, filling the gaps. It was so lovely Evie felt like her smile was smiling.

Until Armand asked, "What did you call me?"

And like that Evie fell into her own trap. No way was she about to give up the fact she'd called him Hot Stuff in the Swanky Suit. Or—heaven forbid—her Train Boyfriend. She frantically searched for something believable.

What did he do, apart from sit there scowling, and looking gorgeous—?

"Reading Guy. We called you Reading Guy."

"Mmm..." he grunted. "That's fair."

*Phew.*

The winter sun shone over the artwork scrawled into the walls of the alleyway as they neared the Montrose offices. Armand wasn't sure he'd actually noticed the artwork before. Or that Jonathon's entrance was in an alley.

In fact, he tried to remember the last couple of dozen times he'd walked from the train station but it was a blur of grey. Shapes. Streets crossed. Corners turned. But today...

"Can you smell coffee?" he asked. "And buttered toast?"

Evie looked at him sideways. Then tipped her chin over his shoulder to the doorway of a café that seemed to have sprung suddenly from the wall to his right.

"Was that always there?"

"Not since the beginning of time, but yeah."

Armand only half heard, as his senses were all talking to him at once.

Birdsong in the roof gutters, car tyres whistling against the damp bitumen. The tell-tale rainbow shimmer of oil on the path ahead. The sun glinting off the threads in Evie's shiny jacket, the misshapen curve of her knitted hat.

Cool at his collar, Armand lifted his hand to find he'd forgotten to put on his tie.

"Look," said Evie, grabbing him by the elbow and pulling him up short. "Can we just have one more chat about this?"

"This?" The fact that everything was loud, bright, as if he'd stepped out of a sensory deprivation tank.

"This." She waved a frantic hand between them. "Back in your apartment the thought of being all *laissez-faire* sounded fine, but here…" She glanced up at the building. "When we go in there, can we just keep things normal?"

"Normal."

"I frustrate you. You ruffle me."

"That is true."

She glared at him a moment before bursting into laughter. He'd never known a person so quick to find joy. "I'm serious. I made such a big deal with the others about being one of the guys, if they found out you and I were…"

Armand reached up and tucked in the tag at the neckline of the T-shirt she'd put on back to front. "Worried I'll cramp your style?"

"Are you serious? My cred would level up."

She sank her face into both hands and gave her head a wild shake, dark hair floating over her shoulders. "But what about Jonathon? He put his faith in us to work together, not…you know. What if I lose his respect?"

A memory swam to the surface; Jonathon assuring him he Did Not Care if they did anything HR would not approve of. He tucked it back away.

"Evie, are you planning on embezzling from the company?"

Her head whipped up so fast her hair caught in her lashes.

"There she is," said Armand. "Will your work suffer because of last night?"

She held up finger and thumb and held them a millimetre apart.

Armand couldn't help but laugh. *Laugh*. Before coming to this part of the world he couldn't remember the last time he'd smiled.

"Your fifty percent is everyone else's one hundred, so that's a moot point. It is none of anyone's business. Including Jonathon. Yet you are determined we seal our lips?"

She nodded vigorously. Then her gaze dropped to his lips, her wide-open face giving him everything he needed to know.

"Then sealed they are," he said. "You Australians, so uptight."

Her gaze slunk back to his, eyes narrowed. Then she quickly checked the alley way, lifted up onto her toes, kissed him hard and fast, then ducked through the door and inside.

Armand counted to thirty, looked into the camera that had no doubt filmed their entire conversation, gave it a jaunty wave, then opened the door and went to work.

"Mate."

Armand pulled up as Jonathon came out of his office. "Morning."

"Evie just scooted past like she had a dragon at her heels. Everything all right?"

"As far as I know."

Jonathon looked at him a moment. "Great. So how was last night?"

The fingers of his right hand curled into his palm until he realised Jonathon was asking about the Escape Room.

Now who was acting uptight? "A corporate espionage soldier story? Subtle."

"Imogen found it. Worth her weight in microchips, that one. I hear you aced it. Jamie couldn't hold it in this morning. I think someone has a little crush."

Armand's fingers were again starting to tingle. "You only just noticed. He's had his eye on her from day dot."

Jonathon's mouth twitched. "I was talking about you. The kid totally wants to be you when he grows up."

Armand breathed out hard and counted to three. "Okay, then. I have a job to do—"

"All in good time. Now, what were we talking about?"

"When you think you might grow up."

"Right."

As one they turned to look over the railing at the Bullpen below, then they were off and running, reminiscing about their uni days, when growing up was the last thing on their minds. Deliberately leaving out the Turkish trip, during which they had both grown up overnight.

Again Armand only listened with half an ear but by then his senses had well and truly recalibrated. And they were twanging like a plucked violin string.

Something Jonathon said niggled at him. Not Jamie. Not this time. *Time*. He'd said "*All in good time*". The man was so concerned about his huge new project he'd all but cried on the phone to convince Armand to come all the way over here to help him, and now he was saying it could be sorted out "all in good time".

Out of the corner of his eye Armand catalogued Jonathon's fidgeting fingers, the way he shifted as if his shoes were too tight. The fact his gaze couldn't quite stick.

Dammit. Jonathon was hiding something. Knowing Jonathon, it could be anything—a new woman in his life, a new invention he'd patented, but it wasn't.

It was something to do with this project.

"Everything all right with you?" Armand asked when Jonathon took a breath.

"Sure, mate," he said. Silence hung between them, taut and loaded. Until Jonathon sparked up with his trademark grin. "Why do you ask?"

Armand considered pushing the matter. But he wasn't prepared to go into battle without a further reconnaissance. He pushed away from the railing. "I'd better get to it."

Jonathon glanced down the hall to where Evie was no doubt already hard at work and said, "Go get 'em, cowboy."

Evie stood beside Armand on the train platform, waiting for the evening ride back to his place. He was busy scowling and texting on his ancient cell phone—it was painful to watch—so she left him be.

It had been the longest day of her life. Stuck in their small room, trying to concentrate on her work. She'd had to stop and go back more than once, which was not like her. In the end she'd begged if she could pack up her laptop and go to the cafeteria.

Fully expecting a blanket "not on your life" and a lecture on the importance of security, she'd found herself disappointed when Armand had suggested she ask Jonathon.

When Jonathon had told her to do whatever her heart desired, Armand's response was instant. Storm clouds rolled in and he'd grunted at her like in the days of old. Lucky she enjoyed that side of him. The caveman in the designer suit.

Deciding it was between them, she'd given Armand a quick kiss on the cheek before shooting off to the Yum Lounge. Surrounded by food and coffee, and a fort of chairs to keep the scavengers away, she'd powered through acres of code.

Either the problem was deeply hidden in striations within the code, or Jonathon, in fact, had himself a fantastic new product. She'd felt productive either way, until she'd headed back to the office to find Armand still fuming.

"Still don't want to tell me what has put a bee in your bonnet?" she asked.

He rolled a shoulder, checked his phone again and moved a little further up the train platform.

She rolled her eyes and followed, not about to let him go back into his mental man cave. For she couldn't quite work out how she'd managed to lure him out of there in the first place and wasn't sure enough of her own allure to know she could do it again.

"Armand, what's going on?"

"Nothing. Nothing important."

"I don't believe you."

"And yet I have nothing more to add."

She threw her hands in the air. "Is this the way it's going to be? Because I'm not going back to your place to hide in my room. I can do that at Zoe's."

His attention finally shot back to her. He reached out and took her by the elbow. Began to draw her in—

Then his phone rang. He looked at her—she could have sworn it was a look of fraught despair.

He let go and answered the phone. "Jonathon, I've been trying to get you all damn day." Then he turned and moved further up the way.

Giving in, for now, Evie watched as two of the triplets she recognised as belonging to Frazzled Mum chased one another across the platform. She glanced back to find the mum coming along behind them, one boy asleep in the pram, the other seats filled with discount shopping bags.

Evie looked to see where Armand had gone when she saw he had stilled. His mouth moved as he spoke on the phone, his eyes on the boys as if he were a tiger preparing to pounce.

One toddler had hit the yellow line—the one behind which grown-ups knew to wait. The other, on the other hand…

Evie stepped forward, a country girl's instinct to help warring with a city girl's learned response to stay the heck out of other people's business.

Then the ground beneath her feet began to buzz, and rumble, and the clatter of metal wheels on train tracks split the air.

Everything from that moment happened in a blur.

Toddler number one stopped at the yellow line. While toddler number two saw his chance to win the race and kept on running, waddling to the edge of the platform before tipping right over the edge.

Someone screamed. It might even have been Evie.

The taste of bile rose up in her throat as fear and horror slammed her from all sides, her vision contracting to a tunnel as she ran to grab the other boy.

Before she was anywhere near him, Armand was at the edge of the platform, his coat flying out behind him like a cape.

Everything from that point slowed—as if it had been choreographed for a movie. He scooped up one toddler under his arm, handing the boy off to a random stranger. Then, with a glance up the tunnel, towards the now heavy rumbling and screeching of the oncoming train, he leapt onto the tracks.

Evie's heart slammed up into her throat. Her legs collapsed out from under her till she stumbled to her knees. But she didn't stop, crawling towards the edge, her usually sharp mind in a tailspin.

She would have followed him too—right over the edge—when out of the corner of her eye she saw the mother, mouth open in a silent scream, a bag of apples spilling from the pram and over the edge of the platform.

Evie was on her feet, with suddenly superhuman strength stopping the crying woman from hurling herself and her other boy onto the track too.

Then, with the screech of brakes and a siren tripped no doubt by Armand's leap, the commuter train braked hard as it barrelled into the station.

Evie slammed her eyes closed as she was hit with a blast of air from the train as it passed—relentless, unstoppable—

smacking against her over-sensitised skin till she felt as if it was going to peel right off.

A million years later, the train finally stopped.

When Evie opened her eyes, it was to find the doors remaining closed. The people inside looking bewildered, talking and pointing towards the source of the siren splitting the otherwise deathly silence of the station.

Then, through the translucent train windows, she saw, on the far platform on the other side of the tracks, dark hair, a suit jacket, no tie. Armand. Hands on his knees, breathing heavily.

"They're okay," she said on a sob, grabbing the mother hard. "Both of them. They're okay."

"Are you sure?"

"Look," she said, pointing through the gaps to the other side of the train, where an official in a blue uniform had a crying two-year-old in her arms.

The mother broke down, her cries racking her in deep, thankful sobs.

The stranger to whom Armand had handed the first toddler came up to Evie and the mother. The mother grabbed her child, too shocked to say thank you.

The stranger gave Evie a look. A mix of shock and relief.

To which Evie mumbled, "You have no idea."

It was ages, *for ever*, before the doors opened and the commuters poured onto the platform, the siren still wailing.

Evie shifted to see through the window to find a mob of security guards with unhappy faces and dark uniforms talking into walkie-talkies and sweeping commuters back up the stairs, leaving the far platform clear.

In the centre was Armand. Organising, retelling, looking for all intents and purposes like a general. Till each guard shook his hand, or slapped him on the shoulder, then slowly moved away.

Armand stood looking out into the dark, dirty well of

the gap where the train now stood. He brought a hand to his mouth, held it there a moment, before wiping his face hard and putting both hands on his hips.

Then he lifted his gaze.

Through the dusty double windows, he found her.

The storm in his eyes…it had cleared. His shoulders were back. His breaths long and deep. As if he'd woken from a slumber.

"Let's get her to her baby," the stranger beside her said.

Evie nodded, taking the pram while the other stranger comforted the mother and they herded her towards the lift that would get them to the other platform.

Evie kept glancing over her shoulder, trying to catch Armand's eye once more.

She'd always known her brain was special. Quick and curious and clever. But in that moment, when the world had been about to tip into the worst kind of tragedy, compared to Armand her thoughts had been sluggish, like wading through thick mud.

He clearly didn't like to think of himself as heroic—merely fulfilling his duty—as a son, a Frenchman, a friend. Didn't mean Evie couldn't quietly think it for him.

Evie managed to find a tight smile as she explained to the guard that both she and the woman with the pram needed to get down to the platform, investigation scene or not, and that nobody was going to stop them.

Her heart was thundering by the time the lift doors opened. When she saw Armand—big, dark and cool as a cucumber—the urge to run into his arms was only stoppered by the number of police with guns in their holsters milling about.

In the end it didn't matter, as Armand made a direct beeline for her. And said, "What the hell were you thinking?"

"Excuse me?"

Armand took her by the elbow and dragged her into a quiet

spot around the corner by the stairs. "I saw what you were about to do. You were about to climb down there yourself."

"And?"

"You would have been killed."

"You made it."

"I am trained for that kind of thing!"

"Really? Is there a Rescuing Toddlers Who've Fallen onto Train Tracks Only Moments Before a Train Zooms into the Station battalion in the French Foreign Legion? That's lucky."

His cheek twitched but there was no humour in it. "This isn't funny."

"I never said it was, Armand. I'm the one who should be doing the yelling here, but I'm not because you were amazing. So amazing I could jump your bones, right here and now."

He looked at her with solemn dark eyes and she remembered belatedly what he'd told her about his ex. About how she'd been stuck on him "playing the hero". Dammit. That was not what she'd meant at all.

She was just deeply glad he was okay.

"We can go," he said, stepping back.

"Great. I just want to check on Frazzled Mum."

Which she did. The woman's husband was on his way. All three of her children had crayons and colouring books. And she was cradling a hot cup of tea.

She found Armand scowling at the bottom of the stairs, and without having to say a word they headed up to street level, where a car awaited them.

Not another word was said on the car ride back to Armand's apartment. There were no words. Nothing he could say he would not wish to take back. The tension was loud enough, shimmering in the air around them like a mirage.

Once they were through the door the tension spilled over, and before he knew it Armand had Evie with her back to the wall and her leg around his waist as they kissed as if it was their last time.

He pulled back, dragging in breaths, placing a hand on the wall behind her head to steady himself, his jacket and hers in puddles at their feet. His shirt missing a button. Her hair like a wild, dark cloud about her face. His eyes lifted to hers and he'd never seen such emotion in his life.

Confusion and lust, worry and fear.

She sank a hand into his hair, holding him in place.

He waited for a continuation of the argument from the train station. In his experience that was how these things went.

But her voice was soft, emotional, rough as she said, "Take me to bed."

And just like that Armand's heart cracked in two. "You scared the hell out of me, Evie."

"I know."

"I scared the hell out of me too."

"What do you mean?"

"I haven't worked in the field in a long time. I wasn't sure I could ever again. But since you…because of you… I feel like that part of me is back. That I can contribute. That I can help. I couldn't have done that without you."

"I did nothing," she said, her voice cracking. "I just stood there and watched. That little boy is alive because of you."

"And I," said Armand, "feel alive again because of you."

For this woman had switched him back on. Calling to his humanity, to the innocence he had spent years trying to bury. Leaving him looking not to yesterday, to regret, to how he could have done better, but to tomorrow and whatever it might bring.

"Armand," she croaked as a single tear rushed down her cheek.

He kissed it away.

Then lifted her off her feet and carried her to his bed. Where he felt every sensation, every touch, every smile and every tear in three dimensions and technicolour and made damn sure Evie felt the same.

# CHAPTER ELEVEN

AFTER SPENDING THE weekend in bed, Evie somehow made it to Monday.

She made herself a little nest on the couch at work—piling cushions around her back until she was comfortable. She made sure the plate of neatly lined-up chocolate buttons was within reach, clamped her headphones to her ears, found the playlist she'd made to connect her to the job and got to work.

Or at least she tried.

It was hard with Armand sitting behind his heavy wooden desk, banker's lamp streaming golden light over his sleek profile. Knowing the missing tie was all down to her.

"Need something?" he asked.

She quickly looked back at her laptop. "Hmm?" came her response, as if she hadn't been wholly attuned to his every blink, every breath, every scrape of fingernails over the stubble on his jaw.

Even after the transcendental weekend, during which Evie could safely say she'd never felt more real, more understood, more cherished by another human being in all her life, Armand was in a mood.

Not that she minded. It was that darkly delicious, stormy-eyed, messy-haired gravity that had drawn her to him in the first place. The urge to go over there, to climb on his lap and tame the tangles was a strong one.

"Everything okay over there?" she asked.

He didn't say a word.

"Armand?"

When he remained silent, still a niggle of concern edged

its way past the bliss as she realised he was deep inside his cave. The person she had been a few weeks ago would have left him there and backed away quietly.

But she'd been willing to accept very little for so long—with regards to work, living arrangements, friendships. And he was the one who'd made her realise it didn't have to be that way.

She could risk big. She could close her eyes and leap. And falling wasn't always bad. Falling could be the ride of your life.

She put her laptop on the coffee table and ambled over to his desk, put both hands flat on the top and said, "Armand, if you don't tell me right now why you are so gloomy I'm going to make you."

He looked up and a glimmer flashed into his eyes before being swallowed by the storm. "And how are you going to do that?"

"Scream? Stomp my feet? Go to Jonathon?"

The absolute quiet of his response sent a chill up her spine. This was no brooding; it was completely devoid of the passion that made him care so much.

Her gaze dropped to the papers gripped in Armand's hand. "What have you found?"

"Nothing."

She lifted a foot, ready to stomp, hoping to get a laugh out of him, or an answer. Anything but this stillness.

Then from one second to the next she realised what he meant. And the breadcrumbs in her mind lined up in a perfect row.

"There's nothing wrong with the program, is there?"

Armand slowly shook his head.

Evie smacked the table and bounced back. "Ha! I knew it. I mean, it was odd that I hadn't found even a single breadcrumb by now. Just a line of code here and there that needed streamlining. First I thought it was because Jonathon knew his stuff—that he'd bought some seriously sophisticated programming. But I had begun to think I was missing things because I was distracted. You are very distracting, you know. Now I can stop feeling guilty on that score. What do we do now?"

"We don't have to do anything."

"We have to tell Jonathon. He'll be stoked."

It took a few moments for Evie to realise that Armand had not said a word. He just gripped that piece of paper so hard his knuckles had turned white.

And it hit her. "He knows. He always knew." She threw her hands in the air and paced. "Why? Why would he do that to me? To us? To you? Was that the test? To see how long it would take us to figure it out?"

She stopped pacing and stared into the middle distance. "That might actually make sense."

Head spinning, Evie landed back on the couch with a bounce.

"Wow. Does this mean…?" Her waterfall of words came to a stop as she realised exactly what it meant. "It's over. The contract. The project. The team. No man—or woman— left behind."

She tilted her head to find Armand watching her. He looked—not sad, not angry. He looked empty.

Her skin came over cold, clammy. "You knew, didn't you?"

"I had begun to suspect."

"When?"

"A few days ago."

"A few… *What?*"

"The fact that I had found nothing—or more precisely that you had found nothing… It was too clean. Almost as if it had been homogenised. Like one of your games. Virtually real, only completely not."

"And why didn't you tell me then? In the shower this morning? On the train?"

Could it be because he too was feeling the squeeze around his chest, not knowing what this meant for them?

No. Not Armand. His response? "Because it's my fault."

Evie flinched. "What? No. Jeez, Armand. Not this time."

She pulled herself to standing and moved around behind Armand's desk, sitting on the edge. "Stuff happens. People fall pregnant, fall in love with the wrong people, die of aneurisms before they are even thirty. No matter how clever you are, how prepared, how big and strong, you can't protect everyone from everything. If it's anyone's fault, it's Jonathon's."

She reached over and pressed the red button on Armand's phone and yelled, "Jonathon!"

"What can I help you with, Ms Croft?" crooned his disembodied voice.

"Why don't you come on over and I'll tell you all about it?"

"I'll see you in a jiffy."

Evie shrugged at Armand. "See, we can sort this thing out in a jiffy?"

"Evie," Armand said, lifting out of his chair. No longer empty, his eyes were stormier than she'd ever seen them.

Her belly quivered at the sight. But she didn't have the chance to decipher if it was fear or lust making it happen as Jonathon burst through the door holding a coffee mug in his hand.

He took one look at them, Evie perched on Armand's desk, and Armand standing by her side, and smiled like the cat who'd found the cream. "What can I do for you?"

Evie looked to Armand but feared what he might do, so she spun around and said, "We were wondering why you've had us trying to find a problem in a program that has no problem."

"Whatever do you mean?"

"Jonathon." Armand had found his voice. "It's time to put an end to this."

After a few tense moments Jonathon looked to Evie and began a slow clap. "Well done you."

For half a second Evie thought about taking the applause when she saw her future—working for Game Plan, mentored by the man she'd called her hero. But that was before she'd known what that word really meant.

"It was Armand," she said. "He figured it out days ago."

"I don't doubt it. Cleverest man I know. Days ago, you say? Then I wonder why he didn't confront me sooner, don't you?"

Armand moved around Evie with the grace of a man half his size. "You know why."

"Tell me," Jonathon said. "Better yet, tell her."

Evie looked between them, realising there was an undercurrent slipping and sliding beneath their words. "Tell me what?"

Armand took a deep breath in and turned to face her, blocking her completely from Jonathon's view. "I didn't say anything because it would mean that this was over."

Evie made herself swallow. "Armand, that's sweet. But I knew once we were done here you'd be going home." She'd counted on it, needing to put this experience behind her so she could start her life afresh. Not that it stopped the pressure around her heart.

"I don't mean for me, Evie. It's over for you."

Evie made to look past him to Jonathon, but Armand moved, blocking her. Snagging her gaze and not letting go.

Armand's grip tightened on her arm before easing up, his body rigid with barely checked tension. "Jonathon didn't give you this job because he thought you were ready for it. He gave you the job for me."

"For you? I don't understand."

"He knew I was in a bad way. That I'd been living in a fugue for a long time. He brought me out here in an effort to wake me up. It wasn't working, until the day you came into his office. Don't you remember? When he saw us together he hired you on the spot."

"You *knew* this was why? And you let it happen anyway?"

"I thought he was being facetious. I'd convinced myself that the spark he'd claimed to see was all in his head. I was wrong."

Head spinning, heart aching, foundation shaking beneath her, Evie pushed Armand aside and stalked up to Jonathon Montrose. Her boss. Her one-time hero. Right now a person she wanted to smack. Hard.

"Is that true? Did you hire me as some kind of lure?"

Jonathon took a sip of his coffee while he considered his response. "I saw an opportunity for an interesting collaboration. I think we can all agree, here and now, that it worked a treat."

Evie's stomach sank and in the same breath anger so bright it filled her vision with a burning white light filled her entire body.

Before she knew it she was off the ground, legs kicking, arms flailing, as Armand lifted her bodily out of the way. "Let me at him," she cried. "You said you wanted to kill him with your bare hands at times. Let me at him."

"No," Armand crooned, "killing him won't solve anything. I'd rather see him suffer."

Then he gave her a smile, his mouth kicking up at one side, his eyes glinting in that way that made her feel as if to him she was a natural wonder.

When she went limp he held her close and let her slide down his body.

And damn it if her body didn't respond. Her skin warmed up. He lungs squeezed tight. Her heart skipped a beat. "Screw him," she said, her voice soft, just for him. "Don't leave."

No, she hadn't just said that. But yes, she had. And she meant it. Because, despite telling herself it would be okay, that losing him was how it was meant to be, looking into the reality of watching him walk away was heart-breaking. She wasn't strong enough.

"Stay," she said again. "Stay."

Then she made the mistake of looking into Armand's eyes. And what she saw—the heady mix of desire and regret—made her want to weep.

He hadn't trusted her enough to include her in his concerns. That hurt. Now it was clear he didn't want her enough to even consider staying, years of abandonment fell in on her like walls in a demolished building.

She braced herself against the side of the chair as her knees gave way. Armand, being Armand, held out a hand to help her.

"I don't need your help, Armand. Or your protection. I'm tough, tougher than I look." And she was, she realised, as in a case of really wretched timing she felt her heart harden. "I'm an orphan. I'm farm stock. I'm educated. I'm capable. No matter what befalls me I will land on my feet because I say that I will."

"I know you will," he said, his accent, that warm, rough voice of his, nearly undoing her completely. "You are the strongest, sweetest, most fearless woman I have ever known."

*Then stay*, she begged inwardly; *fight for me. Love me.*

"While every time I let someone close they get hurt. If this doesn't show you that, I don't know what will. This is all my fault, Evie, and I cannot apologise to you enough."

He cared about her. He'd just said so. And she *knew* it. Deep down in that place that could read his eyes, his smiles, his tells, in a way she'd never been able to read another living soul. But to hear him say it took her knees out from under her.

"I care about you too," she said. "But for me, caring takes the form of sticking around. When anyone offers you attention, affection, love, you push them away, telling yourself it's because you're terrified that anyone who comes into contact with you would be poisoned by mere association. When the truth is, you're just terrified."

As tears burned the backs of her eyes, Evie moved around Armand and reached out a hand to Jonathon. "Thank you, Mr Montrose. For giving me a shot, for forcing me to take a risk and for teaching me a life lesson. Armand, it's been an education."

She grabbed her backpack, her beanie, her keyboard, and headed for the door.

"Take the rest of the day off, Ms Croft," said Jonathon. "You deserve it."

"I will, thanks. Because I need to find myself a new apartment. And a new job."

As she headed out the office door she heard Jonathon's murmur: "What just happened? I don't understand."

"She quit, you fool. That woman is the best thing that ever happened to your sorry soul and you never had a clue."

Jonathon's voice lifted as if shouting at a departing back as he said, "Maybe you should look in a mirror as you say those words."

When she heard footsteps following her, Evie ran down the stairs. Armand's strides were bigger; he caught up fast, taking her by the elbow, turning her to face him. "Evie. Don't do this."

"Which part?"

Mercury swirled behind his eyes, shifting with his mercurial thoughts. "Don't give up."

"Give up what? On us? On you?" She knew what he'd meant but she needed to hear him say it. For that connection that had drawn them to one another from that very first day made her refuse to believe he could simply let her go.

"Don't give up this opportunity. I warned you, that first day, that this place could eat you alive. But now I know better. You would flourish here. Jonathon is a manipulative bastard, but he's the best there is. Use him. Whatever gig, whatever pay, whatever you want, it will be yours."

Evie reached out and gave him a shove. Then another. "I do not need Jonathon Montrose to get what I want. And if you can't see that…"

She'd risked, she'd leapt, she'd put herself further out on a limb than she'd ever intended. And she had fallen. Landed badly. And now felt broken—in her ego, in her head, in her heart, and seventeen other places besides.

She'd thought breaking the fortune's curse would set her free. Instead she'd banked her future on a mirage.

The other shoe had finally dropped.

She was done with this city. Done with trying to do the right thing and failing anyway.

As she walked out through the door and into the alleyway the bright, beautiful Melbourne winter's sky beaming down on her, she felt as if she was falling still.

There was only one place she could think of that would cushion her landing.

It was time to go home.

# CHAPTER TWELVE

THE RETIREMENT VILLAGE where Evie's granddad now lived was light, bright and inviting. No wind whistling through the old walls the way it had on the old farm. Central heating rather than a tetchy fireplace. And plenty of company of people his own age.

It must have been someone's birthday, as helium balloons bobbed about on the ceiling.

She spotted her granddad through the crowd the moment he spotted her.

"Evie, love!" he cried. "Christmas Evie. Happily Evie After." He came at her with a plate full of cake. And when she fell into her granddad's wiry hug she felt as though she could cry for a year.

"Come," he said, "Sit."

Evie came. She sat. Perched on the edge of a cool plastic chair. A table covered in paper plates, with half-eaten cake, scones and smatterings of cut soft fruit.

"Evie!" a woman called, and the word went around, "It's Evie."

She knew what they were after. She handed over her bag of beanies, and the women snapped them up, oohing and ahhing over the pom-poms, the cats' ears, the lurid colours.

Her granddad frowned at the stash. "Hope you haven't been spending all your spare time knitting for this lot."

"Hush," said one, giving him a nudge. And a smiling side eye. *Norma*, Evie thought, giving herself a mental note to ask about that later.

"Not all," Evie said. "I've been working a lot. Hanging out. Making new friends. Just like you wanted me to do."

"And Zoe?"

"Lance is back. For good. He's moved in with her, in fact. They are blissed out."

"Good for them. And you, Evie, love," said Granddad. "Have you found yourself a nice young man who…blisses you out?"

Evie smiled even while her heart throbbed painfully. "I didn't come here to talk about me, I came here to talk about you. And the latest JD Robb. How good was it?"

She'd dropped the magic word and now her table mates were off and running.

Soothing her with their touches on the hand. Quieting her pain with their ribald jokes. Easing her mind that, while she'd left her granddad behind, he was doing just fine. Better, even, than she'd ever imagined.

It gave her the tiniest kernel of hope she could one day feel that way too.

Not today.

But one day.


Borrowing her granddad's ancient truck, she swung by the farm.

She waved to Farmer Steve, son of their closest neighbour, who now rented the farm. He'd offered to buy her out, more than once. She told herself she'd kept it so her granddad could know that he'd left out of choice, not because she and his doctors had pushed.

But as she pulled up to the old farmhouse she knew. She'd kept it for herself. A back-up plan. A reason not to give herself completely to the Melbourne experiment in case it all went belly-up.

"Evie," Steve called, heading over to the fence, cattle dog in tow.

She hopped out of the truck and gave the dog a quick pat. "How's things?"

"You know."

She did. The life of a farmer was a difficult one.

"You staying?" he said, nudging his chin towards the house. "Your old room is the guest room."

She hadn't actually planned anything beyond fleeing the city, but in the end she said, "Sure. That'd be great."

Evie slept like the dead, waking hours after the dairy farm had been up and at 'em. More proof she was a city girl now—her body clock clearly no longer on farm time.

By the time she sauntered out to the kitchen the wildlings were at school, Steve was out fixing fences and his wife, Stacey, had headed into work at the local supermarket. The logs in the old fireplace had burned down to embers.

There was a note on the old kitchen table.

*Eggs, bacon and fresh milk in the fridge. Warm your*
*towel over the heating rod in the bathroom.*

She put some bread in the ancient toaster and while she waited for it to pop she took a quiet tour about her childhood home—finding the burn mark from when she'd discovered chemistry, the notches of her growth chart behind the pantry door. She'd passed her mother's height when she was thirteen.

As she slathered the hot toast in homemade butter and jam, she let herself wonder what it might be like if she decided to stay. She could teach senior citizens how to use the internet, fix computers, get contracts with the local schools to help out with their IT programs.

It was a beautiful town. Slow and quiet, lovely and dear. But it wasn't her home. Not any more.

Armand might have let her down but he had changed her too. With his deeply held sense of duty and love. His spirit of adventure. His bravery, his determination to stand up for what he thought was right.

There was no going back after that. No more cautiously

hacking her way through the levels of her life—she wanted to meet it head-on. There would be bumps and bruises, there would be mistakes made. But that was okay. More than okay. More challenging. More engaging. More wonderful. For that was life.

And she wasn't going to go another day not living it.

Sticking the toast between her teeth, she grabbed the notepaper from the kitchen table and turned it over to scribble a note to Steve:

*If you want the farm, it's all yours.*

As soon as she wrote the words down she felt a sense of relief. Of letting go of the final shackles holding her back.

Now to figure out what it was she truly wanted so she could go out and get it.

Top of that list: Hot Stuff in the Swanky Suit.

For Armand was her "it" and had been from the moment she'd set eyes on him. And she was his. He might have taken longer to realise it—because he was stubborn and brooding and a man—but she knew he felt it too.

He'd told her so. In his own way.

But, while he claimed he was no hero, he felt it was up to him to fix everything, save everyone, all on his own. When things went wrong he shouldered all the blame. That was why he'd let her go. Not because he didn't care, but because he did.

All she had to do was make him see he wasn't alone any more. She'd be there, backing him up, patching him up, holding his hand, listening, caring right on back.

She'd been too scared to look for her life's passion, but she'd found it anyway.

She moved to the height chart and placed a kiss on her mother's last notch, then took one last turn about the farm kitchen to say goodbye.

Now what? Evie turned right, then left, like a chicken with its head chopped off.

*Stop. Think. Finish breakfast, put on clothes, get the car back to Granddad and head to the city.*

Wrapping herself in a blanket off the back of a couch, she bit down on her toast and stepped out onto the porch to see if she could see Steve out in the field to let him know she was heading off, when...

She choked, spraying crumbs all over her clothes. "Armand?"

Armand looked up at the sound of his name, his shiny brogues stopping halfway up the farmhouse stairs, his gaze travelling over her as if making sure what he was seeing was true. Or maybe it was her wild bed-hair, old brown blanket and scuzzy old Ugg boots that had him transfixed.

"How did you find me?" she asked, mind scrambled, senses in a tizz.

While, in his elegant chinos, button-down shirt and cashmere sweater, he looked the picture of cool. Only his eyes gave him away, all tempestuous stormy blue and focussed on her like a laser beam. "I asked Zoe, but even after using extensive torture techniques she didn't budge."

"And you with all your training."

At her sass a spark lit within the stormy depths of Armand's eyes.

Her voice was husky as she said, "Jonathon."

"He owed me. He went to HR. Your granddad is your next of kin. The farm is his address."

"Your friend has no respect for propriety."

"For which I am extremely grateful."

Evie took another step forward. Then, caught in the man's magnetic pull, she stepped forward again.

A muscle worked in Armand's jaw as he took the final step up onto the porch so Evie had to tilt her chin. He looked...tired, fraught and beautiful.

Evie hitched the blanket up. Curled her toes into her socks. Asked, "Why are you here?"

"You know why," he said, that accent sending delicious shivers down her spine.

And okay, maybe she did. Because she was smart and he wasn't a man to make empty gestures. Yet her heart thumped hard enough against her ribs that it knocked her forwards a step.

Right as Armand reached out to wrap an arm about her waist, haul her to him and kiss her.

Evie threw her arms around his neck and kissed him right on back.

*This*, she thought. *This is what life is all about.*

Then she didn't think much at all for quite some time.

When Evie pulled back she breathed deeply of the chill farm air, of Armand. The feel of him filling her with warmth, with hope, with bliss.

*I'm blissed out, Granddad!* she thought. Already looking forward to introducing her two favourite men in the world.

With a sigh she tipped up onto her toes, wrapped her arms around Armand and buried her face in his neck. Then tossed the toast still gripped in her cold fingers out onto the dry grass, the chickens and ducks squawking as they swarmed to tear it apart.

"Evie," said Armand as she looked up into his eyes, "I should have told you the moment I realised what Jonathon had done."

"You should. But you thought you were protecting me, which is a nice thing to think. Next time know that including me is nicer still."

"Next time?"

"Yes, please."

He kissed her again, on the tip of the nose. On the edge of her eye. On her mouth. Marking his place.

"I truly wanted to kill Jonathon for putting us through

all that. Yet at the same time I feel like I should hug him for putting us through all that."

Armand smiled against her mouth before sealing it with a long, knee-melting kiss. "An urge I have had to subdue more times than you can count. The killing part, not the hugging."

"I can count pretty high."

"And yet…"

Evie shivered at the rough note in Armand's voice. To stave off more shivers, she found the edges of the blanket and wrapped them around him too.

"Now," he said, "I have a question for you."

"Bring it on."

"Did you come here because you finally realised dairy farming was your life's dream?"

Evie laughed. "I did not."

"Excellent. And what about working for Jonathon? I know he is putting together an extremely generous proposal in the hopes of luring you back."

"Been there," she said. "Done that."

"I'm glad, because the conversation we had about following curiosity stuck. And I have an idea that I hope piques yours."

"I'm finally going to be a bus driver? No ballerina firefighter!"

"If that is your dream then I support it wholeheartedly. If you are teasing me, then I have a generous offer of my own."

"I'm teasing you. Offer away."

"How would you feel about working for me?"

"For you, or with you?"

Armand's smile was quick and bright and glorious. And gave nothing away. "I'm setting up an Australian office."

"Of your company? The Action Adventure All-Stars? You're getting the band back together!"

"In a way. Only this time I would like to be proactive rather than reactive."

"Okay."

"Much of the planning happened on my trip up here on the train, so the details are sketchy at best. But how would you feel about helping me design safety apps for commuters travelling at night? For starters. Apps for travellers, how to be aware, safety conscious. Self-defence class apps. The sky is the limit. You could have your own team, hand-picked, with the side benefit of doing work that makes the world a better place. What do you think?"

Evie wondered if it was possible to smile from the bottoms of your feet to the top of your head, because that was what it felt like. "I think you only kissed me to soften me up to get me to work for you." She also thought he was wonderful. "If so you're sneakier than Jonathon ever was."

When Armand's brows lowered and his smile took on a predatory gleam the feeling rushing about in her body was far more fun than a mere smile.

"I didn't come all this way to offer you a job. I came all this way to offer you a life. My life. With all that that means. I know I am flawed, and stubborn, and struggle to ask for help."

"You are also generous. Astute. Forgiving. Loyal. Steadfast. And devastatingly handsome."

He pulled her closer and her entire body sighed. "Taking all that into account, I hope that you can take me as I am."

"I'll take you any way I can get you." Evie lifted a hand to swipe the hair from Armand's eyes.

"You have no idea how glad I am to hear you say that." He breathed in, his eyes travelling slowly over her face as if he couldn't believe what he was seeing. "That moment—when I thought you were about to leap onto the train tracks—my life literally flashed before my eyes. A life in which you were no more. Every horror I had witnessed in my life coalesced into a ball of lead inside me and I could not get the image out of my head."

*Oh, Armand.*

He went on. "After you left—no, after I pushed you

away—I had every intention of going back to Paris, deliberately choosing the fugue in which I had been existing, as it seemed a lesser evil than a life without you. Until I realised the thing I had feared most had—in its own way— happened anyway. You would be gone to me. I would never see you again. And it was my fault."

Evie opened her mouth to contradict him, to admit to her own part in the whole mess, but he leaned down and pressed his forehead to hers and her words dried up in her mouth.

"I love you, Evie. And the thought of life without you is no life at all. I want you with all the risk and joy you bring. And I came here hoping to convince you to give me a second chance."

Evie could barely breathe. Her heart was full, her mind reeling, her blood singing in her veins because of this big, strong man with his grand, poetic heart.

Evie smiled, then grinned, then laughed. Rubbing her forehead against his, she said, "Armand, I've been a little bit in love with you since you were no more to me than my train boyfriend, Hot Stuff in the Swanky Suit. Now that I know you, the real you, flesh and blood and heart and soul, I love you with everything I have."

She felt Armand's body shift as if with shock.

He lifted away, to look into her eyes, his own swirling with emotion. Before they narrowed. "I thought I was Reading Guy."

"That's right. You were Reading Guy. Why am I telling all this to you?"

She made to pull away before he wrapped her up tight.

His mouth kicked up at one side. He had a hell of a smile when he let it loose. "I can go one better, *ma chérie*. I have loved you longer still. Since before we even met."

"Oh, really?"

"Picture the darkest, roughest, farthest reaches of the planet. My spent body protesting every movement, my exhausted mind struggling to form coherent thought, I looked up one night to find the sky awash with more stars than I had ever seen before. And in that darkness, not knowing if any of us would survive the night, I prayed that somewhere in the world a woman had looked to those same stars. A woman whose joy and determination, quirks and kindness and light could fill the very edges of the darkness."

Evie didn't even know she was crying until Armand brushed the pad of a thumb over her cheek.

This time she kissed him, sinking against the long, strong lines of his body as she loved him with all her heart.

"You are my girl in the stars, Evie. My counterpoint. My way out of the dark. The Girl with the Perfect Aim who got me right through the heart. This is the day my life truly begins. No games. No rules. And I want to spend every day of that life with you."

Evie didn't have to think, overthink, or think twice. "Yes, yes, yes, yes, *yes*!"

"That's a yes?"

"Yes!"

Grinning, indulgently, Armand squeezed her tighter still, lifting her feet off the ground. Then he spun her about until she laughed so hard she could scarcely catch her breath, the sound carrying off into the sharp, wintry sky.

"Then let's get the hell out of here," he said.

Evie nodded. "Let's go home."

# EPILOGUE

EVIE SAT ON the train heading into the city, giving into the rock and roll of the carriage.

It had been three months since that day at the farm, when Armand had literally swept her off her feet. It had been a whirlwind since.

She'd gone back to Zoe's, packed her things and spent a week of sleepovers there to unravel their living arrangements and to say goodbye to their single-girl days together.

Then she'd moved her one bag of stuff to Armand's—leaving the futon behind.

Together they'd gone to see Jonathon. She'd thanked him properly for the opportunity and told him she had found a position more suited to her skills. A bittersweet moment, to be sure.

Though watching Armand demand free space in Jonathon's building for the Australian offices of the Action Adventure All-Stars—not their real name—had been far more fun. He was a keen negotiator all spit and fire while cool as ice. She banked it for future alone time.

Armand could afford to buy his own building, but the demand was down to his innate sense of justice. And Jonathon had acquiesced, appearing honestly chagrined at the part he'd played in deceiving them both.

Emphasis on the "appearing", as when they'd left the office Evie had looked back to see him puffing out his chest and looking well pleased with himself. Jonathon was a manipulative bastard, but thankfully he was their manipulative bastard.

And now she really did have the best job ever—heading up the cyber-security division of Armand's company. She had staff—and what do you know, it was really easy to find plenty of super-smart, super-talented, IT-savvy women to work for her. Once Armand had met Lance—who'd just left his position in the army—he'd offered him a job on the spot too.

"Do you have enough room?" Armand asked, shifting to give her more space.

Evie ate up the inches, snuggling closer. She sneaked her hand into the crook of Armand's arm and leant her head on his shoulder. Her eyes slid over the frazzled mother, the schoolboys with their huge bags and glazed eyes, the suits and the yoga queens and the grinders and the hipsters. All of them on a mission to live their best lives—all dealing as best they could with the hiccups and detours and falls and successes along the way.

Evie smiled at them all, each and every one of them helping to make this city of hers the vibrant melting pot of possibility that it was.

"Look."

At the rumble of Armand's voice Evie turned to look at him. The storm in his eyes had cleared, making way for acres of blue. A glint shone within as he took her by the chin and turned her head away. "Over there."

Another couple sat a couple of rows down, all snuggled up too. A young man with short blond hair and Harry Potter glasses was reading from a small hardcover book to a girl with tufts of short dark hair poking out at the bottom of a navy beanie covered in little gold stars, and a big, soppy smile on her face.

Evie wondered about the knitting pattern. Machine-made, perhaps? Those stars would be seriously challenging to...

She sat bolt upright.

Then let go of Armand to grab her phone. She frantically found the app she was looking for and scrolled back

weeks, months, till she found the right page. Then she stuck
it under Armand's nose, listening with half an ear as he read:

> *New to your orbit, I find myself struck*
> *By your raven locks, your starlit eyes. What luck*
> *That I find myself able to see you twice a day.*
> *A beacon in a sea of strangers. I must say*
> *Your sunshine smiles are my good morning.*
> *Your evening sighs my goodnight.*
> *If I had the courage I'd say hello.*
> *Till then I remain alone in my delight.*

"Well, what do you know?" said Armand.

*Not much,* thought Evie, *clearly.*

"Funny," he said, giving her a sideways glance as he
handed back her phone. "One could think it was written
about you."

Evie merely smiled and gave him a quick kiss.

He'd found the fortune cookie message scrunched up
in her wallet when he'd gone looking for coins and he'd
listened with impressive patience while she'd talked him
through the story that went along with it.

They'd get to the poem in good time. But not yet. Armand had taught her that a little mystery could go a long
way.

How funny though, she thought, all the external forces
that had worked to get them together. The dodgy fortune,
someone else's poem and an unlikely fairy godfather in the
shape of Jonathon Montrose.

But the truth was they had found one another on the train
before any of that had even come to pass. Harbouring quiet
fascinations for one another while at points in their lives
where the idea of love at first sight was too momentous a
leap to believe in.

"Would you like me to read to you?" he asked.

"Depends what you are reading, Reading Guy," Evie

said, knowing he could read the back of a cereal box and that voice of his would make her knees quiver.

He pulled out the book he'd tucked inside his coat— *Cyrano de Bergerac*.

"In French?" she asked.

"Of course," he said, taken aback that she would suggest otherwise.

"I thought you read fiction to keep your language skills up to scratch."

"I read fiction because it exists."

"Armand Debussey, you're a romantic."

"That is like telling me I am French," he said, with not a lick of irony.

Evie realised she'd only scratched the surface of this man. That his code went deep. And, while she had the feeling he could be the one project she might never fully crack, that was okay with her.

She'd have a wonderful time trying.

\* \* \* \* \*

# HER SECRET
# TEXAS VALENTINE

## HELEN LACEY

For my parents,
who always encouraged me to read, to write and
to dream. I miss you both more than words can say.

# Chapter One

Twenty-four-year-old real estate agent Valene Fortunado had no illusions about her love life.

She didn't have one.

One lousy date after another over the past six months had made that abundantly clear.

It wasn't like she needed a man to *complete* her. After all, she wasn't the kind of woman to get caught up in grand gestures or romantic nonsense. Okay…maybe she *was*. Maybe she only acted as though she was a career woman, first and foremost.

Still…a *good* date every now and then would fill some of her lonelier nights.

And not that she was really lonely, either. It was just that since both her sisters and two of her brothers had found love, they kept insisting that her white knight was around the corner. Valene wasn't so sure. Maybe her white knight had galloped past on his way through her neck of the woods and failed to notice she was standing there. Maybe she had been too wrapped up in her latest open house or contract negotiation to spot him riding by. She *had* been known to have blinders on when it came to the opposite sex.

Which was why she decided to log into My Perfect Match and let an app find her a date.

*How bad could it be?*

That was the question she *should* have asked herself two disastrous dates ago.

Date number one was so dull he could have been a cardboard cutout. And he spent the whole two and a half excruciating hours talking about himself, his license plate collection and his beloved mother. Date number two barely said a word and was so scruffy he looked like he'd been wearing the same clothes for a week. Not that Valene was hung up on appearances…but at the very least she expected her date to wear a clean shirt and take off his baseball cap during dinner. Novice mistake— first dates should be over coffee, not dinner. There was no easy escape during a three-course sit-down meal that might include a bottle of wine and several hours of conversation. Next time, she would meet someone over coffee and make sure she had a quick exit strategy in case it turned into a disaster.

Because there would be a next time.

Valene wasn't about to give up simply because she'd made a few rookie errors.

She was mostly well behaved and did the right thing. Her parents adored her, and she wanted to make them proud. Plus, she'd always endeavored to be a proactive kind of girl and had never been accused of lacking gumption or courage. But she was determined to be more prudent in her choices. If both her sisters, Schuyler and Maddie, could find love with the men of their dreams, Valene expected nothing less for herself. As long as he ticked all the right boxes.

*Looks*…well, she wasn't too fussy, but nice eyes and broad shoulders would be a bonus.

*Money*…enough that he didn't expect her to pay for every meal and had a nice car.

*Smarts*…a college education and a good job were a must.

How hard could it be? Her sisters had managed it— so could she. Not that she was going to let the whole idea take up too much time or attention. She had more important things on her mind.

It had been a busy few months with way too much drama for her liking. And too much family. Hers and everyone else's. Fortunados. Robinsons. Fortunes. Mendozas. Family life wasn't simple anymore. She had relatives coming out of the woodwork. And things to do. Like saving the family business.

Too many things had gone pear-shaped at Fortunado Real Estate in the past couple of months. Too many deals had been lost for it to be simple coincidence. And she loathed thinking it was merely bad judgment on their part. Sure, they'd lost sales and contracts to other real estate agents before, but this felt different. It felt… *personal*. As though someone was specifically targeting her family's business. And Valene wouldn't sit by and allow that to happen—not on her watch.

Still, she needed to make time for herself. Which was why she was on her way to meet date number three.

As she headed for the Houston coffee place, she caught a glimpse of herself in a flower shop window, pleased that she'd worn a dress and heels that flattered her curves and made her look taller than her five foot three. She glanced at her expression. Not too eager. Not too resistant, either. Just ready for whatever happened. And she was ready. She had her sister's number on speed dial in her cell phone and knew every exit in the coffee place to escape in two seconds if need be.

Valene took a deep breath that added some resolve to her suddenly dwindling courage.

*Third time lucky,* she told herself.

She remained in the doorway and looked around. Blue shirt, she reminded herself. Look for a man wearing a blue shirt. That was the text message she'd received. She spotted three potentials. The first was a guy at the counter paying for two tall frappés. Right age. Tallish. Dark hair. Then she heard him haggling with the barista about a tip before he grabbed the drinks and walked directly past her without her being so much as a blip on his radar. *Not him, thank God.* Valene took another deep breath. She looked toward the second blue-shirted candidate. Not as tall, and thicker set. But he had a nice face and actually looked up and smiled at her. *Okay...he looks normal enough.* She was about to smile back when another woman passed her and headed for his table. The pair kissed briefly and then the woman sat down. Right. Not him, either.

She glanced toward the booth seat and saw candidate number three had his back to her. Broad shoulders and short blond hair, and a nice blue shirt. He looked so good from the back, she hoped it was him. From his online profile, she knew her date's name was Jake and that he worked outside the city. The few texts they'd exchanged had been articulate and humorous enough to pique her interest and make her want to meet him.

*Nothing ventured...nothing gained.*

She'd always had gumption, according to her family. Now was the time to show some. And if it didn't work out, so be it.

Valene pushed back her shoulders and walked through the coffeehouse.

*Dating apps.*

Jake Brockton figured that signing on to one was up there as one of the stupidest things he'd ever done. But he'd promised his sister he'd try it, and he was a man of his word. And it was just coffee. Not a date. Nothing that required too much time or attention. And he could bail as soon as felt the interaction going south.

He glanced at his watch. She was late. He hated that.

Jake had no tolerance for tardiness. He hadn't gotten to where he was by being lazy or disorganized. It had been through grit and a steely determination to be the best version of himself he could possibly be.

Too bad his ex-wife hadn't thought so.

He pushed the memory from his mind and tapped his fingers on the table. He really didn't have time to waste on romantic entanglements. The ranch kept him busy 24/7 and he wasn't about to get seriously involved with anyone. Still, he'd promised Cassidy, and he always kept his promises to his baby sister.

Conscious that someone was standing by the booth seat, Jake turned his head and quickly sucked in a sharp breath.

A woman stood barely two feet away. She was petite but surprisingly curvy, with long blond hair and brown eyes the color of Belgian chocolate. His gut recognized an instant reaction, and he swallowed hard, taking in her perfectly aligned features and lovely curves. She smiled, and her mouth curled at the corners.

His date.

They'd shared a few text messages the day before. Nothing too personal. Just their first names, interests and a time and place to meet. She'd seemed friendly and had added humorous emojis to her texts.

He got to his feet in a microsecond and held out his hand.

"Hi," he said quietly. "I'm Jake Brockton."

She stepped a little closer and took his hand, and he experienced an inexplicable tightening in his chest as their skin connected. Her eyes widened fractionally, as though she was experiencing the same reaction and then she quickly withdrew her hand.

"Valene Fortunado," she said, her voice huskier than he'd expected. "But everyone calls me Val."

Fortunado? He'd heard the name but wasn't sure where. Jake nodded and signaled to the waitress. "Coffee?"

"That would be nice," she said as she placed her small bag on the seat. "I've been here before. You?"

Jake shook his head. "But my sister told me the coffee is good."

As small talk went, it was pretty benign, and he ignored the way his insides twitched. She was very attractive…more than he'd expected. More than he wanted. In his experience, beautiful women were nothing but trouble and potential heartache.

The waitress arrived and he listened, amused, as his date ordered a single-shot, low-fat, vanilla soy latte with extra cinnamon. He asked for a tall black and waited until the waitress disappeared before he spoke again.

"You're very pretty."

She raised one brow, clearly not expecting the compliment. "Thank you. You're not so bad yourself."

Jake laughed softly. "Can I ask you something?"

She nodded. "Sure."

"Why are you using a dating app?"

"Why are you?" she shot back, smiling.

"My sister made me do it," he admitted. "She thinks I spend too much time alone."

Her lovely brow arched higher. "And do you?"

"Probably. Occupational habit."

"What do you do?" she asked.

Jake expelled an even breath. "I work on a ranch."

She sat back in her seat, her head tilted at a gentle angle. "Doing what?"

"Ranching stuff."

She smiled slightly. "I'm a city girl, so I'll need a little more information."

"Ranching," he replied. "Mustering cattle. Horse breaking."

Her brows came together. "Like…a cowboy?"

He nodded. "Exactly."

"I've never been on a date with a cowboy before."

"Really?" He grinned. "Then you've led a sheltered life. This is Texas—cowboy capital of the nation."

She laughed, and the sound reverberated in his chest. "I know that, too. I was born and raised in Houston. What about you?"

"I was raised in San Antonio until I was twelve, but I was born in Stafford, just outside Houston," he said.

"That's a nice spot. I sold a dude ranch there once," she said idly. "Property values hold steady."

Jake rested his elbows on the table. "You owned a dude ranch?"

She shook her head and grinned, waiting while the waitress approached with their order before speaking again. "No, it's what I do for a living."

"Selling dude ranches?"

"Selling real estate," she corrected. "I work in my family's business."

He recalled seeing that she was self-employed on her profile. And now he knew why her surname seemed familiar. He knew of Fortunado Real Estate. They were one of the biggest in the city, and her family was connected to the famous Fortunes of Texas. "Do you enjoy it?"

"Mostly," she replied. "I split my time between both the Austin and Houston offices and like any business, it has its ups and downs. It's a little more down than up at the moment, but I always look on the bright side."

Jake stirred a little sugar into his coffee. "I'm glad to hear it. So, you didn't answer my question."

"Which one?"

He met her gaze. "Why the dating app?"

She shrugged fractionally. "It's simply a way to meet people."

"People?"

Her cheeks spotted with color. "Guys. Or *a* guy. You know, Mr. Wonderful and all that." She spooned the froth off her beverage. "But the truth is, if you'd turned out to be a cardboard cutout or one of the great unwashed, I was going to make this my third and last attempt."

Jake laughed softly. "You've done this before?"

She held up two fingers. "And both disastrous."

"I take it one was dull and the other had an issue with personal hygiene?"

She chuckled and he noticed that her brown eyes had flecks of gold in them. Damn, she really was pretty.

"Exactly," she said on a sigh.

"And how am I comparing so far?"

Her eyes widened, and she bit her lower lip for a moment. "Well, from here you look very much like flesh and blood. And you smell nice."

He laughed again and realized he'd done quite a lot of that since she'd arrived. "So, Valene, tell me about yourself."

She didn't break their gaze. "I'm twenty-four. Single, obviously. I work for my family's real estate business. My parents are wonderful and still happily in love after thirtysomething years of marriage. I'm the youngest of six children and am considered to be somewhat spoiled. I have my own condo in the city and a fiercely protective bulldog. I'm allergic to passion fruit and I love chocolate. You?"

Jake drank some coffee and looked at her. "I'm thirty-two. Single, obviously," he said, echoing her words. "I work on a ranch near Fulshear, outside Houston. My father died over a decade ago, and my mom still grieves him every day. I have a younger sister named Cassidy who is considered somewhat spoiled. I have a very *unprotective* collie mix called Sheba who tries to sleep on the end of my bed every night. I'm not allergic to anything I know of and I can take or leave chocolate."

It was a vague introduction, since he wasn't about to start saying too much about himself to a stranger. But she seemed nice enough, and what harm could a little flirtation do?

"It's nice to meet you, Jake," she said, still smiling.

"Likewise, Valene."

"Do you like being a cowboy?" she asked.

"It has its up and downs," he said, mimicking her earlier words as he smiled. "It's physically hard work, but rewarding. It's all I've done since I left college."

"Where did you graduate?" She sipped her latte and

looked at him over the rim of her mug. "The University of Houston?"

"No."

"Rice University?"

"I dropped out before the second semester."

Jake waited for her expression to change, for disappointment or censure to show on her pretty face. But to her credit, she didn't appear fazed by what he'd described as his meager education. Or his occupation.

"Oh, I see," she said and continued to sip her coffee. "And you said you've been working on the ranch ever since?"

Jake nodded. "We moved from San Antonio to the ranch when I was twelve. My father worked there for a long time."

"And when he died you took over his job?" she asked.

Jake shrugged. "Someone had to fill his boots. So, Valene, why are you single?" he asked, abruptly changing the subject.

"I'm high maintenance," she said and grinned.

"Scared?"

"Not at all," he replied, watching the way her mouth curled at the edges and thinking how sexy it was. It had been a long time since he'd been attracted to someone. But she was funny and flirtatious, and he was discovering that he enjoyed her company. "But I'm not sure I believe you."

She shrugged. "I work long hours, and that doesn't leave me a lot of time for socializing. But lately…"

Her words trailed off and he raised both brows questioningly. "Lately?"

"Both my sisters and one of my brothers have recently gotten married, and another brother got engaged," she explained and sighed. "I feel left out, I guess, as if romance and love have passed me by."

"And is that what you want?" he queried. "Romance and love?"

She shrugged again. "Doesn't everyone?" She turned back and then made a face. "To be honest, I'd settle for someone to share a pizza, watch a movie and snuggle with."

Jake smiled, trying to recall the last time he'd snuggled with anyone. His ex-wife, Patrice, hadn't exactly been the *snuggling* type. But Valene Fortunado, with her lovely hair, soft brown eyes and subtle curves, made him think that it was time he got back to really living and reconnecting with the world.

"What kind of movies do you like?" he asked and finished his coffee.

She chuckled. "Ah…actually, I like a little zombie action."

Jake laughed. "No chick flicks?"

She shook her head. "Not really. Just zombies and fright-night kinds of films."

Jake winced. "Then I guess we're not going to do that pizza and a movie thing," he said, smiling as he shrugged. "Pity."

Her lips curled. "You don't like scary movies?"

"I don't like clowns," he admitted. "And one always seems to turn up in that kind of movie."

She laughed again, so softly, so delightfully, that Jake's belly rolled over.

"You're scared of clowns?"

"Not scared," he corrected quickly. "I just don't like them all that much."

"Tough guy like you," she shot back, still chuckling. "In the movies, cowboys aren't afraid of anything."

"I'm not afraid," he reiterated, enjoying her teasing. "Just…cautious. It's those big feet and red noses… they're kinda freaky."

She laughed again. "Well, if we ever go on a date to a carnival or circus, I promise to protect you from the clowns terrorizing the midway."

Jake stared at her, relaxed back in the booth seat and spoke. "Would you like to?"

Her head tilted fractionally. "Would I like to what?"

"Go on a date?"

Valene's heart was beating like a jackhammer. Jake Brockton was utterly gorgeous. His eyes were clear blue, his face perfectly angled and proportioned, his blond hair the kind that begged for fingers to thread through it. And the rest of him was to-die-for hot. His shoulders were broad, his arms well muscled, and she was certain the rest of him would hold up to her and every other woman on the planet's scrutiny. She couldn't recall ever seeing a man fill out a chambray shirt the way he did. And he had nice hands—strong looking, with long blunt fingers, neat nails and a few calluses that signified hard work. Yes, Jake Brockton was about as masculine and attractive a man as she'd ever met.

Plus, he seemed to like her.

Unfortunately, the good-looking cowboy didn't tick any of her boxes.

No career. No college education. And probably no money. She couldn't be certain, but surely ranch hands weren't paid extravagant salaries. She was disappointed through to her core.

But what harm could a single date do?

It wasn't a marriage proposal. Or a lifelong commitment. And she didn't have anyone else knocking on her door asking for her time and attention. She thought about it, looking at his handsome face again. And decided she'd live a little.

"Sure," she said as casually as she could manage. "Why not."

"Friday night?"

She nodded. "Where?"

He named a small Italian restaurant a few streets away. "Shall I pick you up?"

"I'll meet you there," she replied. "Um…that's a popular place. I'm not sure we could get a reservation this late. Perhaps somewhere else would be easier."

He looked amused by her caution. "I'll text you a time once I make a reservation."

She wasn't convinced he'd get a table, but she agreed. "Ah…great."

"Would you like more coffee?"

She smiled a little. The man certainly wasn't short on manners, and she realized he was an intriguing mix of rough and smooth. There was no denying his earthy roots. His clothes were clean and tidy, but the closer she looked, the more she noticed how the shirt was frayed a little around the cuffs, and how the Stetson sitting on the seat beside him was clearly well used. And despite the air of civility oozing from him, there was nothing urban about Jake Brockton. He was country through and through. Not what she wanted. Not anything like what she wanted. Except…his blue eyes were unbelievably mesmerizing. And his clean-shaven jaw made her fingertips itch with the urge to trace a pattern along his cheek and chin.

Awareness and attraction mingled through her blood and she managed a tight smile, conscious that he was watching her intently. She tried to recall the last time she'd been as interested in a man, and the lingering memory of her first real boyfriend flittered along the edges of her mind. But Diego hadn't hung around. And it turned out he was only ambitious and interested in her family's money and connections rather than her. He wanted a career in real estate and thought she was his meal ticket, and he showed little shame in making it clear he deserved it after putting up with being her boyfriend for a year. After that, a little older and wiser, she'd dated Hugh. He was handsome and polite and from a nice family—his father was a friend of her father's, and they'd been set up with the expectation that they would be perfect for one another. Yes, Hugh was perfect—he had perfect looks and manners and a career in the finance sector, and for five months she'd been convinced they would have a predictable happily-ever-after. But there was very little spark between them. Actually, no spark. Zilch. So it was an easy decision to end things between them. He was disappointed. She was wife material, he said. She shouldn't have high expectations. After that, she'd begun to believe that maybe the spark thing was a myth. But then, over the course of the past year, both her sisters and two of her brothers had fallen madly in love and it got Val thinking that maybe that big love really did exist.

"Why are *you* single, Jake?" she asked bluntly.

"I've been too busy," he said vaguely.

She gave him a disbelieving look. "Really?"

"That's the truth, but I guess I'm still looking for my perfect match."

She chuckled. "Do you think there's such a thing?"

He shrugged lightly. "I'd like to think so. I'm not so sure anymore."

"Do you want kids?"

His expression altered for a nanosecond, as though he was lost in thought. Finally, he spoke again. "Yes, one day. You?"

"I'm pretty sure I want kids...one day."

"You're only twenty-four," he reminded her. "You have plenty of time to think about kids."

Her belly did an odd kind of dive. "I know. But I think it's more about being with the right person, rather than being the right age."

He nodded. "I think you're right. So, tell me about your two disastrous dates."

She laughed lightly. "Oh, my God, they were unbelievably bad. The first guy collected license plates from every state and talked nonstop about his mother. And the second one—he wore a baseball cap backward. But," she said and flashed him a smile, "third time's the charm."

He met her gaze. "I'm really glad your first two dates were duds."

Valene kept the visual contact. "Me too. Anyhow, I should probably get going. I have an open house at noon and need to get back to the office beforehand. But it was nice to meet you."

"You too," he said and waited for her to stand before he got to his feet.

He excused himself for a moment and headed for the counter to pay the check before Valene had a chance to offer to pay her share. When he returned to her, she was halfway to the entrance. He opened the door and let her pass, and they stepped out into the sunlight.

"My car's right here," she said and used the beeper to unlock her silver Lexus, which was parked directly outside the coffeehouse. "Yours?"

He jerked a thumb in the direction of a beaten-up blue Ranger parked on the other side of the road. There was faded writing on the side of the truck that she couldn't make out. Okay…so he had a crappy car. The fact that he was utterly gorgeous made up for that shortcoming. Valene tried to drag her gaze away but couldn't help looking him up and down. It should be illegal, she thought to herself as her skin prickled all over, for a man to look that good in chambray and denim.

"Well, thanks for meeting me, Jake," she said easily and held out her hand. "I had a nice time."

He took her hand, and electricity shot up her arm. "Likewise, Valene. I'll see you Friday."

For a moment, she could have sworn he swayed a little closer. Of course, he wouldn't try to kiss her. That would be outrageous, presumptuous and completely out of line. But still, her lips tingled foolishly and she let out a long and disappointed sigh.

*Don't get ahead of yourself, Val. It was just coffee and conversation.*

He released her hand and she quickly got into her car. When she pulled away from the curb and caught a glimpse of him in the rearview mirror, her thought surprised her. She'd suddenly developed a thing for cowboys.

## Chapter Two

"So," Schuyler asked over brunch the following day. "How did it go?"

They were eating at the office, chowing down on gourmet chicken salads and freshly squeezed juice that their other sister, Maddie, had supplied. Her oldest sister commuted between Austin and Houston most weeks, and Schuyler had driven in from Austin the day before and was staying for a couple of days. They had ditched the break room and were seated around the big oak table in the boardroom.

"It was nice," Valene replied and sipped on a guava and pineapple drink. "Like I said."

"But he's a penniless cowboy?" Maddie asked bluntly.

Val shrugged. "I didn't ask to see his bank statements. He was nice, very charming and funny."

Maddie, always the most serious of the trio, looked

skeptical. "I can't believe you got matched up with a ranch hand. Didn't you say you specifically wanted an educated, white-collar kind of guy?"

She shrugged again. "I don't know. Perhaps he fudged the questionnaire."

"It's possible," Schuyler said and frowned.

"What a jerk," Maddie added.

But the more Val thought about it, the less likely Maddie's opinion seemed. There was something refreshingly candid and honest about Jake. Of course, it could be that she was still gaga over his broad shoulders and blue eyes and didn't want to see the truth right in front of her. But she was convinced that he was exactly as he appeared—a workingman, honest and down to earth. And as hot as Hades.

"We could google him," Schuyler suggested.

Val waved a hand. "Absolutely not. I'm not going to go stalker and start checking out social media profiles and that sort of thing. I want to be a grown-up about this. And I know this might sound silly, but I don't want to jinx it, okay?"

"What do you mean?" Schuyler asked.

"It means," Val said, a little impatiently, "that he was nice, and we had a good time over coffee, like I said. And we're going out for dinner tomorrow night."

"Do you think that's a good idea?" Maddie asked soberly. "I mean, if he's not the kind of guy you think you could get serious about, why bother getting to know him?"

Schuyler laughed. "You're such a snob, Maddie."

"I'm a realist," her sister defended. "And you've said it yourself, you want a man who ticks certain boxes. Sounds like he only ticks the 'looks good in a pair of jeans' box."

Both her sisters laughed, but Val wasn't amused. They were making fun, and for some reason, that bothered her. "We'll just see what happens."

"Well," Schuyler said dramatically, "I think it's great that you're getting out. And if this one doesn't work out, you can try again. But maybe redefine your criteria a little."

Maddie had a serious look on her face. "I'm not trying to be a party pooper, but you need to tread carefully and slowly when it comes to romance."

"Like you did?" Val shot back, brows up. "Weren't you the one who took you and Zach out of the colleague and friend zone when you planted that kiss on him at the Thirsty Ox? How long did it take you to jump into Zach's bed after that?"

Schuyler started wagging a few fingers and counting before Maddie shushed them both. "Okay…don't take *my* lead. All I'm saying is, don't be hasty. If he's right for you, then he'll wait. You're my baby sister and I'll always worry about you."

"I know," Val obliged. "And I appreciate your concern. But believe me, I'm not about to rush into anything. I know how everyone thinks I'm impulsive, but in this instance, I'm going to take my time and get to know someone before I make any big moves. Besides, I'm too busy with work to spend too much time on romance. If I don't start closing more deals," she said and glanced toward Maddie, who along with her überhandsome husband, Zach McCarter, had become joint CEO of Fortunado Real Estate since their father had retired, "Dad's going to insist you fire me."

"Ha," Schuyler said with mock horror. "No chance. You're Daddy's girl. He'll never allow Maddie or Zach to fire you. You are the golden girl and his number two protégée."

Val laughed, because they all knew Maddie had been their father's number one protégée.

"That's true," Val said and grinned. "I am Dad's favorite."

Maddie tossed a piece of lettuce in her direction. "And modest. Speaking of which, do our parents know you're on the hunt for a man?" Maddie asked.

Val rolled her eyes. "I'd hardly call it a hunt. I met Jake for coffee, not a commitment ceremony. And Dad and Mom generally stay out of my love life."

"Except for Hugh," Schuyler reminded her. "He was handpicked."

"Dad worries about gold diggers," Maddie said on a sigh. "And since you're so easily influenced and like to party, they probably thought they were doing the right thing."

"Gosh, I have a terrible reputation," she said tartly, trying to remember the last time she actually *did* go to a party. "Young and impulsive and likely to get into all kinds of trouble. Oh, hang on," she said and smiled. "That was you, Schuyler, getting cozy with the Mendozas so you could wrangle an introduction to our newly discovered Fortune relatives. And then falling in love with one of the sexy Mendoza men."

Of course, every word was true. Schuyler had integrated herself into the Mendoza family, specifically by getting a job working at the Mendoza Winery, and then by falling in love with Carlo Mendoza. It was a series of events, jump-started by discovering that the Fortunados were related to the infamous Fortune family. The very idea that they were connected to the Fortunes had sent a curious Schuyler on a mission to find

out the whole truth. They discovered that their grand-
father was actually Julius Fortune, and that their dad,
Kenneth Fortunado, was one of his many illegitimate
children dotted around the state and even the country.
Their grandmother had signed a confidentiality agreement with Julius, but also being something of a free
spirit, had changed Kenneth's name to Fortunado as a
way of not completely complying to Julius's demands.
Learning that, Schuyler had been determined to get acquainted with the Fortune branch of the family. That's
how she ended up at the Mendoza Winery, pretending to be a waitress. The Mendozas and the Fortunes
were interlaced by marriage. Turned out Julius's son Jerome Fortune, who was known as tech billionaire Gerald Robinson—their uncle—had a daughter who was
married to one of the Mendoza cousins. The link was
enough to get Schuyler's crazy mind into thinking she
could somehow bring the families together.

Valene hadn't taken much interest at the time, since
she'd been neck-deep in work and wanted to prove she
could be as ambitious and successful at Fortunado
Real Estate as her sister Maddie. But now the truth
was out. They were really Fortunes—as their free-spirited grandmother had enjoyed an affair with the phi-
landering Julius. Valene had learned to accept the fact
that she had an incredibly complicated family tree. It
wasn't unusual to see an article on the internet or in the
paper about the family. In fact, it wasn't that long ago
that a journalist named Ariana Lamonte had done an
exposé on *all* of Gerald Robinson's children, including
the ones he'd sired out of wedlock. Yeah, complicated
didn't really cover it. Particularly now that Gerald Robinson, aka Jerome Fortune, had left his embittered wife,
Charlotte, and had sought refuge in the arms of the first

and only love of his life, Deborah—who had borne him three illegitimate sons decades earlier.

Yes, the Fortunado/Fortune/Mendoza connection was about as complicated as it got.

"Okay," Schuyler said and grinned. "I'll admit that I'm the flake in the family."

"What does that make me?" Maddie queried.

"The workaholic," Val said lightly. "And I'm the spoiled brat. I know, since our brothers have told me that repeatedly over the years."

"You're not spoiled," Schuyler defended. "But you're the youngest, and since we've already established that you're Daddy's favorite, you know you have to get labeled as something. But now I think we should check out this Jake on social media and see what he's hiding."

Val rolled her eyes. "He's not hiding anything."

"Everyone is hiding something," Maddie said, her mouth flattened. "What's his last name?"

"I'm not saying," Val replied, standing her ground. "I'm not going to do anything other than go on a nice and respectable date with the man."

Schuyler made a dramatic sound. "Oh, I see, you actually *like* him."

Val waved an impatient hand. She loved her sisters… but sometimes they were impossibly bossy and interfering. "We spent an hour together. I'd hardly call that enough time to form any kind of opinion."

"I'm not so sure about that," Maddie said seriously. "I was pining for Zach for years after the first time I laid eyes on him."

"But underneath your corporate and workaholic demeanor, you're a soppy sentimentalist," Val said and chuckled. "And I'm a realist."

They all laughed, and it was so nice to spend some

quality time with her sisters. Since both of them had married, and Schuyler had moved to Austin to be with Carlo, she'd missed their company. Of course, she still regularly saw Maddie at both the Houston and Austin offices, but that was work. She had friends, but other than her bestie, Adele, no one came close to the affection she felt for her siblings. She even missed hanging out with her brothers. Particularly Connor, who lived in Denver and was always a great source of advice and counsel.

Growing up as the youngest Fortunado child had had its difficult moments. For one, her parents were overprotective of her and often treated her as though she were eighteen and not twenty-four. Since her father had retired and he and her mother had begun traveling, their stranglehold had lessened a little, but she still spoke to both her parents every few days. Case in point: she hadn't told her parents she was using My Perfect Match to find a man, otherwise she knew her father would start handing out her number to people he thought were suitable for his youngest, beloved child.

She packed up what was left of her lunch and gave each of her sisters a hug. "I have to get back to work. I'm showing an estate in Bunker Hill this afternoon."

"The McGovern place?" Maddie inquired, quickly in CEO mode.

"That's the one," she said and shrugged. "I have a buyer from Arizona, a couple who are transferring to Houston for work. We video chatted last time I did an open house, and they seem interested in the property."

"But?" Maddie asked, always picking up on Val's body language.

"They're going in at under three fifty per square foot."

"Median price is what?" Maddie queried. "About four hundred?"

She nodded. "Yeah...so we'll see. The husband really likes the place, but his wife is a banker and is naturally going to try to screw the owners with a lower offer."

Maddie's brows rose quickly. "Please tell me you're not using that terminology with the clients?"

Val laughed. She loved Maddie, but sometimes her oldest sister was too uptight. "Of course not," she assured her boss and smoothed a hand over her perfectly tight chignon. "I am always at my professional best when I'm with a client."

"Well, as long as you let your hair down with your hot cowboy on Friday night," Schuyler said and chuckled.

*Your hot cowboy...*

Her skin turned uncharacteristically warm at the thought of Jake Brockton.

"Would you stop encouraging her to be as reckless as you?" Maddie scolded her sister.

Val was still smiling as she left the boardroom and headed up the hall. She passed her brother-in-law Zach McCarter and hiked a thumb in the direction of the boardroom. He nodded and grinned, clearly amused that she knew he would be looking for the wife he obviously adored. Val liked Zach; he was a good boss and a great businessman. She'd learned a lot from him since he'd moved to Houston from the San Antonio office. The transition had been at her father's behest, of course, before her dad had retired. Kenneth had pitted Maddie and Zach against one another in a contest to secure the top job once he retired, and over the course of the rivalry, they had fallen crazily in love.

She was still smiling as she entered her office and

was moving around her desk when her cell phone beeped. She checked the text message instantly.

It was her hot cowboy.

Toscano's. Seven o'clock. Looking forward to it. Jake.

She grinned when she noticed the smiling emoji, wondering how he'd wrangled a reservation at one of the most popular restaurants in Houston. She texted back quickly and tucked the cell into her pocket.

She had a date.

And for the first time in a long time, Val didn't feel quite so alone.

"Seriously, could you be any more evasive?"

Jake made an impatient sound at the whiny voice rattling in his ear. The same voice that had been demanding answers to a barrage of personal questions for the last five minutes.

"Cass," he said quietly, "I told you, it's none of your business."

"But it was my idea," she wailed and came around his left side, ignoring the fact he was hitching up the cinch on his horse and she was very much in the way. "I suggested the dating app to begin with."

The big gelding sidestepped and stomped its foot. Jake loved his baby sister, but sometimes she was as annoying as a buzzing mosquito. And about as relentless. She'd been at him the moment she got home from college for the weekend, demanding to know how his coffee dates went. Well, date, in the singular, because he'd canceled the two other dates he'd made once he'd met the vivacious and beautiful Valene Fortunado. He'd never been a player, and dating more than one woman didn't sit right.

"Cassidy," he said, calling his sister by her full name, "button up, will you. I've got work to do."

She huffed and swished her flaming-red ponytail. "Sometimes you are such a killjoy, Jake. If you hadn't taken my advice, you never would have met this goddess."

He turned his head and frowned. "And not once did I use that word," he reminded her. "Remember that when you start telling Mom how you're playing cupid."

His sister laughed. "You said she was pretty."

"She was. She is. But I don't want to make more of it than it was. Coffee and conversation," he said, his voice sterner. "That's it."

"But you're seeing her tonight, right?"

He nodded slowly. "Right."

"You should take flowers," Cassidy suggested. "Women love flowers. And wear a suit. And don't take that crappy old truck of yours. Make sure you drive the Sierra. I don't know why you bought the thing— you never take it out of the garage. You'd rather drive around in that old Ranger that you've had since you were sixteen."

Jake wasn't about to argue, since Cassidy had a point. He did prefer the Ranger. But he often had business dealings that required more class than the beat-up Ford that his father had taught him to drive in so many years ago. Sentiment made him hang on to the old truck. And memory. And the acknowledgment of where he had come from, where his roots were, and how far he'd come since his dad had been the foreman of the Double Rock Ranch.

Jake had been raised on the ranch since he was

twelve and Cassidy a newborn. Along with their mother, they'd lived in the cottage behind the main house, and their life had been happy and fulfilling. Jake loved the land and the work, but he'd also gotten good grades in high school, so college was the obvious next step. But when his father had died suddenly from a heart attack when he was eighteen, he'd quickly hightailed it back home from school and stepped into his father's boots. If he hadn't, his mom and sister would have been forced to leave the ranch, and that was unthinkable.

But he understood why Cassidy made the comment about the suit and the truck. Jake had no illusions. Valene was city while he was country. But he wasn't an uneducated hick, even though she might think he was. True, she hadn't made any condescending remarks when he'd admitted to dropping out of college, but he sensed some level of disappointment. He did admire the way she'd kept that feeling to herself, though. And he liked how she had asked him about his work and hadn't made any negative remarks about his occupation. He knew from experience that some women measured a man's worth by the weight of his wallet.

Like Patrice…

He'd pined for her through high school, but she was with the it crowd, and Jake was definitely not on her radar. Years later, that changed. Patrice did notice him. And because he was still stuck on her, Jake didn't hesitate in falling head over heels in love with her, not realizing she was cold and calculating and not to be trusted. He learned his life lessons the hard way. Through Patrice's betrayal and humiliation, his heart hardened, and he was determined he'd never be made a fool of again.

Jake gently grabbed Cassidy's shoulders and ushered her out of the way. He checked the cinch, grabbed the reins and effortlessly sprang into the saddle. "Try to stay out of trouble, will you. I'll be back in an hour or so."

"We haven't finished this conversation," she reminded him, hands on hips.

Jake shook his head. "See ya, kid. Don't forget to study while you're here this weekend."

Cassidy was in her third year at college, but she was easily distracted. He loved her, though, and would walk through fire for her and his mom. He reined the gelding and headed from the corral, meeting up with two of the ranch hands who'd been waiting patiently by the stables.

"Sorry, boys," he said, though no apology was necessary. They all knew how irritating and adorable Cassidy could be.

"No worries, boss," the older of the duo replied. Kris had been on the Double Rock Ranch longer than he had. Jake still winced every time one of the ranch hands called him boss, but he'd worked hard to get where he was, and everyone on the Double Rock knew it and respected him for it. "I got a younger sister myself. Nothin' but trouble."

They all laughed as they headed off. When they passed the main house, Jake slowed down a fraction. The renovations were finally being finished, something that was a long time coming. For years the previous owners had let the home fall into disrepair, but things on the Double Rock were slowly changing. The ranch, situated in Fort Bend County, was a forty-minute drive to Houston and just under four hundred acres. Prime land, dotted with oak and pecan trees, it was predominantly cattle and horses and operated a highly lucrative Wagyu beef business. Jake loved the Double Rock and couldn't imagine living anywhere else.

He spent the following hour checking the perimeter

fences on the west side of the property, ending up down by the creek. From there he had a great view of the rear of the house and the back deck that was currently being redone. Several contractors were working on the place, and he waved to a couple when they spotted him.

By the time he was finished with the fences, it was past four o'clock. He headed for the office in the stables and did paperwork for an hour and then made his way to the bunkhouse to shower and change. Since Cassidy was staying for the weekend, he'd planned on bunking with the ranch hands for a couple of days, giving up his room in the cottage to his sister. He'd been staying with his mom for the last few weeks while the upstairs rooms in the main house were painted and the new flooring went down. Their mother had turned the third bedroom in the cottage into a craft room a couple of years earlier, and he wasn't about to let his baby sister sleep on the couch.

He showered and dressed, dismissing the idea of a suit and settling on dark jeans, a white shirt and a jacket. Suits and ties were not his thing. Sure, Valene was a sophisticated and educated woman, but Jake wasn't about to become someone he wasn't to impress her. He was a rancher, a cowboy, more at home in his Stetson and denim than hand-tailored suits. He kept the suits for business and the denim for pleasure.

And a date with Valene Fortunado was definitely about pleasure.

For two long days he'd been thinking about her, remembering her lovely brown eyes and the perfectly shaped mouth he was hopeful he'd get to kiss at some point.

He drove the Sierra, despite some misgivings, and had to park down the street from the restaurant because the vehicle was so big. Toscano's was a nice place, well regarded and hard to get a reservation at. But he'd been there a lot, with Patrice when they were married and many times for business lunches and for dinner. The owner, Serge, knew him, since the Double Rock supplied their beef, and he'd been happy to make a reservation for Jake.

Jake lingered by the door a few minutes to seven and felt relief pitch in his chest when he saw Valene's familiar-looking Lexus pull into a newly vacant parking space down the block. He met her by the driver's side and closed the door once she got out.

"Evening," he said and held out his hand.

Her fingers curled around his and she met his gaze. It was dark, and a chilly February night, but he felt the connection between them instantly. She wore a long coat, and her beautiful hair was down and framed her face. She was, he thought, as lovely as he remembered. Attraction skittered down his spine, and he experienced an unusual shortness of breath. It had been a long time since he had been so aware of a woman. Too long. And he liked the sensation that being around her evoked. It made him feel as though he was alive, and not the version of himself he'd allowed to take the lead since Patrice had left.

"Hello, Jake, it's nice to see you again."

"Likewise, Valene."

She smiled and withdrew her hand. "You can call me Val."

"I kinda like Valene," he admitted and waited until she'd moved onto the sidewalk before discreetly placing a hand beneath her elbow and ushering her toward the restaurant. "Is that okay?"

She smiled. "Only my dad calls me Valene. And Glammy."

"Glammy?"

She nodded and suddenly looked a little sad. "She was my grandmother. When we were kids, my sister Schuyler had a lisp and couldn't say Grammy...so the word Glammy sort of stuck. She died last year."

"I'm sorry."

"Thank you. She was a wonderful woman. One of a kind. I miss her a lot. How did you manage to get a table?" she asked as they reached the door, changing the subject. "Did you bribe the maître d'?"

He smiled and led her inside, speaking close to her ear. "Something like that."

Once they were inside, she took off her coat to reveal a stunning black-and-white dress that was modest but enhanced her lovely curves. It took about ten seconds for them to be seated and for Serge to seek Jake out. The owner, a Sicilian in his late sixties, greeted him with a friendly handshake.

"So good to see you again, Jake. It's been too long. I saved the best table for you."

Jake could only agree and figured the restaurateur had probably shuffled reservations around to give them the table situated between the small front window and the bar that was away from other diners and offered plenty of privacy.

"Thank you, Serge," he said and then introduced Valene.

The rakish Sicilian grasped Valene's hand and kissed her knuckles. "A pleasure, lovely lady. I have seen you here before, yes?"

She nodded and briefly met Jake's gaze. "Yes, mostly for business lunches. However," she said and smiled warmly, "I have never sat at the *best* table before."

The older man gave a flirtatious laugh. "Ha...nothing is too good for my friend Jake. I shall leave you the wine list and come back soon."

Once Serge left, Valene stared at Jake, brows up questioningly. "So…how?"

"How what?"

"How did you get to be on a first-name basis with the owner of one of the most popular restaurants in the city?"

Jake perused the wine list for a second and then met her inquiring gaze. "I told you I work on a ranch. It supplies the beef for the restaurant. Serge is simply a satisfied customer. Good beef equals the good table."

Her mouth curled at the edges. "You're full of surprises."

Yeah, he thought, to a woman like Valene Fortunado, it would seem like that.

And then he wondered how she'd react if he told her that the beef the Double Rock Ranch supplied to the restaurant actually belonged to him. Because everything on the ranch—the house, the stables, the cattle, the horses—was his, and had been since he'd bought the place eight years earlier.

# Chapter Three

*Yes...he is as gorgeous as I remember.*

Valene couldn't think of anything else as she watched him look over the wine list. She wasn't sure she'd ever seen eyes his color before. They were an old movie-star blue—deep and glittering and framed by the most unfairly long lashes she'd ever seen on a man. And he smelled so good—not some fancy and expensively over-powering and cloying cologne, but a woodsy, totally masculine scent that was wreaking havoc on her dormant libido.

*Sex...*

How long had it been since she'd thought about sex in any real terms? A long time. Even when she was with Hugh, their relationship had been so lukewarm she rarely gave intimacy a thought. But right now, sitting opposite Jake, admiring his broad shoulders and bedroom eyes, she was suddenly thinking about it. Big-time.

"Do you have a wine preference?" he asked, looking at her over the list.

She shrugged lightly. "I prefer white."

He nodded, and within seconds Serge returned and Jake ordered a vintage from the Mendoza Winery. She wondered if he knew of her connection with the family and then figured it didn't matter. He could easily find out her background by going online. She had several social media accounts and often posted frivolous things about food and clothes and the latest pair of must-have shoes she'd purchased. It certainly wouldn't be difficult to trace her family tree and figure out she came from the Fortune family. A very rich family. Maddie's warning suddenly pealed inside her head. *Don't go too fast. Don't trust too easily.*

A waitress arrived and handed them a couple of menus. Valene was looking over the selection when he spoke.

"Everything okay, Valene?"

She looked up and nodded. "Fine. So, what's good here?"

"The beef," he replied and grinned. "Although I may be a little biased."

Valene chose the ravioli and pursed her lips. "I shall take you to task if it's inferior to my palate."

He chuckled at her playful banter. "I look forward to it."

The waitress returned with the wine and to take their order, and once they were alone, Valene spoke again. "So, Jake, have you ever had your heart broken?"

His gaze narrowed fractionally. "Yes. You?"

"Sort of."

He gave her a quizzical look. "Sort of?"

She shrugged. "Not broken…just cracked a little. It

turned out my first boyfriend, Diego, was more interested in courting my father than me."

He sat back. "Well, I can assure you that your father isn't my type."

Valene laughed. He had a lovely sense of humor and she was discovering that she liked that quality very much. "I'll have you know that my dad is very charming."

He chuckled. "I'll take your word for it."

"And he's a good judge of character," she added and sipped her wine. "He saw through Diego long before I did."

"It's good he's there to watch out for you."

"Or smother me," she said and sighed. "My parents can be a little...overprotective."

"You're their youngest child, correct?" he asked.

"Yes."

"Natural then," he said quietly, "that they would want to protect you from jerks and gold diggers."

"I suppose," she said and sighed. "And I shouldn't complain about being loved so much, I know. Tell me about your parents."

He shrugged loosely. "Not much to tell. My parents had a happy marriage. My mom never found anyone else after my father died."

"He was the love of her life?" Val suggested, thinking how wonderful it would be to feel such devotion for someone.

"I guess he was. She works three days a week at the local elementary school and has a small circle of friends. She's happy enough, I suppose. What about your mom?" he asked, turning the conversation back to her.

"My mother's name is Barbara. She and my dad love

one another like crazy. She works in a charity organization that helps women and children. I've always envied the way she can do that."

"Do what?" he inquired.

Val pressed her lips together for a moment. "Help people unselfishly. Without an agenda. She was never overly ambitious for a career—I guess my dad made up for that. But she always seems to be the best version of herself. Maybe doing things for other people makes a person their authentic best."

"I'm sure it does," Jake said evenly. "But I think when we're young, most of us are wrapped up in ourselves. It's not a character flaw...just part of growing up. Don't be too hard on yourself, Valene, I'm sure you do more for others than you realize."

Val stared at him. There was something about the rich timbre of his voice that soothed her. It also occurred to her that he wasn't the roughneck that men who worked the land were often assumed to be.

"You know, you're very...nice," she said and drank some wine. "You said you'd had your heart broken. Will you tell me about it?"

His gaze didn't waver. "There's not much to tell. We went to high school together but weren't in the same crowd. A few years after school we met up again. I loved her. I thought she loved me in return. I was mistaken. We split up."

Val knew there had to be more to the story, but she wasn't going to pry any deeper. They barely knew one another, and she had to respect his privacy. If he wanted to say more about it, he would.

Their meals arrived, and for the following hour, Valene was entertained by Jake's quiet humor and easy conversation. They talked about movies and music; he entertained her with stories about working on the ranch and she did the same with tales of selling houses and dealing with clients. She told him about Maddie and Zach's rivalry and how they fell in love. She talked about Schuyler's whirlwind romance with one of the Mendozas, and he didn't flinch at the mention of anyone's name. If he knew of her connection to the Mendozas or the Fortunes, he had a great poker face.

"Do you enjoy selling houses?" he asked once their plates had been cleared away and she was perusing the dessert menu.

Valene nodded. "Yes. But I travel a lot between Houston and Austin at the moment and the hours can be long. Not as long as yours, I imagine, from sunrise to sunset. But I often work weekends doing open houses or catching up on paperwork. In fact, I'm working tomorrow morning for a few hours."

"What's your favorite part of your job?"

She let out a long breath. "My favorite part is when I show someone a house and they have that 'this is the one' look on their face. The funny thing is, sometimes the house they finally choose is nothing like what they were originally looking for."

"I imagine it's a competitive industry."

"Fiercely," she replied. "Even among people working in the same office. Landing an exclusive listing is so important but often difficult in today's climate. Different agents offer different incentives, but I try not to get wrapped up in the theatrics. I simply match up my listing and prospective buyers the best I can. I mean, buying property is a *considered* purchase, not something people do on a whim. So I get to know the clients as real people. Their history, their family, their dreams. Buying a home is usually the biggest financial commitment someone will make in their lifetime, so I try to make the experience as stress-free as possible."

As she spoke, she longed to feel a surge of passion for what she did. Val liked her job. But she didn't *love* it. She enjoyed working in the family business and strove to be the best she could be. She wasn't as ambitious as Maddie and had little interest in climbing the corporate ladder or being in charge, but the selling, the brokering of deals, the influence she had when she clinched a sale, were challenging and had their rewards.

"I imagine you're very good at getting people to trust you," he remarked, sipping his wine.

Val smiled. "I'd like to think so. And you're right, my clients, both buyers and sellers, put a lot of trust in my hands. So I'm always up front about what the home is worth, how it presents, how it feels. And I believe they appreciate that. Honesty is the key."

His blue eyes glittered brilliantly. "You're right. And since we're on the subject of honesty, I should come clean and tell you that I never order dessert."

Val smiled. "Well, I don't see how this is ever going to work, then."

There was something hypnotic about his gaze, and she couldn't have dragged her eyes away from his even if she'd wanted to. With every look, every word, Valene felt herself getting dragged further into his vortex.

"You can order dessert if you want," he told her. "I hear the cheesecake is good."

She shook her head. "I like my sweets in the morning. There's this place down the road from my office, the Moon Beam Bakery, that does the most amazing blueberry and cream cheese bagels." She moaned her delight.

"So, then, instead of dessert, would you like to go dancing?" he asked.

Oh, God, he danced, too.

The man was perfect. Well, except for every other way that he wasn't. The clothes, although neat and well fitted, were cowboy garb, and of course there was his beat-up truck and the fact he was a ranch hand. But still…he really was incredibly attractive. And smart. And funny.

She nodded. "I would."

"Let's go."

He signaled the waitress, paid the check with a credit card and said a quick farewell to Serge before helping her into her coat. It was chilly outside, and she pulled up the collar around her neck.

"Where are we going?" she asked as they stepped onto the sidewalk.

"Just down the block," he replied. "Are you happy to walk or would you prefer we drive?"

She looked down at her pointy shoes and nodded, thinking that Maddie would blow a gasket if she agreed to get into a car with a man she barely knew. But Valene didn't feel as though she was in any danger with Jake. There was something unwaveringly trustworthy about him. He possessed an aura of enviable integrity, as though it was ingrained within his DNA.

Still, it was such a short distance, she opted to walk.

He grasped her elbow, and even through the woolen coat, she could feel the heat coming off his skin. They walked down the block and then across the road, passing several couples along the way before they reached their destination. She'd been anticipating the fashionable jazz club a few doors down from where they stood. But no. This wasn't the jazz place.

Valene came to an abrupt halt once she heard the music emanating from the very country, very cowboy bar and grill. Of course, she'd passed the place many times, but she had never ventured through the doors of the Red Elk. It was honky-tonk style, with a bar and booth seats and a dance floor toward the back. The place was surprisingly subdued and nowhere near as rowdy and noisy as she'd imagined.

"Ah... I don't really know how to dance to cowboy songs," she said as he ushered her through the doorway and toward a table near the dance floor.

He was smiling. "It's easy," he replied and took her coat, hanging it over the back of a chair. "You just hold on and sway."

Val wasn't convinced. There were a few other couples on the dance floor, and the song changed just as Jake took her hand. Electricity rushed up her arm and she was sure her cheeks spotted with color. And then like magic, she was in his arms. He didn't grope her, didn't do anything other than hold her one hand and then place his other respectfully at her waist. Val reached up and placed her hand on his shoulder and then followed his lead. Of course, he knew what he was doing, and slow dancing clearly came to him as easily as breathing. And the song, a romantic Brett Young number, was exactly the right kind of melody for the mood she was in.

He might be a penniless cowboy, but Jake Brockton knew how to dance. In fact, she was pretty sure he was one of those men who mastered everything he did. And then, of course, she knew he'd be a spectacular kisser. Which was why she looked up, her lips parted slightly as she met his gaze, her eyes clearly betraying her.

Because what she wanted in that moment, more than anything, was his mouth on hers, and she was absolutely certain that he knew it!

\* \* \*

Jake had never in his life wanted to kiss anyone as much as he wanted to kiss Valene Fortunado. Of course, he wouldn't. But he was tempted. It didn't help that her slumberous chocolate-brown eyes were regarding him with seductive invitation. Or that every time she moved, her lovely curves brushed against him.

But it was too soon.

He liked her. He liked her a lot. More than he'd been prepared for when he'd asked her out to dinner. Or suggested they go dancing. But Jake wasn't a hasty man. And even though Valene was delightful and beautiful, he had to show some sense and some self-control.

"See," he said easily, ignoring the way his heart was beating, "you *can* dance to a cowboy song."

She smiled. "I'm just swaying."

"That's all you gotta do, sweetheart."

She smiled again, and the expression reached him way down low. It had been forever since he'd danced with a woman, and he'd forgotten how much he liked it. There was something intoxicating about the way they moved together, and he suspected she felt it, too. Valene was unashamedly honest and the knowledge caused a jolt of shame to slice between his shoulder blades. He needed to come clean, to tell her the truth about himself. But his resistance lingered. He'd already had one woman rip his heart out—he wasn't ready to allow someone else in to do the same. Not just yet.

And he didn't want to ruin the mood or change the dynamic of the evening. He liked that she hadn't made a big deal about his life or occupation. He liked that she hadn't balked outside the honky-tonk and refused to go inside, even though he was sure she'd never set foot in a place like it before. She had gumption and spine and was a strong, independent woman, probably stronger than she knew.

They danced for a while, all slow numbers that suited him and the mood that had developed between them. When the music finally changed to an upbeat number, he took her hand and led her back to their table.

"There are peanut shells on the floor," she remarked when he returned with a drink for them both, light beer for him and bottled water for her.

"It's a cowboy bar," he said and smiled. "Goes with the territory."

"Until someone slips on a shell and then sues the proprietor."

Jake watched her over the rim of his glass. "That wouldn't happen."

"Cowboy code, huh?" she suggested, brows up a little.

"I guess you could call it that. You know, we're not so different from you city folk. We eat, dance, make love…do all the things that the urban dwellers do."

She smiled so sexily he had to shift in his seat. Damn, she was hot.

"That's reassuring," she said quietly and unscrewed the lid off her drink. "We've mastered two out of three."

She was flirting. Unabashedly and provocatively. And Jake was so turned on he could have hauled her into his arms and kissed her without hesitation.

"You're very beautiful, Valene," he said quietly. "Probably more than you know. But I'm not going to rush into anything, okay?"

He felt like a conceited fool for saying it…but he wanted the air clear between them. He didn't want her thinking he was some randy cowboy who simply wanted to get laid and have a little fun. Well, of course he wanted to have fun, and he wanted to get laid...but he also wanted to get to know her. The real Valene Fortunado. Not just the sweet, if somewhat spoiled, party-girl image she had on social media. He'd checked her out, of course, having no choice once he'd told Cassidy who she was. His sister had brought up page after page of highlights from Valene's life and lifestyle and forced Jake to take a look.

He wondered if she'd done the same. He didn't have any personal social media accounts, but if she dug a little deeper, she'd find him easily enough, through articles and interviews and local business affiliations. Valene was a smart and resourceful woman, and it occurred to Jake that she might know exactly who he was, and all about his portfolio and net worth. It unnerved him a little, since she'd bleated on about honesty and transparency. But he didn't think she was underhanded. On the other hand, he hadn't believed Patrice was a liar or a cheat, either—until his life and marriage spectacularly blew up in his face.

"Okay," she said softly. "To be honest, Jake, I'm not the rushing type. I don't jump into bed with every man I meet."

He knew that, of course. There was a sweetness and an innocence about Valene that simmered underneath the surface. And she was young, just twenty-four. Plus, she'd clearly been protected and watched over all her life. He was glad about that, hating to think that she'd ever suffered adversity or real heartbreak.

"Then we agree...slow is best?"

She nodded and smiled in a way that made his insides contract. "Sure...just not *too* slow, okay, Jake?"

Laughter rumbled in his chest, and he spent the next half hour listening to her talk about dancing, the best places to get coffee in town, her beloved dog, and her close relationship with her sisters and how much she missed them since one had moved to Austin to be with the man she loved, and the other had recently married and commuted between Houston and Austin.

"Maddie and Zach are the perfect couple," she said. "He gets her need to be in charge of everything and everyone, and even though he's as business focused as she is, he has a good sense of fun. And Carlo and Schuyler are perfect for one another, too. He knows how to deal with her craziness. All my siblings are either married or engaged now...well, except for Connor. I think he's determined to *never* fall in love."

"What about you?" he asked, knowing her answer even before she replied. But caution told him that Valene Fortunado might be in love with the idea of being in love.

"Of course I want to be in love," she replied. "But I don't want it to be too distracting. With everything that's going on with the family business, I need to stay focused."

"Is something wrong with your business?" he asked, his gaze narrowing.

She shrugged, looking as though she'd said too much. "Nothing we can't handle."

"Big business can be tough."

She nodded. "But I like the challenge. And Maddie is giving me more opportunity to shine, which is great. In fact, she and Zach have recently let me take the lead on signing a really important client. Which we need."

Jake backed off, but he made a mental note to do a little investigating. From all accounts, the Fortunado family was wealthy and successful. If that was a facade, he figured he needed to know before he got in any deeper with Valene.

"You father is a self-made man, I presume?" he asked quietly.

She shrugged. "Kind of. He was lucky enough to have had a lottery win some years ago. He invested wisely, made a few good decisions and started the real estate business. The business grew, and we now have offices in San Antonio and Austin as well as Houston."

It occurred to Jake that Kenneth Fortunado was much like himself. Jake had invested the sum he'd inherited from his father's life insurance, plus the money he'd earned working at the ranch and also packing shelves at Mason's Minimart just outside Fulshear. Five years later he had enough to make an offer when the ranch came up for sale. A few years and some sound business decisions later, including his investment in the lucrative Wagyu beef market, and he owned the ranch outright and had more money in the bank than he could ever spend.

"You admire him a lot?"

She nodded. "I admire people who make their dreams come true. My dad did that and created a legacy that will continue to grow. My sister Maddie is now CEO alongside her husband, so the business is in good hands."

"And what are your ambitions?"

"To be the best I can be," she replied. "At whatever I do. When I graduated college, I went directly into the business and haven't regretted it. I enjoy the work and get to spend my days helping people find the home of their dreams. It's a win-win."

Jake realized he could easily get hooked on her passion for life. She was definitely a glass-half-full kind of girl. He liked that about her. The truth was, he liked everything about her.

They stayed for a little while longer, but by ten she

said she'd had enough. Jake helped her into her coat and then walked her from the bar and back down the street. Once they reached her car, she fished inside her small bag for her keys and unlocked the vehicle.

"Well, thank you for a lovely evening," she said and held out her hand.

He stared down into her face, watching as her mouth parted slightly and his own mouth tingled in response. She was eminently kissable. But he wasn't about to have his first kiss with Valene Fortunado in the middle of a busy street with people walking past.

He took her hand and enclosed his fingers around hers. "Good night, Valene. I'll call you."

"Are you sure?" she asked quietly, almost nervously.

"Positive."

She nodded fractionally. "Okay, see you soon."

As she stepped into the car and drove off down the street, Jake remained on the sidewalk, hands on his hips, staring after the fading taillights. And he knew one thing. He fully intended on seeing Valene again.

And the sooner, the better.

## Chapter Four

Two dates. Two really enjoyable interactions. Good company. Dancing. And not one kiss.

So maybe Jake wasn't interested in her in that way. Perhaps he wasn't attracted to her and had put her in the friend zone. Maybe she had misread the connection they appeared to have. It wouldn't be the first time she'd been misled by a man's intentions, after all.

When Val arrived home, Bruce greeted her with slobbery enthusiasm and bounded around her feet. Her ground-floor condo had a small garden and Bruce had a doggy door to come and go, but he mostly spent his days curled up on the couch or sprawled in the middle of her bed. Perhaps it was just as well she wasn't sharing the sheets with anyone, she thought and laughed to herself. It would certainly put Bruce's nose out of joint if she did.

She started humming the Brett Young tune as she

slipped off her dress and shoes and put on her pajamas. She cleaned off her makeup, brushed her teeth, slathered on hand cream and sat on the edge of her bed, thinking, wondering.

Okay…so Jake didn't find her particularly attractive, that had to be it. And he was too polite to say anything. Although he had said she was pretty *and* called her "sweetheart." And he didn't look at her as though she was in the friends-only category. Val was certain she'd seen attraction and awareness in his eyes. He had said he wanted to go slow. And she'd agreed.

*Then why am I making a big deal out of him not kissing me good-night?*

Because she'd wanted to kiss him, that's why.

She'd wanted to feel his arms around her and his mouth on hers. She was achingly attracted to him, even though she knew he was nothing like the kind of man she'd convinced herself was right for her. She'd wanted to find someone as driven and ambitious as Zach, or as charming and sophisticated as Carlo. Someone from her world.

Perhaps Jake understood that and that's why he'd kept the evening casual. And she liked him, so maybe friendship might be enough. Or perhaps he was seeing someone else at the same time, some other woman, or women, that he met on the dating app. Of course, he could do what he wanted. Still, the notion wounded her just a little.

Val was still mulling over her predicament the following morning as she sat at her desk, half-heartedly working on a proposal for one of her clients. She hated that she was preoccupied and had tried to pull herself together since she'd arrived at the office an hour earlier. But she was in a funk. And it was all Jake Brockton's fault. That, and a disappointing email she'd received from her sister that she kept reading over and over.

"Got a minute?" said a voice, and then Maddie stuck her head around the door.

Val look up from her computer, saw that Maddie had a furrow between her brows and nodded. "Sure."

"Did you get the email I sent you?" she asked. "About the Waterson estate?"

The owner of the estate was now deceased, and every agent in Houston had been vying for the opportunity to sell the mansion and the three commercial properties the owner had left to his only grandson, a young man who resided in California and had no interest in living on the estate. Val had spent weeks talking with the man, and a week earlier he'd committed to listing the places with Fortunado Real Estate. At least, that's what she'd believed…until Maddie had forwarded his email, informing the office that he'd decided to go with someone else, a firm that was their biggest competitor. A firm she believed had no scruples and that certainly didn't offer the service her family's company did. It was a big blow. Maddie and Zach had entrusted the client to her, and she felt as though she had seriously let them down.

"I don't know what happened." She shrugged. "It was all going well. I have the contracts almost ready to go. I've booked photographers and stylists for a shoot. I just…" Her words trailed off and she shrugged again. "I can't explain it."

"Are you sure?"

Val frowned. "What does that mean?"

"You've been distracted this week," Maddie said bluntly. "You've had that cowboy on your mind for days."

Val tried to keep a lid on her temper. She loved Maddie, and her sister wasn't being deliberately mean, but she had a responsibility to the firm, and Val understood she needed to ask the tough questions.

"This has nothing to do with Jake," she defended quietly.

"It's the second deal you've had go sour this week," Maddie reminded her, and Val quickly recalled the other owner who'd pulled a listing. "And the only thing that is different from last week to this one is your new boyfriend."

"He's not my boyfriend," Val stated firmly. "We've been on two dates. If you must know, he hasn't even tried to kiss me. So, I'm not distracted. I'm no different than I was last week or last month. And I can't explain why I've lost two listings this week. I'm so sorry about the Waterson deal. I know it would have meant a lot to the firm. I can call him and—"

"No point." Maddie waved a hand. "Zach put through a call early this morning, and it doesn't look as though the owner will change his mind. He said he was going with a firm who had a more *experienced* team. If Zach couldn't talk this around, no one can. We've lost this one, Val. I'd like you to start running things by Zach again, like you used to."

Val's insides hurt. Her sister looked so disappointed in her and she had no words of explanation to offer, no excuses or justification for what had happened. She'd bombed, big-time. And she didn't blame Maddie for being annoyed. But it hurt. Her big sister's approval had always been important to her, especially since Maddie had become her boss.

She waited until her sister left her office and then let out a long and painful sigh, resting her face in her hands. What a mess. Missing out on the Waterson deal was a huge loss. The commission and kudos would have been so good for the business. And for her. Now she felt like a monumental failure.

"Everything okay, Valene?"

She knew that voice. It had haunted her dreams the night before. Val looked up and spotted Jake standing in the doorway, a small brown bag in one hand, a take-out coffee cup in the other. She hadn't expected to see him, and it was a delightful surprise.

Her breath shuddered. "What are you doing here?" she asked and straightened immediately.

He took a few steps into the room. "I had a few things to do in town." He dropped the brown bag on her desk. "Blueberry cream cheese bagel. And a low-fat, single-shot, extra cinnamon vanilla soy latte," he said and placed the coffee by the computer. "From your favorite bakery."

Val let out a long sigh, touched that he'd remembered. "Thank you. How did you know how to find me?"

"The receptionist at the front desk," he supplied. "And last night you said you were working for a few hours this morning. I knew the location of the office and took my chances, hoping you'd still be here. But next time I can call first if you prefer."

Val didn't prefer. She was very happy to see him. She got to her feet, wrapping her fingers around the coffee, and took a sip. "You can stop by anytime you like. And thank you. I needed to see a friendly face."

His gaze narrowed. "Bad morning?"

"The worst." She briefly explained about losing the account and then backpedaled a little because she knew she probably shouldn't be talking about the family business to a man she hardly knew. "Sorry... I didn't mean to vent."

He smiled. "No problem. Actually, the reason I'm here is I was wondering if you were free tomorrow?"

Tomorrow. Sunday. If she had any sense, she would tell him she had work to do, reports to catch up on, plans to make about how to reel the Waterson deal back in. But it *was* Sunday. And all work and no play was no way to function.

Plus, he looked so damned appealing in his jeans, beige chambray shirt and sheepskin-lined jacket. And the fact that he'd brought her the coffee and bagel she liked…well, she couldn't be blamed for being a little smitten with him.

"Free for what?" she asked him.

His gaze narrowed a fraction, and she wondered if he'd picked up in the flirtation in her reply. He smiled then, and she saw that he had. "I thought we could spend the morning together."

It sounded like a great idea, and she was just about to say so when her sister Schuyler walked into the office. One thing about her crazy sibling, she had impeccable timing. Not.

"Oh, sorry," Schuyler gushed and quickly gave the man standing by her desk a deliberate once-over. "Didn't mean to interrupt."

Val raised a brow. "This is Jake. This is my sister Schuyler. She lives in Austin and is leaving soon, right?"

Schuyler chuckled and shook Jake's hand. "Tomorrow morning. Carlo is back from his business thing tomorrow and I want to be home when he returns. We're still newlyweds," she told Jake with a wicked grin, and Val envied her sister's ability to sound so effortlessly flirtatious. "I miss him madly. And my baby sister is right. But I just wanted to remind you about dinner tonight with me and Maddie. Unless," she added and gave Jake another long and deliberate perusal, "you have other plans."

Val waved her hand. "I'll see you tonight. At seven. *Goodbye*, Schuyler." Once her sister left, Val let out a long sigh. "Sorry about that. My sister is—"

"Probably as annoying as mine," he said, cutting her off and smiling. "But that's why we love 'em, right?"

Val laughed. "Absolutely. I adore Schuyler. She's like this force of nature and has incredibly positive energy."

"You're not so different," he remarked.

Val's insides crunched up. How often had she envied her sister's ability to remain a free spirit but stay true to who she was? Like she'd also sought to be more like Maddie—focused and completely on track with her life.

Her cell beeped with a text, and she excused herself for a moment as she was expecting a message from a client who had a showing on Monday. But it wasn't a client. It was Schuyler.

OMG! He's so hot. Who cares if he doesn't have two pennies to rub together. Go for it, kid!

Val's skin burned. Trust her sister to say exactly what she was thinking.

"Sorry," she said and put down the phone. "So, you were saying something about tomorrow?"

He nodded. "I'll pick you up around nine, unless that's too early?"

"No," she replied. "I'm a morning person. I rarely sleep past six."

"Something else we have in common."

She liked that notion. "I imagine your work demands

an early start. I usually hit the treadmill for half an hour in the morning. Or hang out with my dog, Bruce."

He nodded. "You told me about him last night. I'm glad you like dogs."

"I like cats, too," she admitted. "But it's more challenging to take a cat for a walk in the park."

He laughed, and the lovely sound filled her with a silly kind of happiness. She liked that she could make him laugh.

"Okay, I'll pick you up at nine, as long as you text me your address. Or I can meet you somewhere in town."

Val thought about it for a moment. She could take the safe road and meet him on neutral ground. But nothing about Jake felt threatening to her. "You can pick me up. I'll text you."

He half smiled. "Okay. Oh, and wear something comfortable."

Once he left, Val got her mind back to work. She left around lunchtime, grabbing a few groceries on the way home. She did some much-needed housework in the afternoon and arrived at Maddie and Zach's home just before seven. They also rented a place in Austin, but she knew her sister enjoyed spending weekends in their hometown. Schuyler was already there, legs dangling over the edge of a counter stool in the kitchen, sipping on a margarita.

Val declined the alcohol, preferring club soda, which Zach poured for her just before he announced he had work to do and would be tucked away in his office well out of the way of their girl time.

"So, I was just telling Maddie how sexy your cowboy is," Schuyler said with a wicked chuckle.

"Please don't," Val protested. "She already thinks I'm distracted from my work."

"There's more to life than work, ladies," Schuyler said and gave them both a playful grin. "There's fun and friendship and…sex. Which Maddie here knows all about since she hooked up with our gorgeous brother-in-law. And I absolutely forbid us to talk about work tonight."

Val met Maddie's gaze. "I'm sorry about the Waterson deal," she said, ignoring Schuyler's protest.

"I know," Maddie said gently. "And I'm not angry. *Or* disappointed. I do want you to be happy, Val. I'm not saying you shouldn't have a social life…you absolutely should. Just tread carefully. You don't know anything about this guy."

*I know he's handsome and charming and considerate and nice…and sexy.*

"Okay," she said quietly, knowing Maddie wouldn't give up her lioness mode. "I'll tread carefully. I promise."

"He really is ridiculously good-looking," Schuyler sighed. "So, where's he taking you tomorrow?"

Val shrugged. "I have no idea. He simply said to wear something casual."

Maddie frowned. "Like sweats kind of casual, or jeans and a Calvin Klein T-shirt casual?"

"I was thinking I'd go for something in between," she replied and grinned.

"Maybe he's taking you horseback riding?" Schuyler suggested. "Isn't that what cowboys do in their spare time? A nice, long, romantic ride on that ranch he works at. You know, if you tell me his last name, I will happily snoop on the internet and find out everything there is to know about him."

"No," Val said firmly. "I don't want to start out that way."

"Safety first," Maddie said wryly. "You should be more cautious. What if he takes you to some isolated spot and—"

"Oh, for heaven's sake, he's not an ax murderer," Val responded, her irritation rising. "And stop smothering me."

"Mom and Dad asked me to look out for you while they were away," Maddie said matter-of-factly. "If they knew you were seeing someone you met off a dating app, they would blow a gasket."

"Um, wasn't it your idea?" Val reminded her sister.

Maddie hooked a thumb in Schuyler's direction. "Her idea. I didn't think you'd actually go through with it."

"We can't all meet the man of our dreams in the workplace," she said and smiled sweetly. "And leave Mom and Dad out of this. They're not back from their trip for another couple of weeks."

"Plenty of time for you to get into trouble."

"Ha. I'm not interested in trouble."

"But you are interested in this cowboy," Maddie said flatly. "Even though he is nothing like the kind of man you said you wanted."

Val shrugged. "So…maybe I've changed my mind about what I want."

"He could be a player, or some kind of heartless philanderer."

Val laughed so loud she snorted. "Seriously, have you been reading Brontë and Austen again?" She looked toward Schuyler and raised both hands. "Do something, will you?"

Schuyler grinned. "She doesn't listen to me."

"I just think you need to be careful," Maddie said, still serious. "With everything that has been going on, we can't be too careful."

*Everything...*

Val knew what she meant. Losing contracts at Fortunado Real Estate was one thing, but there had been other signs that things were awry. Like the fact that Robinson Tech had recently been hacked and an attempt had been made to sabotage their operating systems. Or worse—the fire at the Robinson estate and the even more disturbing fact that their cousin Ben Fortune Robinson had almost been killed. Yes, things had been happening. Unexplained things. But Val had no reason to suspect that her meeting Jake was in any way connected to these events. Val stared at one sister, then the other, thinking that neither truly understood how she felt. Of course, she took stock of Maddie's warnings, but she was also keen to adopt Schuyler's philosophy about embracing life.

And she figured that hanging out with Jake Brockton was doing exactly that.

Jake whistled under his breath when he pulled up outside Val's luxury condo in the River Oaks district. It was a high-end spot, one of the best in the city, and he let the engine run on the Ranger but put it in Park and got out, waiting for her by the security gate. The complex was one of many that had risen in the city in the past decade and was designed to be hurricane-proof. There was a small pond and several bench seats and an abundance of trees and gardens behind the tall fence.

Val appeared a couple of minutes later, in jeans, a bright red shirt, knee-high boots and a fitted dark jacket. Her hair was down and she smiled as she greeted him, allowing the gate to lock automatically behind her. She looked beautiful and vibrant and so enticing he could barely stop himself from staring at her like an enraptured fool.

"Hi there," she said cheerfully.

"Good morning. Nice spot," he said and opened the passenger door.

She smiled, and his insides flipped over. "When I moved out, my dad insisted I relocate to a gated community for security reasons. This place came up, and he pitched in so I could afford it."

Jake's brows rose. "Pitched in?"

She shrugged. "Okay...so he pitched in the whole amount. But I fully intend to pay him back one day. And he got the place for a song because it was part of an ugly divorce."

Jake's back straightened. He knew all about bitter divorces. He'd had the worst breakup of the century. And Val's flippant reaction to something so emotionally devastating stung a little. But she was young. Probably too young for him. And probably, as he had suspected from their first meeting, more in love with the idea of being in love than wanting a real and messy relationship.

It should have registered on his radar.

But being around her, sharing molecules of space with her, was inexplicably soothing. Which was at odds with the blistering attraction he felt for her. It was a heady mix of lust and like, something he couldn't remember experiencing before. And for a man who only a few days ago had firmly denied he'd get seriously involved with anyone, he knew he was stupidly back-pedaling.

"Let's go."

She got in the truck, dropped her tote between her feet and buckled up. "I think this rig is older than me," she said when he got in.

Jake half smiled. "A second-class drive is better than a first-class walk."

She laughed loudly and fiddled with the magnetic religious medal attached to the center console. "That's so true. What's this?"

"Saint Eligius," he replied.

"Who?"

"Patron saint of horses."

She looked impressed. "Are you an expert on the saints?"

"Not all," he replied and grinned. "I'm not sure I'm an expert on anything. What about you? Do you have a particular talent?"

She looked directly ahead. "Well, I recently learned how to dance cowboy style. And I know how to order a fancy cup of coffee."

"That's quite a skill."

"I know," she said and laughed. "I am envied in several states."

God, she was intoxicating. He couldn't recall ever being as aware of a woman as he was of Valene. The perfume she wore, something flowery and subtle, touched his senses and he inhaled discreetly, allowing the memory of the fragrance to linger in his brain like a rush of endorphins.

Jake pulled away from the sidewalk and turned the vehicle south, heading out of the city.

"Where are we going?" she asked. "I need to let my sister know, otherwise she's going to worry all morning. Maddie can be overprotective."

He quickly told her the address. "Understandable. I'd probably demand Cassidy do exactly the same thing. Older siblings tend to think they have to do all of the protecting. But I promise you, Valene, I'm not a threat to you."

"I know that," she said and sent a quick text. "Can I ask you something?"

His chest tightened, thinking perhaps she'd discovered he wasn't exactly who he'd said he was. "Of course."

She took a sharp breath. "Are you…are you doing this with anyone else?"

"This?" he echoed and then quickly realized her meaning. "I don't—"

"I know," she said and waved a dismissive hand. "You don't have to explain yourself to me. I mean, this is only our third date and I have no claim on your time. I mean, this is just a friends thing for you, right? And it's not like you're attracted to me or anything, and so I understand if you want to see other—"

"Valene," Jake said quietly, cutting off her impassioned speech, his gaze directly on the road ahead. "I'm not seeing anyone else, I assure you. And I am definitely attracted to you."

He heard her soft sigh. "Oh, okay."

"Are you always so nervous around men?"

Her chuckle was whisper quiet. "Actually, I think this is the least nervous I've ever been."

He smiled and relaxed a little. Despite her bravado, despite her enthusiasm for life and her delightful sense of humor, there was an earnestness about Valene that he found incredibly alluring. Sure, she was probably a little spoiled and definitely overprotected, but there was nothing deliberately arrogant or condescending about her. Even her trite remark about the truck had been more humorous than insulting. And despite what she knew about him—or rather, didn't know—she appeared to genuinely want to pursue something between them.

"I won't ever deliberately hurt you, Valene, not physically or emotionally. I've been there, and it's a dark place."

Her head turned. "You mean your last relationship?"

He nodded. "Yep. It ended badly."

"If you ever want to talk about it," she said softly, "you can."

Jake shrugged. He'd stopped talking about Patrice because the memories of all she had put him through, and all he had lost, made him ache inside. "I know. And thank you. One day, okay?"

"Sure," she replied.

Jake turned the truck left and pulled into a parking lot. "We're here."

She looked around and then swiveled in her seat. "An animal shelter?"

He shrugged. "Is it okay?"

"Of course," she replied. "I'm just surprised. My sister was convinced we were going horseback riding."

He smiled, amused that he'd been the topic of conversation with her sisters. "Maybe next time."

She nodded, and he noticed that her cheeks were flushed. "So, what are we doing here? Are you looking for a puppy?"

"I volunteer here sometimes," he said, feeling faintly embarrassed by her sudden and intense scrutiny.

She smiled, nodded and quickly grabbed her tote and got out of the truck.

Jake watched her as she strolled up the path leading to the front door, actually admiring the way she didn't hang back and wait for him. Valene clearly wasn't afraid of new things.

He caught up with her and they walked through to the reception desk side by side. He'd been volunteering at the Sweet Pines Shelter since he was a teenager. It was where he'd found his first canine companion, Rudy. The old dog was long gone now, but he had fond memories of the day he'd brought him home, sitting alongside him and his dad in the same old truck that was now parked outside.

"Good morning, sunshine!"

The familiar singsong voice that greeted them belonged to Florence, a volunteer who had been working at the shelter for close to twenty years. The sixtysomething-year-old woman was the heart and soul of the shelter. Jake introduced her to Valene, and Florence was clearly intrigued.

"A girl?" Florence queried and chuckled.

"I brought supplies, too," he replied and tugged a little at his collar. "I'll drive the truck around the back and unload." He looked toward Valene. "Be back in a sec."

Jake grinned and walked back through the front door, thinking that hanging out with Valene was just about the best way to spend a Sunday morning. Unless he was spending it in her bed.

Which he figured wasn't too far off in his future, either.

# Chapter Five

"He's such a sweet boy."

Valene stared at the older woman and smiled. *Boy?* Jake was about as far from a boy as you could get. But it was quite adorable that Florence thought so.

"I take it you've known Jake for a long time?" Valene asked.

She nodded. "Oh, yes, since he was a teenager. When he was young, he used to come and help tend to the animals, particularly the ones that had been abused or neglected. Of course he's so busy these days he doesn't have time to do that, but he's here without fail once a month, donating food and bedding and cat litter. And he always helps out by fixing things around the place when he's here," she added, clearly adoring him. "If I'd had a son, I'd want him to be just like Jake. Not that I'd trade my daughters for a son, but you know what I mean. There was a time when I hoped my youngest might be a good match for him," Florence said and shrugged. "But she married a house painter and moved to New Mexico. I was starting to think Jake would never find someone again after the way he got his heart broke. But," she said and gently patted Valene's arm, "I'm glad to see that he has."

"Oh, we're not—"

"He's a special man," Florence said, cutting her off gently. "But my guess is you already know that."

Valene didn't disagree and didn't try to correct the other woman again. At that moment Jake came striding down the corridor from the rear of the building and rejoined them.

"Do you mind if I whisk Valene away now?"

Florence laughed. "Of course not. And I told Digby that you were going to be here today, so he's been running around in his pen all morning."

Jake laughed and gently grasped Valene's elbow. "Catch you later, Florrie."

Florrie? Digby? Valene chuckled to herself as they walked down the corridor. The sound of dogs barking hit her ears the moment they reached the rear door. The shelter was obviously well run, clean and tidy. The dog pens were spacious and each one had a bed. And sadly, every single one had a resident locked inside.

"Jake?"

He was a couple of steps ahead, but quickly turned. "Yes?"

"Who's Digby?"

He pointed to a pen a couple of doors down and she followed him, to come face-to-face with the most adorable little dog. A mixed breed, perhaps spaniel and collie, with white and brown patches and the fluffiest feet she'd ever seen.

"This is Digby." At the sound of Jake's voice, the pooch started yelping excitedly, and when Jake opened the pen, the dog raced out and jumped around his legs. "He's a long-term resident," he explained and bent down to pick up the dog. "And an old-timer. His owner passed away and there were no relatives or neighbors to take him in. So he ended up here and has called this place home for nine months."

Valene's heart lurched. The poor little thing. And he clearly adored Jake.

"You should adopt him."

"I'd love to," he replied. "But this little guy likes to run off, and I'm afraid he might end up in all kinds of trouble if he tangled with some of the local wildlife around the ranch. Plus I'm not sure how Sheba would take to sharing the bottom of my bed." He ushered the dog back into the pen and looked at her. "I gotta unload the truck. Feel like keeping me company?"

She nodded enthusiastically. "I can help."

They passed a couple of volunteers, a pair of twenty-something women who knew Jake by name and made goo-goo eyes at him when he greeted them. It was enough to straighten Valene's spine and make her stare daggers. Thankfully, Jake seemed perfectly immune to their flirtation, intent on unloading his truck. Once they were outside, he pulled the tarp off the truck bed and Valene saw a huge pile of supplies.

"You donate this every month?" she queried, both startled and impressed by his generosity.

"More or less. Local funding doesn't quite cover the costs of the place. And it's just a small way of helping out."

"Small way?" she echoed as she stared at the supplies. "This must have cost you hundreds."

He shrugged, looking acutely embarrassed, and quickly began unloading the large bags of dog food. Valene helped with the smaller bags, stacking them in the shed, and they finished the task within ten minutes.

"What now?" she asked.

"I've got a couple of chores to do," he replied. "A few maintenance things. You can be my apprentice or hang out with Florence."

"I'd like to hang out with you," she said and smiled. "If that's okay."

"Perfectly," he said and the warmth in his voice made Valene's body heat from head to toe.

It was, she decided a couple of hours later, the most unorthodox date she had ever been on. And yet, it was surprisingly the most fun. Of course she knew that Jake was good company, but away from the standard date scenario, he was even more relaxed and funny and engaging.

*And perfect boyfriend material.*

It took Valene about two seconds to snap herself out of such thoughts, even if traces of the idea lingered around the edges of her mind for most of the morning.

By midday, while Jake was repairing one of the large dog runs with one of the other volunteers, who she quickly discovered was Florence's husband, Valene ended up back in the reception area, photocopying flyers for an upcoming fund-raiser.

"You're welcome to come and help us," Florence said and grinned. "Jake can bring you. It's a really fun day, and we get to do so many adoptions."

Valene was tempted, particularly since she'd witnessed three adoptions that morning—two dogs and a crazy, one-eyed ginger cat. It was delightful to watch the three separate groups choose a new family member.

She'd couldn't help feeling emotional when she watched the small child hug his new puppy, or the elderly couple who were replacing the cat they'd recently lost.

When Jake was finished with the repairs, he returned to the reception area, two coffee cups in his hands. Florence had left Val in charge of meeting and greeting, and she was having a lovely time talking to potential adopters.

Jake came around the counter and perched himself on the edge of the desk. "Everything okay?"

Valene nodded, watching the way the denim stretched over his thighs and his shirt fit across his broad shoulders. She swallowed hard, feeling the intimacy of the space between them, meeting his gaze and noticing everything about his perfectly handsome face. He had slight stubble across his jaw, as though he hadn't shaved for a day or so, and a tiny scar above his left temple. She wondered how he'd gotten that scar, just like she wondered how she'd managed to capture the attention of such a complex yet stunningly normal man. He was confident and clearly comfortable in his own skin. He didn't brag, didn't gloat, didn't name-drop or go on about his life, his work or any accomplishments. He was funny and self-effacing and had a kind of effortless charm. He was also, she realized, the polar opposite of any other man she had dated.

"I'm glad you brought me here," she said and smiled "It feels good to do something for someone else. I don't get the chance very often."

"The chance?" he queried, his gaze locked with hers.

Val sighed. "Okay, I don't *take* the opportunity. I know I should. My mother does so much for charity, particularly her work with the Fortunado Foundation.

I envy how generous she is with herself. Maybe I'd be a better person if I did more for others. Like you."

"It's not a contest, Valene," he said softly. "And perhaps it's something you could do *with* your mom. After my dad died, I spent a lot of time wishing I'd spent more time with him, made more of an effort, you know. But you can't live in the past, either. If you want to change, then change. But frankly, I think you're a very good person. You're smart and beautiful and funny and great to be around."

Val stared at him, mesmerized by the deepness of his voice and the intensity of his gaze. She wondered, briefly, if she'd ever met a man with bluer eyes, or a stronger jawline, or more innate integrity. And all she could think was no.

They left the shelter shortly after, stopping on the way to grab some lunch. They sat in a small café in the park a few streets away, eating burgers and sharing a side of fries, sitting close together at the tiny table for two. Jake had ordered them sodas and she sipped her beverage in between bites of her food.

"I've had a nice time today," she said quietly. "Thank you."

He smiled. "Anytime."

"So…does that mean you'd like to see me again?"

"Absolutely."

She was delighted to hear it, ignoring the tiny voice in her head telling her that he wasn't what she was looking for. The truth was, Valene had never come close to finding the right man. Until now. Everything about Jake *felt* right. The fact that he was a cowboy in worn denim and drove a twenty-year-old truck somehow didn't bother her one bit. She'd parted ways with Diego because he'd wanted a job, and when that hadn't panned out he'd moved on to the daughter of another moneyed man. But Jake Brockton didn't seem interested in her money or family connections. And she'd broken up with Hugh because there was zero chemistry between them and she didn't want to tie herself to a man she didn't feel any passion for, who simply wanted a suitable wife. But with Jake, her libido was jumping all over the place.

Sure, she didn't know everything about him, but that would change with time. And she wasn't about to start being paranoid, even if her sister believed she was crazy for trusting a man she hardly knew. Maddie had been pining for Zach for years before she summoned the courage to do something about it, and although Valene wanted to settle down and start nesting, she wanted to be in a relationship with someone who cared about her.

"Would you like to meet the man in my life?" she asked suddenly.

His blue eyes widened. "The what?"

Valene smiled. "My dog."

His mouth curled at the edges. "I'd like that very much."

She pushed the plate aside and quickly finished her drink. "Then let's go."

Jake was conscious of how quiet Valene was on the drive to her place. She lived on the ground floor, and as she opened the door to her condo, he heard the rattle of excited feet clamoring over floorboards.

The short but powerful-looking bulldog came rushing down the hall to greet her and turned around in frenzied circles at her feet, making guttural sounds low in his throat. He had an underbite and slobber oozing from one side of his mouth.

"Isn't he adorable?" she said and crouched down to pet the animal. "My beautiful boy."

Jake laughed. He had several working dogs on the ranch, but Sheba was his pet. She was dainty and fluffy and considered herself quite the princess. Quite the opposite of the very unattractive dog who suddenly registered Jake's presence and started barking like crazy. He woofed and growled and was clearly standing his ground and making it known who was the boss around the place.

"Beautiful?" he queried, ignoring the growling.

"He is to me," she said and stood. "Bruce, this is Jake and he's a friend of mine, and he's very nice and I like him a lot, so be a good boy and don't slobber over his jeans or chew his feet off, okay?"

The dog stopped barking, angled his head to the side and let out a loud woof before he briefly rubbed against Jake's ankles, sniffed his boots and, clearly making the decision that Jake was not a threat to his beloved owner, trotted off down the hallway.

"You passed the test." Valene grinned.

"There was a test?"

She laughed. "Well, of course. Bruce always gets to meet my friends."

Jake liked that she considered him a friend. However, he certainly didn't want to get stuck in that category. Not when he was so attracted to her. "Well, I'm glad he approves."

She laughed again and invited him to take a tour of the condo. It was large and spacious, with polished wood floors, two bedrooms and bathrooms, its own laundry facility, a huge French provincial–style kitchen, and spacious dining and living room areas. A wall of windows overlooked the yard, and yet the place was surprisingly private. Showcasing her good taste, the furnishings were quality and understated, and it occurred to him that they had that in common, too.

"Would you like coffee?"

Jake turned and discovered she was directly behind him. They were close, barely a foot apart, and the proximity sent his body into high-alert mode. She was looking up, her chin tilted at an alluring angle, her brown eyes warm and eminently welcoming. Jake reached out and touched her hair, threading the silky strands through his fingers.

"Valene," he said softly, the blood simmering in his veins. "Would it be okay if I kissed you now?"

Her eyes darkened, and after a moment she spoke. "Yes."

Jake curled one hand around her nape and drew her closer. Her mouth parted slightly, as though she was thinking, waiting, anticipating his kiss. He bent his head and looked directly into her eyes, feeling the connection between them down to the soles of his feet. He urged her a little closer and she pressed against him. His other arm moved around her and settled on her hip as he bent down and touched her mouth with his own. He gently anchored her head and slowly deepened the kiss. Her lips parted and she sighed against his mouth, driving away all coherent thought as she accepted his tongue into her mouth. The kiss was hot and intense and blisteringly arousing, but Jake wasn't about to ask for anything else. He just kissed her. He didn't move his hands to her rib cage like he longed to do, he didn't stroke the swell of her breasts, he didn't press closer to make his arousal more obvious. He simply enjoyed the taste and feel of her tongue dancing around with his for those few intoxicating moments.

In the end, it was Valene who pulled back, and Jake released her instantly. She took a step backward, her breath coming out sharply, her eyes darkened with a heady kind of desire that shook him to the very core.

And then she spoke.

"I'm not going to have sex with you today," she said quietly and crossed her arms. "If that's what you—"

"It's not," he assured her. "It was a kiss. I've told you that I'm not interested in rushing into this, Valene, and I mean it. I like you, and I'm clearly very attracted to you."

"Actually, up until about two minutes ago I was almost convinced you'd put me into the friend zone. I'm pleased to know you haven't."

He smiled, captivated by her honesty. "I thought the same about you."

She smiled. "I'm not used to being around a man who can show so much restraint."

Jake laughed. "Restraint? It's not that. The truth is, I don't want to screw things up with you. We hardly know each other and we need to spend a lot more time together. And frankly, you don't strike me as a casual-sex kind of woman."

"I'm not," she said flatly. "I've had two relationships and they were both disappointing. I've never had a one-night stand. I've never picked a guy up in a bar. I've never had sex outside of a serious relationship. I'm boring and straitlaced in that way. The most outrageous thing I've ever done in my romantic life is use that dating app."

"Ditto," he said quietly. "And, Valene, you are anything but boring. But I hear you. I've had three serious relationships and the last one ended really badly, so I'm cautious about getting caught up in something too quickly. I like you a lot," he admitted. "And I want to get to know you. I'd like to date you. And kiss you. And yeah," he said, pausing as he took a long breath, "at some point I would like to make love to you. But, for now, let's just get to know one another, okay?"

She looked instantly relieved. And then she regarded him thoughtfully. "Why was your last breakup so bad?"

"It just didn't work out," he replied quickly. "I think I told you how we knew one another in high school and a few years back we reconnected. But it was a mistake. We were too different."

Jake wasn't about to admit that he'd caught Patrice in bed with one of the contractors he'd hired to remodel the ranch house—a renovation she'd insisted on because the house, like him, wasn't good enough for her. Maybe one day he'd tell Valene the real story, but for now she didn't need to know the sordid details.

"I know what you mean," she said and then spent a moment telling him about her last boyfriend and how he was handpicked by her overprotective father. "I guess after the way things went with Diego, I can't blame Dad for smothering me a little."

The reminder that her ex-boyfriend had been after her family's money struck a guilty chord in Jake's gut. He hadn't told Valene the truth about himself because he didn't want his wealth to muddy the waters between them, when the truth was, she'd been on the receiving end of a gold-digging ex and would probably understand. But something held him back from admitting the truth. For one, he'd heard rumors that the Fortunado empire wasn't as rock solid as it had once been. According to his friends and business acquaintances and word on the street, there had been some shady things going on with everyone associated with the Fortune family—including Kenneth Fortunado.

"I thought you were making coffee," he said casually and walked toward the kitchen counter.

She looked relieved by the digression and quickly prepared two cups of coffee. "Cookie?" she asked and held out a small cookie jar.

"Did you bake them?"

She laughed. "Ha, are you serious? I can't cook. I suppose you can?"

Jake smiled. "A little. Enough to get by. Can I ask you a question?"

She nodded. "Sure."

"You're related to the Fortune family, correct?"

Her brows instantly came together. "Yes."

"But you don't talk about it?"

She shrugged. "No," she replied, handing him his coffee. "My dad prefers not to talk about it," she said after a moment. "So, we don't."

"Is there bad blood?"

She let out a sigh and came around the counter, perching herself on the edge of a stool. "More like no blood. My dad didn't know about his family tree until recently. He found out he was Julius Fortune's son and had a few other illegitimate half brothers. It's been kind of messy ever since. My grandmother chose the name Fortunado as a way of enabling my dad to have a link with his family, but he doesn't have any interest in being a part of them."

"Do you?" Jake asked and sipped his coffee.

"I'm not sure," she replied. "I mean, I am *intrigued*, of course. How could I not be? It's the Fortunes. They're legendary in this state, for one reason or another. Plus, my father and Gerald Robinson of Robinson Tech are half brothers, since Gerald Robinson is really Jerome Fortune and Julius's son. The last year has been full of surprises, to say the least. And one of Gerald's daughters is married to a Mendoza and my sister Schuyler is also married to a Mendoza...so the huge disconnect between the families is not as wide as it used to be. It's been difficult for everyone. Particularly since so many strange things have happened."

Jake met her gaze. "What kind of strange things?"

"Robinson Tech was hacked. We've been losing clients at both the Austin and Houston offices, which almost seems less like coincidence and more like sabotage according to my sister and her husband, Zach. And there was a terrible fire at the Robinson estate."

"I heard about that," Jake said. "Makes me kind of pleased that you don't have anything to do with them."

"It's complicated," she said quietly. "I have a crazy family tree."

"Not me," he admitted. "Dull as dishwater. Mom and Dad loved each other. No family skeletons. We're boring and uneventful."

"I envy you," she said on a sigh. "In my family, every day is potentially a disaster waiting to happen. And it doesn't help that my dad won't talk about it, not even to Mom. He used to talk to my grandmother, I guess, but I think he's just over the whole Fortune thing. It's probably why he vacations so much now. I mean, he and Mom did plan on doing a lot of trips once he retired, so they haven't spent much time at home lately. They came back for Maddie's wedding and then took off again."

"You miss them?" Jake suggested.

She nodded, suddenly looking incredibly young. "I do," she admitted. "I guess I'm one of those crazy people who actually like their parents."

"You're not crazy," Jake assured her. "I like my parents, too. In fact, my mother is going to want to meet you at some point in the near future. She thinks I've been in a much better mood this week."

Valene laughed loudly. "I think I like your mom already."

"And of course Cassidy is taking all the credit." He grinned. "My sister is quite the matchmaker."

"Well, you can tell her she does good work," she said quietly. "Speaking of which, I really need to get some work done this afternoon, or Maddie is going to fire me."

Jake didn't believe her. "Of course she won't do that."

"She might." Valene shrugged. "I've lost two listings in the past week, and the company lost several more in the last month. No listing, no sales...it's a vicious circle."

Jake experienced an acute sense of concern. "Do you know why?"

"No," she replied. "I think I've lost my mojo."

"I'm sure you'll get it back."

"I hope so," she said. "I need to get a few more exclusive clients to prove myself. Which means I have to start pounding the pavement this week." She took a sip of her coffee, then looked up at him. "Um, there's a charity thing I have to go to on Friday night. My sister Maddie and her husband will be there. It's at one of the hotels in town, a fund-raiser for the Fortunado Foundation. Would you like to accompany me?"

Jake's gaze narrowed. "As your date?"

She nodded fractionally. "Do you have a suit?"

Jake heard the uncertainty in her voice, and for some reason it irked him. "Yes, I do."

She looked relieved. "So...you'll go?"

"Sure."

"Great. You can meet me here and we'll go in my car."

Her car? He didn't need her to spell out what that meant, since she'd only seen him driving the old Ranger. Jake drained the coffee cup and got to his feet. "I should bail and let you get some work done."

She slid off the stool. "Thank you for a lovely day."

"Anytime."

She stood on her toes and kissed his cheek and then again, a little closer to his mouth. Jake grasped her shoulders and kissed her gently on the lips. She sighed against him, and it made him smile. He lingered for a few seconds, kissing her again, inhaling the scent of her hair and her lovely skin, tasting the sweetness of her mouth.

And as he left her condo and walked back toward his truck and then drove off, Jake realized one thing. He liked Valene. A lot. Which meant he had to come clean about his past and his present. And soon.

# Chapter Six

"You went where?"

Valene was standing by the water cooler in the lunch room on Monday morning, talking to Maddie and getting the third degree about her date with Jake. "An animal shelter."

She saw Maddie's frown. "Why?"

"He volunteers there. He has since he was a teenager. He's really perfect."

Maddie didn't look convinced. "Did you sleep with him last night?"

Valene no doubt looked as affronted as she felt. "Of course not. I'm not like that. And neither is Jake, which you'd know if you would stop being all judgmental about him not being wealthy or successful. Frankly, Maddie, I didn't realize you were so bigoted."

Maddie didn't bother to disguise her displeasure. "You can be as smart with me as you want, but I can see you're really falling for this guy, and I'm concerned. I'm certainly not judging him. I'm sure he's very nice and really charming, but you can't make a silk purse out of a sow's ear, Val. And I know you're all starry-eyed because he's attractive and something of a novelty, and he's taking you to see puppies and kittens and bringing you your favorite coffee, but do you honestly think he'll fit into your real world? I mean, long-term?"

Truthfully, Valene had no idea. She liked Jake. A lot. She was more attracted to him than she'd ever been to anyone, and his kisses were out of this world. But Maddie had a point. For starters, his lifestyle was the polar opposite of her own. And yet, she didn't care. A warning voice in the back of her mind told her she was heading for heartbreak by falling for a penniless cowboy like Jake but he made her feel so good about herself. So in tune with herself. And Valene had never experienced that before.

"I don't know," she said to her sister with a sigh. "But I know he's the first man I've ever met who makes me feel as though he likes me for me, and who is completely and utterly himself. He's not trying to be someone or something he isn't, and he certainly isn't trying to impress me with some ulterior motive. He's probably the most honorable and self-sufficient man I have ever met. He's honest, Maddie, and with my history, that's something I'm looking for. Please try to understand that I just want to see where this goes."

"I do understand, Val, and I truly want you to be happy. But please go slowly."

"I will," she said. "I promise. As long as you promise to let me live my own life and not judge Jake too quickly or harshly."

"I promise," she assured her.

"You can prove it on Friday night," Valene said and smiled. "I invited him to be my date to the charity dinner."

Maddie looked dubious, then sighed. "Okay. Now, I had better get back to work. I'm leaving for Austin around lunchtime and will be back Wednesday afternoon. Zach's staying here to connect with a couple of important clients."

"I need to get back to work, too," Val said, grinning. "Or my boss will send me packing."

"No, she won't. You're far too valuable around here."

"Even though I'm losing clients left, right and center?"

"Even then," Maddie said and gave her a quick hug. "And we're all in this together, remember? You're not the only agent who's lost clients. It's happening to us all. See you soon."

The following days were busy for Valene. And surprising. Because on Tuesday morning she received a call from a man who introduced himself as Karl Messer. He was a property developer and his company, the Messer Group, was building one of the new high-rises on the east side of the city, one that was zoned both residential and commercial, and he wanted to meet with her the following day to discuss listing the place exclusively with Fortunado Real Estate. When she ended the call, Valene's hands were shaking. It would be an amazing coup to land an exclusive listing with one of the hottest property developers in Houston. Usually Zach handled the larger accounts, and since Maddie had insisted she run everything by her brother-in-law, Valene tapped on his office door later that day.

"Would you like me to come to the meeting with you?" he asked once she'd told him the details.

Valene bit her lip. "I'd like to have the opportunity to land the deal myself. Is that okay?"

Zach, who was undoubtedly one of the greatest guys she had ever known, nodded. "Of course. You know I'm here to support you."

"Thank you, Zach. I won't let you down."

"I know that, Val. And remember that Maddie and I are one hundred percent behind you."

That thought stayed with her when she met with Karl Messer the following day. The meeting took place at the office on the construction site, and she was instantly impressed. Messer, in his early thirties, clearly was in command of the business he had inherited from his uncle a few years earlier. He was tall and attractive and acted completely professional toward her. The meeting ran for over an hour, and then he gave her a brief tour of the construction site. She ended the meeting with his assurance that he was committed to working with Fortunado Real Estate and would give her exclusivity on both the residential and commercial properties.

When Valene returned to her office, it was after four and she was humming and about to drop off her bag before she headed to see Zach when she noticed a cylindrical package on her desk. She recognized the name of the courier company and assumed it was something work related. But when she opened the package, she discovered a scrolled paper inside. She rolled it out and laughed delightedly. It was a sketch, intricately done, of a bulldog. Her bulldog, it seemed, one poking tooth and drool included. And written at the bottom in a dark and cursive scrawl were a few words.

*From the other man in your life...*

She knew instantly that it was from Jake. So, her sexy cowboy was talented as well as gorgeous. Valene remembered him telling her over dinner that he had liked to draw in high school, after he'd teased her about being on the math squad and the calculus team.

She grabbed her cell and sent him a text.

I love it. Bruce looks adorable. Thank you! V.

She waited a few minutes and then read the reply message.

My pleasure. Looking forward to seeing you again. J.

Valene's entire body thrummed. She texted back immediately.

If you want to call me tonight, that would be okay. V.

It took about two seconds to get a reply.

It's a date. Eight o'clock. J.

"Why do you look so happy?"

She turned to see both her sister and brother-in-law standing in the doorway. Valene rolled up the scroll and smiled. "I had a good meeting," she said, deciding not to show them the picture Jake had sent her, because it felt personal and ridiculously intimate and she didn't want to share her enjoyment with anyone.

She spent the next five minutes outlining every detail of the meeting she had with Karl Messer and how he'd promised her exclusivity and, if the arrangement was successful, the same entitlement for his next high-rise project, as well. It was the biggest deal she had ever brokered, and she knew both Maddie and Zach would be proud of her. And they were.

"How did you meet Mr. Messer?" her sister asked.

Valene shrugged. "He called me. He said he'd heard good things about Fortunado."

Maddie nodded. "He's got a good reputation as a builder. Good safety record. I think Gavin knows him," she said of their recently engaged lawyer brother. "I'll ask for a rundown next time I talk to him."

"I wonder if Gavin recommended us?" Val mused. "Well, if he did, Mr. Messer didn't mention it. And it appears to be a genuine offer, so I'll have the contracts started tomorrow."

Both Maddie and Zach nodded. "Good work," Maddie said and smiled. "It will help ease the sting when I tell you that we lost the McGovern place this afternoon."

Valene's stomach sank. "That's not possible. Just last week I took—"

"It's possible," Zach said gently. "I spoke to the owner myself."

"Was it something I did?" she asked.

"No," Zach promised her. "Just business. Don't take this personally, Val."

But she did. Because it felt personal. It felt as though her career was slipping from her fingertips. Sure, the Messer deal was huge, but she'd worked hard to cultivate the other clients and couldn't believe so many were dropping off the Fortunado books. Not only her clients, but two of the other agents in the office had lost clients in the last month.

Which was what she told Jake when she spoke to him later that night. He'd called at exactly eight o'clock and Valene was eagerly waiting for his call, keen to hear his voice and listen to his words of encouragement and steady reasoning. Which she did. He was exactly the tonic she needed.

"I'm sure you'll work this out," he said assuredly. "Every business goes through tough times, Valene."

"I know," she sighed. "I just hate letting people down."

"Didn't you say both your sister and brother-in-law told you not to take it to heart?"

"Yes," she replied. "But I always do. I always have. And I know Maddie is worried. With Dad retired and out of town, it just feels like we're under attack. I know that sounds dramatic, and I know I probably sound like a spoiled little girl whose daddy isn't around to pick up the pieces of the disaster she's gotten herself into, but I can't help how I feel."

"You're not a little girl and you're not spoiled," Jake said evenly. "You're an accomplished young woman with a great career. Did you know that your name means strong?"

She chuckled softly. "Yes, I know. Did you look that up?"

"I was curious," he replied. "It also means you are dynamic and visionary. Use that part of yourself to your advantage. Like you did today with the new client you got."

"I'm not sure I did much," she said honestly. "He came to me. I didn't have to pound the pavement to find him."

"Sometimes it's not how you get opportunity that makes you successful. It's what you do with it."

She took a breath and felt the air fill her lungs, calming her immediately. "Thank you. I always feel better when I talk to you."

He was silent, and she wondered if she'd gone too far,

said too much, made him feel uncomfortable by intimating that there was more going on between them than there actually was. But oddly, it didn't feel as though they had only known one another a week. It felt as though they had been friends for a long time.

"Valentine's Day is a little over a week away," he reminded her. "Save the date, okay? I'd like to spend the day with you."

Valene's heart skipped a beat. Never in her wildest dreams had she imagined she'd have a date for Valentine's Day. "I'd love to spend the day with you. So, I'll see you Friday night for the dinner."

"For sure. Sweet dreams, Valene."

She ended the call and spent the next hour or so thinking about him. For a man who made his living on the land, he was surprisingly insightful and philosophical.

She dreamed about him that night, imagining his kiss and his touch, and when she awoke she was unusually fatigued. He texted her around nine to wish her a nice day, and it put her in a good mood all morning. Her day brightened around lunchtime when she took a call from another prospective client, a rancher about half an hour out of town who owned a few hundred acres he wanted to sell. He was a gruff kind of man who got straight to the point and said he wouldn't be messing around with other agents as long as he had her word that she would give him one hundred percent loyalty. Valene liked him immediately and made arrangements to visit his place the following Monday.

She spoke to her mother that afternoon, staying mute about the troubles the business was having, figuring it was Maddie and Zach's place to talk to their father about it. Instead, she mentioned that she'd met someone and brushed over the details, just focusing on how nice he was and how much she liked him and how she looked forward to them meeting him when they returned from their vacation.

On Friday afternoon she left work early and headed for the salon, getting her hair and makeup done. She'd bought a new gown for the event, a red halter that showed off way too much skin, so she paired it with a black organza wrap and matching shoes. The color was about as wild as she got and she twirled in front of the mirror a few times, under Bruce's strict scrutiny, and then decided she looked nice enough. She slipped on her coat, grabbed her bag and headed outside, waiting for Jake by the front gate.

He arrived exactly on time, pulling up in a huge, hulking and very new cherry-red SUV. It looked like they weren't taking her Lexus, after all.

When he got out of the vehicle, he looked so hot she almost fainted. He wore a black suit, white shirt, shiny black boots and a bolo tie. He was just about the most gorgeous man she had ever seen. Clean shaven, his jaw was smooth, and she itched with the need to feel his mouth pressed against hers. He kissed her cheek and opened the passenger door.

"Nice rig," she said and hauled herself up. When he came around to the driver's side and got in, she asked, "Borrowed?"

"It belongs on the ranch."

She nodded. "Well, it's good you can borrow it for special occasions. Hey, I got another prospective client yesterday—someone who owns a ranch out near Fulshear. That's your territory, isn't it?"

"Close enough," he replied as he pulled onto the road. "So, where are we going?"

She gave him the directions and they headed off.

The hotel was one of the best in town, and she knew the ballroom would be transformed for the event. A jazz band was expected to perform, along with several well-known entertainers. The tables seated ten and had cost a fortune, so the attendees would be a who's who of Houston society. The funds raised would go directly to the Fortunado Foundation and then be funneled out to several other charities that helped women and children.

Jake helped her from the SUV, dropped the keys into the valet's hand and then led her into the hotel.

She checked in her coat and heard Jake's breath suck in as he stared at her, wide-eyed.

"You look incredible."

"Thank you," she said and placed her hand on his lapel. "You look sharp yourself. Thank you for dressing up. I know you're probably more comfortable in jeans and a Stetson. In fact, I prefer jeans and a T-shirt myself most of the time, but every now and then I have to dress up for one of Mom's galas."

His gaze lingered on her bare shoulders. "I'm starting to like your mom more and more."

Valene grinned. "She's disappointed she couldn't be here tonight, but the dates conflicted with the vacation she and Dad had planned. I'm sure Maddie will be in charge in her usual way. Actually, I think Zach is doing the honors as MC."

He nodded. "So, jazz?" he queried close to her ear as they entered the ballroom and made their way to their table. "Is this payback for the cowboy dancing?"

Valene chuckled. Gosh, he was sexy. The feel of his breath so close to her skin heated her blood, and she swayed toward him. The place was buzzing with people and she noticed that their table was already filling with couples. Jake pulled out her seat politely, and as she sat down it occurred to her that he was incredibly well mannered.

Before she had a chance to look around the table, he introduced himself, and Valene recognized two of the other couples sitting there. They were business associates of Zach's, nice enough people, but rich and often acting just a little too entitled for her taste. Perhaps that's why Val didn't have a lot of friends in her circle. She had two close friends from college who still regularly kept in contact with her, and her friend Adele, but most of her socializing was done with her work colleagues or her sisters when they were in town. Friday nights were often download time at the Thirsty Ox, an English-style pub just down the street from the office, but Val hadn't been for a few weeks. And since meeting Jake, most of her spare time had been filled with seeing him or thinking about him.

For a moment she worried he might be out of his depth with their tablemates. But no, he was clearly at ease and making conversation. Then she felt small-minded for thinking such a thing. Jake Brockton was no small-town hick. Lack of college education aside, he was smart and articulate and obviously at home in any scenario. She was about to join the conversation when her sister and brother-in-law appeared.

Jake was on his feet in a microsecond and took Maddie's hand, then he shook Zach's. Val quickly noticed Maddie's surprise and the gathering approval once her sister looked him over. Val felt vindicated, and also a little resentful. She hadn't brought Jake to the gala so he could be on show: she'd brought him because she wanted to be with him. Her sister's reaction simply proved what Val had suspected, that everyone stood in judgment.

And she realized that she'd been like that herself. Asking him to wear a suit. Suggesting they arrive in her car. Intimating that he had to be someone other than who he was to be acceptable company. Everything about those comments screamed entitled, spoiled, snobby, and she was deeply ashamed of herself.

"Are you okay, Valene?"

Jake's voice, close and whisper soft, brought her out of her thoughts. He was back in his seat and regarding her with concern.

"I'm fine," she assured him quietly, discreetly touching his arm. "I just wanted to say I'm glad you're here with me tonight and I like you...just as you are. I like your integrity and your honesty."

His gaze narrowed. "Valene...we need to talk about some things."

"What things?"

He was about to reply when the band played an introduction number, indicating the show was about to commence. "Later," he said and leaned in to kiss her cheek. "Nothing will change between us, I promise."

Oddly, she was put instantly at ease. Because Jake could do that. His deep voice and quiet confidence made her believe that anything was possible...including a real future with him...a man she was falling for. Big time.

Jake shifted in his seat as Valene's brother-in-law took to the stage. He'd never met the man before tonight, but he was well acquainted with several other people he'd spotted in the room. The irony of the situation was not lost on him. Last year he'd bought a table for the event for several of his customers. He hadn't attended himself, since he was neck-deep in divorcing Patrice at the time, but he felt foolish for not remembering why the Fortunado name was so familiar to him when he'd first met Valene.

He listened to the MC, conscious that Valene's fingers were resting on his arm, curling around his bicep. After the first speech, a comedian took to the stage, a well-known performer who cleverly dissed politics and social media and several self-obsessed celebrities. Beside him, Valene's soft laughter filled his chest with a heady kind of happiness. He enjoyed her company a lot. Too much, probably. And they were getting closer every time they were together. Becoming lovers was inevitable and he didn't want there to be any secrets between them, but… A warning voice lingered in his head. Something wasn't right with the Fortunado family. Something he suspected had everything to do with their link to the Fortunes and Robinsons. He wasn't sure why he felt there was a connection—instinct perhaps, or the street smarts he'd picked up over the years. They rarely failed him.

The band started shortly afterward, and they were entertained by a jazz singer. Sure, jazz wasn't his thing, but Jake could appreciate talent. As he listened, he thought of Valene's sister. Maddie had spoken to him a little, her curious expression making it plain that she was keeping a watchful eye on her little sister. She was a very beautiful woman and was clearly besotted with her husband and business partner. Jake admired the way they had made both their personal and professional relationships work. In a way, he envied them, since it looked so easy. But he knew from experience that it wasn't. Patrice had done a great job at convincing him that marriage was hard work. Still, he had good memories of his parents' marriage, and Valene often talked about how much in love her mother and father still were. And he was pleased that Valene was well loved and that her family was watching out for her.

Family was everything to Jake.

Which was why he'd been happy when Patrice had told him she was pregnant. They were already separated, already in the throes of divorce, but he'd believed her when she'd said the baby was his. Looking back, Jake couldn't believe he'd been so foolishly naive. He'd offered to raise the child with a shared custody arrangement, or alone if that's what she preferred. But that wasn't Patrice's endgame. Her motive was the same as it had always been—to grab as much of his money as she could. It was only when he said he wasn't about to pay for the privilege of being a parent that she admitted the child wasn't his.

The announcement had hurt more than he'd believed possible. And it turned him hurt to stone for a while. Or at the very least, made him overcautious of getting involved with anyone.

Until Valene.

Of course, the warning bells were pealing like crazy.

The possibility of marriage and kids was way off into the future, but being around Valene gave him hope that he could open himself up again to feel something for someone. And it wasn't simply desire. Of course, he wanted her. She was beautiful and sexy and drove him crazy, but there was more to her than a pretty face, seductive brown eyes and incredible curves. Valene had gumption and intelligence and wit. She was the whole package. There didn't seem to be anything narcissistic or covetous about her. Sure, she was young and inexperienced and a little spoiled, but she carried herself like a woman who knew exactly who and what she was, even if she sometimes didn't believe it.

*Then why can't I tell her the truth?*

Jake knew why.

Fear.

If she knew who he really was, what he'd made of himself, how could he be certain that her feelings for him were real? Were pure? Were what he needed to get the taste of bitterness and betrayal from his mouth? She liked him. She'd said it several times, and he was savvy enough to see the desire and genuine attraction in her eyes. But since both her sisters had recently found partners, how could Jake be sure she wasn't simply in love with the idea of being in love? He couldn't. Only time would tell if their budding relationship would go the distance. And with time came the very real chance that she would discover who and what he was before he took the opportunity to tell her himself. She believed he was a simple ranch hand and in a way that was true. Jake still worked the ranch as he had done since before he'd bought the place. But she had him pegged as a ranch hand who lived week to week, who owned a beat-up truck and who could afford jeans, not jewels. Someone she had to ask to wear a suit to a fancy shindig like a gala dinner. Someone who couldn't get a reservation at one of the busiest restaurants in town. Someone without influence.

When the truth was quite the opposite.

He was a successful ranch owner who had a considerable portfolio of other properties and investments in several developments around town—including one with Karl Messer. They'd been friends since high school and were now connected through business, even though Jake insisted on being a silent partner in any venture he invested in. And Karl was discreet, which was why he'd set him up with Valene. He'd wanted to help her, to let her shimmer the way she was destined to shine. He wasn't sure she'd be entirely pleased that he'd interfered, however, so staying quiet about his involvement was probably the best option at the moment.

"Would you like to dance, cowboy?"

Valene's soft and seductive voice whispered close to his ear. He noticed there were several couples on the dance floor. "Love to."

He took her hand and got to his feet, and within seconds they were on the dance floor.

"You know," she said as she swayed, resting a hand on his shoulder while the other was enclosed firmly within his, "this isn't so different from dancing cowboy style."

Jake urged her a little closer. "Not so different at all."

Someone he knew was dancing nearby and recognized him, and Jake responded with a brief nod. The last thing he wanted was to be outed on the dance floor. He pressed his face against her hair, inhaling the intoxicating scent. And he was a goner. He was so into Valene he couldn't think straight. Even the guys who worked for him had mentioned he was distracted. He was thinking about Valene when he should have been doing a dozen other things. He was dreaming about Valene. He was fantasizing about her.

He was, Jake realized foolishly, half in love with a woman he'd known a little over a week.

## Chapter Seven

Valene lost sight of Jake in the room and scanned the crowd. They'd parted company for a while when Maddie had insisted she help meet and greet the band and guest artists who had all donated their time for the charity event. It took about ten seconds to find him, though, near the bar area, talking to three other men of various ages. The oldest of the group said something and the rest of them laughed, Jake included, and then one of them slapped him on the back as though they had been acquainted for years. It struck her as odd behavior, as she was sure he didn't know anyone in the room besides her.

She made a direct line to him through the crowd when he looked her way, as though they were connected by some invisible radar. He quickly excused himself and met her halfway across the room.

"Having a good time?" she asked when he took her hand and raised it to his mouth.

"Of course. You?"

Valene's brows rose high at his benign reply. "My sister thinks you're ridiculously good-looking."

He laughed softly. "And what do you think?"

"I think you were making friends over there," she remarked. "*And* I think you are perfectly at ease in a room full of people."

"People are just people, Valene. There's no mystery to making conversation."

"I'm not so sure," she said and allowed him to lead her away from the crowd and back to their now vacant table. "I've always been considered something of a party girl, but the truth is, I've never been that great in crowds. I think I'm really more of an introvert, despite my reputation."

He chuckled and kissed her cheek, lingering around the soft skin beneath her lobe. The sensation turned her bones to liquid and she sighed, curling her fingers around his arm. In all her life, Val had never had such an intense physical reaction to anyone.

"I think," he whispered against her skin, "that you are perfect, Ms. Fortunado."

Val pulled back a fraction and met his gaze, conscious that to anyone watching, they would appear like lovers who had known one another intimately. There was an intensity about the connection they shared that defied logic, considering the short time they had known one another. She'd heard about it, of course, about instant attraction, the lightning-bolt kind. Even her sister Schuyler had declared that she believed in lust at first sight since she'd met Carlo. But as attracted as she was to Jake, there was also something else going on. Something deeper than pure sexual attraction. She enjoyed his company, experienced pleasure when he spoke or laughed, found herself thinking of him every day.

*It's like at first sight.*

*Who am I kidding?*

Valene wasn't an expert at deep emotion, but she'd witnessed real love firsthand by watching her parents' happy and successful marriage. It was something she wanted to emulate, like Maddie and Schuyler had recently done. It was important to her that she spend her life with one man, someone she could have children with, walk alongside through the challenges of life.

Someone like Jake.

He was strong and sincere and clearly valued honesty and integrity. She liked that about him. She knew it was what she was looking for.

"I've never met a man like you," she said softly.

Jake touched her cheek. "Like what?"

"So…together. So…real."

He chuckled. "I've been called a lot of things, but never that."

"Who were you talking to back there?" she asked.

He shrugged. "Just someone I know from the ranch. So, would you like to dance some more?"

"Sure."

They spent the next half hour on the dance floor, and she spotted Maddie and Zach swaying to a romantic number, engrossed in each other and clearly in love. And surprisingly, the spike of envy she expected didn't come, because somehow, she was in the middle of her own romantic fairy tale. Valene pressed herself into Jake's embrace, inhaling the sexy, woodsy scent of his cologne, feeling his strong chest beneath her cheek. She noticed a few things about him as they danced close together, like the fact that his cuff links were stamped with his initials, and his tie bar was made of solid silver. It seemed at odds, somehow, with his workingman, ranch hand image.

"I like your cuff links," she said and touched the ornate bar with her finger.

"They were my grandfather's," he supplied. "I was named after him."

Val nodded. "You have a strong sense of family."

He pressed a hand into the small of her back. "Family is everything."

"I agree," she said and swayed against him, loving the feel of his hand on her, even through her gown, and the heat it created on her skin. "I love my family very much. And I really want to have a family of my own one day. You said you wanted kids, right?"

"Yes."

It was a simple response. Too simple. Because Valone picked up on something hollow about the way he said it, as though he was suddenly filled with memory, and sadness.

"Jake...is everything okay?"

"Fine."

"If you've had enough, we can leave."

He shook his head. "And miss out on dancing this close with you?" he replied. "Not a chance."

Val felt light-headed, and for a second she wondered if women still swooned, because being around Jake made her feel all kinds of things she wasn't sure existed.

They danced for a while longer, and then once they returned to the table, she told him she was ready to go. Val found her sister, congratulated her and Zach on a fabulous event, and said she'd see them both the following week.

"Why don't you stop by the house tomorrow night

and bring Jake?" her sister suggested. "I'll cook. Or Zach will cook." Maddie grinned. "Or we'll order take-out."

An evening under the microscope with her very opinionated and judgmental sister? Val was about to refuse the invitation when she saw Jake nod slightly and relax. "Ah...okay. I'll bring dessert."

"No need," Maddie said and waved a hand. "I have it covered."

They were driving back to her apartment about ten minutes later when she spoke about her sister's offer. "We don't have to go if you don't want to."

Jake glanced her way for a second. "I'm happy to do whatever makes *you* happy, Valene. You've said many times that family is important to you. And your sister and her husband are nice people."

"She'll give you the third degree," Val said and made a face. "Are you up for that?"

Jake chuckled. "I'll cope. If Cassidy brought home someone I didn't know, I'd do the same thing."

"She's so lucky to have you."

"Likewise for your siblings," he said quietly. "Maddie is only watching out for you. Don't get frustrated because she loves you so much."

Val sighed and relaxed in the seat. "You make everything seem easier."

"Family isn't easy. But they're who we have, so there's no point fighting it. I'm sure there are days when Cassidy feels as though she's smothered and overprotected and that's why she went away to college. It's instinct, I guess, to want to protect the people we love."

He had a point. For most of her life, Val had been overprotected by her parents and siblings. She hadn't balked against it, hadn't overreacted, but sometimes her resentment had simmered along the surface, looking for an escape route. She'd never acted out, never done anything wild or outrageous, but she'd also never complained about the attention, either.

"If I told my parents they smothered me, they'd be so hurt."

"Then don't," Jake replied as they drove through the city. "You can be independent without being alone."

She sighed. "I live in a condo my father bought. I work in a place run by my sister. That doesn't sound like the life of an independent person, does it?"

"We can all look for ways to devalue the meaning of our life," he remarked quietly. "I guess it's how we manage our good fortune that matters the most."

"Like my mom does," she remarked. "Working with the Fortunado Foundation. Or you do at the shelter." She let out a long breath. "Do you know, the last pair of jeans I bought cost nearly four hundred dollars? Imagine how many rescue animals that money could feed at the shelter. Or how many people it could help through the Fortunado Foundation. Gah... I'm a spoiled child."

Jake chuckled softly and grabbed her hand, holding it firmly within his. "You're incredible, Valene. You're passionate and funny, and the world needs that kind of passion."

She looked down at their linked hands. "Do you?"

"That's a loaded question."

She laughed. "I really like being with you. And flirting with you," she added.

"I've noticed."

A few minutes later he parked outside her condo and quickly came around to the passenger side, where he held her door for her.

"Do you want to come inside?" she asked.

"Yes," he replied and gathered her into his strong arms. "Which is why I'm going to kiss you good-night and then leave."

Val experienced a mix of disappointment and appreciation. He was right. It was still too soon for her to have sex with him. Even though she wanted it more and more every time they were together. But she appreciated the fact that he knew it.

He kissed her, slowly and deeply, and by the time he raised his head she was clinging to him, desperate for more of his mouth on hers. She touched his face, felt how his skin was cool from the night air and was instantly caught up in his glittering gaze.

"Good night, Jake."

He made arrangements to pick her up the following evening, kissed her again before wishing her sweet dreams and then waited until she was safely inside before leaving.

She sent him a text about an hour later, when she knew he would be home and not driving.

I had a lovely time tonight. Thank you. Part of me wishes you'd stayed. V.

A message came back within seconds.

Ditto. Stop text torturing me. Good night, sweetheart. J.

Val was still smiling, still ridiculously happy when she awoke the next morning. She went in to work for a couple of hours to facilitate the Messer listing and took a call from Schuyler around eleven. They chatted for a while, mostly about Jake, and Schuyler squealed in delight that Val was so happy. Later, she made plans to meet with a couple of clients in Austin the following week and locked in several appointments.

She dropped by the supermarket after work to load up the rear of her Lexus with dog and cat food and then headed for the animal shelter, specifically to see Florence and drop off the donation, but also to spend a few minutes petting Digby, who'd become something of a favorite of hers. When she returned home she took Bruce for a walk, did some laundry, spent an idle half hour on Instagram and then went to the gym at the complex. By six she was showered and dressed and waiting for Jake.

He picked her up on time as always, in his old truck, and kissed her softly, and they headed for her sister's place. Maddie, of course, was her usual reserved and cautious self, but Zach was entertaining and a great host. Jake had stopped off to buy imported beer and wine, and soon after arriving they were all settled in the huge dining room. Maddie had gone all out ordering takeout, offering appetizers first and then a main meal that was delicious and loaded with carbs.

"Toscano's," Maddie announced when Jake complimented the porcini pasta dish. "It really is the best Italian place in the city, in my opinion. They do the most amazing beef ravioli."

Val glanced toward Jake and smiled. He hadn't flinched, hadn't moved a muscle, and Val was certain she had never met a more self-assured, quietly confident man in her life.

"You should take the Messer Group people there," Maddie told her. "A good meal is always a great way to break the ice with a new client. Probably best to try for lunch, though. It's impossible to get a dinner reservation. The place is always booked weeks ahead."

Val's mouth curled at the edges and when her gaze

met Jake's again, she saw the humor in his expression. She wasn't about to brag and say that her new boyfriend had only had to make a phone call to score them the best table in the place at a day's notice.

*New boyfriend?*

*Is that what he is?*

Val had been desperate not to label what they had, but they were into the second week of their acquaintance and it certainly felt like more than something casual. It felt real. Perhaps the most real relationship she had ever had.

Equally surprisingly, the evening at her sister's was pleasant. Maddie and Zach were perfect hosts, the food was wonderful and the conversation easy. Till Maddie brought up Jake's lack of a college education.

"Val said you left college in your first year?"

He nodded, unflinching. "That's right."

"What were you studying?"

"Art."

Valene wasn't surprised, considering the quality of the adorable portrait of Bruce he'd drawn freehand. But she was stunned that she hadn't asked him that question herself. They did, she realized, spend a lot more time talking about her than they did about his life or his past. It was something she intended to remedy. She certainly didn't want her sister learning things about him before she did.

"Why did you leave school?" Maddie asked, relentless.

"My father passed away and I was needed at home."

"That must have been a difficult decision."

"Not really," he replied. "My family needed me. And at the end of the day, family is all that matters. But of course, you know that."

It was the perfect shutdown. Val noticed the edge of "mind your own business" in his tone, but he was too polite to say it outright. And Maddie didn't know him well enough to pick up on anything other than his calm and quiet courtesy. They stayed another couple of hours, talking over dessert, which Jake declined, and then playing a few rounds of pool, two of which Jake won, much to Zach's good-humored irritation. As soon as they were in his truck and heading back to her condo, Val apologized.

"I'm so sorry about Maddie. She can be a pain in the neck about some things."

He chuckled. "You worry too much. She wasn't so bad."

Val sighed. "That's generous."

"She was right about one thing," Jake said and took a left onto the highway. "The beef ravioli at Toscano's is the best around."

Val laughed so loudly she snorted, which made Jake laugh. It was such a wonderful moment, and her heart fluttered madly. The more time she spent with Jake, the more she wanted to spend with him.

When they pulled up at her building, he was out of the vehicle and around to her side in seconds.

"So," she said, "are you coming in?"

Jake gently hauled her into his arms and kissed her soundly. "You know, Valene, I've never been the self-sacrificing type, so you better stop asking me that question."

She groaned and pressed against him, snaking her arms around his waist. "I'm sorry I didn't know about what you were studying in college. I should have known," she said and rested her ear against his heart. "I should have realized after that wonderful portrait you did of Bruce."

"Stop apologizing," he said softly. "And you better get inside, because it's getting colder out here, and I don't want either of us to catch pneumonia."

He left as soon as she was inside, and Val was uncharacteristically unhappy afterward, moping around her place for an hour or so before she showered and headed to bed, with Bruce firmly taking up his spot on one side.

"You better get used to the floor, buddy," she said playfully and petted him. "I'm pretty sure that spot is going to be taken up soon."

And as she drifted off to sleep, her thoughts and dreams were filled with images of the man who had captured her heart.

Val headed to Austin early on Tuesday morning and worked through until Wednesday afternoon and was back in Houston by six in the evening. On Thursday morning she headed out to Fulshear to meet with the owner whose listing she'd acquired the week before. It had been an eventful couple of days in Austin, and now she was back home she needed to focus on the week ahead. The Messer building was now hers to sell exclusively, and she had scored another prospective new client, a woman who owned a large estate in River Oaks and who had been recommended to her by Karl Messer. For her, things were definitely looking up, but the agency had lost another two clients and Zach was now talking conspiracy and sabotage. After what had happened to the Robinsons, and what were clearly more than coincidental losses at Fortunado Real Estate, everyone was taking the possibility of it being a real threat very seriously.

The upside was that she talked to Jake every night. He called her at eight o'clock in the evenings and they chatted for close to half an hour, discussing their days and anything else that came to mind. It was a lovely way to finish off the day, and she looked forward to hearing his voice each night more than she'd believed possible.

The land in Fulshear was cleared and fenced and had a small, neat dwelling and several water holes—it would be perfect for running stock. Val spent half an hour with the owner, Otis McAvoy, an ornery man in his midsixties who clearly had no tolerance for fools. But Val didn't mind straight talk and quite liked him. He would be a no-nonsense, no-fuss client who only wanted the best and fairest price for his land.

It was simple providence that made her drive past the Double Rock Ranch. Her GPS had diverted her down a shortcut and she spotted the ranch where Jake worked and lived. There was a huge picture of a dark stud bull on a sign beside the gate, along with the letters *JJB* and a phone number beneath.

She drove through the gates and up a long driveway, which was blanketed by lush coastal grasses, and pasture, which was dotted with mature oak and pecan trees. It was a postcard-perfect scene. As she drove farther she spotted a ranch house at the end of the driveway. The home was clearly in the midst of a renovation, as it was surrounded by scaffolding and there were tarps attached to several sections of the roof. Behind the house she saw several other dwellings, including one that had a perfectly beautiful cottage garden. She looked around and noticed several round yards, cattle pens, stalls with turnout areas, a huge barn and three tall windmills.

She sighed, finding it odd that for the first time, she wasn't thinking about how easily or quickly she might be able to make a sale should the place ever go on the market. Instead, she thought about how lovely it would be to live somewhere so beautifully idyllic.

She parked the car in the driveway and got out, looking around, hoping to find some sign of Jake, hoping it wasn't too inconvenient or inappropriate that she'd stopped by. She quickly called him, but it went directly to voice mail and she left a brief response, asking him to call her back if he wasn't too busy. She could hear music coming from the barn, and when she didn't get a reply after a few minutes Val grabbed her coat, slipped it on and then walked in that direction.

She spotted a young man, about nineteen, swaggering out from the barn, a saddle perched on one hip. "Hi," she said and managed a tight smile. "I'm looking for Jake Brockton. Is he here?"

The young man gave her a quick once-over, rubbed his whiskerless chin and half shook his head. "He's out musterin' strays with a coupla the guys. He left me here to clean some of the gear."

"I tried to call him," Val said and motioned to the cell phone in her hand.

He grinned. "You ain't gonna get no good reception from where they're at, ma'am. Too much rock."

The way he called her *ma'am* made Val feel about sixty years old. But there was a genuine politeness about the young man that was impossible to disregard, and she quickly thanked him and headed back to her car. She decided to check out the house and walked up the path and started heading around the side.

"Can I help you?"

The sound of a cheerful voice quickly grabbed her

attention, and she spotted a middle-aged woman walking the path from around the rear of the house. She was a tall, thin, fair-haired woman who wore jeans, a thick sweater and a long multicolored vest. A friendly-looking small dog stood at her side, and the woman was smiling.

"Oh, hi," Val said and took a right turn toward the other woman. "Actually, I'm looking for Jake Brockton."

The woman regarded her curiously, looked her up and down, tilted her head to the side, and then responded. "You must be Valene."

Val stiffened. "Ah…yes."

"I'm Lynda… Jake's mom."

Val felt both relief and embarrassment. She certainly hadn't expected to come face-to-face with his mother. She moved forward and held out her hand. "It's lovely to meet you. I was passing by here and thought I'd stop to see Jake. I called his cell, but it went directly to voice mail."

The other woman nodded. "He's out mustering a few strays down past the creek. There's a lot of rock around that way and it makes for poor cell reception."

"I met one of the hands by the barn and he said the same thing."

Lynda grinned. "That'll be Ricky. He's been working here a few months. Jake should be back soon. Why don't you come up to the house and I'll make tea?"

Val resisted the urge to check her watch. She had a later appointment at the office but could certainly spend some time with his mother. She nodded and followed the woman up the path. The dog wound itself around Val's legs, and she petted the animal on the top of the head.

"Jake's spoiled baby," his mother said and grinned. "Sheba?"

The dog barked at the mention of her name, which made Val smile. When they reached the cottage behind the house, Val stopped in her tracks. The garden was like something out of a fairy tale, with a well and small pond, plus rows of colorful shrubs whose survival defied any logic since it was winter and chillier than usual.

"Everything okay?"

Val nodded. "This is such a beautiful garden."

"Thank you," Lynda said and headed up the cobbled pathway. "My little piece of heaven. An English cottage garden in the middle of Texas. My daughter thinks I'm crazy for putting so much effort into it, but it makes me happy."

"How do you get these flowers and shrubs to grow?"

"Love and kindness," Lynda replied. "Plants really aren't all that different from people. They thrive on both of those things."

Val smiled and decided she liked Jake's mother very much, particularly when she discovered that the inside of the house was as adorable as the outside. From the mahogany furniture to the soft pastel accessories, the place was like something she'd seen on one of those old BBC shows about living in the English countryside. Val was tempted to grab her camera from the car and take a few snapshots.

"Your home is lovely," she said and half twirled around. "Jake said you've lived here for a long time."

Lynda nodded and moved into the kitchen. "Twenty years. My husband got a job as ranch foreman, and this cottage was where we lived. When he died so unexpectedly, I thought we might have to leave. Cassidy was still a child, and I was working a few days a week at the local elementary school. But then Jake came home, and everything worked out. And Cassidy was so happy she got to stay on the ranch." As she spoke Lynda moved around the small kitchen, gathering cups and filling the teapot.

There was a large framed sketch on the wall, of a herd of mustangs galloping through a creek bed, and Val recognized the strokes immediately. "Jake did this?"

Lynda nodded. "When he was about sixteen. He's very talented. And you work for your family's business, right?"

"Yes," she replied. "We sell real estate."

Lynda nodded again. "It's lovely when family can work together. You know, my son likes you very much."

Val's insides leaped. "I like him very much."

Lynda smiled. "He's been through a lot. Don't break his heart, okay?"

She was obviously referring to his last relationship, and as warnings went, it was mild and said with the utmost warmth. Val didn't mind. "I won't, I promise," she said and walked toward the fireplace.

There were several photographs on the mantel and she lingered over one that was of three men, one younger, one older and another older still, arms linked companionably at the shoulders. They all shared the same sandy-blond hair and glittering blue eyes. Jake and his father and grandfather. The picture made Val experience several different emotions. There was love and affection in the photograph, but she also knew it represented loss, of both his dad and grandparent. And suddenly it made her miss Glammy more than she usually allowed herself to. She knew how much Schuyler grieved the loss of their beloved grandmother, and Val made a mental note to talk more about Glammy to her sister.

"Is this your daughter? She's very beautiful," Val

said, moving to the next photograph of a young woman standing beside a tall palomino horse.

Lynda nodded. "Yes, that's Cassidy. My late husband, Mike, and I weren't expecting we'd have any more children after Jake since I had complications after the birth. But then along came Cassidy, and she has truly blessed our lives. And she adores her big brother."

Who wouldn't adore Jake, Val thought as she perused the photographs and then spotted one of Lynda and Jake. He was dressed in a cap and gown. He was younger, maybe midtwenties.

She frowned and pointed to the picture. "Jake's graduation?"

Lynda nodded proudly. "That was when he got his MBA. He worked so hard and graduated with honors."

Val's insides were suddenly and unexpectedly hollow. Jake had told her he'd dropped out of college. "He said he'd left school when his father passed away."

"He did," Lynda replied, her gaze narrowing a little. "But he went back to school online a year or so later. He's not one to boast or talk about himself. He gets that from his dad. My husband was a very humble and yet strong man. And he was such a wonderful father. And Jake will be the same," Lynda added, a gleam in her eyes.

Val swallowed hard, irritated and a little hurt by the fact that Jake hadn't told her about graduating college, particularly after Maddie had grilled him about it. Suddenly everything about him began to make sense. He was smart and articulate. He knew some of the people at the charity benefit. The young man she'd talked to by the stables clearly regarded him as an authority figure. He wasn't an uneducated hick. He was obviously more than a simple ranch hand.

And he had some serious explaining to do!

## *Chapter Eight*

Jake knew he was in hot water the moment he entered his mom's living room. He wasn't sure how much his mother had told Valene—not too much, he hoped, because there were things he needed to tell her himself. Plus, he'd made it clear to his mom that he hadn't mentioned his money or owning the ranch to the woman he was dating. And although Lynda had warned him about the perils of deception, Jake was determined to see how his relationship with Valene progressed before he told her everything about himself.

Valene was sitting on the sofa in the small living room, sipping tea, and shot him daggers when their gazes connected. Seeing her in her work garb, and her hair in a neat ponytail, he remembered she'd told him she was meeting up with a client who lived close by, which should have registered the possibility that she would drop in at the ranch. Jake knew Otis McAvoy very well, since the older man had been a good friend of his father's. He noticed that his mother looked delighted that she was getting the opportunity to hang out with the woman who had taken up so much of his time and attention.

Jake kissed her cheek, saw his mother's approval and then sat down.

"Sorry I missed your call, but the cell reception can be a little hit or miss at times."

"I was in the neighborhood," she said flatly. "So I thought I'd come and see you. Is that okay?"

"Of course."

They all chatted for a couple of minutes, about the weather and the cottage and Sheba, who had perched herself at his booted feet, and once Valene finished her tea, she thanked his mother and stood up.

"I have to go," she said and collected her bag. "But thank you, Lynda. It was lovely to meet you."

"Likewise. Please come and visit again."

Once they were outside, she didn't wait for him, but charged down the path and circumnavigated the ranch house. The contractors were done for the day, but when Jake reached her, one of the young ranch hands passed by and smiled at Jake.

"Afternoon, ma'am. Afternoon, boss."

Jake saw her back stiffen, and when she reached the front of the house she turned, hands on hips. Her brown eyes were dark and her expression clearly unhappy.

"Your father's boots?"

"What?"

"Exactly," she shot back. "You told me someone had to fill your father's boots. At the time I thought you meant because of your mom and your sister, but it was more than that. You meant his job. He was the ranch foreman. And now you are. You're in charge here, right?"

Jake wasn't sure how to answer. He was in charge, so technically her assumption was correct.

"Yes."

"And you have an MBA?"

He nodded. "That's correct."

"And you didn't say anything about it because you don't like talking about yourself?"

"Something like that," he replied, seeing the fire in her eyes and suddenly itching with the need to kiss her. She looked so beautiful and it had been days since they'd been so close.

"It's really annoying how you do that, you know," she said flatly.

"Do what?"

"Make everything seem so damned reasonable. Drives me crazy. I really want to be mad at you right now."

Jake laughed softly. "Does that mean we get to make up and make out afterward?"

She crossed her arms. "Only if you show me inside this house," she replied, nodding at the ranch house. "If that's allowed."

"Sure."

He held out his hand and she took it, and a bolt of electricity raced up his arm. He wondered if he'd ever get used to that, or if the scent of her perfume would always stay with him for days after he'd held her in his arms.

Jake walked up the steps, crossed the wide veranda and opened the front door. Most of the furniture was covered in protective sheets, and any decorative items were safely stored in boxes. He'd started the renovation over two years ago and put a halt on it during the divorce. Since then, his mind had gotten clearer, and now he wanted the place finished so he could move back in and start his life over.

*With someone like Valene...*

It occurred to him that he'd never fallen so hard and so quickly before, and the realization made warning bells peal in his head. With Patrice, he'd spent high school desiring her, and when she had made her move, he had been flattered and a little relieved, thinking his search to find someone to share his life with was over. Of course, then she'd busted his heart into a thousand pieces and made a mockery of everything he'd believed they had.

"Wow," Valene said as they entered the hallway, taking in the raked ceilings, polished floors and wood accents throughout the house. "This is incredible. Are you sure the owners won't mind me looking?"

"Positive."

"Are they here?"

"Not they. He," Jake corrected. "And yeah, he's around."

"Well, if he ever wants to put this place on the market, let me know," she said and grinned. "Not that I want to put you out of a job by selling the place. But it's such a lovely home," she said as she traced her fingertips along the edge of the walnut newel post at the bottom of the stairs. "How long before the renovations are finished?"

"Another month or so, I should think. Would you like to see the upstairs?"

She nodded. "Love to."

Jake grasped her hand and led her up the stairway and down the hall. There were three bedrooms, one of which was a master suite with its own bathroom and small living area, and there was another bathroom that serviced both the other bedrooms. There was a balcony off the main bedroom that offered a fabulous view of the rear of the ranch, including the creek and the undulating pasture. The furniture was covered in sheets, and she lingered for a moment at the foot of the large four-poster bed. Jake stared at the intricately carved piece Patrice had insisted he pay a fortune for. He'd never liked it, thinking it too old-fashioned and heavy for his taste. Jake intended to ditch the bed, particularly since he'd discovered his ex-wife between the sheets with another man.

"This room doesn't look like it's been used in a while," she said.

"It hasn't," he replied.

She glanced around the room. "I'm guessing there hasn't been a whole lot of happiness in this house."

"Not especially," he replied. "Ugly divorce."

"That's sad," she said and walked out onto the balcony. "You know, I can't tell how many of those ugly divorces I've used to my advantage in the last year or so...you know, to get a client motivated for a quick sale. Sometimes I feel like a used furniture salesman scouring the death notices in the newspaper. What an amazing view," Valene remarked as she wandered around the perimeter of the balcony. "Is that an orchard?" she asked, pointing to the left.

"Pecans," he replied. "And not exactly an orchard, but there's potential, I guess."

When the cows began to bellow, she smiled. "It's so peaceful here. I'm not sure I would ever sell this place if it was mine. You're lucky to have spent so many years in such a beautiful spot. It must have been a wonderful experience to be raised here."

"It was. That's why I—"

"It's why you quit school," she said and turned to face him. "So that your mom and Cassidy could stay here. You did the job your dad used to do, so they wouldn't have to leave."

He shrugged. "This is home."

She moved in front of him and settled her hands at his waist, linking her thumbs through the loops on his jeans. It was an incredibly intimate gesture and one that had the temperature of his blood skyrocketing. Jake kept his arms at his sides, even though all he wanted to do was haul her close and kiss her.

"And then you went back to college and your mom said you graduated with honors," she said and sighed. "Jake, I'm sorry if I ever inferred that you were—"

"An uneducated hick more interested in peanut shells and beer than anything else?" he said, cutting her off. "No," he assured her. "You haven't. But I appreciate your apology."

She pressed closer. "Sometimes I put my foot in my mouth and say inappropriate things."

Jake wound his arms around her. "But I'll bet you have pretty feet."

She chuckled. "Actually, I do have nice feet. I'll have to show you sometime."

"I'm looking forward to it."

He kissed her and felt the breath sucked from his lungs like a vacuum. The moment her tongue wound around his, Jake was lost. She was like tonic, like air and food and everything he needed for sustenance.

"Jake," she whispered against his mouth. "Would you like to make love to me?"

It was a sweet, tempting invitation. One he fully intended accepting. "Absolutely."

"When?"

"Soon," he promised. "But first, I need to tell you—"

His words were interrupted by the sound of a cell phone ringing. She sighed and stepped back, removing her hands from his belt before diving into her handbag for her phone. The call lasted less than a minute and then she slipped the cell back into her bag.

"I'm sorry," she said quickly. "I have to go."

"Everything okay?" he asked, seeing the furrow between her brows.

"A family thing," she explained. "That was Maddie. She wants me to come to the office right away. Trouble at work."

Jake nodded, understanding immediately. "If there's anything I can do, let me know."

"I will," she assured him.

"And I'll see you Saturday?"

"Yes," she replied and kissed him softly on the mouth. "Thanks for the tour. And the kiss."

"I'll call you tonight," he said once they were back at her car. "Take care."

Jake watched her drive off, his heart unusually heavy. He hated seeing her out of sorts, and the phone call had definitely not been a good one. He was just about to turn on his heels when his mother stepped up beside him.

"She's a nice girl."

"I know," he remarked.

"But you don't trust her?"

Guilt hit him between the shoulder blades. "I'm not sure what I feel."

"She's not Patrice," his mother reminded him. "And I don't think she's the mercenary type. She comes from a wealthy family, so I'm pretty sure she isn't after your money."

"It's not that, Mom."

"I know," his mother said. "But you need to tell her the truth, before someone else does."

The first thing that Valene noticed when she returned to the office was the fact that the secretary at reception looked frazzled and barely acknowledged her. Maddie's earlier phone call had been fraught with tension and urgency, demanding her presence. She headed straight for the conference room and was stunned to see Schuyler standing by the window.

And her parents!

They weren't due back for another week, and Val immediately wondered what had happened to make them abort their vacation so abruptly.

"Mom! Dad!" she exclaimed and rushed directly toward them, delighted to see them both.

They embraced her affectionately, and she was certain her father clung to her longer than usual. When she stepped back, she noticed that Maddie and Zach were also in the room, along with her brother-in-law Carlo and her brother Everett, who looked particularly grim.

"What's going on?" she demanded.

"Trouble," Maddie said and sighed. "We lost the Butterworth account."

Val knew what that meant. Fortunado had been selling Butterworth property for close to two decades. Laurence Butterworth had been a family friend for just as long. Butterworth Industries was responsible for most of the residential development on the outskirts of the city—affordable, middle-class real estate that turned over quickly and was highly profitable for both the developer and Fortunado—as well as the commercially zoned development in the heart of town, which included Fortunado's exclusive listing for most of the shopping malls.

It was a huge blow. Butterworth was Fortunado Real Estate's most important client.

And the loss was one they might not recover from.

Val winced when her father thumped his fist on the conference table. "I'll be damned if I'm going to let decades of work go down the drain overnight. Someone is responsible for this."

"But who?" It was Schuyler who voiced what they were all thinking.

"I don't know," Kenneth replied, red faced. "But I'm sure as hell going to find out."

"We've hired a private detective to do some digging," Zach said and dropped a stack of files on the table. "These are the clients we've lost in the last three months. These," he said, dropping another stack of files, "are all the clients we think might be at risk. And this," he said for dramatic effect as he held up a piece of paper, "is a list of anyone we think might be worth investigating. Feel free to add names to it. The more people we look at, the better chance we have of finding out who is responsible."

Val wasn't interested in any cloak-and-dagger subterfuge, but she did want to know who was trying to ruin the family business. She also wanted to remain positive. "We've signed on a few new clients in the past couple weeks, like the Messer Group account, so surely that will help with the loss of Butterworth."

"Of course," Zach said. "But I don't think we can ignore the fact that someone is deliberately doing damage to this company. Which is why everyone we know needs to be put under the microscope."

"Like who?" Val asked.

"Like your new boyfriend."

Maddie's voice was filled with suspicion, and Val saw that her father was frowning. "Jake has nothing to do with this. We were losing clients a long time before I even met Jake. He works on a ranch, for goodness' sake, and he's certainly no threat to Fortunado Real Estate."

"You can't know that, Val," Zach said gently. "We can't leave anything or anyone to chance."

"Maybe he sought you out because he wants to get close to the family," Everett suggested. "You know, to get information."

Val was shocked by the intimation. The very idea that her family believed Jake might be using her for information about her family *or* be responsible for any of the disasters that had landed in the company's lap lately made her seethe. They didn't know Jake and they had no right to make assumptions.

"Please don't do this," she implored and then looked at her father. "Daddy, I'm asking you to respect his privacy and believe me when I say there is no way he is involved in this."

"Sorry, Val, everyone is a suspect," her father said calmly. "With everything that has been happening with us and with the Fortunes, we need to investigate everyone. Particularly after the fire at the Robinson estate and the fact that Ben Robinson was nearly killed. This is serious…too serious to waste time worrying about what your new beau might think is his right to privacy. I'm not taking any chances when it comes to my family."

Val's heart sank. She knew her father was relentless when it came to family matters. And since the business was part of the family, it became very clear that he believed they were in the middle of a full-on attack. It was made worse by the fact that she was still reeling from what she'd learned about Jake that afternoon, and she certainly didn't want her family poking around in his business. Jake was a private man and would not appreciate being investigated. On the other hand, there was no way she could tell him what was happening without being disloyal to her family.

She was at an impasse.

Which was exactly what she told her brother Connor when she called him at his home in Denver later that evening.

Out of all her siblings, Connor was the one she always leaned on for advice. He was a straight-talking, no-nonsense kind of man, and one who could be trusted implicitly.

"I don't know what to tell you, kid. You know how complicated this family is now," Connor said and laughed a little. "With the Fortune connection, we're bound to be a target for some unscrupulous characters. And if you think this new guy of yours has nothing to hide, what are you worrying about?"

"Because it's invasive and completely unnecessary." She sighed heavily. "I wish you were here to help sort this mess out."

"I will be," he assured her. "I'll be back in Houston in a few weeks."

Val made an excited sound. "Wonderful. I miss you. Mom and Dad miss you. But what brought on this upcoming visit?"

"I just need to talk to everyone in person about something."

"What?" Val asked, instantly suspicious. "Is something wrong? Are you okay? Should I be worried?"

"No, yes and no," he replied, answering her three questions. "You see, that's why I don't tell you and Maddie and Schuyler anything. You all jump to conclusions. I'm perfectly fine."

"I thought you might be getting married or something," she teased.

"Not a chance," he flipped back. "You know I'm not the marrying kind."

"You might be," she ventured, "if you meet the right girl."

"You're the one all caught up in this romance thing," he shot back and laughed. "Not me. This cowboy of yours has got you all hot and bothered."

"You're making fun of me."

"A little. Good night, kid. See you soon."

She ended the call, took a shower, fed Bruce and then heated up soup for herself. She played with the dog for a while, thinking that she had been ignoring him too much lately and hadn't been as strict about his walking and grooming. The truth was, she was out all day, every day, and she knew he must be lonely. Maybe he needed a friend. She had the room, and the yard was certainly large enough for another pet. She hopped onto her laptop and sent an inquiry email to the breeder she'd purchased Bruce from, and by eight o'clock, Jake called. They talked for about twenty minutes, about everything and anything and nothing in particular, and Val avoided saying anything about Fortunado Real Estate. He seemed unusually distant, and she wondered if he was annoyed that she'd dropped in unexpectedly at the ranch but was too polite to say anything. But when she asked him, he quickly brushed off her concerns. And when she reminded him that he'd said he wanted to tell her something before they were interrupted by Maddie's phone call earlier that day, he said they'd talk on the weekend.

As she drifted off to sleep later that night, Val tried not to make a big deal out of his evasiveness, or the guilt pressing down between her shoulders because she knew her father and Zach were about to start snooping into his life.

On Friday morning, the day before Valentine's Day, she received a box of heart-shaped cookies from the local bakery and knew immediately they were from Jake even though there was no note attached. An hour later, a bouquet of flowers arrived for her via a delivery service. They were cottage-garden flowers, the kind you would find in an English garden and not the kind ordered from a florist. The fact that he'd picked them himself and arranged for a courier to drop them off filled her heart with happiness. Again, there was no note or card, but she knew they were from Jake and she couldn't have imagined a more romantic gesture even if she'd tried. Realizing he knew she would prefer the wildflowers to something flashy and store bought, like roses or oriental lilies, amplified every feeling she had for him. It was turning out to be the perfect Valentine's Day weekend.

She stepped out of the office at midday, at Schuyler's insistence. After her sister had snooped around and noticed the flowers and cookies, she insisted Valene reciprocate and get Jake the perfect Valentine's Day gift. She loved spending time with her sister and was touched to know Schuyler always made time for her when she was in town.

"It's cute that he's sending you gifts today," her sister said. "I'll have to get Carlo to up his game. So, what do you think of this?" Schuyler queried, holding up a dark Aran sweater. "For my handsome husband? Or your hot cowboy?"

"Nice," Val said as she wandered around the small and exclusive men's boutique. "But it doesn't help me. I can't buy Jake a sweater. It's too soon for that. Besides, I don't know his size."

Schuyler raised her brows provocatively. "You will once you get his clothes off."

Val waved a hand, walked around the leather goods cabinet and spotted a tray of tie pins and slides. One of the slides caught her attention, and she asked the sales clerk if she could take a closer look. It was perfect, fine platinum edged in gold and engraved with a horse standing on its hind legs. She purchased the item immediately and had it gift wrapped while Schuyler went on behind her about how boring she was.

"So, where is soon-to-be lover boy taking you tomorrow?" Schuyler asked once she'd paid for the sweater.

"I have no idea," Val replied as they left the store. "He just said we'd be spending the day together."

"He certainly is romantic."

Val's skin warmed. "I know."

"Have you told him about the private investigator?"

She shook her head. "No."

"Divided loyalties, huh?"

She sighed. "It's difficult."

Schuyler nodded. "I imagine it would be. I remember when I was falling for Carlo, I was so wrapped up in him, so completely in lust, I don't think I would have been able to keep that kind of secret. But then, you've always been better at keeping your feelings under wraps than I have."

"You mean I don't wear my heart on my sleeve. I know, I'm uptight like Maddie."

Schuyler sighed. "No one is as uptight as Maddie, although she has mellowed some since marrying Zach. And you've always been the most considerate one out of all of us. You've never liked hurting people. Or keeping secrets. It's why we all love you so much."

Val's eyes burned. "I don't know what to do."

"What does your heart tell you?"

"That Jake is exactly what I've been looking for."

"Even though he doesn't tick all those boxes you were so hung up about a few weeks ago?" her sister asked as they walked through the door of the Fortunado building.

Valene shrugged. "You mean the money and the sophistication? I think those qualities are overrated. And actually, he's highly intelligent and articulate and—"

"I get the picture," Schuyler said, waving a hand. "But you must know that regardless of all the drama that's happening in the business right now, Dad would always want to check out anyone you started dating that he hasn't handpicked. When he called two days ago and said he and Mom were coming home early from their vacation and that he wanted me here, he also asked me if I'd met your new boyfriend."

"Jake's not my boyfriend," she corrected. "We hardly know one another."

"I think I knew Carlo about three days when I realized how much I liked him. It doesn't matter how long you've known him. Look at Maddie and Zach. It took them five years to admit how they felt about one another. But you and I aren't as cautious as that, Val. We're a little more free-spirited and less afraid than Maddie. Go with that. If you like him, then like him. You don't need anyone's permission other than your own."

Val was still thinking about her sister's words when

she left the building for the afternoon. Jake called at eight and they made arrangements for him to pick her up at nine the following morning. He instructed her to wear jeans and boots and, as expected, announced they were going horseback riding the next day.

"You know I can't ride a horse," she warned him as they headed to the ranch on Valentine's Day.

"I know, but you'll be perfectly safe," he said and grinned, looking gorgeous in worn jeans and a blue chambray shirt—the same shirt he'd worn on their first date at the coffeehouse.

"I like that shirt on you," she remarked and reached across to touch the soft fabric for a moment.

"This old thing." He smiled. "It's my lucky shirt."

"So, you're planning on getting lucky?"

He laughed. "I meant it brings me luck."

Val smiled. "Does it?"

"Well, I'm here with you, so I'd say it's working just fine."

Her heart rolled over. "You're very sweet."

"Sweet?" he echoed. "I'm not sure I've been called that before."

She laughed and then sighed. "It's so nice to relax and not think about work or anything else."

"Like what?"

"Fortunes or Robinsons," she replied and then gave a brittle laugh. "I don't want to bore you with the details."

"Nothing about you bores me, Valene."

Her heart rolled over, but she still didn't feel right about saying too much about what was going on with her family.

She shrugged lightly. "We've lost a few more clients, and it's at critical mass. My folks came home early from their vacation to try to sort things out."

He glanced sideways and she saw the concern in his expression. And something else. Wariness. "Is there anything I can do to help you?"

"Besides exactly what we're doing now?" She shook her head. "Not a thing. I'd just like to forget everything today."

"I'll see what I can do," he said quietly. "And I'll cook you breakfast in the morning."

Val was about to respond when she got the real meaning behind his words. "Oh…okay. My place or yours?"

"Yours," he replied. "Unless you want to spend the night in the bunkhouse. It can get a little crowded."

She chuckled. "My place it is, then. Besides, I'm sure Bruce is keen to see you again. I've been thinking of getting him a companion."

"Good idea. Puppy or rescue dog?"

"Puppy," she replied and then saw his brows shoot up. "Okay…rescue dog. See what a good influence you are?"

"I'm not sure you'd agree if you knew what I was thinking right now."

Val's skin warmed. "Then tell me."

"I want to turn this truck around, take you home and make love to you all day long."

She turned in her seat, noticing that his hands were tightly gripping the steering wheel. "Then turn the truck around, take me home and make love to me all day long."

"Don't tempt me," he said and cast her a long and sexy look.

Val laughed freely, feeling so completely at ease, so completely *in like* with him that she could barely contain her happiness. "I'm glad you wore that shirt today."

His brows rose. "Why?"

"Because it means we're both going to get lucky."

## Chapter Nine

Jake tried very hard to concentrate on what he was doing for the following few hours, but it was damned difficult when everything that came out of Valene's mouth was flirtation and pure seduction. She had him at her mercy and he was pretty sure she knew it.

And he didn't mind one iota.

The air between them sizzled, fired up by the knowledge of how the day would end.

Once they were at the ranch, he took Valene straight to the stables and introduced her to her ride, an old chestnut mare called Agnes whom he trusted implicitly. Then he spent an agonizing twenty minutes standing behind her, explaining how to hold the reins, mount and keep her seat in the saddle. She was an excellent student, asking questions, not assuming she knew anything, and was clearly eager to get it right. But she was so close that every time she moved her hip would collide with his, which sent his libido skyrocketing like the space shuttle.

He'd given most of the ranch hands the day off and was pleased that they were making themselves scarce, except for Ricky, who made it his business to properly introduce himself to Valene and looked a little smitten. Not that Jake blamed the young man, since Valene was incredibly beautiful.

He led her into the small corral by the stables and got her to mount the horse, tucked her feet into the stirrups and, once she was holding the reins correctly, led her around the yard for a while until he believed she was confident enough to handle the mare out in the open. He quickly tacked up his gelding, attached a couple of saddlebags and checked over Valene one more time, which included making sure she wore a safety helmet. He clipped a long rein from her horse to his, then they headed off down toward the creek.

It was a picture-perfect day, cool, but the sun shone brightly and the sky was a vivid blue. She looked good in the saddle, too, he noticed, like she was born to ride. Her hips moved to the rhythm of Agnes's amble and she held the reins softly. She had a strong and well-balanced seat, and like with everything she did, she had purpose in her actions.

"Is that tether necessary?" she asked and pointed to the long rein connecting the two horses.

"Yep," Jake said and tipped his Stetson a fraction. "I'll take it off next time."

"How much trouble could I possibly get into?"

"Enough," he replied and motioned to the rocks and trees surrounding them. "I trust Agnes completely, but horses sometimes spook and I don't want you falling off and hitting your head on anything."

"I've got a tough head," she said and laughed, tapping the helmet.

"I couldn't bear it if anything happened to you."

As he said the words, Jake experienced a sharp pain in the center of his chest. Since his marriage had ended, he hadn't allowed himself to feel much of anything—not joy or humor or passion. But around Valene, he experienced all those emotions. And a couple of weeks ago he wouldn't have imagined it was possible to fall so hard and so fast. But he had. He liked her with an intensity that seemed at odds with the measured, calm and ordered way he'd lived in the past. Even with Patrice, he'd known exactly what he was doing. Marriage had been simply another step in the right direction, one that would lead to happiness and children and a lifelong commitment. Looking back, as much as he'd wanted her in high school, he hadn't spared her much thought until she reentered his life several years later. Courting her, marrying her, had seemed the logical thing to do. But with Valene, his usual controlled resolve had disappeared. For starters, he'd never considered himself the romantic type…but he was compelled to woo her in whatever romantic and sappy fashion he could think of. Because it made him feel good, and that had been in short supply during the last couple of years. And Valene, as passionate and vibrant as she seemed, was also something of an old-fashioned girl from an over-protective family and was worthy of all his attention, and not just so he could get her into his bed.

"Besides, your father would be after me with a shotgun if I allowed you to get hurt," he said, trying to lighten the mood.

But at the mention of her father, she frowned. "Jake,

about my dad…he's a good man, you know. And he always acts with the best intentions."

"Of course. I guess at some point I should meet you parents?"

She nodded. "I'm sure my mom would like that."

"And your father?"

"He's a touch more protective. I'm sure you'll be the same when you have a daughter."

Jake's insides contracted. After what had transpired with Patrice, children had seemed way out of reach. But now, not so much. Of course, it was way too soon to start considering that kind of commitment with Valene. But he liked knowing that he had hope in his heart again, and not just regret and pain.

Jake led them down toward the creek, conscious of keeping Agnes on the track. When they reached a tree near the edge of the water, Jake came to a halt and dismounted and then moved around to help Valene. Once she was on the ground, Jake tethered the horses and then helped Valene take the helmet off.

"I guess I have hat hair now?' she asked and laughed, fluffing out the waves.

"You look as lovely as always."

She reached up and briefly touched his face. "Thank you. What a magical spot," she said, hands now on her hips as she surveyed the area. "It's so beautiful."

Jake watched her, enthralled by the passion in her voice as she kept talking, and by the way she noticed everything, from the wildflowers to the birds to the gentle ripple of the water over the colored stones in the creek bed. Several head of cattle were drinking on the other side of the creek, and she ventured across a few rocks, her booted heels clicking over the stones. She stood alone, one hand up to shield her eyes from the sun, the other at her side, and he experienced a consuming feeling of attraction and longing that almost knocked him off at the knees. But it wasn't simply her physical beauty that attracted him…it was her intense zest for life. She'd grown up wanting for nothing, with an adoring family, the best education money could buy, fancy cars and luxury most people never knew. And yet something as simple as the bellow of a cow, the call of a bird or the sound of water rushing over rocks captured her attention in a way that was mesmerizing to witness.

She turned and met his gaze, smiling warmly. "Thank you for bringing me here. I'm so glad you got the day off today. Your boss must be—"

"Valene," he said, cutting her off. "There's something I have to tell you."

"I know," she said and skipped back across the rocks. "You sent me the cookies and the flowers yesterday. And they were lovely. Although," she said a little more seriously, "you shouldn't have wasted your hard-earned money on a delivery service. I would have been just as delighted to get them in person today."

Jake's gut dropped. "Valene, about the money. You know I—"

"I don't care about money, Jake," she implored, moving closer and resting her hands on his chest. "I never have. I care about *you*. More than I imagined possible. Everything you are—honest and strong and caring—that's the important stuff. That's what I want."

Guilt hit him directly in the center of his chest. *Honest.* Right… He really had to come clean. "Valene… I'm not without flaws, you know."

"I don't believe you," she said and smiled. "And can we ditch this serious talk and simply enjoy the moment?"

Jake considered his options. And he decided now was not the time to come clean. "Sure. Go and take a seat over there," he said and pointed to a large log by the edge of the creek. "I'll be back in a minute."

She strolled off and Jake headed back to the horses. He took off the saddlebags and rejoined her by the water's edge.

"What's this?" she asked, spying the saddlebags.

Jake extracted a small plastic container and two sodas from the saddlebag. "My mom made brownies yesterday. I snatched a couple for you."

She grabbed the box and dug in, laughing delightfully. "My absolute favorite thing in the whole world."

"I know," he said and wiped a smear of chocolate off her lower lip. Then he kissed her, softly, slowly, not asking for too much, not taking anything she wasn't prepared to give him freely.

They stayed like that for a while, eating brownies, talking, kissing, staring out at the creek. It was a sweet and lovely way to spend an idle couple of hours. About noon they rode back to the stables and he left instructions for Ricky to unsaddle and strap down both horses. He waited for a moment while Valene petted and hugged Agnes and thanked her for being such a trustworthy mount. His mother had gone out to her quilting class for the afternoon, and he ushered Valene into the cottage and made lunch for them both. Nothing fancy, just ham and cheese sandwiches, but she seemed content to simply sit on the counter stool and watch him, chatting about the horses and the creek and asking questions about the beef industry.

"So, you sleep in the bunkhouse?" she asked, drinking the coffee he'd made.

"At the moment," he replied, thinking he had the perfect opportunity to explain that he was only there until the renovations on the ranch house were completed. "Sometimes I stay with Mom, unless Cassidy is home from school." Before he could say anything more, she spoke again.

"I guess you used to live with your ex?"

He nodded. "Yes, I did."

"Would you consider moving in with someone else?" she queried, shrugging. "I mean, down the road...you know...after a while."

Jake stopped what he was doing, holding his sandwich in midair. "Of course. But the thing is, I could never live in the city. My work is here."

She nodded and smiled. "Well, after spending some time here, I can see that the city is not all it's cracked up to be. And I kinda like the idea of cowboy boots at the end of my bed. Maybe I'll buy a place around here," she mused and smiled. "Land prices are good. Did I tell you that I already have someone interested in that listing I got not far from here? The owner is a bit of a cranky pants, but I think he'll come around."

"I'm sure he will succumb to your charms."

She laughed delightedly. "Getting new listings is all that's keeping me sane at work these days."

"I take it things haven't improved?"

"We lost our most important client," she said on a heavy sigh. "It will have a huge impact on the business and my dad is convinced we're being deliberately targeted."

"What do you think?"

She shrugged. "My dad has good instincts. So does Zach. All I can say is thank goodness I managed to get the exclusive contract with that property developer—you know, Karl Messer. At least that will alleviate some of the financial burden on the agency."

Her admission rattled him a little. "Are things that grim?"

"I'm not sure. But we can't keep hemorrhaging clients. I mean, imagine if someone rustled all the cattle off this ranch. Would the owner remain solvent?"

"I'm pretty sure he'd be okay," Jake replied casually. "He's invested wisely in other things."

"He's obviously a sensible businessman. So is my dad, but a real estate business relies on selling real estate. No clients equals no income. But please don't say anything about this to anyone," she said quietly.

Jake nodded assuredly. "You have my word."

"Anyway," she said on a long sigh, "let's not talk about it anymore." She dug into her jacket pocket and pulled out a small box. "Happy Valentine's Day, Jake."

He opened the box and examined the tie slide. "It's lovely, thank you."

"You can wear it to the next charity dinner I rope you into."

"That happens a lot?"

"Now that my mom's back in town, I'm sure there'll be plenty of charity functions to attend. Speaking of which, I promised Florrie I'd be at the fund-raiser for the shelter next weekend. And now," she said as she rose from the stool and cradled his face in her palms, "I'd like you to drive me home."

He saw the desire shining in her eyes. "Really?"

"Really," she echoed. "Because as much as I like you in that lucky shirt, all I want to do right now is get you out of it."

Val had never considered herself particularly seductive or flirtatious—but being around Jake gave her a kind of sexual confidence she hadn't known she possessed. They left about twenty minutes later, after Jake had grabbed an overnight bag with a few personal items and a change of clothes. It seemed oddly mechanical and yet infinitely sexy, and as she waited for him by his truck, Val experienced a heady kind of longing that made her knees weak and her blood simmer. He hadn't touched her or kissed her since their make-out session by the creek, but the heat and awareness between them clung to the air. There was no mistaking it, no denying the inevitability of what was going to happen between them.

They didn't talk much on the trip back to her condo, nor when she opened the security gate and walked up the path and then headed inside. Bruce came to greet them at racing pace, tail wagging and tongue lolling. Val discreetly locked him in the laundry with his bedding and favorite toys and returned to find Jake standing in the middle of the living room, his overnight bag at his feet, looking sexier than any man had the right to look.

She glanced down at her jeans and shirt. "I think I'll take a shower." She took a couple of steps and then turned. "Are you joining me?"

His eyes widened. "Is that an invitation?"

"Absolutely."

He picked up his bag and wordlessly followed her down the hall. Strangely, her bedroom seemed smaller with the both of them in it. She'd never had a man in this bed before, as she'd moved into the place the week after she ended things with Hugh. Since then she hadn't been intimate with anyone.

She stalled at the end of the bed. "I haven't done this for a while."

"Me either," he said and dropped the bag. "But I'm pretty sure we'll make out just fine."

Val smiled. As always, he had a way of putting her at ease. "Birth control?"

He withdrew a box of condoms from his bag and placed it on the bedside table. "Got it."

She ditched her jacket and draped it over the chair in the corner of the room and then quickly closed the shutters. She flicked on the bedside lamp, kicked off her boots, removed her socks and returned to the end of the bed.

Jake hadn't moved an inch. He stared at her, long and blistering, and the desire in his expression fueled her confidence. She reached for the buttons on her shirt, ignoring her trembling fingers as she slowly undid them. Then he finally moved, pulling his own shirt free of his jeans and dispensing with the buttons quickly. His chest was spectacular, his skin like satin stretched over pressed steel, with a sexy smattering of blond hair on his pecs. Val swallowed hard, stepping backward, dispensing with her shirt and jeans with record speed as she made her way to the bathroom. The large shower could easily accommodate two people, and once she was naked, she turned on the water and stepped inside, waiting as steam filled the space. He joined her moments later.

Never in her life had she seen a man with more masculine angles, more muscle, more sinew and strength. He was perfectly proportioned, generously so, and she swallowed hard as her gaze lowered and then moved back up to his handsome face.

He looked at her, her face, her shoulders, her breasts, her waist, her hips and legs, and with every second of their visual connection, Val was drawn further into his world. He didn't touch her, didn't speak, didn't move, didn't do anything other than offer complete and unadulterated appraisal as the water sluiced over them, creating an erotic image that would remain with her forever.

"You're so very beautiful, Valene," he said finally.

She stepped forward, making contact, feeling his skin, so hot and wet and so utterly desirable she almost buckled at the knees. He must have sensed her reaction, because his arms came around her, settling on her hips, urging her closer. And then he kissed her, taking her mouth in a wild and erotic way that defied anything she'd experienced before. With the hot water beating down on them, with their skin slipping against each other, with his big hands splayed against her hips, Val lost all coherent thought. His tongue was in her mouth, his desire undeniable, his passion for her like a potent force, and she longed for it, craved it, needed it like she needed air in her lungs. She wrapped her arms around his waist and slid them upward, feeling his muscles clench firmer with every stroke of her hands. And she kissed him back, hotly and passionately. She gave up her lips and her tongue and reveled in the feelings he evoked throughout her entire body. As he kissed her, he touched her breasts, rousing the nipples to life, placing his mouth there and driving her wild. And he touched her intimately and so expertly she had to lean back against the cool tiles for support, craving the release he incited in her. His touch was addictive, his caress firm yet gentle, and she couldn't get enough of him.

"We have to get out of here," he muttered raggedly against her mouth.

Val managed to garner some strength in her legs and quickly turned off the water. She passed him a towel and grabbed one for herself and took a few moments to dry herself before she padded back into the bedroom, unbelievably unselfconscious. She'd never been so at ease with a lover, so in tune, so…free. She'd never wanted to make love with someone like she wanted to with Jake.

Once they were on the bed, he took her into his arms, holding her head steady, gazing into her upturned face. "Tell me what you're feeling," he whispered.

Val reached up and pulled his head toward hers. "Happy."

He kissed her again, smiling against her lips. And he touched her. He made her scorch, he made her writhe, he made her ache. He traced his tongue across her nipples over and over; he ran his fingers along every part of her, finding unbelievably erogenous places Val had never known she possessed. He caressed between her thighs skillfully, drawing her higher and higher toward release, kissing her in time with the rhythm his fingers created.

And when she could stand no more of the incredible erotic torture he was bestowing, he quickly grabbed a condom, sheathed himself and moved over her, holding her head gently between his hands, kissing her mouth in a deeply erotic way that made her instinctively lift her hips to meet him.

He entered her slowly, not breaking their visual contact, and in that moment, Val realized what she'd suspected for the past week and now couldn't deny. She was falling in love with Jake. And the passion she felt, the connection she experienced with him, was real. It was intense. It was everything she had dreamed of.

She kissed him, saying his name, gripping his hips in a message as old as time, and he moved inside her, his body a part of hers, her body a part of his. The rhythm he created was steady, not rushed, not hasty or self-serving. It didn't take long for her to succumb, and she flew higher than she ever had before, feeling the white-hot rush of release sweep through her entire body as wave after wave of pleasure coursed through her. And then she felt him shudder and she held on, experiencing both power and acquiescence in the moment he found that same release.

He rolled over, his breathing hard, his broad chest rising up and down as he dragged air into his lungs. "Be back in a second," he said and swung his legs off the bed and then headed for the bathroom.

By the time he returned, Val had moved the coverlet down and ditched some of the pillows. He slid back into bed and pushed away the sheet she was suddenly desperate to have covering her nakedness.

"Oh, no," he said and kissed her soundly. "We're past the self-conscious stage, sweetheart."

"Easy for you to say," she breathed and traced her fingers through the slight smatter of hair on his chest. "You're perfect in every way. And I'm not."

He eased her onto her side and ran a hand along her hip. "You look pretty perfect from here."

"That's just your post-sex vision," she said and pouted a little. "In a couple of hours, you'll see things differently."

"In a couple of hours," he said as he rubbed his thumb gently over one budded nipple, "I intend to make love to you again."

Val moaned. "I've never had anyone make me feel like this before."

"Ditto."

It wasn't a declaration of love. It wasn't even close. But it was…something.

"I need to send a great big thank-you to the dating

app people," she said on a dreamy sigh. "You know, it's a Robinson Tech app."

"I know," he replied and kissed her, lingering a little. "I signed on, remember?"

She chuckled. "That's right, your sister's suggestion. I think I like your sister."

"Well, I'm sure she'll like you, too. Now," he said as he rolled her over until she was lying on top of him, "how about we stop talking about anyone else who's not in this room. And you can tell me exactly what you would like me to do, Ms. Fortunado, to make you happy."

Val's entire body thrummed. "This," she said, feeling his arousal, "makes me happy."

They made love again, taking time to stroke and touch and get to know each other, and Val knew she had never been as intimate or as close to another human being in her entire life. When he was inside her again, she was on top of him, feeling so sexy and powerful, so in tune with her entire body, she could barely get enough breath into her lungs. Jake gripped her hips, guiding her in a way that gifted them both the most mind-blowing pleasure and cemented in her mind and heart what she had suspected. She *wasn't* falling in love with Jake. She *was* in love with him.

Completely and irrevocably.

Afterward they slept for a while, and then Val slipped out of bed to make coffee. It was after six o'clock and they'd been in bed for several hours. She was behind the counter, wearing his lucky shirt, when he appeared in the doorway, in nothing but his jeans with the snap undone. Her libido did a crazy leap.

"Hey," she said and smiled. "Hungry? I have the

makings of a somewhat great pasta dish in my refrigerator."

He smiled. "Or we could order takeout from Toscano's."

Val glanced at the clock on the wall. "At this hour, and on Valentine's Day? I don't like our chances."

"Serge owes me a favor. You know, you look very sexy in my shirt."

She touched the fabric with idle fingers. "It's soft."

"Are you okay?"

"I'm fine. You?"

"Never better."

That was how she felt, too. As though she had finally found exactly where she wanted to be. And with whom. Well, not exactly where, because she knew that city living wasn't appealing to Jake. But Val wondered if there was a middle road for them.

He nodded. "I have something for you."

Her gaze roved up and down him possessively and then she grinned. "Something else?"

He laughed and then disappeared back into the bedroom for a moment. By the time he returned, Val had the dinner ingredients laid out on the countertop. He carried a small, flat parcel wrapped in bright pink tissue paper. There was a card attached, and she read that first. The sentiment inside was romantic and exactly what she would expect from a man like Jake. Val sat on a counter stool and opened the gift, sighing when she saw what he'd given her. A picture of herself and Bruce, sketched in intricate detail and beautifully showcased in a silver frame. She looked at the likeness, saw something in the expression he'd drawn, how he'd made her look good, and she glanced at him.

"Is this how you really see me? No little bump in my nose, no pointy chin, no flaws?"

"Exactly."

"Thank you," she said on a sigh. "I love it."

Jake moved forward and stood between her legs, settling his hand lightly on her shoulders. "What to get the girl who has everything," he said and rested his chin on the top of her head.

Valene inhaled the musky and intoxicating scent of him. "I don't have everything."

He reached down and grasped her chin, tilting her head backward. "No?"

She met his gaze. "Well, actually, at the moment, it feels like I do."

And as he kissed her, as their mouths met and he pulled her close, Val knew she had everything she'd ever wanted. His friendship. His body. His trust.

And, if she was lucky, his heart.

## Chapter Ten

On Monday, life returned to normal. Sort of. Val was still in a kind of dreamy, post-Valentine's weekend of sensual bliss, recalling every romantic and passionate moment they had spent together, when Maddie popped her head around the doorway to her office at eleven o'clock.

"How was your weekend?" her sister asked.

Val looked up, smiled and felt heat scorch her cheeks. "Perfect."

"Really?" Her sister looked skeptical.

"I'm not going to pretend I don't care simply because I haven't known him very long."

"It's only been a few weeks," ever-practical Maddie reminded her.

"Some of us don't need five years to figure out who we want to be with," Val said pointedly. "Although we are all glad that you and Zach came to your senses and realized you were meant to be together."

Maddie's steep brows rose significantly. "Oh, I see... you're in love with Jake now?"

She didn't bother denying it. "Yes."

"And is he in love with you?" Maddie asked and stepped into her office.

Val shrugged. "I don't know. It's not like we've said the words or anything. But I feel... I feel very strongly about Jake."

Her sister's expression softened. "I hope he's everything you believe he is."

"He's more," Val assured her sister. "He's got integrity and strength, and he's so incredibly nice. As it turns out, I don't care about wealth or power or career. I care that he makes me laugh, that I feel like I'm my genuine self when we're together. That he's not judging me, not resenting me, not trying to get something from me, and not with me because we're from the same kind of family."

"Are you sure?" Maddie asked quietly.

"Positive. He's not after our money or our name. If you could see the way the people around him look up to him," she said and sighed, "you'd realize that Jake is very much his own man."

"You slept with him?"

She nodded. "And it was incredible. I've never experienced real passion, or desire, or real chemistry before. I mean, I've imagined feeling like this, but I never quite believed I'd find it. But with Jake I feel all of those things. Don't ask me to play the caution card, Maddie. It's not in my nature, and I like feeling this way."

When her sister left shortly afterward, Val got back to work, but her mind wasn't completely focused on the task. She took a call from Karl Messer and another from a potential new client in Austin she was seeing the following week. Despite losing the Butterworth account, Valene had never been busier. It was her time to shine, she thought. Her time to prove to her family that she could have a serious career and not simply playact. She knew that's what they thought. Oh, they loved and supported her too much to say so, but in her heart she knew none of her family truly believed she was cut out for business. She knew they figured she'd grow tired of the work soon enough and then get married and have a family. And maybe she would. Because the more she considered the idea of getting married and having babies, the more the notion appealed to her.

Beautiful little blond babies with glittering blue eyes. *Jake's babies.*

She sent him a playful text at lunchtime.

You're distracting me. V.

A few minutes later, her cell pinged in response.

I don't see how. I'm in the corral branding calves. J.

Val swooned over the heart emoji he added to the end of the message.

Call me tonight. V.

He did call, and they talked for half an hour, about random and mundane things. And she loved how they could talk about the simple stuff—even the weather— and it was still fresh and exciting.

She drove to Austin Tuesday morning for a meeting

and stayed the night, returning Wednesday. In the evening Jake came to her place and Val had every intention of making dinner. Until he kissed her and then she was lost. They made love quickly and passionately and she was stripped of every thread of self-control as she came apart in his arms. Afterward, they took a shower together and he helped her prepare dinner and she accepted that he was a much better cook than she was. Later, once the food was eaten and the dishes cleared, he suggested they watch a movie.

He even supplied the DVD. A zombie flick, one she hadn't seen.

"How did you know which one to get?" she asked as they snuggled on the couch, with Bruce doing his best to get into a comfy spot between them. In the end, the dog made do with his basket at the foot of the sofa. "This kind of movie isn't your thing."

He laughed. "My sister made a few suggestions. It's something you two have in common."

"What's that?" she teased. "That we're both crazy about you? Me especially."

He kissed her mouth. "You know, if there are any clowns in this flick, we're sleeping with the light on tonight."

"Oh, you think you're going to be sleeping," she said and turned, straddling him and moving her hips in a way that was deliberately provocative. "Not a chance."

As it turned out, there weren't any clowns in the movie, but Val quickly lost interest in watching once Jake began kissing her neck. They went to bed around ten, leaving the light on because he insisted on seeing her, and she experienced such acute and mind-blowing pleasure in his arms, Val thought she might pass out. There was something impossibly erotic about watching him reach the peak of pleasure, knowing she was giving him every part of herself, knowing every touch, every kiss, every slide of her hand and mouth were just for him. Just as his touch was for her alone. The night became a voyage of sensual discovery, of pleasure and release, and there were quiet moments of gentle vulnerability that filled her heart with so much love, she wasn't sure where he ended and she began. His every touch was like worship against her skin, every kiss was like a brand, every sigh a memento she would treasure forever.

In the morning they woke early and took the dog for a walk and then returned to eat breakfast together. He was ready to leave at eight, and she kissed him goodbye with the promise of seeing him Saturday morning at the shelter.

But he lingered in the doorway, looking down into her upturned face, his expression suddenly serious. "How about you come and stay at the ranch on Saturday night?"

She raised a brow. "Is that allowed?"

His blue eyes glittered brilliantly. "We need to talk, Valene, and I'd like to show you the ranch. I mean, really show you."

She pressed against him. "Like the hayloft in the barn?"

"Everything," he said and sighed heavily. "And what it means to me."

He sounded somber, not like his usual self, and she was immediately concerned. "Um…okay. Of course I'll stay. I'll take Bruce over to my parents for the evening."

They said goodbye, and she was already missing him by the time she returned inside and collected her bag and laptop. She wanted to tell him she loved him. Of course it was too soon. But the words burned on the end of her tongue. The condo seemed so much fuller with him in it, and standing alone in the living room now, Val realized how incredibly lonely she had been before Jake had entered her life.

He'd said they needed to talk and she was filled with anticipation and some fear. Talking sounded serious. Perhaps he was ready to admit that their relationship was headed to the next level—like real commitment. Or maybe he thought they were moving too fast? The notion that he might want to slow things down hurt more than bore thinking about. She didn't want to go slow—she wanted to jump headfirst into a serious relationship with him.

She'd been at work for less than half an hour when her father called her into his office. Even though her dad was retired, and Maddie and Zach were in charge, he still kept his office and used it on the odd occasion he was in the building. Val tapped on the door and entered the room, spotting her father immediately by the window, arms crossed, looking grimmer than she'd seen for a long time.

"Come in, Valene," he said and moved across the room to close the door.

"Is everything okay, Dad?"

He met her gaze, his brown eyes appearing tired. "Not exactly. I've discovered something that I would like to discuss with you."

"Something?" She frowned. "Do you mean you know who's responsible for us losing so many—"

"Sit down, Valene," he instructed.

Val stilled immediately and then took a seat. "Dad, what's going on?"

He took a breath and grabbed a thin folder from his desk. "You know your mom and I love you."

She nodded. "I know. I love you both, too."

"And you know I only want to see you happy?"

"Yes, of course."

He sighed heavily. "I want you to tell me everything you know about Jake Brockton."

Val rolled her eyes. "Not this again. I told you that Jake has nothing to do with what's been happening with the company and—"

"I know that," her father said quietly, cutting her off. "But please, answer the question."

She took a heavy breath. Okay, this was about her father being her *dad*. "You don't have to worry about me. I'm fine. In fact, I've never been better or happier."

"You seem happy," he said. "Answer the question, Valene."

She frowned. "Look, I know you have reservations, but I'll introduce you and Mom to Jake and you'll see that he is—"

"Answer the question," her father said again, firmer and more impatiently.

Val sat back in the chair. "He's very nice. We've been dating a few weeks. He works on a ranch near Fulshear. He's got a mother and a younger sister. He's kind and considerate and handsome and I like him very much. In fact, I more than—"

"Works on a ranch, you say?" her father queried, dropping the file in front of her. "Valene." He said her name with deliberate emphasis. "Your new beau, Jake Brockton, *owns* the Double Rock Ranch."

Val heard white noise so loud it screeched through her ears, then she thought about the absurdity of her father's words and laughed humorlessly. "That's ridiculous, Dad. Jake *works* on the ranch. He quit college when his father died and took over the job as foreman and studied for his degree online a few years later to get his MBA."

"That much is true," he father said and pointed to the file. "It's all in there. It also documents how he purchased the Double Rock Ranch eight years ago and has turned it into a very successful and highly lucrative business."

The white noise returned. "That doesn't make sense. What are you saying, Dad? That Jake is—"

"Wealthy," he supplied. "Very wealthy. In fact, he's so wealthy that at the moment he could probably buy us out ten times over."

It made no sense. Val kept shaking her head, refuting her father's claims. "I don't believe this."

"Believe it," he assured her. "I have no reason to lie to you about this, Valene. However, your boyfriend is another story."

Val's insides ached. "It can't be true. Jake wouldn't deliberately deceive me. Why would he pretend to be a penniless ranch hand?"

"It might have something to do with the fact that his ex-wife took him to the cleaner's in the divorce."

Ex-wife?

Val wanted to throw up. Jake had been married? He was wealthy? He had lied to her over and over? It couldn't be true!

The look on her face must have given her away, because her father quickly responded.

"You weren't aware he'd been married?"

She shook her head. "I thought he had an ex-girl-friend."

"An ex-wife," her father amended. "A pregnant ex-wife, in fact. Take a look, it's all in the investigator's report."

*A pregnant ex-wife?*

Could he have stooped any lower?

The sickness in her belly reached her heart and she stared at the damning file, refusing to open it up and look. She didn't want to hear any more, because none of it made any sense. Why would Jake lie to her? Why would he pretend to be someone he wasn't?

"I'm sorry, kiddo," her father said quietly. "This wasn't what we were looking for when we started this investigation. It's just a little collateral damage, I'm afraid."

Had he really just equated her relationship with Jake to collateral damage?

Val grabbed the file and left the room without saying another word to her father. What could she possible say to assuage the humiliation and embarrassment coursing through her veins? There was no logical reason, no explanation Jake could offer that would undo the betrayal she felt. While she had been going on about gold diggers and money not being important to her, what a great laugh he must have been having at her expense.

When she returned to her office, she slammed the door and dropped into her chair. She noticed two unread text messages on her cell phone from Jake.

Lying, deceitful rat!

She ignored the messages and looked through the file, flicking through the pages with furious fingers.

Multimillionaire, divorced, baby with his ex-wife.

The list of his sins kept getting longer and longer.

She remembered the conversation they'd had in the upstairs bedroom at the ranch. The owner had gotten the place in an ugly divorce, he'd said. While that might have been true, he'd neglected to tell her *he* was the owner! He must have been laughing his ass off behind her back the whole time he was trying to get her into bed. Because that's clearly all they were about—the wildflowers, her favorite bagel, the sketches of her beloved dog, the trip to the animal shelter, the horseback riding, the agonizing wait for his first kiss…the man certainly had the seduction thing down to a fine art. What was worse, he knew how important honesty was to her. She'd told him, when they were wrapped in each other's arms, how difficult it had been to learn to trust again after Diego's blatant disregard for her feelings once she'd discovered he was only interested in the Fortunado name and money. What a gullible and utter fool he must think her to be.

*Jerk! Jerk! Jerk!*

She hated him.

"Hey, sis?"

She looked up, not realizing she was holding her head in her hands. And also not realizing she had tears on her cheeks. Maddie stood in the half-open doorway, her expression filled with compassion and worse, pity.

"I know, you told me so, right?" she said and shrugged. "You said not to trust him, and I didn't listen and now—"

"Don't blame yourself," Maddie said gently and closed the door. "You didn't know he was pretending to be someone he wasn't."

Val scowled. "Why would he do it? Why act like a poor man when…" Her words trailed off and she gave a brittle laugh. "He took me to Toscano's for our first real date. I asked him how he managed to get a reservation on such short notice, and he said he knew the owner through the beef business. *His* beef business. He picked me up in a brand-new truck the night of the charity benefit, and when I asked him who owned it, he said it belonged to the ranch. *His* ranch. He gave me a tour of the ranch house that's being renovated and said the owner had been through an ugly divorce. *His* ugly divorce. And there's a child," she added, her rage gaining momentum. "He has a *child* and he didn't tell me. And I…I fell for it… I fell for his sexy, workingman charm, and within a couple of dates I was putty in his hands. I fell in love with a man I know *nothing* about, Maddie. Everything he said to me was twisted around and manipulated and said for a purpose—because he wanted to deceive me into thinking he was someone else—someone with values and integrity and honor. I feel like such a complete fool. And a condescending one, at that, because I know there were times over the past few weeks when I said things that made me sound like a spoiled snob. And all this time he was probably laughing at me."

"Perhaps there's an explanation," Maddie said, clearly trying to be a voice of reason.

Val shook her head. "There's nothing he can say to me that will erase the lies."

Maddie sighed. "What are you going to do, Val?"

She took a breath and squared her shoulders. "I'm going to do what I should have done the first time we met. I'm going to tell him to go straight to hell!"

Jake was standing in front of the house on Friday morning, listening to the drywall contractor complain about unreasonable time frames to get the place finished when he spotted Valene's car coming down the driveway.

He hadn't spoken to her the evening before. Instead she'd sent a text message pleading a headache and promising she would talk to him the following day. He certainly hadn't expected to see her. But he wasn't unhappy. All he needed to do was get the contractor to stop talking.

"Okay, okay," he said and held up his hand. "Another week, but that's it. I want it finished and your crew out of here by the end of the month."

He turned and walked down the path, greeting her as she pulled up and turned off the engine. She got out and as always, his heart skipped a beat. She looked tired, he thought, as though she hadn't slept, and he wondered if she was still struggling with a headache.

"Hey there, this is a nice surprise." He bent his head to kiss her and she twisted unexpectedly, so he only managed to feel her cheek beneath his mouth. "Everything okay?"

She looked up, her brown eyes darker than he'd ever seen them. "Perfect. Things have never seemed clearer."

He noticed she was wearing her work attire, as though she'd come directly from the office, and her hair was up in a tight ponytail. "Valene, I—"

"I was wondering if you could show me around some more," she said and took a few steps toward the house. "You know, give me the full tour experience. Take me into every room of the house, and every stall and stable. I mean, I know you'd planned on giving me the full tour tomorrow, but since I'm here," she said and held up her arms, "how about right now?"

The tone of her voice sent alarms bells ringing, and since the tension emanating from her was palpable, it took him about two seconds to figure out what was wrong.

*She knows...*

"Valene," he said quietly. "Let's go inside and—"

"Inside?" she said shrilly. "Inside where? The bunkhouse? Your mom's house? The ranch house? Oh, hang on," she said and pointed to the house. "I mean, *your* house."

The air sucked from his lungs. "I wanted to tell you."

"When?" she demanded. "On our first date? Our second date? The first time you kissed me? The first time you got me into bed?"

It was then that he realized they had an audience. His mother, for one, and several of the contractors who were trying to look uninterested from their spot on the scaffolding.

"Let me explain," he said quietly.

"Explain what?" she shot back. "That you're not a penniless ranch hand?"

"I never actually said I was. You just assumed I—"

"I made an assumption based on what you told me," she said angrily. "On what I believed was the truth. The fact that nothing you have said to me so far *is* the truth makes it very clear what you think of me and this thing between us."

Jake could see the hurt etched on every line on her face. "I know I deceived you, Valene, but it wasn't ever intentionally malicious. And I tried to tell you several times about the ranch, but it—"

"I must have missed that part," she said, cutting him off. "And the part about your ex-wife!"

"Okay," he said, exasperated. "I also should have told you about Patrice. But frankly, it didn't seem important."

She laughed. "Not important? What about the baby, Jake? I guess that isn't important, either?"

His gut clenched. "It's not what you think."

"I don't believe it matters what I think. If it did, you wouldn't have been lying your ass off to me for the past three weeks."

He understood her anger, but it still annoyed the hell out of him. She wasn't listening. She wasn't even *trying* to listen. "I planned on telling you tomorrow night."

"Too little, too late."

Irritation curled up his spine. "That's an immature response, Valene. Yes, okay, I'm wealthy. I bought this ranch eight years ago, and with a lot of hard work I've made a lot of money, some that I've invested, some I've given to charity. And yes, I was married and now I'm divorced. And yes, my ex-wife *was* pregnant when we separated. But none of that," he emphasized, "has anything to do with you and me."

She shook her head, clearly bemused. And furious.

"It has everything to do with you and me," she shot back. "I trusted you."

"I know. I'm sorry."

"That doesn't cut it. Because I believed you trusted me, too. But I can see that clearly it was a one-way street. You had your own agenda and I was too gullible and naive to see it for what it was. I have to hand it to you, Jake, you gave a damned fine performance of being a humble ranch hand—right up to the cowboy dancing and wildflowers."

"It wasn't a performance, Valene. It was real, all of it. And the money doesn't change who I am."

She didn't look convinced. "Well, it shouldn't…but I'll never know, will I? You duped me. You made me believe you were someone you're not, and at times you made me feel small-minded and spoiled and overindulged. I've admitted things to you about myself that I've never told anyone, and as I was driving over here to say goodbye to you, it occurred to me that you really didn't let me get to know much of you at all."

Jake's belly took a dive. What was she saying? "Goodbye?"

"Yes," she replied. "I don't want to see you again."

"You're not serious."

"I'm perfectly serious."

Jake ran a hand through his hair, ignoring the fact that his mother and the contractors were in earshot and could probably hear every word they were saying. "So, we had a fight. We'll get past it."

She shook her head. "I don't want to get past it, Jake. And I'm pleased that I found all this out now, before I got in too deep. Have a nice life."

She turned and opened the car door, flinging it wide for effect.

"Valene…sweetheart, would you please let me—"

"I told my sister I was going to tell you to go to hell," she said and started the ignition. "But I can't want that for you, because I care too much. Damn you, Jake," she said, her eyes glistening with tears. "Damn you for making me fall in love with you."

Then she slammed the door and drove off down the driveway. Through the gates.

And out of his life.

"You just going to stand there," his mother said from behind him, "or are you going after her?"

Jake thrust his hands into his jacket pockets. "You heard her. She said goodbye."

His mother came up beside him. "I heard a very unhappy girl say that she was in love with you."

His insides clenched. "If that was true, she wouldn't have left."

"She's hurting. People act irrationally when they are hurt."

"Valene's in love with the idea of being in love,"

he said, watching her car disappear into the distance, aching all over. "You don't fall for someone in three weeks."

"I did," his mother said. "I knew I loved your father the first time we met. It was a blind date."

"I know the story, Mom."

"And you know how it played out," she reminded him. "We were married seven weeks after we first met. We had two wonderful children and twenty amazing years together. And I still miss him every day of my life."

Jake's throat tightened. "I know you do."

"I don't regret one moment. Losing him was devastating, but I know I wouldn't feel this intense grief if I hadn't experienced such a great love."

Jake sighed heavily. "What's your point, Mom?"

"You've allowed what happened with Patrice to damage your heart, Jake. You've fallen for Valene and you are too afraid to admit it."

"I'm not afraid of anything," he said quietly. "I simply don't believe that falling in love happens overnight. It takes time and—"

"Who are you trying to convince?" his mother queried. "The rest of the world, or yourself?"

It was a question he couldn't answer. He only knew he hurt all over.

And had no idea what he was going to do about it.

## Chapter Eleven

Val had no desire to see Jake on Saturday. But she'd promised Florrie she'd be at the shelter to help out with the fund-raiser, and she wouldn't go back on her word. She spotted his truck in the parking lot. His new truck. Not the old Ranger he'd driven almost every time she'd seen him. Seeing the cherry-red vehicle inflamed her already fuming temper.

And her broken heart.

She'd spoken to both Schuyler and Maddie at length the night before, Schuyler pointing out Jake's many good points, despite his obvious deception. Maddie wasn't quite so forgiving, but even she tried to be more neutral than usual, no doubt because she knew Val was hurting so much. But Val wasn't hearing any of it. He'd lied. End of story. Schuyler, as expected, was more flexible and suggested she talk to him. But Val wasn't going to be manipulated any longer. She'd made her decision.

They were over.

She grabbed the gift basket she'd put together as a raffle prize and headed toward the tent near the entrance. Florrie was there, handing out instructions to the volunteers. A couple of dozen temporary pens had been erected for the dogs going up for adoption, and several cat cages had been set up underneath one of the tents. There was a face painter, some rides for the little tots and several craft stalls.

"Good morning," Florrie greeted her with a wide grin. "I think we're in for a busy day. I'm going to set you up in this tent to collate the adoption applications as they come in. Let's keep our fingers crossed that Digby finds his own special family today."

Val's already vulnerable emotions were pushed to the edge. Poor unwanted Digby. She swallowed the lump in her throat, took a deep breath and plastered on a wide smile. "I'll keep my fingers crossed. So, show me what to do."

Ten minutes later Valene was set up under the tent and had another one of the volunteers, Cam, a young man in his midtwenties, for company.

People started arriving, milling around the pens and strolling past the stalls. She sold raffle tickets and gave out information leaflets, and it wasn't long before she processed her first application for a mixed-breed puppy. She was laughing with Cam when she spotted Jake striding down past the dog pens, with a couple of large bags of dog food piled on one shoulder. He dropped the food in the tent and came around the side of the table, where he squatted beside her.

"Good morning, Valene."

She glanced his way and shrugged. There was nothing good about being forced to spend time with him. "Hello."

"How are you?"

"Fine."

He moved closer. "Can we talk privately?"

She pushed back her shoulders. "I'd rather not."

Cam clearly sensed the tension between them, because he was on his feet in a microsecond and quickly excused himself, making himself useful at the dog pens by chatting with prospective adopters and leaving her alone with Jake.

"Valene, please look at me."

She took a breath and met his gaze. "What?"

"I wasn't expecting you to turn up today."

"I made a commitment to Florrie," she said stiffly. "And I like to think of myself as someone with honor."

It was a direct dig, and they both knew it.

Humiliation burned her skin. She'd told him she was in love with him. God, it was too embarrassing to bear thinking about.

"Would you let me explain?"

"No."

He made an exasperated sound. "You just plan on staying mad at me?"

"Yes."

She *was* being childish, but Val was too hurt to care. She wanted to cry and hate him for all eternity. She'd spent close to forty-eight hours thinking about his lies, his ex-wife, his child and every other truth he hadn't had the decency to come clean about.

He stayed where he was for a moment and then exhaled heavily before straightening and walking off, his shoulders tight, his hands clenched at his sides. Even when she hated him, Val was still achingly attracted to every wretched inch of the man. He looked so gorgeous in his jeans, shirt and sheepskin-lined jacket.

"Never let the sun go down on an argument."

Val turned her head and saw Florrie standing behind her, a curious expression on her face.

She shrugged. "It's complicated."

"Love usually is. But I've known Jake for a long time, and I don't think I've ever seen him as happy as he's been the last few weeks. By my reckoning," Florrie said and grinned, "that's all your doing."

It was a nice fairy tale. But the older woman didn't know the details, and Val wasn't about to admit to anything. She didn't have a chance to respond, because Florrie spoke again.

"He had a hard time with that wife of his. She was bad news. Especially what she put him through with the baby." The older woman sighed thoughtfully. "He really would have taken care of the child. But she knew what she was doing right from the beginning. Hateful woman. He was heartbroken for such a long time."

Val could barely get air into her lungs. She didn't want to hear about Jake's ex-wife or his child or how broken his heart was. She didn't want to *feel* anything. At least, she didn't want to feel anything other than anger and rage, because that's all that was keeping her from crying every single second of the day.

Thankfully, Cam returned with a family looking to adopt one of the older dogs. Not Digby, unfortunately, and after a couple of hours Val walked to his pen and spent some time with the dog. He was such a sweet-natured little thing and clearly adored company. She was closing the door to his pen when she heard Jake's voice.

"I see no one is interested in him."

She glanced sideways and wrapped her arms around herself. "No."

Jake reached into the pen and picked the dog up. "He'll find the right family one day."

The pooch licked Jake's face and he laughed, the sound sending goose bumps across Val's skin. "Not everyone gets their happily-ever-after."

"That's a grim view of things," he said and petted the dog's ears.

"I guess I'm in one of those moods."

"Can I call you later?"

Val's mouth flattened. "No."

His brows rose. "Can I text you?"

"No."

"Can I send a raven?" he suggested and smiled, using a line from *Game of Thrones*, one of her favorite television series.

Val planted her hands on her hips. "No calls, no texts, no ravens. I told you that we were over, Jake," she said and realized that just saying his name hurt.

"You said you were in love with me," he reminded her. "Did you mean it?"

"Of course not," she refuted, hating that he'd brought her admission into the conversation. "I was confused and angry and—"

"You can avoid me, Valene," he said, cutting her off, "if that's what you really want to do."

"That's exactly what I want."

"I don't believe you."

She glared at him. "I don't lie, Jake. That's your department."

Then she walked off.

"Mom said you screwed up big-time."

Jake glared at his sister. Cassidy had the bad habit of saying whatever was on her mind, whenever the mood took her. And all her attention had been focused on him for the last ten minutes. She'd arrived at the ranch half an hour before and met him at the top of the stairs in the main house.

"Just leave it alone, okay?"

She shrugged. "Have you tried talking to her?"

He'd tried. Several times. He'd sent flowers. He'd sent text messages. And nothing. It was as though she'd wiped him from her memory.

"I wish you and Mom would stop gossiping."

"Can't help it. But I can help you," Cassidy said and grinned. "Let's have a look at your profile on the dating app and—"

"Forget it," Jake said, holding up his hands. "No more dating apps, no more dates, no more interfering in my life, okay? Next time I want a date, I'll find one the old-fashioned way."

Cassidy made a face. "Jake, you're so old-school and out of touch. This is how people meet each other these days. We're all busy, we're all trying to juggle careers and school and home life and friends and family. Things like this app simply speed up the process, that's all. Stop being such a stick-in-the-mud about it. If we set your profile back up on Perfect Match, soon you'll have—"

"I don't want to date anyone else, okay?"

"Anyone else?" she queried. "You mean, anyone other than Valene?"

Busted. His sister was too smart for her own good. "I'm not ready."

Cassidy's expression softened. "You really like her?"

Jake nodded. "I do."

"Is she ever going to forgive you?"

He shrugged. "It doesn't seem likely."

"I'm sorry, Jake."

"Yeah, kid, me too."

\* \* \*

It was almost a week later, on Friday afternoon, when Jake headed into Houston to meet with his accountant. He'd been planning for some time to expand the business into Austin, and after spending all week crunching numbers, he decided he could certainly afford to take the chance now. After a productive meeting, he drove directly to the Fortunado Real Estate building.

"Jake?"

Maddie Fortunado-McCarter greeted him in the reception area a few minutes after he'd asked to see either her or Zach McCarter.

"Hello, Maddie."

She looked as guarded as always. "Val's not here. She's doing an open house and then going home afterward."

"It's you I'm here to see," he said swiftly. "Business."

One brow rose, and he remembered how Valene did exactly the same thing. In Maddie's office, twenty minutes later—after a conversation with Maddie and her husband—Jake nodded in agreement.

"Okay, sounds good."

"Val isn't going to be happy about this," Maddie remarked and keyed a few more notes into the laptop on her desk. "She hates you at the moment. With good reason," she added.

Jake wasn't about to get into a conversation about his and Valene's relationship with any of her relatives—as least, not until he spoke to her first. "It's business."

"Are you sure?" Zach asked.

"Do you mean am I sure I would have walked through the door of this building and not one of your competitors' had I not known Valene?" He shrugged. "I think so. Your company has a good reputation. And if you can get me what I want, where I want, for the price I want, then we have a deal."

The other man nodded and shook his hand. "I'll get right on it."

When Jake left, he stopped by Toscano's and ordered some takeout and then drove to Valene's condo, hoping she was home. She was. But she clearly had no intention of letting him in. Or having dinner with him.

"I have a date tonight," she said through the speaker system at the gate. "Go away."

"Please, Valene, I'd like to talk to you. Just talk. And after that, if you want to end things, then I will respect your decision."

Silence stretched between them like brittle elastic. Then she spoke. "Just talk?"

"Yes," he said quickly. "And eat dinner. I picked up Toscano's and I thought – "

"You thought wrong," she said frostily. "Go away."

Jake took a long and steady breath. "Please, Valene?"

Her heard her sigh, feeling her unhappiness through to the marrow in his bones. Then she spoke. "Okay."

Minutes later he was standing on her doorstep.

He held out the food as he crossed the threshold and Bruce came racing down the hallway.

"Make it quick," she said, taking the bag and heading to the kitchen. She placed the food on the countertop and crossed her arms tightly. "Talk."

Jake managed a smile. "You don't want to eat?"

"I told you I had a date."

His gut clenched. "Seriously?"

She nodded. "I didn't realize I needed your permission."

"You don't," he replied and swallowed the ache constricting his throat. "I just thought…"

"What?" she shot back. "That I would sit around moping? Wishing things were different? Pining after you?"

"I've missed you this week," he admitted.

"You mean you missed your weekly sleepover?"

"This isn't about sex," he retorted. "I miss talking to you. I miss our friendship."

"Friends don't lie to each other," she said hotly. "Friends don't make each other feel like a fool."

"If I did that, it wasn't my intention."

She didn't look convinced. "I must have sounded like an entitled snob to you—asking you if you had a suit, making comments about your old truck, acting as though I had any kind of clue what it's like to live paycheck to paycheck. What a joke I must have been to you. I insulted you every time I opened my mouth and I didn't even know it. But you did. That's quite the power play, Jake. I bet you play a good game of poker."

Even angry with him, she looked so passionate, so beautiful. It was everything he liked about her. Everything he *loved* about her.

Because he *did* love her.

Maybe it was too soon. Maybe he was crazy for allowing himself to feel something so intense after such a short time. But he didn't care.

And she deserved his truth, even if she didn't want to hear it.

Jake walked into the living room and sat down, pressing his hands onto his knees. He waited for her, hoping she'd sit beside him, but she chose a seat across the room. Finally, he spoke.

"Nothing about our relationship is a joke to me, Valene."

"I don't know how to believe anything you say."

"You can," he assured her. "Because you *know* me."

She looked uncertain. "Do I?"

"All right, you want the truth, here it goes. I was married," he said heavily. "For a few years. Her name was Patrice. I knew her in high school, but back then she never looked in my direction. I was working class, blue collar, and her father was a lawyer and she was part of the it crowd. But I noticed her. I was young and she was beautiful…but sort of cold, like one of those mannequins in a department store. When school ended I went to college and put all thought of Patrice out of my mind. And then my dad died," he said and let out a long and painful breath, "and I had to go home. The people who owned the ranch would have made my mom and Cassidy leave."

He paused, sensing she wanted to say something.

"That seems harsh."

"Just the way things are." He shrugged. "I came home and started working as a ranch hand, and in a year or so I was made foreman. My dad had left an insurance policy, which my mom invested and I worked a second job packing shelves at a store not far from the ranch. I studied for my degree and waited for the opportunity I sensed was coming. It happened when the owners said they were selling. I knew my mom didn't want to leave, and Cassidy was still in school. So I got a mortgage and with Mom's help I bought a ranch at a ridiculously low price because it had pretty much been insolvent for the previous decade."

"That's quite a risk," she said quietly.

Jake shrugged. "I had to try. My family was at stake."

"And the business?"

"I got lucky. I made a few good decisions and found a place in the market for a high-end product. I invested well, and in a couple of years the ranch was financially viable."

It was a gross understatement. Jake had made his first million within two short years.

"And then?" she asked.

"Patrice came back into my life," he supplied. "Only now I was successful enough to get her attention. But the marriage was a disaster, and neither of us was ever happy. It turned out that her father had a gambling problem, and I bailed him out more than once. And Patrice had her own demons. She demanded we renovate the house, so I agreed. Frankly, at that point I was prepared to do whatever I could to help salvage our marriage. But nothing was ever good enough. She went through money like it was water."

"Is that why you divorced her?"

He sighed. "I divorced her because I found her in bed with one of the contractors I'd hired to renovate the house."

Valene gasped and placed her hand to her mouth for a moment. "How despicable."

The pain and memory from those days had lessened with time, but the muscles between Jake's shoulders still twitched. "Like I said, Patrice had her troubles."

Silence stretched between them, and Jake forced himself to remain on the couch. He wanted to touch her so badly, to hold her in his arms and feel the tonic of her touch through to his very soul.

"And your child?"

A sharper, more intense pain twisted in his chest. "Not mine."

"Then why did Florrie tell me you would have raised the baby?"

"Patrice told me she was pregnant after we separated," he explained. "I'm certain she hoped it would mean a reconciliation."

"But that's not what you wanted?"

"God, no," he replied. "I've never believed that monogamy is a big price to pay when you're in a committed relationship. So for me, it was a deal breaker. But I would have raised the child with her, even though we weren't together anymore. However, that's not what she wanted to hear. That's when she said the baby wasn't mine and that she'd only married me for my money. She said that it didn't matter how big my bank balance was, I would always be working class. And that I would never be good enough for her. That I would never be successful enough. Never rich enough. After that, what ensued was a very bitter and very ugly divorce that cost me a lot of money and my pride and eventually robbed me of my ability to trust anyone."

It was the first time he'd admitted it out loud. And the first time he'd told anyone other than his attorney how bitter and recriminatory things had become between himself and his ex-wife. But he wanted Valene to know what he was feeling. And why he'd kept the truth from her about the ranch and his considerable wealth.

Val stared at him, feeling the connection between them with a blistering intensity. Her head was jumbled with so many emotions—compassion and understanding and then rage and resentment toward the woman who had hurt him so badly.

But that still didn't absolve Jake of his decision to lie to her.

"And the child?" she asked.

"She lost the baby. The last I heard she was living in New Orleans."

"She broke your heart?"

He shrugged. "More like my spirit."

Val pressed her knees together. "Why are you telling me this now?"

"Because you wanted my story."

"I wanted your story weeks ago," she said and got to her feet. "Before the feelings started."

"I couldn't," he admitted. "I didn't know you well enough. I didn't know if I could trust you."

"Trust me to do what?"

He stood and paced the room for a few seconds, seemingly oblivious to Bruce dancing around his feet. "To like me for me," he said softly. "To want me…for me."

Val couldn't believe what she was hearing. Insecurity. Vulnerability. Things she knew a man like Jake would consider a weakness.

"You thought I might only be interested in your bank account, and that's why you didn't tell me who you really were?"

He shrugged, his broad shoulders sagging. "I had to be sure."

Val heard the pain in his words, overwhelmed by the reality of what he was feeling. After Diego, she'd also questioned her worth, and she hadn't experienced anywhere near the betrayal that Jake had. But she still didn't entirely understand his feelings, considering she came from the Fortunado family.

"I never hid who I was from you, Jake," she said quietly. "I might not have been shouting my family tree from the rooftops, but it was never a secret. My family is well off and—"

"In trouble," he added and then shrugged again.

Val's spine straightened. Suddenly she understood

him completely. "You didn't trust me because you believed my family's business is in financial trouble and that somehow I might be a threat to your precious bank balance."

"I couldn't be sure."

Her disbelief turned to anger. "Are you that self-absorbed, Jake?"

"Of course not. I'm not saying this to hurt you, Valene. You wanted the truth," he reminded her. "This is it. I have trust issues, okay? Big trust issues. But I have genuine feelings for you and I don't want to—"

"Genuine feelings?" she echoed. "Yes, I can tell. I can feel every one of those *feelings* each time you insinuate that my family and I are after your money."

"That's not what I said," he remarked, clearly frustrated. "You're mixing up my words. I care about you. I want to pursue our relationship further. I want to date you. I want to make love to you and wake up next to you. I want all those things, Valene. And I'm hoping that we can have them now that we've cleared the air."

"Cleared the air?" She laughed loudly. "Is that what you think? For the record, the air is not cleared. It's about as hazy as it gets. My family doesn't need your money."

He sighed heavily. "I'm not trying to insult your family."

"Maybe you're not, but you're doing a great job, regardless." She checked her watch. "You need to leave now."

He looked skeptical. "Is your date running late?"

"No, I'm sure he'll be on time as always."

She wasn't about to tell him that her parents were picking her up and they were going out to dinner together. Jake had no right to assume anything about her. He'd done enough of that already!

"Please don't go out with another man...not while we're in the middle of this."

Pity for the obvious anguish in his voice quickly took hold of her. "It's not that kind of date. If you must know, I'm meeting my parents for dinner. But I still want you to leave." She gave him the takeout food she'd placed on the counter. "Go home, Jake. I need some time to digest all this information."

"When can I see you again?"

She shrugged. "I'm not sure."

"I don't want this to be the end of us, Valene."

She didn't want that either...not really. But she was hurting through to her bones.

"Good night, Jake."

Once he was gone, Val sagged against the back of the door, propped up on knees she had to lock into place. Damn his gorgeous hide. She shouldn't have let him in. She shouldn't have listened to his explanation. Because now she was more conflicted than she was before.

The problem was, Val was as much in love with Jake Brockton as she'd ever been.

And she was pretty sure he knew it.

## *Chapter Twelve*

Valene didn't hear from Jake for three days. Three of the longest days of her life. She knew he was giving her space, exactly as she'd requested, but she couldn't believe how much she yearned to hear the sound of his voice, or taste his kiss, or feel his breath against her skin.

On Monday he sent her flowers, lots of them—the store-bought variety—which irritated her to no end, even though all the women in the office thought it was hopelessly romantic. On Tuesday it was a stuffed toy in the shape of a bulldog, and Wednesday it was a poster from her favorite zombie television show. Even Maddie sighed a little at his efforts.

"Since when did you become the president of Jake's fan club?" she queried in the lunchroom when her sister asked if she'd seen him.

"I'm not," Maddie replied. "Just wondering how you feel about him at the moment."

"Angry," she replied. "Hurt. Disappointed. He truly thought I would be after his money."

"Well," Maddie said and shrugged, "people are often motivated by a lot less."

Val's gaze narrowed. "What are you suggesting, Maddie, that I simply forgive him and move on?"

"Maybe that's not such a bad idea."

Val stirred extra sugar into her coffee. "I'm not so sure you'd be as forgiving of Zach if you were in my situation."

Maddie rested her hip against the countertop. "Do you remember when Dad pitted Zach and me against one another for the CEO position?"

"Of course."

"Do you remember how I thought Zach had deliberately gone behind my back with a client?"

Val remembered the whole situation. It was the first time she'd witnessed her usually reserved sister at the mercy of her emotions. "I remember."

"And of course, that wasn't the case. But I jumped to conclusions based on the facts I believed I knew."

"It's hardly the same scenario," Val pointed out. "For one, Zach was crazy in love with you."

Maddie's brows rose. "And you don't believe Jake is in love with you?"

"I think he wants me," she admitted, hurting all over. "I think the sex is great and we get along and we became friends and enjoy spending time together and somehow that started to feel like more. But he lied to me, over and over. I believed he was someone else. In all that time when we were getting to know one another, I thought he was a certain kind of man, and he's not. He's rich and successful, and as Dad pointed out, he could buy us out ten times over."

"You almost sound as though you'd prefer he be a penniless ranch hand."

Val sighed. "I'd prefer he was honest from the beginning. I'd prefer that what we had was real and not simply Jake moving me around like a piece on a chessboard. It feels like Diego all over again."

"Except that Jake *isn't* Diego," Maddie reminded her. "He hasn't asked for anything from you other than *you*. What are you so scared of facing, Val?"

"The truth," she said dully. "I was duped. Made to look foolish."

"In whose eyes?"

"Mine," she admitted.

"So, your reaction is about pride?"

Val swallowed the heat in her throat. "It's about value. How I value myself. And that I'm not just *little* Valene, the spoiled daughter of Kenneth Fortunado, who will tolerate anything because I'm compliant and good-natured and easily manipulated. I know I'm not going to change the world, Maddie. I'm not extreme—I'm not passionate about causes like Schuyler is or driven by a need for success like you are. I'm middle-of-the-road. I'm reliable and predictable in the feelings department. I'm the person who always buys an extra gift on the holidays just in case someone unexpected turns up. I'm the person who will always be the designated driver on a night out. I'm the person a gold-digging creep like Diego would target, because I am gullible and have an insatiable need to be liked. I'm the person a man like Hugh would want to be with, because I will never be chaotic or unpredictable."

"And Jake?"

"Honestly," she replied, "I have no idea why Jake is attracted to me."

"Why don't you ask him?"

"I'm not sure I want to hear the answer."

Maddie reached out and unexpectedly hugged her. "You're strong and beautiful and kind, and being around you is like balm for the soul, Val. That's why Jake is attracted to you. It's why we all love you. Why we all need to be around you. You make our lives better. You make the world better."

Val's eyes filled with tears. "I love him, Maddie."

Her sister squeezed her tightly. "I know you do."

"I just don't know if I can forgive him."

"Well, the only way you're going to find out is if you talk to him."

Val knew Maddie was right. When she returned to her office, she stared at the flowers for a few minutes. It took about an hour of emotional yo-yoing before she garnered the courage to grab her phone.

I think we should talk. V.

The text reply came back in about ten seconds.

Love to. Tell me when. J.

She took a breath and sent another message.

Coffee. Tomorrow. Eleven. You know the place. V.

He replied with a thumbs-up emoji. They had a date. It would be make or break. Being in love with Jake was one thing—it was out of her control—but forgiveness was harder. Because if she did forgive him for deceiving her, she'd open herself up to vulnerability and potential heartbreak. It was a giant leap for Val.

Being with Diego, and even Hugh, had switched off something inside her. Diego had used her. Hugh had admitted he didn't love her but she was suitable wife material. She thought about Jake's words about being wanted for *who* he was, not his bank balance, and Val understood. Neither of her previous relationships had been about her. For Diego, it was the money, for Hugh, her family tree. The realization had left her with envy in her heart when her two sisters had found love. Not jealousy—because she wasn't that mean-spirited and she truly adored both Maddie and Schuyler—but she knew she wanted the same kind of deep connection with someone. The way Zach adored Maddie, the way he relaxed her often prickly defenses through love and commitment and support. And the way Carlo clearly loved Schuyler more than life itself, revering her craziness, keeping her grounded. It's why she'd logged on to the dating app. Why she'd punched in her details and opened herself up to the possibility of meeting a man that a computer program insisted was her perfect match.

And she'd met him.

Hardworking, successful, strong, funny, a man who possessed a strict moral compass. A man who cared for the people around him, who'd quit college to protect his family, who'd built a business from the ground up using sweat and smarts and steely determination.

Too bad he'd also deceived her like the lousy rat he was.

When Val walked into the coffeehouse the following morning, she realized she was more nervous than when she'd done the same thing a month earlier.

A lot had happened since then.

The place was empty except for someone ordering at the counter and a young couple sitting at a table in the back. Val looked around, seeing no sign of Jake, and walked toward the same booth where they'd sat on their first meeting.

A few minutes later, Jake strode through the doors. He looked so gorgeous, so tall and broad and familiar. He spotted her immediately and headed for the booth.

"Mornin'," he said and sat down.

A waiter approached and took their order, and once the young man left, Val spoke.

"Thank you for meeting me."

He met her gaze. "It's good to see you. How are you?"

"Okay. You?"

"Better for seeing you," he said candidly. "I have some news from the shelter. It looks as though Digby will get his own family."

Val's heart rolled over. "I'm so glad."

"See, sometimes everyone does get their happily-ever-after."

She placed her hands on the table. "Thank you for the zombie poster."

He grinned. "My pleasure."

"The flowers and stuffed toy were a bit over-the-top."

He shrugged. "I just want to make sure you keep thinking about me."

Val made a face. "I don't think I could stop thinking about you even if I tried. But I'm still mad at you."

"I know."

"However, I'm trying to be a grown-up about it," she admitted. "I'm trying to keep things in perspective."

"Like how?"

"Like, I know you didn't tell me who you were because you didn't want to be judged...but by not telling me, you were judging *me*. And my family. Something I take very personally."

"I'm sorry I hurt you, Valene."

Val heard the earnestness in his voice, took a breath and was about to speak when they were interrupted by the waiter with their coffees. After he left, she said, "Okay, let's take a small step and have a do-over."

"A do-over?"

"Yes." She held out her hand. "Hi, my name is Valene Fortunado. I'm twenty-four, single, I work in my family's business, where things have been a little tough recently. I live in a condo my father bought for me, I have a dog called Bruce, and I once paid twelve hundred dollars for a pair of shoes. I'm spoiled and have an opinion about pretty much everything."

He grinned as he shook her hand. "I'm Jake Brockton. Thirty-two, divorced, with major trust issues. I own a very successful ranch outside Fulshear and worry that I'm going to be wanted for my money and not myself."

"See," Val said with a fake smile. "That wasn't so difficult, was it?"

"Harder than you can possibly imagine."

"Don't keep things from me again, Jake. Trust goes both ways."

"I know," he said quietly. "I'm learning to let go of the past, Valene."

She nodded. "I understand. All my life I've been overprotected and looked after. It's as though my family doesn't believe I can handle the hard stuff. But I can," she assured him. "I can handle whatever I need to. I can fight fires and slay dragons—and of course I don't mean that in the literal sense, but you get the drift. I know my parents treat me differently because I'm the youngest, and in many ways, I appreciate being shielded from the world…but sometimes I wish everyone in my family would treat me as though I am a grown-up and able to fully contribute in a meaningful way."

"You think they don't?"

"I think I got the job at Fortunado Real Estate as a way of keeping me close. My parents were worried that I was planning on going to college out of state—which was never the case. I love Houston and I love being close to my family. But still, sometimes I'm smothered by their need to keep a watchful eye on everything I do."

"Family is all that matters, Valene, and if they smother you, it's only because they care."

"That's a nice sentiment, Jake, but I wouldn't expect a self-made man to understand." She laughed humorlessly. "You know, the irony is, my father would really like you."

"I'd like to meet him. And your mom."

Val took a breath. "Okay. Friday night. My parents are having a family get-together. Schuyler and Carlo are driving in from Austin, and my brother Everett and his wife, Lila, will be there—I think I told you that he's a doctor. And my other brother Gavin and his fiancée, who I haven't seen since Maddie's wedding last month. He's a workaholic lawyer. Plus Maddie and Zach."

"Will I be there as your date?"

"I haven't decided," she replied. "To be honest, I haven't decided if I'll forgive you, either."

He leaned forward and rested his elbows on the table. "I think for both our sakes you should. You know, I haven't forgotten what you said to me at the ranch last week."

Val knew immediately what he was referring to. "That was a heat-of-the-moment thing. I was angry and worked up and I can't be blamed for things that might have been said rashly and without proper consideration."

He laughed. "Have you been practicing that perfectly eloquent backpedal, Valene?"

Val's skin heated. "You're such a horse's ass, Jake. I'm not going to incriminate myself any further. Are you accepting the invitation to meet my parents or not?"

"Of course."

Val drank her latte and then wiggled a little in the booth, indicating she was ready to leave. "I'll text you my parents' home address."

"I'll pick you up and we'll go together."

She wasn't about to let him have his own way. "That's the offer, Jake. Meet me there or don't show."

His mouth flattened. "Okay, I accept your terms."

She nodded. "See you Friday. Seven o'clock."

And then she left as swiftly as her legs allowed.

*The Fortunado estate is impressive*, Jake thought as he pulled in the driveway. He spotted Val's Lexus immediately and parked the Sierra behind a white Volvo and a red BMW. He got out, strode onto the wide front porch and then knocked on the huge wooden double doors. A few minutes later, the door opened and a middle-aged woman appeared. She was tall and attractive, and he recognized Valene's brown eyes.

"You must be Jake," she said, her voice soft and cultured and *very* southern. "I'm Barbara Fortunado. It's lovely to meet you."

Jake shook her hand and was politely ushered inside. The house, as expected, was well appointed and tasteful, and the floors gleamed with polish. "Thank you for inviting me."

Barbara smiled. "My daughter is quite taken with you."

Jake chuckled. "Yeah, but I don't think she likes me very much at the moment."

"She's stubborn," the older woman said quietly. "She gets that from her father. She's also unwaveringly honest. She gets that from me. We've spoiled her, of course, but I imagine you know that. That being said, she has such a kind and forgiving heart, I don't imagine she will stay angry with you forever."

He grinned. "I hope not."

"For the record, when one of my cubs is hurting, I do tend to get a little lioness about things."

"Oh, God, Mom, let him at least get in the house before you start giving him the talk."

Jake heard Valene's voice and then spotted her when she appeared in the hallway, her heels clicking over the floorboards. Bruce was bounding behind her, followed by a fluff ball that he suspected was Maddie's pet, Ramona. Valene had told him all about her sister's very pampered pooch the day they'd spent volunteering at the animal shelter.

He met Valene's gaze, wanting desperately to haul her into his arms and kiss her. But he didn't. For one thing, Barbara Fortunado was watching them keenly, and for another, he was certain Valene would take a swing at him if he tried.

"Valene has told me about the good work you're doing with the Fortunado Foundation," he told her mother. "I'd like to talk with you about it sometime."

"You're interested in charity work?"

He nodded. "I'm interested in learning more about your foundation. I support a few local charitable organizations, but if I can help with your charity, I will."

Valene was frowning. "Yes, Mom, he is perfectly serious. Jake's a born do-gooder. You two will get along famously."

He passed Valene the two bottles of wine he'd brought, and she grabbed his arm. She looked so good, so sexy in a short red tunic dress and black boots.

"Cute outfit."

She gave a wide smile. "You don't look so bad yourself."

He glanced down, pleased he'd ditched his usual jeans and Western shirt for taupe cargos, a white shirt and a leather aviator-style jacket. "I can tone down the cowboy thing every now and then."

"So I see," she said and moved closer, leading him into the kitchen. "But you know, I've kinda gotten used to that cowboy thing you've got going."

Before he could reply, the room erupted in a series of greetings and introductions. Kenneth Fortunado was naturally reserved at first, but the rest of her family was friendly and talkative. Her brother Everett and his wife, Lila, were nice people, as were Gavin and his fiancée, and Maddie surprisingly kissed his cheek.

Before dinner, Kenneth cornered him, but Jake didn't mind. He figured he'd be equally suspicious if he had a daughter. Which only made him imagine what it would be like to have a child with Valene. Which was, he realized, something he genuinely wanted.

"My daughter spoke very highly of you," the older man said.

*Spoke.* Past tense. "She's quite a woman."

Kenneth nodded. "Of course, she told you I had an investigator check out your history. I had to, you understand, as there have been attempts to sabotage my business, and with everything that is going on with the

Robinson family and the Fortunes—" He paused. "I suppose you know about that, too?"

"Valene mentioned it."

"If I had my way, I would forget the Fortunes exist, particularly the fact that I'm related to them. But I have to protect my family."

"I understand," Jake replied, trying not to feel too outraged at the blatant invasion of his privacy. "I trust Valene has explained to you some of the details of my divorce?"

"She said enough," Kenneth replied. "She's still very upset with you for deceiving her."

"I know," Jake said as he caught her laughter from the other side of the room.

"My wife and I have overprotected her," Kenneth admitted. "Naturally, with the last child, you try to learn from the mistakes you made with the others. Not that she needed it. But we indulged her and tried to make things as easy as possible for her. But she's stubborn—she gets that from her mother," he said and grinned. "Anyway, I wanted to apologize for digging into your past."

Jake wondered if Kenneth would have been less apologetic had he not discovered Jake's net worth, but he shrugged off the thought. He didn't want to resent Valene's family, and he was genuinely interested in helping the Fortunado Foundation, about which he'd heard great things. It was time he got back to living a full life and started doing things that were important to him. His work at the shelter was important, but with his resources, Jake knew he could do so much more.

"No sweat," he said and smiled. "Are you any closer to finding out who is behind all of the trouble?"

Kenneth shrugged. "Not yet. But I know one thing— there are a few too many coincidences for it to be mere chance. And I'll tell you, when I find the person or persons responsible, they will regret the day they took on my family and expected to win."

"Well, if you need someone in your corner, let me know."

"Thank you, son, that's very generous."

Dinner was served in the dining room, a delicious meal of selected meats and vegetables. Valene was on one side of him, Barbara Fortunado on the other, and he was complimenting the chef when Schuyler Mendoza spoke.

"So, you're, like, some kind of mega-rich beef magnate?" she asked Jake.

Jake felt Valene's arm press against his, and since it was the most intimate contact they'd had in weeks, he didn't flinch. "Something like that."

"You're well off the social media grid. I'm not sure how you've managed to do that."

He wasn't about to admit that he'd avoided all social media since his divorce because he knew Patrice would try to keep track of his movements.

"I don't do the selfie thing."

Valene's brothers groaned in agreement, and Schuyler shrugged when Valene made a protesting sound. "Well, of course I tried to find out what I could about you, since my sister has old-fashioned ideas about a person's right to privacy and all that."

Jake pushed back in his chair, aware that everyone at the table was waiting for his response. But Valene had told him enough about her beloved sister to know the other woman was simply good-natured and nosy. Even though her husband was giving her a cautious glance.

"What would you like to know?" he inquired.

Both her brows rose high. "How old were you when you made your first million?"

"Twenty-six."

"How much are you worth now?" she asked.

"A lot."

Everyone laughed, and Jake did his best to keep a straight face. Only Valene looked outraged. He touched her hand reassuringly, making it clear he was very capable of handling a few inappropriate questions.

"Really, Sky, is this necessary?" Valene demanded.

"No," her sister replied. "But I've got a curious nature. What else do you do besides sell really expensive steaks?"

Jake smiled. "I donate to charity. I invest in some property development. I buy overpriced horses. I'm currently renovating my home. Anything else?"

The mood shifted, laughter rang around the table and he urged Valene to relax once everyone continued eating their meals.

"Stop being such a worrier," he said softly so only she could hear.

"I'm sorry Schuyler is such a pain. She doesn't have a filter and thinks that—"

"Wait until you meet my sister," he said, cutting her off. "She's the pain of the century."

"I'd like to meet her."

"I'm sure she'd like that, too."

"Jake." Gavin Fortunado said his name and diverted his attention from Valene for a moment. "I believe you know a client of mine. He mentioned you the other day. Karl Messer? From the Messer Group? He does those high-rises and shopping malls."

Jake's back straightened, because even though people around him continued to chatter, Valene was suddenly as still as a statue. He looked directly at Gavin as he replied. "We went to school together."

"You know Karl Messer?"

Valene's voice was ice-cold.

"Yes."

He watched as her throat rolled convulsively. "Are you one of his silent investors?"

"At times."

She jumped to the obvious and correct conclusion. "Are you the reason he called me?"

Jake knew there was no getting away from the truth. "I gave him your number."

She was on her feet in a microsecond, tossing her napkin on the table. "I've lost my appetite."

She stormed off, leaving everyone at the table sitting in stunned silence. Until Schuyler spoke again.

"Um, what just happened?"

Maddie sighed heavily, Kenneth was shaking his head and Zach shrugged.

"I should go to her," Maddie said and started to get up.

Jake stood immediately and held out a hand. "It's my medicine," he said as he pushed the chair in. "I'll take it."

He left the room and headed for the kitchen. Valene was by the sink, a glass of cold water pressed against her temple, her eyes closed. But she clearly sensed his presence, because she spoke first.

"I don't want to talk to you."

"I'm pretty sure you do," he said and moved around the counter. "Because I know you want an explanation."

She harrumphed. "Oh, I think I can figure this one out for myself. You called your old school buddy Karl and asked him to help me out because I'm such an utter failure at what I do and clearly unable to do my job without interference from my knight in shining armor.

Does that about cover it?" she asked him, opening her eyes and spearing him with a look.

"I gave him your number," Jake insisted, "and that's all. Any business agreements that were made between the Messer Group and Fortunado Real Estate were made because of you, not me."

She didn't look convinced. "You gave him my number? You asked him to call me. *Told* him, is probably more to the point. Do you think I can't read between the lines here, Jake?"

"Read what?" he shot back. "Karl and I went to school together. We sometimes do business together. He's a trustworthy and successful operator. Having him as an exclusive client will be good for your business."

"And good for *me*, right?"

Jake sighed, exasperated. "Why are you getting so worked up?"

"Why?" she shot back. "Because I don't need help to be successful. I don't need to be spoon-fed to do my job."

"That's hardly what I did."

She was glaring, her beautiful cheeks scorched with color. "What about Otis McAvoy? Did you send him to me, too?"

Jake nodded. "He was a friend of my dad's."

"Ha," she said sarcastically. "I guess I need to screen every single client I've taken on in the last month to make sure they weren't setups by my stupid, thoughtless, controlling, multimillionaire boyfriend!"

Jake rocked back on his heels. "At least you're calling me your boyfriend."

She glared at him, her hands on her hips. "Is that all you got from that? Can you not see why I'm so angry?"

"I know why, but I think you're overreacting."

She moved around the marble island, her chest heaving. "I guess you would. That's the standard reply from a control freak."

"I'm not a control freak, Valene. I saw that you were in trouble and wanted to help you."

"I don't need help. Don't you get it, Jake? For the first time in my life, I actually believed I had done something on my own, without my father or my family making things easier. But it was just a lie," she said quietly. "Like everything with you."

Jake sighed heavily. "Valene, this is just your pride talking. If you take some time and think about—"

"This isn't pride," she insisted. "It's respect. Self-respect. I don't want to be another notch on your charity bedpost, Jake. I'm not like one of those homeless puppies at the animal shelter who need you to fix things. I don't need fixing. Like you, I want to make my own way in the world. I want to be successful and make a difference. But I won't do that on the coattails of someone else's influence."

She inhaled deeply, and Jake noticed how much her hands were shaking. He desperately wanted to take her into his arms, to make her see sense, to show her that anything he did, he did because he cared about her.

"My intention wasn't to—"

"Your intention," she said hotly, cutting him off, "is to get whatever you want, in whatever way you can get it. I've been around men like you all my life. Money and success is a breeding ground for that kind of arrogance. But I don't want to be a part of that environment. I never have. Perhaps that's why I'm below par in the successful career department. Why I'm mediocre at best at what I do."

Jake couldn't believe what he was hearing. "You're not mediocre, Valene."

"No? I guess I'll never know, since everyone around me thinks I need propping up. Well," she said, laughing humorlessly, "I'm over being treated like the weak link. I guess in a way I should thank you. If it wasn't for you, Jake, I might have continued to walk in the shadow of everyone around me for the rest of my life."

He frowned. "What does that mean?"

"It means that we're done," she said and walked past him. Jake followed her back down the hallway and into the dining room. He noticed the startled expressions on the faces of everyone in the room. And Valene—vibrant and passionate and unbelievably sexy as she strode around the table, her shoulders back, her chin held at a defiant tilt—wasn't finished yet.

"Dad, Maddie, Zach," she said and took a deep breath. "I quit!"

## Chapter Thirteen

It was day five of #CowboyGate, and the Fortunado Real Estate office was still in a kind of vibrating shock.

Val had dropped her resignation letter on Maddie's desk first thing Monday morning, before she'd headed to Austin to meet with a client and also to cool off for a day or so. Now it was Wednesday and she was back in Houston.

And the place was still in an uproar.

But she held her resolve. Val had no intention of being swayed from her decision. She was about to embark on a new and totally independent phase in her life and wasn't allowing anyone to change her mind.

Of course, "anyone" hadn't made contact.

Jake had been unusually quiet since the drama that had ensued at her parents' home the previous Friday. Naturally, her family all thought he was quite wonderful. Both Schuyler and her mother thought he was Mr. Romance of the Century, Maddie told her she was overreacting, Gavin said he shouldn't have made any comment about Karl Messer, and her father told her not to be hasty. But Val wasn't backing down. Jake had gone too far. She wasn't anyone's charity case, particularly for a tall, good-looking cowboy who believed he owned enough of the world to ensnare her in his web of deceit and lies and manipulation.

Yep, she had made the right decision calling things off.

It wasn't as though she still loved him or anything.

It had been a passing phase. Just sexual chemistry. She had been in love with the idea of being in love. And now she was completely over her fleeting infatuation. Besides, the lying, underhanded rat didn't deserve her.

Val got up from her desk and headed from the office, making her way down the hall to Maddie's much larger office that overlooked the street. Her sister was on the phone, but she beckoned her into the room the moment she spotted her in the doorway. She ended the call and gave Val her complete attention.

"Hey, Val, what's up?"

Of course, everyone was being extra nice to her, extra sensitive, extra understanding.

"I sent through the Messer file to your email. You can decide what you want to do with it."

Maddie sighed. "You're sure that's what you want, Val?"

"Positive." She lingered for a moment. "And the McAvoy account is on Zach's desk. Where is Zach, anyway? I've called him twice this morning. And his office door is closed."

"He's in a meeting with a client."

Val nodded. Zach rarely took meetings behind closed doors. "Important client, huh?"

"You could say that. I'm just heading there now. So…

you're sure you want to quit?" she queried as she got to her feet. "Seems like you're still interested in what's going on around here."

"You have my notice," she replied. "And I'll continue to work up until my last day, which is next Friday."

"And then what?"

She shrugged. "I haven't completely decided. I have some money saved, so I thought I'd take a sabbatical and do some charity work."

"I'm sure Mom would find a place for you at the Fortunado Foundation, if that's what you want."

Val's spine straightened. "Oh, you mean take another family handout because I'm too incompetent to make it on my own?"

"That's not what I mean."

Val shrugged, tired of the conversation, tired of everyone thinking they knew what was best for her. "I'm going to sort through my client list today and make sure everything is up to date. I'll be in my office if you need me."

She headed back down the hall and slumped in her chair. She pulled up her client listing on her laptop, made a few notes, then got into the folder she kept for Maddie's clients who overlapped with her own and almost reeled back when she saw a file named Brockton. Of course it was password protected, but that didn't stop Val's imagination from surging into overdrive. She raced from the room and headed to Maddie's office. She walked around her sister's desk and stared at the open day planner. For all Maddie's ability to embrace technology, her uptight sister still preferred an old-fashioned way of diarizing her appointments. And there, on today's docket, she saw it in black and white.

*Jake Brockton. Eleven o'clock.*

Anger surged through her blood.

She strode out of the room and headed to Zach's office, the room next to Maddie's. She knocked and then opened the door, not waiting for an invitation to enter.

And then she stared, long and hard, at the three people sitting around the huge desk.

Her sister. Her brother-in-law. And her former lover. Former friend. Former *everything*.

"Val?" Maddie's voice sounded higher-pitched than usual.

"What's going on?" she demanded, hands on hips, so fired up she thought she was going to bust a blood vessel.

"Valene," Jake said, on his feet in a second and taking a step toward her. "I can explain."

Val glared at him and ignored the two other people in the room. "Why is there a client file with your name on it? And why are you in a meeting with the CEOs of this company? The company my father started. The company I've worked for."

"It's business."

"Funny business," she shot back with a brittle laugh.

"I've been planning to expand the business into Austin for some time, so Maddie and Zach are looking for potential sites in that area. There's nothing sinister going on, Valene."

It sounded simple and logical. She looked at her sister. "And you think, despite the situation, it's acceptable to do this?"

"It's business, like Jake said," Maddie replied.

She turned her attention back to Jake. "And this is the only real estate agency in Houston that can assist in this sudden grand plan you have to carve out a beef empire?" she asked sarcastically, refusing to think about how gorgeous he looked in his regulation jeans, Western shirt and dark jacket. She'd missed him so much. More than she'd believed she could miss anyone. She missed his nightly phone calls, his silly jokes, his willingness to watch zombie flicks even though she knew he didn't like them. And she missed his arms around her. So much.

"Of course not, but Fortunado is the best, correct?"

He was right, but Val wasn't convinced of his motives. In fact, she knew exactly what he was doing. And what Maddie and Zach were up to. Since the family had discovered that Jake was dipped in gold, they'd spent hours talking about him, so she wasn't convinced of the purity of their motives, either. In fact, the whole situation reeked of manipulation and greed. And she wasn't sure whom she was madder at in that moment—Jake or Maddie and Zach.

"It's not enough that you threw Messer and McAvoy in my path?" she demanded. "Now this?"

"I was trying to help you."

"That's exactly my point," she said hotly. "I don't need anyone's help. And it's not your place to help me."

His head tilted fractionally. "Are you sure about that?"

"I'm *sure* that you don't have the right to run interference just because we've had sex a few times."

Maddie gasped, clearly uncomfortable by the tone of the conversation. "Maybe Zach and I should leave you both alone and—"

"Don't bother," Val snapped. "*I'm* leaving."

"Avoiding this, or me," Jake said quietly, "isn't going to make the situation go away, Valene."

"Want to bet?" She laughed humorlessly. "Keep in mind that we wouldn't have a situation if you hadn't lied your ass off when we first met, or you hadn't gotten your friends to take pity and make me look good in my job, or if my *bosses* hadn't suddenly decided to help you expand your empire. Cut the crap, Jake. This is about one thing. You did all this because of me."

"Well, of course it's because of you!" he said, clearly exasperated.

Val rolled back on her heels. "But…why?"

He stared at her, his glittering blue eyes unwavering in their intensity. "Why do you think?"

She swallowed hard, unsure of what she saw in his expression. "Because…because you want to control me and—"

"If you could look past your pride for one minute," he said quietly, cutting her off, his breath heavy, "you'd know why. I don't want to control you, Valene. Frankly, that would be like trying to hold back the tide. But ask yourself why you're so determined to think the worst of me, and why things changed the moment you found out I *wasn't* that working-class ranch hand you seemed to like so much. You want to talk about control?" he said. "Think about that!"

He left then, striding from the room with a brief farewell to Zach and Maddie and saying nothing more to her. Once he was out of sight, Val slumped back against one of the office chairs.

"Val," Maddie said softly. "Go after him."

She shook her head, hurting all over. "Why would you both think it's okay to be in business with him? Why did you approach him? Why did you—"

"We didn't," Zach explained. "He approached us."

That didn't make her feel any better. "And you both thought it would be okay to take advantage of his… of his…"

"Of his feelings for you?" Maddie offered, regarding her gently.

*His feelings…*

Val had been so wound up, so angry, so vehement and hurt she hadn't spent a second considering he had a motive other than his need to control her. "I'm not sure he has—"

"Val," Zach said with an impatient groan, "for pity's sake, the guy is obviously crazy in love with you."

Her heart almost stopped. Could that be true? Of course, she knew he cared. And she knew they had chemistry and an amazing connection unlike any she'd known before. But love? When she'd blurted out her own feelings weeks earlier, he hadn't responded, hadn't said anything. Sure, he'd still pursued her…but love?

"Even if he does…feel…you know, whatever," she said, stumbling over her words as heat suffused her cheeks, "that doesn't give you the right to use that to the advantage of the business. We don't operate that way, and I have always believed that both of you had more scruples. And I won't have anyone using me as a pawn or a reason to fleece him."

Maddie clapped her hands, smiling broadly. "It's good to see you fighting for what you want, Val. But honestly, I don't think anyone could take advantage of Jake. He's very much his own man. The only person who has that kind of influence is you. And he's right in what he said," Maddie reminded her. "Ever since you found out he was wealthy, you have backed off and looked for reasons to end your relationship. Which, logically, makes no sense. You said you wanted someone who ticked all your boxes. Well, kiddo, he does. And that terrifies you. He's not after your connections like Diego, and he's not after a compliant and suitable match like Hugh. But you're still cautious, and there's a reason for that. Maybe it's time to face what that is?"

Val stared at her sister, dumbstruck. Because Maddie's point was irrefutable. She had fallen for Jake when she believed he was exactly the opposite of what she wanted. And she'd hidden behind her outrage at his deception as a shield against the real issue: she was terrified he would really see her. Every flaw. Every failing. Her lack of real ambition. Her average grades in school and college. Her constant fear that she wasn't reaching her potential, that she was one of the *lesser* Fortunados. And that what she really wanted—to find a man who loved her, to raise a family, to nurture—would be seen as an easy out, settling, taking the uncomplicated route.

But what Val really wanted, what she yearned for, was a family of her own.

She'd never been motivated by ambition or money or kudos. But she was a Fortunado, and there were expectations. Perhaps if she'd been a free spirit like Schuyler, creative and energetic in her approach to life, she might have been given a free pass. But she was Valene—the youngest—the girl who was the apple of her parents' eyes and could do no wrong. So, she did no wrong. She went to school, college, began working at Fortunado Real Estate. For a while she'd even dated a man handpicked by her father, because after the disaster with Diego, it was obvious she couldn't choose someone herself.

And then there was Jake.

Handsome and hardworking. A man who knew who he was. A man who she believed didn't tick any of her boxes—and yet, she was drawn to him unlike she'd ever been to anyone before. And with him, she didn't have to be Valene Fortunado—she could be Val, exactly who *she* was. No expectations. No judgment. Because she'd believed he was also unambitious and happy to live his life in the present. And he was right…she had judged him. She had all the control while she believed he was a penniless ranch hand. In retrospect, she'd been arrogant and haughty and completely self-obsessed. Everything she despised.

She was ashamed of herself. Of her condemnation. Of her blatant condescension, her self-serving superiority. It was a wonder he hadn't run a mile in the opposite direction the moment she'd raised a brow at his crappy old truck or asked him if he owned a suit. And she'd stayed angry at him for weeks because she was trapped by her own egotistical pride. When the truth was, she loved him. She loved everything about him. And she wanted to spend the rest of her life showing him how much.

She just hoped it wasn't too late.

On Sunday afternoon, Jake was finally able to pull the covers off all the furniture in the ranch house. It had been a long time since the place had been dusted or cleaned, and as he piled up the covers in the downstairs living room, he realized he needed to give the place a thorough going-over. He'd slept in the house for the past three nights, having replaced the furniture in the upstairs bedroom. The work, he figured, would do him some good. It would exorcize his demons and maybe help alleviate the constant ache in his heart.

"Is that the last of them?"

He looked up as his mom walked in from the kitchen. "Yep."

She glanced around. "You need some new furniture."

It was true. There were several empty spaces around the room, including where the antique armoire had been, and the matching dining table and chairs. Patrice had taken them, along with most of the other antiquities he'd sourced over the years.

"I think I might ditch all of this stuff," he said, looking around at the pieces that were left, some of them worth a small fortune. Patrice had liked antiques, but Jake wanted to add some more modern furniture into the place. "Maybe we'll have a yard sale."

She crossed her arms. "Great idea."

"You know," he said and tossed the stack of covers into a box, "you can move in here if you want. There's plenty of room."

"And cramp your style?" she queried and smiled. "No, I'm very happy in my little cottage out in the back. This is a house that needs to have a family in it—a mom, a dad and a whole bunch of kids. A family you need to make, son."

Jake shoved the lid down on the box. "Not much chance of that," he muttered.

His mother sighed. "Well, have you called her?"

*No...*

But he missed her. He wasn't sure how he would stop missing her.

"She made her opinion very clear, Mom," he said as he closed up another box.

"She's upset," Lynda said quietly. "Naturally so. But you should talk to her, try to work things out."

He wanted to. But he didn't want to get another dose of her rejection. He was still stinging, still hurting, still trying to figure out what he could have done differently.

*Everything...*

He should have been up front from the beginning. He should have told her who and what he was. And he sure as hell shouldn't have started interfering in her work. He'd gotten, he figured, exactly what he deserved. But even knowing he'd behaved like a jackass, he still couldn't believe she wouldn't see the real reason behind his behavior. That's what tortured him, that she didn't understand. He'd believed she knew him better. But he'd been wrong. While Jake had fallen headlong and crazy in love with her, it was obvious that Valene had only been in love with the idea of being in love. And *that* couldn't last. Still, part of him wanted to believe that her feelings were real and as intense as his own. He remembered how she'd cursed at him for making her fall in love with him, as though it was the last thing she wanted, and then backpedaled when he called her out on it.

Beside him, Sheba gave a loud bark, and he heard a vehicle pull up outside. "Someone's here," he said, ending the conversation with his mother. Jake grabbed the box and headed for the door, crossing the threshold before he came to an abrupt halt.

Valene stood at the bottom of the steps. Dressed in jeans, high boots, a black sweater and a long white woolen coat, she looked more beautiful than he had ever seen her. Her hair was loose, framing her face, and since it was a chilly afternoon, her cheeks and nose were rosy.

He dropped the box as Sheba raced down the steps to greet her. He watched, aching inside, as she bent down to pet the dog and then straightened. "Hi," she said softly, placing a foot on the bottom step.

"Hello."

He heard his mother shuffling behind him. "I'll make myself scarce," she said discreetly, quickly moving down the steps and grabbing Sheba's collar. "I'll take her with me. It's good to see you, Val," his mom said and then hurriedly took the path leading to the cottage.

"Can we talk?"

Jake pulled himself from his trance and quickly beckoned her inside. "Of course, come on in out of the cold."

She took the steps wordlessly and entered the house,

walking down the hall and into the living room. She took off her jacket and draped it over a chair and stood by the fireplace, then she turned. "You've finished renovating?"

He nodded. "I need to clean up and refurnish the place now."

She looked around. "It's such a lovely house, Jake."

"It's big," he said quietly. "I mean, for one person."

She met his gaze for a second, then looked away. "I thought perhaps your mom and sister might—"

"Mom says she's happy in the cottage," he said, cutting her off. "And Cassidy only comes back every month or so. Besides, it's the kind of house that should have a family in it. You know, kids..."

She traced her hand along the mantel. "Do you...is that what you want?" she asked.

"What I want," he said, taking a breath, "is for you to look at me."

She slowly met his gaze again. Her eyes glistened, and Jake fought every instinct he possessed to not stride across the room and take her into his arms. She looked lost. And hurt. And incredibly vulnerable.

"Why are you here?"

"I didn't... I didn't tell you my whole story," she said raggedly, swallowing hard. "Do you remember our first date when I introduced myself? I didn't tell you everything. I didn't tell you that I worked in my family's business but I was never really happy doing it. I didn't tell you that I've never been very ambitious. I didn't tell you that I had to work extra hard in school to get respectable grades because it's what my parents expected of me. I didn't tell you that I hate my condo but couldn't say that because my father bought it for me, and that's why I got Bruce, because I feel so incredibly alone there. I didn't tell you that when I found out my ex-boyfriend was only interested in me because he wanted a job at Fortunado and I confronted him about it, he called me weak and dull and said I would never amount to anything. And I believed him," she admitted, tears in her eyes. "That's why I dated Hugh. Because he knew what I was and didn't care. Which was worse, in a way, because he was indifferent, and that became a daily reminder of my shortcomings."

Jake's chest ached hearing her admission. "You don't have any shortcomings. You're quite extraordinary."

She stared at him, the tears now on her cheeks, and she managed a small smile.

"Jake..." Her words trailed off. "I'm in love with you."

The ache in his chest vanished, replaced by a tight swell of emotion that sucked the air from his lungs. But he needed to know for certain. "Valene, are you sure you're not simply in love with the idea of being in love?" he asked softly.

"Positive," she replied. "And anyway, I told you I loved you the last time I was here."

"I know you did," he said and took three strides toward her. "I just didn't dare let myself really believe it."

"Believe it," she insisted and laughed through her tears. "But, Jake...are you...are you..."

"Am I what?" he queried, taking her hands gently in his. "Am I in love with you?" He pulled her close. "I am so madly and completely in love with you, Valene, I can barely draw a breath when we're this close."

He kissed her hotly, and she clung to him, her wet cheeks touching his, her mouth exquisitely sweet beneath his. He kissed her again. And again. And she kissed him back, her hands on his shoulders, her soft sighs echoing around the room.

"Are you really sure, Valene?" he whispered against her mouth. "Are you positive it's enough, and not—"

"It's more," she assured him. "I love you, Jake. I love you even if you *are* rich."

He laughed, and it felt so good. "Ah, sweetheart, I'm sorry, you know," he said and dragged her toward the chaise by the window. He sat down and urged her beside him. "I never meant to keep so many secrets, but I had to know. I had to be sure that any feelings you had were for me and not anything else. My ex-wife hammered me, and I—"

She shushed him and placed her fingertips against his mouth. "I know what she did. I know she hurt you and betrayed you. I know she couldn't value what she had, and it made you wary of getting close to anyone. I get it," she said and made a self-deprecating sound. "I understand. And I know it took courage for you to let me into your life," she said and touched his chest. "And into your heart. I love who I am when I'm with you. And I want to spend as much time with you as I can."

Jake grasped her hands. "I don't ever want to be away from you again. And I'm sorry, Valene, about Messer and the whole—"

"We don't have to talk about that," she said quickly.

"Yes, we do," he replied. "Anything I did wasn't done to undermine you or manipulate you. I honestly wanted to help you. And Messer knows good business. I simply pointed him in your direction. You did the rest. The same with Otis. If I overstepped, I apologize. I saw you were hurting, and that your family was in trouble, and it pushed at my overprotective side. If I embarrassed you, I'm sorry. It won't happen again."

"I'm pretty sure it will," she teased and pressed closer. "Let's face it, Jake, you're a good guy. You like helping people, like you did when your dad passed away and you came home so your mom and sister could still live here.

That part of you. That generous, protective side is one of the things I love about you." She sighed and smiled. "I'm not going to pick and choose parts of you to love. I love all of you. I won't pretend I wasn't shocked to learn about your wealth and owning this place and your apparent plans to expand your empire…but I love that you're not obsessed by it."

"I'm not," he said and then chuckled. "Don't get me wrong, I like that I can support the people I care about, and I try to do some good in the community, but the money isn't why I work."

"But," she said, "I don't want you to think you have to *fix* everything."

"Everything?"

"Like my family's business," she replied. "I do know you were trying to help, but I don't want anyone taking advantage of that, either. Particularly Maddie and Zach. If they start bombarding you with business opportunities, they'll have to deal with me."

He chuckled. "My fearless love," he said, loving that she would go to bat to protect him. "But stop fretting. I've planned on expanding the business into other places for a couple of years. But from here on out I will run everything by you beforehand, okay, sweetheart?"

She sighed. "I know Maddie and Zach are worried. And I know my dad said they were getting closer to finding out who is responsible, but I won't allow anyone to manipulate the situation because we fell in love."

He kissed her again, and they stayed on the chaise for a while, making out, holding one another, and then he took her upstairs to his bedroom.

"You got a new bed?" she said when they walked through the doorway.

"I did," he replied. "The old one had too many memories attached to it."

"I'm sorry she hurt you, Jake."

"You know something, I think it stopped hurting the day I met you."

She smiled. "Do you know when I fell in love with you? That day at the animal shelter."

"It took you that long?" he teased. "I knew the moment you ordered that low-fat, single-shot vanilla soy latte with extra cinnamon. And I thought, my God, she's so beautiful, I hope she stays, I hope she likes me, I hope I find out that she wants what I want—marriage, children, family."

She laughed delightfully. "She does. *I do*, Jake. It's all I want. I want to get married one day and make babies with you."

Jake took her hand. "So, once I ask your dad's permission, you'll let me ask you to marry me?"

"Yes, absolutely."

He groaned and led her to the bed. They undressed and then made love slowly, taking time to reacquaint themselves with one another. Jake had never experienced such intense release, such a soul-deep connection to anyone.

Afterward, they lay together, side by side, talking, touching.

"So, are you still intent on leaving Fortunado Real Estate?" he asked, gently stroking her cheek.

She nodded. "I want my work to have value. I want to make a difference."

"Have you given any thought to working at the Fortunado Foundation?

She sighed. "Maddie suggested it. But I'm worried that people might think I —"

"It's what you think that matters, Valene. And I really believe that the foundation is a place where you really could make a difference. Don't let pride stand in your way."

She kissed him and smiled against his mouth. "I'll think about it."

"Okay. And when I told your mom I would like to help at the foundation, I meant it. But I promise you, I won't overstep."

"Sure you will," she teased again. "But I'm learning to lessen my resistance to your knight-in-shining-armor gig. Also, I've decided to put my condo on the market," she said softly.

He touched her cheek. "So, it looks like you will be needing somewhere to stay. Well, since you just agreed you were going to marry me, you may as well move in with me now. Besides, I need someone to pick out furniture and drapes and all that nesting kind of stuff."

"I'd love to nest here," she declared. "And marry you and have your babies. But what about the other man in my life?"

He raised a brow. "Other man?"

"Bruce," she replied. "How will he get along with Sheba? And there's no fenced yard here and I —"

"I'll build a fence," he promised. "And a huge doghouse. And a dollhouse. And a cubbyhouse for when our kids come along."

She pressed closer. "I can't wait to start our life together."

"Me either," he said.

And as he kissed her again, Jake left any doubts and insecurities behind. He was exactly where he wanted to be, with the woman of his dreams.

Life was sweet.

## *Epilogue*

"Are you sure about this?"

Val looked up at her incredibly handsome, amazingly sexy, super-smart fiancé and nodded.

"Yes, positive. I really want to do this."

"There's no going back once we sign on the dotted line."

"I know," she said and touched his cheek. "You know, we've been talking about this all week."

"I only want you to be sure," he said and shrugged.

Val laughed softly and then sighed. It had been a whirlwind couple of weeks. First, their hasty engagement. Val had a rock on her finger that was so beautiful it defied belief. Of course, her parents had voiced their concerns about the swiftness of their relationship, but they weren't swayed. She loved Jake. He loved her. Marriage was the obvious next step. Then kids. It was everything Val had dreamed about. She had most of her personal possessions already moved into the ranch house, and other than a few furniture items left at the condo, the transition had been seamless.

She was taking a month off to get herself sorted out and then would be starting at the Fortunado Foundation. Her mother had welcomed her wholeheartedly, and even though her father was clearly disappointed she'd left the family business, he said he understood her need to do what made her happy. And both her parents adored Jake, even though they thought they were rushing into a serious relationship. Jake had gallantly asked her father for her hand, and her dad had given it—with a couple of provisos that Val wasn't privy to, as Jake had no intention of breaking her father's confidence.

But today was the big commitment day.

She got out of the truck and opened the back door, while Jake did the same on the other side. Bruce was yapping excitedly, and she grabbed his lead while Jake called a much better behaved Sheba to heel. Val was amazed at how quickly Sheba and Bruce had bonded and become good friends. Neither of them was pleased about having to use baskets to sleep in, since they had both been permanently ousted from the end of their bed. Jake had built a sturdy fence around the back of the house, and the large yard was plenty big enough for the dogs to roam around during the day. At night they spent all their time inside.

Val hadn't believed she could be so happy.

Their wedding was in the planning stage. Nothing too extravagant, although Jake had offered whatever kind of wedding she desired. But Val wasn't interested in a circus-style event. Just their families and a few close friends, with Adele and her sisters and Cassidy as attendants. She already adored Jake's younger sister and was pretty sure the feeling was reciprocated.

The wedding would take place on the ranch, down by the creek, and then a reception under a tent in Lynda's English garden. She knew it would be perfect. First, they had to get through their upcoming engagement party, which had been eagerly arranged by her family.

"Ready?"

She nodded. "Let's do it."

When they walked through the doors of the animal shelter, Florrie greeted them with wide smiles. "Hello! Everyone ready for the next big adventure?"

Val nodded, although she could see Jake was still a little skeptical. "It will work out, you'll see."

Half an hour later, they were all relieved. And delighted.

Adopting Digby had been a no-brainer. After the old dog had been passed over by the people who had put in an application a few weeks earlier, Val had secretly been delighted, because she knew he was meant to be a part of their family.

But only if he got along with Sheba and Bruce.

Which turned out just fine. Bruce bounded and slobbered around, while a more polite Sheba sniffed and then lost interest. And Digby was clearly thrilled to be put on the leash and led out to the truck. Once the three pooches were strapped in the back seat, Val jumped into the front and waited for Jake.

"All set?" he asked.

Val nodded, so happy she could barely breathe. "And raring to go."

He smiled. "I love you."

Her heart rolled over. "I love you, too."

She had so much to be grateful for. For Jake, of course, for the three happy pooches in the back, for her family, for the babies they hoped to have, for the love that had come to complete them both. And she would be eternally grateful for the silly dating app that made it all possible.

She sighed with happiness. "Let's get this adventure started."

\* \* \* \* \*

# COMING SOON!

We really hope you enjoyed reading this book. If you're looking for more romance, be sure to head to the shops when new books are available on

# Thursday 7th February

To see which titles are coming soon, please visit
**millsandboon.co.uk/nextmonth**

MILLS & BOON

# MILLS & BOON

## Coming next month

### CARRYING THE GREEK TYCOON'S BABY
Jennifer Faye

"I'm pregnant."

Xander stumbled back as though Lea's words had physically slugged him in the chest. The back of his knees hit the edge of the bed. He slumped down onto the mattress. Maybe he'd heard her incorrectly.

"Could you say that again?"

"Xander, I'm pregnant. And you're the father."

That's what he thought she'd said.

But this can't be true. Could it?

Xander knew all too well that it was quite possible. They'd spent that not-so-long-ago weekend in bed…and there was the time on the floor…in the living room—

He halted his rambling memories. He didn't normally let loose like that. In fact, he'd never had a weekend like that one. It was unforgettable. And apparently in more than one way.

The silence dragged on. He should say something. Anything. But what? He'd never been in this position before.

He needed time to think because right now all that was going around in his mind was that he was going to be a father. He wondered if this was what shock felt like.

"I…I need a little time to absorb this," he said. "We'll talk soon."

He wasn't even sure if he said goodbye before disconnecting the call. He had no idea how long he laid there staring into space before an incoming text jarred him back to reality.

I'm going to be a father.

The profound words echoed in his mind.

How could this be? Well, of course he knew how it happened. It was a weekend that he would never forget, much as he had tried. Lea's stunning image was imprinted upon his mind.

Still, he never thought he'd hear that he was going to be a father. A father. His heart was racing and his palms were damp.

His mind slipped back to the time he'd spent on Infinity Island. He never thought that it would change his life. But it had. And now he had to figure out a plan. He was known for thinking on his toes, but this was different. This was a baby. His baby.

And he had to do whatever was best for the child.

But what was that?

Continue reading
**CARRYING THE GREEK TYCOON'S BABY**
Jennifer Faye

*Available next month*
www.millsandboon.co.uk

# LET'S TALK
## Romance

For exclusive extracts, competitions
and special offers, find us online:

 facebook.com/millsandboon

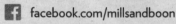 @MillsandBoon

@MillsandBoonUK

**Get in touch on 01413 063232**

For all the latest titles coming soon, visit
**millsandboon.co.uk/nextmonth**